Praise for *The Piano Teacher*:

'Two love stories lie at the centre of this impressive debut, which explores the moral ambiguities of war, culture, race and romantic love. Intriguing, sad, rivetingly detailed…'
ELIZABETH BUCHAN, *Daily Mail*

'A lovely novel – it has an old-fashioned solidity and crafts-manship and effortlessly recreates the atmosphere of post-war Hong Kong'   *The Times*

'This cleverly crafted debut novel is a winner'   *Marie Claire*

'A beautifully written novel that evokes passion and heartache in a bitter period for Hong Kong'
Waterstones Books Quarterly magazine

'This season's *Atonement*…a first-class steamer ticket to a disappearing Hong Kong'   *Elle* magazine

'A heartfelt debut [that] illuminates World War II's lesser-known chapters'   *Vogue*

'Laced with intrigue…Readers will be enthralled by Lee's depiction of Will's relationships with his two lovers…and the unsparing way Lee unravels them'   *New York Times*

'War, love, betrayal – an exquisite fugue of a first novel… intensely readable'   *O* magazine

'This cinematic tale of two love affairs in mid-century Hong Kong shows colonial pretensions tainted by wartime truths

...Lee unfolds each story, and flits between them, with the brisk grace and discretion of the society she describes'

New Yorker

'War. Love. Betrayal. The harsh lessons of history. These are big subjects for any veteran writer, and yet, in her first novel, Janice Y.K. Lee confronts them admirably'   *Washington Post*

'Evocative, poignant and skilfully crafted, *The Piano Teacher* is more than an epic tale of war and a tangled, tortured love story. It is the kind of novel one consumes in great, greedy gulps, pausing (grudgingly) only when absolutely necessary'

Chicago Tribune

'Rarely does one encounter a debut work as beguiling and assured as *The Piano Teacher*. Rich with intrigue, romance, and betrayal, this wonderfully written, utterly captivating novel dazzles with its sharp-eyed renderings of beau monde Hong Kong as it is plunged into the crucible of war...a truly transporting – and indeed irresistible – work of fiction'

CHANG-RAE LEE, author of *Aloft*

'One of the most insightful, elegant and atmospheric novels I've read in a long time. Janice Lee is nothing short of brilliant and her novel is impossible to put down'

GARY SHTEYNGART, author of *Absurdistan*

JANICE Y.K. LEE

The Piano Teacher

Harper
Press

HarperPress
An imprint of HarperCollinsPublishers
77–85 Fulham Palace Road
Hammersmith, London W6 8JB

www.harpercollins.co.uk
Visit out authors' blog: www.fifthestate.co.uk
Love this book? www.bookarmy.com

This edition published by HarperPress in 2009
Copyright © Janice Y.K. Lee 2009

1

Janice Y.K. Lee asserts the moral right to
be identified as the author of this work

A catalogue record for this book is available from the British Library

ISBN 978-0-00-728637-9

Typeset in Minion by Newgen Imaging Systems (P) Ltd, Chennai, India

Printed and bound in Great Britain by Clays Ltd, St Ives plc

Mixed Sources

Product group from well-managed
forests and other controlled sources
www.fsc.org Cert no. SW-COC-1806
© 1996 Forest Stewardship Council

FSC is a non-profit international organisation established to promote the
responsible management of the world's forests. Products carrying the FSC
label are independently certified to assure consumers that they come
from forests that are managed to meet the social, economic and
ecological needs of present and future generations.

Find out more about HarperCollins and the environment at
www.harpercollins.co.uk/green

For my parents

PART I

May 1952

It started as an accident. The small Herend rabbit had fallen into Claire's handbag. It had been on the piano and she had been gathering up the sheet music at the end of the lesson when she knocked it off. It fell off the doily (a doily! On the Steinway!) and into her large leather bag. What had happened after that was perplexing, even to her. Locket had been staring down at the keyboard, and hadn't noticed. And then, Claire had just . . . left. It wasn't until she was downstairs and waiting for the bus that she grasped what she had done. And then it had been too late. She went home and buried the expensive porcelain figurine under her sweaters.

Claire and her husband had moved to Hong Kong nine months ago, transferred by the government, which had posted Martin in the Department of Water Services. Churchill had ended rationing and things were starting to return to normal when they had received news of the posting. She had never dreamed of leaving England before.

Martin was an engineer, overseeing the building of the Tai Lam Cheung reservoir, so that there wouldn't need to be so much rationing when the rains ebbed, as they did every several years. It was to hold four and a half billion gallons of water when full. Claire almost couldn't imagine such a number, but Martin said it was barely enough for the people of Hong Kong, and he was sure that by the time they had finished, they'd have to build another. 'More work for me,' he said cheerfully. He was analysing the topography of the hills so that they could install catch-drains for when the rain came. The English government did so much for the colonies, Claire knew. They made their lives much better, but the locals rarely appreciated it. Her mother had warned her about the Chinese before she left – an unscrupulous, conniving people, who would surely try to take advantage of her innocence and goodwill.

Coming over, she had noticed it for days, the increasing wetness in the air, even more than usual. The sea breezes were stronger and the sun's rays more powerful when they broke through cloud. When the P&O *Canton* had finally pulled into Hong Kong harbour in August, she had really felt she was in the tropics, hair frizzing up in curls, face always slightly damp and oily, the constant moisture under her arms and behind her knees. When she had stepped out of her cabin, the heat had assailed her like a physical blow, until she managed to find shade and fan herself.

There had been seven stops along the month-long journey, but after a few grimy hours spent in Algiers and Port Said, Claire had decided to stay on board rather than encounter more frightening peoples and customs. She had never imagined such sights. In Algiers, she had seen a man kiss a donkey and she couldn't discern whether the high odour was coming from one or the other, and in Egypt the markets were the very definition of unhygienic – a fish-monger gutting a fish had licked the knife clean with his tongue.

She had enquired as to whether the ship's provisions were pro-cured locally, at these markets, and the answer had been most unsat-isfactory. An uncle had died from food poisoning in India, making her cautious. She kept to herself, and sustained herself mostly on the beef tea they dispensed in the late morning on the sun deck. The menus, which were distributed every day, were mundane: turnips, potatoes, things that could be stored in the hold, with meat and salads the first few days after port. Martin promenaded on the deck every morning for exercise, and tried to get her to join him, to no avail. She preferred to sit in a deck-chair, wearing a large-brimmed hat and wrap herself in one of the ship's scratchy wool blankets, face shaded from the omnipresent sun.

There had been a scandal on the ship. A woman, going to meet her fiancé in Hong Kong, had spent one too many moonlit nights on the deck with another gentleman, and had disembarked in the Philippines with her new man, leaving only a letter for her intended. Liesl, the girlfriend to whom the woman had entrusted the letter, grew visibly more nervous as the date of arrival drew near. Men joked that she could take Sarah's place, but she wasn't having any of that. Liesl was a serious young woman, who was joining her sister and brother-in-law in Hong Kong, where she intended to educate Unfortunate Chinese Girls in Art: when she held forth about it, it was always with capital letters in Claire's mind.

Before disembarking, Claire separated out all of her thin cotton dresses and skirts; she could tell that was all she would be wearing for a while. They had arrived to a big party on the dock, with paper streamers and shouting vendors selling fresh fruit juice and soy-milk drinks and garish flower arrangements to the people waiting. Groups of revellers had already opened champagne and were toasting the arrival of their friends and family.

'We pop the corks as soon as we see the ship on the horizon,' a man explained to his girl, as he escorted her away. 'It's a big party. We've been here for hours.'

Claire watched Liesl go down the gangplank, looking very nervous, and then she disappeared into the throng. Claire and Martin went down next, treading on the soft, humid wood, luggage behind them, carried by two scantily clad young Chinese boys who had materialized out of nowhere.

Martin had an old schoolfriend, John, who worked at Dodwell's, one of the trading firms, and had promised to greet the ship. He came with two friends and offered the new arrivals freshly squeezed guava drinks. Claire pretended to sip hers as her mother had warned her about the cholera that was rampant in these parts. The men were bachelors and very pleasant. John, Nigel, Leslie. They explained they all lived together in a mess – there were many, known by their companies' names, Dodwell's Mess, Jardine's Mess, et cetera, and they assured Claire and Martin that Dodwell's threw the best parties around.

They accompanied them to the government-approved hotel in Tsim Sha Tsui, where a Chinese man with a long queue, dirty white tunic and shockingly long fingernails showed them to their room. They made an arrangement to meet for tiffin the next day and the men departed, leaving Martin and Claire sitting on the bed, exhausted and staring at one another. They didn't know each other very well. They had been married barely four months.

She had accepted Martin's proposal to escape the dark interior of her house, her bitter mother railing against everything, getting worse, it seemed, with her advancing age, and an uninspiring job as a filing girl in an insurance company. Martin was older, in his forties, and had never had luck with women. The first time he had kissed her, she had had to stifle the urge to wipe her mouth. He was like a cow, slow and steady. And kind. She knew this. She was grateful for it.

She had not had many chances with men. Her parents stayed at home all the time, so she had as well. When she had started seeing Martin – he was the older brother of one of the girls at work – she had had dinner at restaurants, drunk a cocktail at a hotel bar, and seen other young women and men talking, laughing, with an assurance she could not fathom. They had opinions about politics; they had read books she had never heard of and seen foreign films and talked about them with such confidence. She was enthralled and not a little intimidated. And then Martin had come to her, serious: his job was taking him to the Orient, and would she come with him? She was not so attracted to him, but who was she to be choosy? she thought, hearing the voice of her mother. She let him kiss her and nodded yes.

Claire had started to draw a bath in their hotel room when another knock on the door revealed a small Chinese woman, an amah, she was called, who started to unpack their suitcases until Martin shooed her away.

And that was how they had arrived in Hong Kong, which was like nothing Claire had imagined. Apart from the usual colonial haunts – all hush and genteel, potted palms and polished wood in whitewashed buildings – it was loud and crowded and dirty and bustling. The buildings were right next to each other and often had clothing hung out to dry on bamboo poles. There were garish vertical signs hung on every one, advertising massage parlours, pubs and hair salons. Someone had told her that opium dens still existed in back alleys. There was often refuse on the street, sometimes even human filth, and there was a pungent, peppery odour that was oddly clingy, attaching itself to your very skin until you went home for a good scrub.

There were all sorts of people. The local women carried their babies in a sort of back sling. Sikhs served as uniformed security guards – you saw them dozing off on wooden stools outside the banks, turbaned heads hanging heavily above their chests, rifles held loosely between their knees. The Indians had been brought over by the British, of course. Pakistanis ran carpet stores, Portuguese were doctors and Jews ran the dairy farms and other large businesses. There were British businessmen and American bankers, White Russian aristocrats and Peruvian entrepreneurs – all peculiarly well-travelled and sophisticated – and, of course, there were the Chinese, quite different in Hong Kong from the ones in China, she was told.

To her surprise, she didn't detest Hong Kong, as her mother had told her she would – she found the streets busy and distracting, so very different from Croydon, and filled with people and shops and goods she had never seen before. She liked to sample the local bakery goods, the pineapple buns and yellow egg tarts, and sometimes wandered outside Central, where she would quickly find herself in unfamiliar surroundings, where she might be the only non-Chinese around. The fruit stalls were heaped with not only oranges and bananas, still luxuries in post-war England, but spiky, strange-looking fruits she came to try and like: starfruit, durian, lychee. She would buy a dollar's worth and be handed a small, waxy brown bag and she would eat the fruit slowly as she walked. There were small stalls made of crudely nailed wood and corrugated tin, which housed small speciality enterprises: this one sold chops, the stone stamps the Chinese used in place of signatures, this one made only keys, this one had a chair that was rented for half-days by a street dentist and a barber.

The locals ate on the street in tiny restaurants called *daipaidong*, and she had seen three workmen in dirty singlets and trousers crouched over a plate containing a whole fish, spitting out the bones at their feet. One had seen her watching them, and deliberately picked up the fish's eyeball with his chopsticks, raised it up to her, smiling, before he ate it.

Claire hadn't met many Chinese people before, but the ones she had seen in the big towns in England had been serving in restaurants or ironing clothes. There were many of those types in Hong Kong, of course, but what had been eye-opening was the sight of the affluent Chinese, the ones who seemed English in all but their skin colour. It had been quite something to see a Chinese step out of a Rolls-Royce, as she had one day when she was waiting on the steps of the Gloucester Hotel, or in business suits, having lunch with British men who talked to them as if they were the same. She hadn't known that such a world existed. And then, with Locket, she was thrust into this world.

After a few months settling in, finding a flat and furnishing it, Claire had put the word out that she was looking for a job giving piano lessons, 'as a lark', was how she put it – something to fill the day, but the truth was, they could really use the extra money. She had played the piano most of her life and was primarily self-taught, but she didn't think it would matter. Amelia, an acquaintance she had met at a sewing circle, said she would ask around.

She rang a few days later.

'There's a Chinese family, the Chens. They run everything in town. Apparently, they're looking for a piano teacher for their daughter, and they'd prefer an Englishwoman. What do you think?'

'A Chinese family?' Claire said. 'I hadn't thought about that possibility. Aren't there any English families looking?'

'No,' Amelia said. 'Not that I've been able to ascertain.'

'I just don't know . . .' Claire demurred. 'Wouldn't it be odd?' She couldn't imagine teaching a Chinese girl. 'Does she speak English?'

'Probably better than you or me,' Amelia said impatiently. 'They're offering a very adequate fee.' She named a large sum.

'Well,' Claire said slowly, 'I suppose it couldn't do any harm to meet them.'

Victor and Melody Chen lived in the Mid-Levels, in an enormous white two-storey house on May Road. There was a driveway with potted plants lining the sides. Inside, there was the quiet, efficient buzz of a household staffed with plentiful servants. Claire had taken a bus and when she arrived, she was perspiring after the walk from the road to the house.

The amah led her to a sitting room, where she found a fan blowing blessedly cool air. A houseboy adjusted the drapes so that she was properly shaded. Her blue linen skirt, just delivered from the tailor, was wrinkled and she had on a white voile blouse that was splotched with moisture. She hoped the Chens would allow her some time to compose herself. She shifted, feeling a drop of perspiration trickle down her thigh.

No such luck. Mrs Chen swooped through the door, a vision in cool pink, holding a tray of drinks. A small, exquisite woman, with hair cut just so, so that it swung in precise, geometric movements. Her shoulders were fragile and exposed in her sleeveless shift, her face a tiny oval.

'Hello!' she trilled. 'Lovely to meet you. I'm Melody. Locket's just on her way.'

'Locket?' Claire said, uncertain.

'My daughter. She's just back from school and getting changed into something more comfortable. Isn't the heat dreadful?' She set down the tray, which held long glasses of iced tea. 'Have something cool, please.'

'Your English is remarkably good,' Claire said, as she took a glass.

'Oh, is it?' Melody said casually. 'Four years at Wellesley will do that for you, I suppose.'

'You were at university in America?' Claire asked. She hadn't known that Chinese went to university in America.

'Loved every minute,' she said. 'Except for the horrible, horrible food. Americans think a grilled cheese sandwich is a meal! And, as you know, we Chinese take food very seriously.'

'Is Locket going to be schooled in America?'

'We haven't decided but, really, I'd rather talk to you about your education,' Mrs Chen said.

'Oh.' Claire was taken aback.

'You know,' she continued pleasantly, 'where you studied music, and all that.'

Claire settled back in her seat. 'I was a serious student for a number of years. I studied with Mrs Eloise Pollock and was about to apply for a position at the Royal Academy when my family situation changed.'

Mrs Chen sat, waiting, head tilted, with one bird-like ankle crossed over the other, her knees slanted to one side.

'And so, I was unable to continue,' Claire said. Was she supposed to explain it in detail to this stranger? Her father had been let go from the printing company and it had been a black couple of months before he had found a new job as an insurance salesman. His pay had been erratic at best – he was not a natural salesman – and luxuries like piano lessons were unthinkable. Mrs Pollock, a very kind woman, had offered to continue her instruction at a much-reduced fee, but her mother, sensitive and pointlessly proud, had refused to even entertain the idea.

'And what level of studies did you achieve?'

'I was studying for my Seventh Grade examinations.'

'Locket is a beginning student but I want her to be taught seriously, by a serious musician,' Mrs Chen said. 'She should pass all her examinations with distinction.'

'Well, I'm certainly serious about music and, as for passing with distinction, that will be up to Locket,' Claire said. 'I did very well in my examinations.'

Locket entered the room, or rather, she bumbled into it. Where her mother was small and fine, Locket was chubby, all rounded limbs and padded cheeks. Her glossy hair was tied in a thick ponytail.

'Hallo,' she said. She had a distinctly English accent.

'Locket, this is Mrs Pendleton,' Mrs Chen said, stroking her daughter's cheek. 'She's come to see if she'll be your piano teacher so you must be very polite.'

'Do you like the piano, Locket?' Claire said, too slowly, she realized, for a ten-year-old child. She had no experience with children.

'I dunno,' Locket said. 'I suppose so.'

'Locket!' her mother cried. 'You said you wanted to learn. That's why we bought you the new Steinway.'

'Locket's a pretty name,' Claire said. 'How did you come about it?'

'Dunno,' said Locket again. She reached for a glass of iced tea and drank. A small trickle wended its way down her chin. Her mother took a napkin off the silver tray and dabbed it dry.

'Will Mr Chen be arriving soon?' Claire asked.

'Oh, Victor!' Mrs Chen laughed. 'He's far too busy for these household matters. He's always working.'

'I see,' Claire said. She was uncertain as to what came next.

'Would you play us something?' Mrs Chen asked. 'We just got the piano and it would be lovely to hear it played professionally.'

'Of course,' Claire said, because she didn't know what else to say. She felt as if she were being made to perform like a common entertainer – there had been something in the woman's tone – but she couldn't think of a gracious way to refuse.

She played a simple étude, which Mrs Chen seemed to enjoy and Locket squirmed through.

'I think this will be fine,' Mrs Chen said. 'Are you available on Thursdays?'

Claire hesitated. She didn't know whether she was going to take the job.

'It would have to be Thursdays because Locket has lessons the other days,' Mrs Chen said.

'Fine,' said Claire. 'I accept.'

Locket's mother was of a Hong Kong type. Claire saw women like her lunching at Chez Henri, laughing and gossiping with each other. They were called *taitais* and you could spot them at the smart

12

clothing boutiques, trying on the latest fashions or climbing into their chauffeur-driven cars. Sometimes Mrs Chen would come home and put a slim, perfumed hand on Locket's shoulder and comment liltingly on the music. And then, Claire couldn't help it, she really couldn't, she would think to herself, *You people drown your daughters*! Her mother had told her about how the Chinese were just a little above animals and that they would drown their daughters because they preferred sons. Once, Mrs Chen had mentioned a function at the Jockey Club that she and her husband were going to. She had been dressed up in diamonds, a flowing black dress and red, red lipstick. She had not looked like an animal.

Bruce Comstock, the head of the water office, had taken Martin and Claire to the club once, with his wife, and they had drunk pink gin while watching the horse races, the stands filled with shouting gamblers.

The week before the figurine fell into Claire's handbag, she had been leaving the lesson when Victor and Melody Chen came in. It had rung five on the ornate mahogany grandfather clock that had mother-of-pearl Chinese characters inlaid all down the front of it and she had been putting her things away when they walked into the room. They were a tiny couple and they looked like porcelain dolls, with their shiny skin and coal eyes. 'Out the door already?' Mr Chen said drily. He was dressed nattily in a navy-blue pin-striped suit with a burgundy handkerchief peeping out of his breast pocket just so. 'It's five on the dot!' He spoke English with the faintest hint of a Chinese accent.

Claire flushed. 'I was here early. Ten minutes before four, I believe,' she said. She took pride in her punctuality.

'Oh, don't be silly,' Mrs Chen said. 'Victor is just teasing you. Stop it!' She swatted her husband with her little hand.

'The English are so serious all the time,' he said.

13

'Well,' Claire said uncertainly. 'Locket and I spent a productive hour together.'

Locket slipped off the piano bench and under her father's arm. 'Hello, Daddy,' she said shyly. She looked younger than her ten years.

He patted her shoulder. 'How's my little Rachmaninoff?' he said. Locket giggled delightedly.

Mrs Chen was clattering around in her high heels. 'Mrs Pendleton,' she asked, 'would you like to join us for a drink?' She had on a suit that looked like it came out of the fashion magazines. It was almost certainly a Paris original. The jacket was made of a golden silk and buttoned smartly up the front and there was a shimmery yellow skirt underneath that flowed and draped like gossamer.

'Oh, no,' she answered. 'It's very kind of you, but I should go home and start supper.'

'I insist,' Mr Chen said. 'I must hear about my little genius.' His voice didn't allow for any disagreement. 'Run along now, Locket. The adults are having a conversation.'

There was a large velvet divan in the sitting room, and several chairs, upholstered in red silk, along with two matching black lacquered tables. Claire sat down in an armchair that was far more slippery than it looked. She sank too deeply into it, then had to move forward in an ungainly manner until she was perched precariously on the edge. She steadied herself with her arms.

'How are you finding Hong Kong?' Mr Chen said. His wife had gone into the kitchen to ask the amah to bring them drinks.

'Quite well,' she said. 'It's certainly different from England, but it's an adventure.' She smiled at him. He was a well-groomed man, in his well-pressed suit and red and black silk tie. Above him, there was an oil of a Chinese man dressed in robes and a black skull cap. 'What an interesting painting,' she remarked.

He looked up. 'Oh, that,' he said. 'That's Melody's grandfather, who had a large dye factory in Shanghai. He was quite famous.'

'Dyes?' she said. 'How fascinating.'

'Yes, and her father started the First Bank of Shanghai, and did very well indeed.' He smiled. 'Melody comes from a family of entrepreneurs. Her family was all educated in the West, England and America.'

Mrs Chen came back into the room. She had taken off her jacket to reveal a pearly blouse underneath. 'Claire,' she said. 'What will you have?'

'Just soda water for me, please.'

'And I'll have a sherry,' Mr Chen said.

'I know!' Mrs Chen said. She left again.

'And your husband,' he said. 'He's at a bank?'

'He's at the Department of Water Services,' she said. 'Working on the new reservoir.' She paused. 'He's heading it up.'

'Oh, very good,' Mr Chen said carelessly. 'Water's certainly important. And the English do a fair job of making sure it's in the taps when we need it.' He sat back and crossed one leg over the other. 'I miss England,' he said suddenly.

'Oh, did you spend time there?' Claire asked politely.

'I was at Oxford – Balliol,' he said, flapping his tie at her. Claire felt as if he had been waiting to tell her this fact. 'And Melody went to Wellesley, so we're a product of two different systems. I defend England, and Melody just loves the United States.'

'Indeed,' Claire murmured.

Mrs Chen came back into the room and sat down next to her husband. The amah appeared next and offered Claire a napkin. It had blue cornflowers on it.

'These are lovely,' she said, inspecting the embroidered linen.

'They're from Ireland,' Mrs Chen said. 'I just got them!'

'I just bought some lovely Chinese tablecloths at the China Emporium,' Claire said. 'Beautiful lace cut work.'

'You can't compare them with the Irish ones, though,' Mrs Chen said. 'Very crude.'

Mr Chen viewed his wife with amusement. 'Women!' he said to Claire.

The amah brought in a tray of drinks.

Claire sipped at her drink and felt the gassy bubbles in her mouth. Mr Chen looked at her expectantly.

'The Communists are a great threat,' she said. This is what she had heard again and again at gatherings.

Mr Chen laughed. 'Of course! And what will you and Melody do about them?'

'Shut up, darling. Don't tease,' said his wife. She took a sip of her drink. Mr Chen was watching her. 'What's that you're drinking, love?'

'A little cocktail,' she said. 'I've had a long day.' She sounded defensive.

There was a pause.

'Locket is a good student,' Claire said, 'but she needs to practise more.'

'It's not her fault,' Mrs Chen said breezily. 'I'm not here to oversee her practice enough.'

Mr Chen laughed. 'Oh, she'll be fine,' he said. 'I'm sure she knows what she's doing.'

Claire nodded. Parents were all the same. When she had children, she would be sure not to indulge them. She set her drink down. 'I should be going,' she said. 'It's harder to get a seat on the bus after five.'

'Are you sure?' Mrs Chen said. 'Pai was getting us some biscuits.'

'Oh, no, thank you,' she demurred. 'I really should be leaving.'

'We'll have Truesdale drive you home,' Mr Chen offered.

'Oh, no,' Claire said. 'I couldn't put you out.'

'Do you know him?' Mr Chen asked. 'He's English.'

'I haven't had the pleasure,' Claire said.

'Hong Kong is very small,' Mr Chen said. 'It's tiresome that way.'

'It's no trouble at all for Truesdale,' Mrs Chen said. 'He'll be going home anyway. Where do you live?'

'Happy Valley,' answered Claire, feeling put on the spot.

'Oh, that's near where he lives!' Mrs Chen cried, delighted at the coincidence. 'So, it's settled.' She called for Pai in Cantonese and told her to call the driver.

'Chinese is such an intriguing language,' Claire said. 'I hope to pick some up during our time here.'

Mr Chen raised an eyebrow. '*Cantonese*,' he said, 'is very difficult. There are some nine different tones for one sound. It's much more difficult than English. I picked up rudimentary English in a year, but I'm sure I wouldn't have been able to learn Cantonese or Mandarin or Shanghainese in twice that.'

'Well,' she said brightly, 'one always hopes.'

Pai walked in and spoke. Mrs Chen nodded. 'I'm terribly sorry,' she said, 'but the driver seems to have left already.'

'I'll catch the bus,' Claire said.

Mr Chen stood up as she picked up her bag. 'It was very nice to meet you,' he said.

'And you,' she said, and walked out, feeling their eyes on her back.

When she got home, Martin was already there. 'Hello,' he said. 'You're late today.' He was in a vest and his weekend trousers, which were stained and shiny at the knees. He had a drink in his hand.

She took off her jacket and put on a pot of water to boil. 'I was at the Chens' house today,' she said. 'Locket's parents asked me to stay for a drink.'

'Victor Chen, is it?' he asked, impressed. 'He's rather a big deal here.'

'I gathered,' she said. 'He was quite something. Not at all like a Chinaman.'

'You shouldn't use that word, Claire,' Martin said. 'It's very old-fashioned and a bit insulting.'

Claire coloured. 'I've just never . . .' She trailed off. 'I've never seen Chinese people like the Chens.'

'You are in Hong Kong,' Martin said, not unkindly. 'There are all types of Chinese.'

'Where is the amah?' she asked, wanting to change the subject.

Yu Ling came from the back when Claire called. 'Can you help with dinner?' Claire said. 'I bought some meat at the market.'

Yu Ling looked at her impassively. She had a way of making Claire feel uncomfortable, but she couldn't bring herself to sack her. She wondered how the other wives did it – they appeared to handle their servants with an easy aplomb that seemed unfamiliar and unattainable to Claire. Some even joked with them and treated them like family members, but she'd heard that was more the American influence. Her friend Cecilia had her amah brush her hair for her before she went to bed, while she sat at her dressing-table and put on cold cream.

Claire handed Yu Ling the meat she had bought on the way home. Then she went to lie down on the bed with a cold compress over her eyes. How had she got here, to this small flat on the other side of the world? She remembered her quiet childhood in Croydon, an only child sitting at her mother's side while she mended clothes, listening to her talk. Her mother had been bitter at what life had given her, a hand-to-mouth existence, especially after the war, and her father drank too much, perhaps because of it. Claire had never imagined life being much more than that. But marrying Martin had changed it all.

But this was the thing: she herself had changed in Hong Kong. Something about the tropical climate had ripened her appearance, brought everything into harmony. Where the other English women looked as if they were about to wilt in the heat, she thrived, like a hothouse flower. Her hair had lightened in the tropical sun until it was veritably gold. She perspired lightly so that her skin looked dewy, not drenched. She had lost weight so that her body was compact, and her eyes sparkled, cornflower blue. Martin had remarked on it, how the heat seemed to suit her. When she was at the Gripps or at a dinner party, she saw that men looked at her longer than necessary, came over to talk to her, let their hands linger on her back. She was learning how to speak to people at parties, order in a restaurant with confidence. She felt as if she were finally becoming a woman, not the girl she had been when she had left England. She felt as if she were a woman coming into her own.

And then the next week, after Locket's lesson, the porcelain rabbit had fallen into her handbag.

The week after, the phone rang and Locket leaped up to answer it, eager for any excuse to stop mangling the prelude she had been playing, and while she had been chattering away to a schoolmate, Claire saw a silk scarf lying on a chair. It was a beautiful, printed scarf, the kind women tied around their necks. She put it into her bag. A wonderful sense of calm came over her. And when Locket returned, with only a mumbled, 'Sorry, Mrs Pendleton,' Claire smiled instead of giving the little girl a piece of her mind.

When she got home, she went into the bedroom, locked the door and pulled out the scarf. It was an Hermès scarf, from Paris, and had pictures of zebras and lions in vivid oranges and browns. She practised tying it around her neck, and over her head, like an adventurous heiress on safari. She felt very glamorous.

The next month, after a conversation in which Mrs Chen told her she sent all her fine washing to Singapore because 'the girls here don't know how to do it properly and, of course, that means I have to have triple the amount of linens, what a bother', Claire found herself walking out with two of those wonderful Irish napkins in her skirt pocket. She had Yu Ling handwash and iron them so that she and Martin could use them with dinner.

She pocketed three French cloisonné turtles after Locket had abruptly gone to the bathroom – as if the child couldn't take care of nature's business before Claire arrived! A pair of sterling silver salt and pepper shakers found their way into her bag as she was passing through the dining room, and an exquisite Murano perfume bottle left out in the sitting room, as if Melody Chen had dashed some scent on as she was breezing her way through the foyer on her way to a gala event, was discreetly tucked into Claire's skirt pocket.

Another afternoon she was leaving when she heard Victor Chen in his study. He was talking loudly into the telephone and had left his door slightly ajar.

'It's the bloody British,' he said, before lapsing into Cantonese. Then, 'Can't let them,' and then something incomprehensible, which sounded very much like swearing. 'They want to create unrest, digging up skeletons that should be left buried, and all for their own purposes. The Crown Collection didn't belong to them in the first place. It's all our history, our artefacts, that they just took for their own. How'd they have liked it if Chinese explorers had come to their country years ago and made off with all their treasures? It's outrageous. Downing Street's behind all of this, I can assure you. There's no need for this right now.' He was very agitated, and Claire found herself waiting outside, breath held, to see if she couldn't hear anything more. She stood there until Pai appeared and looked at her questioningly. She pretended she had been studying the painting in the hallway, but she could feel Pai's eyes on her as she walked towards the door. She let herself out and went home.

Two weeks later, when Claire went for her lesson, she found Pai gone and a new girl opening the door.

'This is Su Mei,' Locket told her when they entered the room. 'She's from China, from a farm. She just arrived. Do you want something to drink?'

The new girl was small and dark, and would have been pretty if it hadn't been for a large black birthmark on her right cheek. She never looked up from the floor.

'Her family didn't want her because the mark on her face would make her hard to marry off. It's supposedly very bad luck.'

'Did your mother tell you that?' Claire asked.

'Yes,' Locket said. She hesitated. 'Well, I heard her say it on the telephone, and she said she got her very cheap because of it. Su Mei doesn't know anything! She tried to go to the bathroom in the bushes outside and Ah Wing beat her and told her she was like an animal. She's never used a tap before or had running water!'

'I'd like a bitter lemon, please,' Claire said, wanting to change the subject.

Locket spoke to the girl quickly. She left the room silently.

'Pai was stealing from us,' Locket said, eyes wide with the scandal. 'So Mummy had to let her go. Pai cried and cried, and then she beat the floor with her fists. Mummy said she was hysterical and slapped her face to stop her crying. They had to get Mr Wong to carry Pai out. He put her over his shoulder like a sack of potatoes and she was hitting his back with her fists.'

'Oh!' Claire said, before she could stifle the cry.

Locket looked at her curiously. 'Mummy says all servants steal.'

'Does she now?' Claire said. 'How terrible. But you know, Locket, I'm not sure that's true.' She remembered the way Pai had looked at her when she came upon her in the hallway and her chest felt tight.

'Where did she go?' she asked Locket.

'No idea,' she said cheerfully. 'Good riddance I say.'

Claire looked at the placid face of the girl, unruffled by conscience.

'There must be shelters or places for people like her.' Claire's voice quivered. 'She's not on the street, is she? Does she have family in Hong Kong?'

'Haven't a clue.'

'How can you not know? She lived with you!'

'She was a maid, Mrs Pendleton.' Locket looked at her curiously. 'Do you know anything about your servants?'

Claire was shamed into silence. The blood rose in her cheeks. 'Well,' she said. 'I suppose that's enough of that. Did you practise the scales?'

Locket pounded on the piano keys as Claire looked hard at the girl's chubby fingers, trying not to blink so that the tears would not fall.

June 1941

It begins like that. Her lilting laugh at a consular party. A spilled drink. A wet dress and a handkerchief hastily proffered. She is a sleek greyhound among the others – plump, braying women of a certain class. He doesn't want to meet her – he is suspicious of her kind, all chiffon and champagne, nothing underneath, but she has knocked his drink over her silk shift ('There I go again,' she says. 'I'm the clumsiest person in all Hong Kong'), and then commandeers him to escort her to the bathroom where she dabs at herself while peppering him with questions.

She is famous, born of a well-known couple, the mother a Portuguese beauty, the father a Shanghai millionaire with fortunes in trading and money lending.

'Finally, someone new! We can tell right away, you know. I've been stuck with those old bags for ages. We're very good at sniffing out new blood since the community is so wretchedly small and we're all so dreadfully sick of each other. We practically wait at the docks to drag the new people off the ships. Just arrived, yes? Have you a job yet?' she asks, having sat him on the rim of the bath while she reapplies her lipstick. 'Is it for fun or funds?'

'I'm at Asiatic Petrol,' he says, wary of being cast as the amusing newcomer. 'And it's most certainly for funds.' Although that's not the truth. A mother with money.

'How delightful!' she says. 'I'm so sick of meeting all these stuffy people. They don't have the slightest knowledge or ambition.'

'Those without expectations have been known to lack both of those qualities,' he says.

'Aren't you a grumpy grump?' she says. 'But stupidity is much more forgivable in the poor, don't you think?' She pauses, as if to let him think about that. 'Your name? And how do you know the Trotters?'

'I'm Will Truesdale, and I play cricket with Hugh. He knows some of my family, on my mother's side,' he says. 'I'm new to Hong Kong and he's been very decent to me.'

'Hmm,' she says. 'I've known Hugh for a decade and I've never ever thought of him as decent. And do you like Hong Kong?'

'It'll do for now,' he says. 'I came off the ship, decided to stay, rustled up something to do in the meantime. Seems pleasant enough here.'

'An adventurer, how fascinating,' she says, without the slightest bit of interest. Then she snaps her evening bag shut, takes his wrist firmly and waltzes – there is no other word, music seems to accompany her – out of the bathroom.

Conscious of being steered round the room like a pet poodle, her diversion of the moment, he excuses himself to go smoke in the garden. But peace is not to be his. She finds him out there, has him light her cigarette and leans confidentially towards him. 'Tell me,' she says. 'Why do your women get so fat after marriage? If I were an Englishman I'd be quite put out when the comely young lass I proposed to exploded after a few months of marriage or after popping out a child. You know what I'm talking about?' She blows smoke up to the dark sky.

'Not at all,' he says, amused despite himself.

'I'm not as flighty as you think,' she says. 'I do like you so very much. I'll ring you tomorrow, and we'll make a plan.' And then she is gone, wafting smoke and glamour as she trips her way into the resolutely non-smoking house of their hosts – Hugh loathes the smell.

He sees her in the next hour, flitting from group to group, chattering away. The women are dimmed by her, the men bedazzled.

The next day the phone rings in his office. He had been telling Simonds about the party.

'She's Eurasian, is she?' Simonds says. 'Watch out there. It's not as bad as dating a Chinese, but the higher-ups don't like it if you fraternize too much with the locals.'

'That is an outrageous statement,' Will says. He had liked Simonds up to that point.

'You know how it is,' Simonds says. 'At Hong Kong Bank, you get asked to leave if you marry a Chinese. But this girl sounds different, she sounds rather more than a local girl. It's not like she's running a noodle shop.'

'Yes, she is different,' he says. 'Not that it matters,' he adds as he answers the phone. 'I'm not marrying her.'

'Darling, it's Trudy Liang,' she says. 'Who aren't you marrying?'

'Nobody.' He laughs.

'That would have been quick work.'

'Even for you?'

'Wasn't it shocking how many women there were at the party yesterday?' she says, ignoring him. The women in the colony are supposed to have gone, evacuated to safer areas, while the war is simmering, threatening to boil over into their small corner of the world. 'I'm essential, you know. I'm a nurse with the Auxiliary Nursing Service!'

'None of the nurses I've ever had looked like you,' he says.

'If you were injured, you wouldn't want me as a nurse, believe me.' She pauses. 'Listen, I'll be at the races in the Wongs' box this afternoon. Would you care to join us?'

'The Wongs?' he asks.

'Yes, they're my godparents,' she says impatiently. 'Are you coming or not?'

'All right,' he says. This is the first in a long line of acquiescences.

Will muddles his way through the club and into the upper tier where the boxes are filled with chattering people in jackets and silky dresses. He comes through the door of number twenty-eight and Trudy spies him right away, pounces on him, and introduces him to everybody. There are Chinese from Peru, Polish by way of Tokyo, a Frenchman married to Russian royalty. English is spoken.

Trudy pulls him to one side. 'Oh dear,' she says. 'You're just as handsome as I remember. I think I might be in trouble. You've never had any issues with women, I'm sure. Or perhaps you've had too many.' She pauses and takes a theatrical breath. 'I'll give you the lie of the land here. That's my cousin, Dommie.' She points out an elegant, slim Chinese man with a gold pocket watch in his hand. 'He's my best friend and very protective, so you'd better watch out. And avoid her,' she says, pointing to a slight European woman with spectacles. 'Awful. She's just spent twenty minutes telling me the most extraordinary and yet incredibly boring story about barking deer on Lamma Island.'

'Really?' he says, looking at her oval face, her large golden-green eyes.

'And he,' she says, pointing to an owlish Englishman, 'is a bore. Some sort of art historian, keeps talking about the Crown Collection, which is apparently something most colonies have. They either acquire it locally or have pieces shipped from England for the public buildings – important paintings and statues and things like that. Hong Kong's is very impressive, apparently, and he's very worried about what will happen once war comes.' She makes a face. 'Also a bigot.'

She searches the room for others and her eyes narrow. 'There's my other cousin – or cousin by marriage.' She points out a stocky Chinese man in a double-breasted suit. 'Victor Chen. He thinks he's very important indeed. But I just find him tedious. He's married to my cousin, Melody, who used to be nice until she met him.' She pauses. 'Now she's . . .' Her voice trails off.

'Well, here you are,' she says, 'and what a gossip I'm being,' and drags him to the front where she has claimed the two best seats. They watch the races. She wins a thousand dollars and shrieks with pleasure. She insists on giving it all away, to the waiters, to the lavatory attendant, to a little girl they pass on the way out. 'Really,' she says disapprovingly, 'this is no place for children, don't you think?' Later she tells him she practically grew up at the track.

Her real name is Prudence. Trudy came later, when it was apparent that her given name was wholly unsuitable for the little sprite who terrorized her amahs and charmed all the waiters into bringing her forbidden fizzy drinks and sugar lumps.

'You can call me Prudence, though,' she says. Her long arms are draped round his shoulders and her jasmine scent is overwhelming him.

'I think I won't,' he says.

'I'm terribly strong,' she whispers. 'I hope I don't destroy you.'

He laughs. 'Don't worry about that,' he says. But, later, he wonders.

They spend most weekends at her father's large house in Shek-O, where wizened servants bring them buckets of ice and lemonade, which they mix with Plymouth gin, and plates of salty shrimp crackers. Trudy lies in the sun with an enormous floppy hat saying she thinks tans are vulgar, no matter what that Coco Chanel says. 'But I do so enjoy the feel of the sun on me,' she says, reaching for a kiss.

The Liangs' house is spread out on a promontory where it overlooks a placid sea. They keep chickens for fresh eggs – far away, of course, because of the odour – and a slightly fraying but still belligerent peacock roams the grounds, asserting himself to any intruders, except the gardener's Great Dane, with whom it has a mutual treaty. Trudy's father is never there; mostly he is in Macau where he is said to have the largest house on the Praia Grande and a Chinese mistress. Why he doesn't marry her, nobody knows. Trudy's mother disappeared when she was eight – a famous case that is still unsolved. The last anyone saw of her, she was stepping into a car outside the Gloucester Hotel. This is what he likes most about Trudy. With so many questions in her life, she never asks about his.

Trudy has a body like a child's – all slim hips and tiny feet. She is flat as a board, her breasts not even buds. Her arms are as slender as her wrists, her hair a sleek, smoky brown, her eyes wide and Western, with the lid-fold. She wears form-fitting sheaths, sometimes the *qipao*, slim tunics, narrow trousers, always flat silk slippers. She wears gold or brown lipstick, wears her hair shoulder-length, straight, and has black, kohl-lined eyes. She looks nothing like any of the other women at events – with their blowsy, flowing, floral skirts, carefully permanent-waved hair, red lipstick. She hates compliments – when people tell her she's beautiful, she says instantly, 'But I have a moustache!' And she does, a faint golden one you can see only in the sun. She is always in the papers although, she explains, that's more because of her father than because she is beautiful. 'Hong Kong is very practical in that way,' she says. 'Wealth can make a woman beautiful.' She is often the only Chinese at a party, although she says she's not really Chinese – she's not really anything, she says. She's everything, invited everywhere. Cercle Sportif Français, the American Country Club, the Deutsche Garten Club, she is welcome, an honorary member of everything.

Her best friend is her second cousin Dommie, Dominick Wong, the man from the races. They meet every Sunday night for dinner at the Gripps, and gossip over what transpired at the parties over the weekend. They grew up together. Her father and his mother are cousins. Will is starting to see that everyone in Hong Kong is related in one way or another – everyone who matters, that is. Victor Chen, Trudy's other cousin, is always in the papers for his business dealings, or he and his wife, Melody, are smiling out from photographs in the society pages.

Dominick is a fine-chiselled boy-man, a bit effeminate, with a long string of lissome, dissatisfied girlfriends. Will is never invited to Trudy's dinners with Dommie. 'Don't be cross. You wouldn't have fun,' she says, trailing a cool finger over his cheek. 'We chatter away in Shanghainese and it would be so tedious to have to explain everything to you. And Dommie's just about a girl anyway.'

'I don't want to go,' he says, trying to keep his dignity.

'Of course you don't, darling.' She laughs. She pulls him close. 'I'll tell you a secret.'

'What?' Her jasmine smell brings to mind the waxy yellow flower, her skin as smooth, as impermeable.

'Dommie was born with eleven fingers. Six on the left hand. His family had it removed when he was a baby, but it keeps growing back! Isn't that the most extraordinary thing? I tell him it's the devil inside. You can keep pruning it, but it'll always come back,' she whispers. 'Don't tell a soul. You're the first person I've ever told! And Dominick would have my head if he knew! He's quite ashamed of it!'

Hong Kong is a village. At the RAF ball, Dr Richards was found in the linen room at the Gloucester with a chambermaid; at the Sewells' dinner party, Blanca Morehouse had too much to drink and started to take off her blouse – you know about her past, don't you? Trudy, his very opinionated and biased guide to society, finds the English stuffy, the Americans tiresomely earnest, the French boring and self-satisfied, the Japanese horrible. He wonders aloud how she can stand him. 'Well, you're a bit of a mongrel,' she says. 'You don't belong anywhere, just like me.'

He had arrived in Hong Kong with just a letter of introduction to an old family friend, and has found himself defined, before he has done anything to define himself, by a chance meeting with a woman who asks nothing of him except to be with her.

People talk about Trudy all the time – she is always scandalizing someone or other. They talk about her in front of him, to him, as if daring him to say something. He never gives anything away. She came down from Shanghai, where she spent her early twenties in Noël Coward's old suite at the Cathay, and threw lavish parties on the roof terrace. She is rumoured to have fled an affair there, an affair with a top gangster who became obsessed with her; she is rumoured to have spent far too much time in the casinos, rumoured to have friends who are singsong girls, rumoured to have sold herself for a night, rumoured to be an opium addict. She is a lesbian. She is a radical. She assures him that almost none of these rumours are true. She says Shanghai is the place to be, that Hong Kong is dreadfully suburban. She speaks fluent Shanghainese, Cantonese, Mandarin, English, conversational French and a smattering of Portuguese.

In Shanghai, she says, the day starts at four in the afternoon with tea, then drinks at the Cathay or someone's party, then dinner of hairy crab and rice wine if you're inclined to the local, then more drinks and dancing, and you go and go, the night is so long, until it's time for breakfast – eggs and fried tomatoes at the Del Monte. Then you sleep until three, have noodles in broth for the hangover, and get dressed for another round. Such fun. She'll go back one of these days, she says, as soon as her father will let her.

The Biddles hire a cabana at the Lido in Repulse Bay and invite them for a day at the beach. There, they all smoke like mad and drink gimlets while Angeline complains about her life. Angeline Biddle is an old friend of Trudy's, a small and physically unappealing Chinese woman whom she's known since they were at primary school together. She married a very clever British businessman, whom she rules with an iron fist, and has a son away at school. They live in grand style on the Peak, where Angeline's presence causes some discomfort as Chinese are supposed to have permission to live there, except for one family, so rich they are exempt from the rules. There is a feeling, Trudy explains to Will later, that Angeline has somehow pulled a fast one on the British who live there, and she is resented for it, although Trudy admits that Angeline is hardly the most likeable of people to begin with. In the sun, Trudy takes off her top and sunbathes, her small breasts glowing pale in contrast to the rest of her.

'I thought you said a tan was vulgar,' he says.

'Shut up,' she says.

He hears her talking to Angeline: 'I'm just wild about him,' she says. 'He's the most stern, solid person I've ever met.' He supposes she is talking about him. People are not as scandalized as one might think. Simonds admits he was wrong about her.

The Englishwomen in the colony are disappointed: another bachelor taken off the market. Whispered, 'She did swoop down and grab him before anyone even knew he was in town.'

For him, there have been others, of course – the missionary's daughter in New Delhi, always ill and wan, though beautiful; the clever, hopeful spinster on the boat over from Penang – the women who say they're looking for adventure but who are really looking for husbands. He's managed to avoid the inconvenience of love for quite some time, but it seems to have found him in this unlikely place.

Women don't like Trudy. 'Isn't that always the case, darling?' she says, when, indiscreetly, he asks her about it. 'And aren't you a strange one for bringing it up?' She chucks him under the chin and continues making a jug of gin and lemonade. 'No one likes me,' she says. 'Chinese don't because I don't act Chinese enough, Europeans don't because I don't look at all European, and my father doesn't like me because I'm not very filial. Do you like me?'

He assures her he does.

'I wonder,' she says. 'I can tell why people like you. Besides the fact that you're a handsome bachelor with mysterious prospects, of course. They read into you everything they want you to be. They read into me all that they don't like.' She dips her finger into the mix and brings it out to taste. Her face puckers. 'Perfect,' she says. She likes it sour.

Little secrets begin to spill out of Trudy. A temple fortune-teller told her the mole on her forehead signifies death to a future husband. She's been engaged before, but it ended mysteriously. She tells him these secrets, then refuses to elaborate, saying he'll leave her. She seems serious.

Trudy has two amahs. They have 'tied their hair up together', she explains. Two women decide not to marry and put a notice in the newspaper, like vows, declaring they will live together for ever. Ah Lok and Mei Sing are old now, almost sixty, but they live together in a small room with twin beds ('So get that out of your mind right now,' Trudy says lazily, 'although we Chinese are very blasé about that sort of thing and who cares, really?'), a happy couple, except that they are both women. 'It's the best thing,' Trudy says. 'Lots of women know they'll never get married so this is just as good. So civilized, don't you think? All you need is a companion. That sex thing gets in the way after a while. A sisterhood thing. I'm thinking about doing it myself.' She pays them each twenty-five cents a week and they will do anything for her. Once, he came into the living room to find Mei Sing massaging lotion on to Trudy's hands while she was asleep on the sofa.

He never grows used to them. They completely ignore him, always talking to Trudy about him when he's there. They tell her he has a big nose, that he smells funny, that his hands and feet are grotesque. He is beginning to understand a little of what they say, but their disapproving intonation needs no translation. Ah Lok cooks – salty, oily dishes he finds unhealthy and unappealing. Trudy eats them with relish – it's the food she grew up with. She claims Mei Sing cleans, but he finds dust everywhere. The old woman also collects rubbish – used beer bottles, empty cold-cream jars, discarded toothbrushes – and stores it underneath her bed in anticipation of some apocalyptic event. All three women are messy. Trudy has the utter disregard for her surroundings that belongs to those who have been waited on since birth. She never cleans up, never lifts a finger, but neither do the amahs. They have picked up her habits – a peculiar symbiosis. Trudy defends them with the ferocity of a child defending her parents. 'They're old,' she says. 'Leave them alone. I can't bear people who poke at their servants.'

She pokes at them, though. She argues with them when the flower man comes and Ah Lok wants to give him fifty cents and Trudy says to give him what he asks. The flower man is called Fa Wong, king of flowers, and he comes round the neighbourhood once a week, giant woven baskets slung from his brown, wiry shoulders, filled with masses of flowers. He calls, '*Fa yuen, fa yuen,*' in a low monotonous pitch, and people wave him up to their flats. He and the amahs love to spar and they go at it for ages, until Trudy comes to break it up and give the man his money. Then Ah Lok gets angry and scolds her for giving in too easily. The old lady and the lovely young woman, their arms filled with flowers, go into the kitchen, where the blooms will be distributed into vases and scattered around the house. He watches them from his chair, his book spread over his lap, his eyes hooded as if in sleep – he watches her.

***

He is almost never alone, these days, always with her. It is something different for him. He used to like solitude, but now he craves her presence all the time. He's gone without this drug for so long, he's forgotten how compelling it is. When he is at the office, pecking away at the typewriter, he thinks of her laughing, drinking tea, smoking, the rings puffing up in front of her face. 'Why do you work?' she asks. 'It's so dreary.'

Discipline, he thinks. Don't fall down that rabbit hole. But it's useless. She's always there, ringing him on the phone, ready with plans for the evening. When he looks at her, he feels weak and happy. Is that so bad?

They are eating brunch at the Repulse Bay, and reading the Sunday paper when Trudy looks up.

'Why do they let these awful companies have advertisements?' she asks. 'Listen to this one – "Why suffer from agonizing piles?" Is there a need for that? Can't they be a little bit more oblique?' She shakes the newspaper at him. 'There's an illustration of a man suffering from piles! Is that really necessary?'

'My heart,' he says, 'I don't know. I just don't know.' A displaced Russian in a dinner jacket plays the piano behind him.

'Oh,' she says, as if an afterthought. 'My father wants to meet you. He wants to meet the man I've been spending so much time with.' She is nonchalant, too much so. 'Are you free tonight?'

'Of course,' he says.

They go for dinner at the Gloucester, where Trudy tells him the story of her parents' meeting while they're waiting at the bar. She is drinking brandy, unusual for her, which makes him think she might be more nervous than she is letting on. She swirls it, takes a delicate whiff, sips.

'My mother was a great Portuguese beauty – her family had been in Macau for ages. They met there. My father was not as successful then, although he came from a well-to-do family. He had just started up a business selling widgets or something. He's very clever, my father. Don't know why I turned out to be such a dim bulb.' Her face lights up. 'Here he is!' She leaps off the stool and rushes over to give her father a kiss. Will had expected a big, confident man with the aura of power. Instead, Mr Liang is small and diffident, with an ill-cut suit and an air of sweetness. He seems to be over-whelmed by the vitality of his daughter. He lets Trudy wash over him, like a force of nature, much as everyone else in Hong Kong does, Will thinks. The head waiter seats them with much hovering and solicitous hand-waving, which neither Trudy nor her father seems to notice. They speak to each other in Cantonese, which makes her seem like a different person entirely.

Their food is brought to them, as if preordained. 'Should we order?' he ventures, and their faces are astonished.

'You only eat certain dishes here,' they say.

Trudy calls for champagne. 'This is a momentous occasion,' she declares. 'My father's not met many of my beaux. You're over the first hurdle.'

Wan Kee Liang does not ask Will about his life or his work. Instead, they exchange pleasantries, talk about the horse races and the war. When Trudy excuses herself to go to the powder room, her father motions for Will to come closer.

'You are not a rich man,' he says.

'Not like you, but I do all right.' How odd to assume.

'Trudy is very spoiled girl, and want many things.' The man's face betrays nothing.

'Yes,' Will says.

'Not good for woman to pay for anything.'

35

Trudy's father hands him an envelope. 'Here is money for you to take Trudy out. Will cover expenses for a long time. Not good for Trudy to be paying all time.'

Will is taken aback. 'I can't take that,' he says. 'I've never let Trudy pay for a meal.'

'Doesn't matter,' the man waves his hand. 'Good for your relationship.'

Will refuses and puts the envelope on the table, where it sits until they see Trudy approaching. Trudy's father puts it back in his suit jacket. 'Not meant to be insult,' he says. 'I want best for Trudy. So best for her means best for you. This means little to me, but might make difference for you two.'

'I appreciate the thought,' Will says. 'But I can't.' He lets it go at that.

The next week, Will receives letters in the post from restaurants and clubs around town informing him that his accounts have been opened and are ready for use. One has scribbled a note in the margin, 'Just come in. You won't even need to sign. We look forward to seeing you.' The tone: apologetic to a good customer, but deferring to the wishes of their best.

He is a little irritated, but not so much, more bemused than anything. He puts the letters in a drawer. He supposes, to Wan Kee Liang, that everyone looks like a pauper, hoping for handouts. The Chinese are wise, he thinks. Or maybe it's just Trudy's family.

Trudy loves the Parisian Grill, is great friends with the owner, a Greek married to a local Portuguese who sees no irony in the fact that he serves the froggiest of foods. She refuses absolutely to go to a Chinese restaurant with Will, will only go when with Chinese people who, she says, are the only ones who appreciate the food the way it should be.

The Greek who runs the Parisian Grill, his name is now Henri, changed from God knows what, loves Trudy, views her as a daughter, and his wife, Elsbieta, treats her like a sister. She goes there for first drinks almost every night, often ends evenings there as well. Henri and Elsbieta are polite to him, but with a certain reserve. He thinks they have seen too many of Trudy's beaux. He wants to protest that he is the one in danger, protest over the red vinyl banquettes, the smoky white candles burned down to smudgy lumps, but he never does.

They meet everyone at the Parisian Grill. It is the sort of place one goes to when one is new in town or old, or bored. Hong Kong is small, and eventually, everyone ends up there. One night, they have drinks at the bar with a group of visiting Americans and are invited to dinner with them.

Trudy tells their new friends that she loves Americans, their open-handed extravagance, their loud talk and braying confidence. When someone brings up the war, she pretends not to hear, instead going on about the qualities she feels all Americans have. They have a sense of the world being incomparably large, she says and that they are able to . . . not colonize, but spread through all countries, spending their money like water, without guilt or too much self-consciousness. She loves that. The men are tall and rangy, with long faces and quick decisions, and the women leave them be, isn't that wonderful?, because they're so busy with their own committees and plans. They invite all and sundry to their events, and they serve marvellous items like potato salads and ham and cheese sandwiches. And, unless there is a very special type of Englishman present (she tips her head towards Will), they tend to diminish the other men in the room. It's very odd, but she's seen it. Haven't you noticed that? If she had it all to do over again, she says to the dinner-table, she would come back as an American. Lacking that possibility, she'll marry one. Or maybe just move there, if someone objects to her marrying an American – said with eyes cast down demurely as a joke.

Will thinks back to when she complained that Americans were tiresomely earnest, and just smiles. She has free will, he says simply.

He would never do anything to stop her from doing what she wants. The Americans applaud. An enlightened man, says a woman with red lips and an orange dress.

Life is easy. At the office, he is expected in at nine thirty, then a two-hour lunch is not uncommon, and they knock off at five for drinks. He can go out every night, play all weekend, do whatever he wants. Trudy's friends move to London and want someone responsible to take care of their flat, so Will moves to May Road and pays the ludicrous rent of two hundred Hong Kong dollars, and this only after much wrangling to persuade Sudie and Frank Chen to take anything at all. They all go out for dinner, and it's very civilized.

'You're doing us a favour!' they cry, as they pour more champagne.

'You really are, Will,' Trudy says. 'No one in all Hong Kong would agree to do anything so nice for the Chens, you know. They've awful reputations around here – that's why they're leaving.'

'Be that as it may,' Will says. 'I have to pay something.'

'We'll talk about it later,' the Chens say, but they never do. Instead they drink four splits of champagne and end up going to the beach at midnight to hunt for crabs by candlelight.

May Road is different from Happy Valley, his old neighbourhood. Filled with expatriates and their servants, it is a bourgeois suburb of England, or how he'd always imagined one to be. Children walk obediently next to their amahs, matrons climb into the backs of their chauffeured cars; it's much quieter than the chattering bustle of his old haunt. He misses Happy Valley, the vitality of it, the loud, rude locals, the lively shops.

But then there is Trudy. Trudy has a large place not five minutes from him. He walks the winding road to her flat every day, having picked up fresh clothes after work.

'Isn't this nice?' she says, lavishing him with kisses at the door. 'Isn't it delicious that you're so close and not in that dreadful Happy Valley? I do think the only time I'd go there before I met you was when I needed plimsolls for the beach. There's this wonderful shop . . .'

And then she's on to something else, crying out to Ah Lok that the flowers are browning, or that there's a puddle in the foyer. At Trudy's, there's no talk of war, no fighting except squabbling with the servants, no real troubles. There's only ease and her sweet, lilting laugh. He slips gratefully into her world.

June 1952

Claire had been waking at the same time every night. Twenty-two minutes after three. By now, she knew it without even looking at the clock. And every night, after she started awake, she would look over at the hulking shape of her husband as he slept, and she would be calmed from the shock of consciousness. His chest rose and fell evenly as his nose reverberated with a gentle snore. He always slept heavily, aided by the several beers he drank every evening.

She sat up, clapped loudly twice, her hands stiff, the sound like two bullets in the night. Martin shifted at the noise, then breathed freely. That trick was one of the few that her mother had imparted about married life. The clock now showed three twenty-three.

She tried to go back to sleep. She had done it once or twice before, fallen back asleep before her body got too awake. Breathing softly, she lay flat on her back and felt the damp linen sheet beneath and the light weight of the cotton quilt on top. It was so humid she could only wear a thin nightdress to bed, and even that grew sticky after a day or two. She must buy a new fan. The old one had sputtered to a standstill last week, caked with mossy mould. A fan, and also some more electric cord. And lightbulbs. She mustn't forget lightbulbs. She breathed lightly, over the slight rumble of Martin starting up again. Should she write the things down? She would remember, she tried to tell herself. But she knew she would get up and write them down, so as not to forget, so as not to obsess about forgetting, and then she would be up and unable to go back to sleep. It was settled. She got up softly and felt her way out of the mosquito netting, disturbing a resting mosquito that buzzed angrily in her ear before flying away. The pad was lying on a table next to the bed, and she pencilled her list.

Then, the real reason. She reached into the depths of the bureau and felt around carefully for the bag. It was a cloth bag, one she had got for free at a bazaar, and it was large and full. She pulled it out quietly.

Going into the bathroom, she switched on the light. The bath was full of water. There hadn't been rain for several months now, and the government was starting to ration. Yu Ling filled the bath every evening, between five and seven o'clock when the water was on, for their use during the day.

Claire set the bag down, dipped a bucket into the water and wet a cloth to wipe her face. Then she sat on the cool tiled floor and pulled up her nightdress so that she could place the bag between her legs.

She tumbled out the contents.

There were more than thirty items glittering up at her. More than thirty costly necklaces, scarves, ornaments, perfume bottles. They looked almost tawdry, jumbled together in the harsh bathroom light, against the white tiles, so Claire laid down a towel and separated them, so that each had a few inches of space, a cushion against the floor. There. Now they looked like the expensive items they were. Here was a ring, thick, beautifully worked gold, with what was probably turquoise. She slipped it on to her finger. And here was a handkerchief, so sheer she could see the pale pink of her palm underneath it. She sprayed it with perfume, a small round bottle of it, called Jazz. On the bottle, there was a drawing of two women dancing in flapper dresses. She waved the scented handkerchief around. Jasmine. Too heavy. She did her hair with the tortoiseshell comb, rubbed French hand lotion into her fingers, then carefully applied lipstick. Then she clipped on heavy gold earrings and tied a scarf round her head.

She stood in front of the mirror. The woman who looked back was sophisticated and groomed, a woman who travelled the world and knew about art and books and yachts.

She wanted to be someone else. The old Claire seemed provincial, ignorant. She had been to a party at Government House, sipped champagne at the Gripps while women she knew twirled around in silky dresses. She had her nose pressed up against the glass and was watching a different world. She could not name it but she felt as if she was about to be revealed, as if there was another Claire inside, waiting to come out. In these few hours in the morning, dressed in someone else's finery, she could pretend she was part of it, that she had lived in Colombo, eaten frog's legs in France or ridden an elephant in Delhi with a maharajah by her side.

At seven, after she had brewed herself a cup of tea and eaten some buttered toast, she made her way to the bedroom. She stood over her sleeping husband.

'Wake up,' she said quietly.

He stirred, then rolled over to face her.

'Cuckoo,' she said, a little louder.

'Happy birthday, darling,' he said sleepily. He propped himself up on one elbow to offer a kiss. His breath was sour but not unpleasant.

Claire was twenty-eight today.

It was Saturday, and the beginning of summer. Not too hot yet, the mornings had a breeze and a little bit of cool before the sun warmed the afternoons and the hats and fans had to come out.

Martin worked a half-day on Saturday but then there was a party at the Arbogasts', on the Peak. Reginald Arbogast was a very successful businessman and made a point of inviting every English person in the colony to his gatherings, which were famous for his unstinting hand and lavish foods.

'I'll meet you at the funicular at one,' Martin told her.

At one o'clock, Claire was at the tram station waiting. She had on a new dress the tailor had delivered just the day before, a white poplin based on a Paris original. She had found a Mr Hao, an inexpensive man in Causeway Bay, who would come and measure her at home and charge eight Hong Kong dollars a dress. It had turned out quite well. She had sprayed on a bit of Jazz, although she found it strong; she dabbed it on, then rubbed water on it to dilute the smell.

At ten past one, Martin came through the station doors, and gave her a kiss. 'You look nice,' he said. 'New dress?'

'Mm-hmm,' she said.

They took the tram up the mountain, a steep ride that seemed almost vertical at times. They held on to the rail, leaned forward and looked outside, where they could see into people's homes in the Mid-Levels, with curtains pushed to one side, and newspapers and dirty glasses strewn on tables.

'I would think,' Claire said, 'that if I knew people would be looking in my house all day from the tram, I'd make a point of leaving it tidy, wouldn't you?'

At the top, they found that the Arbogasts had hired rickshaws to take their guests to the house from the station. Claire climbed into one. 'I always feel for the men,' she said quietly to Martin. 'Isn't this why we have mules or horses? It's one of these queer Hong Kong customs, isn't it?'

'It's a fact that human labour here often costs less,' Martin said.

Claire stifled her irritation. Martin was always so literal.

The man lifted up the harness with a grunt. They started to roll along and Claire settled into the uncomfortable seat. Around them, the green was overwhelming, tropical trees bursting with leaves that dripped when scratched, bougainvillaea and other flowering bushes springing from the hillsides. Sometimes, she got the feeling that Hong Kong was too alive. It seemed unable to restrain itself. There were insects crawling everywhere, wild dogs on the hills, mosquitoes breeding furiously. They had made roads in the hillsides and buildings sprouted out of the ground, but nature strained at her boundaries – there were always sweaty, shirtless men chopping away at the greenery that seemed to grow overnight. It wasn't India, she supposed, but it certainly wasn't England. The man in front of her strained and sweated. His shirt was thin and grey.

'The Arbogasts apparently had this place undergo a massive cleaning after the war,' Martin said. 'Smythson was telling me about it, how it had been gutted by the Japanese and all that was left was walls, and not many of those. It used to belong to the Bayer representative out here, Thorpe, and he never came back after he was repatriated after the war. He sold it for a song. He'd had enough.'

'The way people lived out here before the war,' Claire said. 'It was very gracious.'

'Arbogast lost his hand during the war as well. He has a hook now. They say he's quite sensitive about it so try not to look at it.'

'Of course,' Claire said.

When they walked in, the party was in full swing. Doors opened on to a large receiving room, which led into a drawing room with french doors that looked over a lawn with a wide, stunning view of the harbour. A violinist sawed away at his instrument while a pianist accompanied him. The house was decorated in the way the

English did their houses in the Orient, with Persian carpets and the occasional wooden Chinese table topped with Burmese silver bowls and other exotic curiosities. Women in light cotton dresses swayed towards each other while men in safari suits or blazers stood with hands in pockets. Swiftly moving servants balanced trays of Pimm's and champagne.

'Why does he do this?' Claire asked Martin. 'Invite the world, I mean.'

'He's done well for himself here, and he didn't have much before, and wants to do something good for the community. What I've heard, anyway.'

'Hello, hello,' said Mrs Arbogast from the hall where she was greeting guests – a thin, elegant woman with a sharp face. Sparkly earrings jangled from her ears.

'Lovely of you to have us,' said Martin. 'A real honour.'

'Don't know you, but perhaps we shall have the pleasure later.' She turned aside, looking for the next guest. They had been dismissed.

'Drink?' Martin said.

'Please,' said Claire.

She saw an acquaintance, Amelia, and walked over. Too late, she saw that Mrs Pinter was in the circle, partially hidden by a potted plant. They all tried to avoid Mrs Pinter. Claire had been cornered by her before, and had spent an excruciating thirty minutes listening to the old woman talk about ant colonies. She wanted to be kind to older people but she had her limits. Mrs Pinter was now obsessed with starting up an Esperanto society, and would reel unwitting newcomers into her ever more complicated and idiotic plans. She was convinced that a universal language would have saved them all from the war.

'I've been thinking about getting a butler,' Mrs Pinter was saying. 'One of those Chinese fellows would do all right with a bit of training.'

'Are you going to teach him Esperanto?' Amelia asked, teasing.

'We have to teach everyone but the Communists,' Mrs Pinter said placidly.

'Isn't the refugee problem alarming?' Marjorie Winter said, ignoring all of them. She was fanning herself with a napkin. She was a fat, kindly woman, with very small sausage-like curls around her face.

'They're coming in by the thousands, I hear,' Claire said.

'I'm starting a new league,' said Marjorie. 'To help them. Those poor Chinese streaming across the border like herded animals, running away from that dreadful government. They live in the most frightful conditions. You must volunteer! I've rented space for an office and everything.'

'You remember in 1950,' Amelia said, 'when some of the locals were practically running hotels, taking care of all their family and friends who had fled? And these were the well-off ones, who were able to book passage. It was quite something.'

'Why are they leaving China?' Claire said. 'Where do they expect to go from here?'

'Well, that's the thing, dear,' Marjorie said. 'They don't have anywhere *to* go. Imagine that. That's why my league is so important.'

Amelia sat down. 'The Chinese come down during war, they go back up, then come down again. It's dizzying. They are these giant waves of displacement. And their different dialects. I do think Mandarin is the ugliest, with its *wer* and its *er* and those strange noises.' She fanned herself. 'It's far too hot to talk about a league,' she said. 'Your energy always astounds me, Marjorie.'

'Amelia,' Marjorie said unsympathetically, 'you're always hot.'

Indeed Amelia *was* always hot, or cold, or vaguely out of sorts. She was not physically suited to life outside of England, which was ironic since she had not lived there for some three decades. She needed her creature comforts and suffered mightily, and not silently, without them. They had been in Hong Kong since before the war. Her husband, Angus, had brought her from India, which she had loathed, to Hong Kong in 1938 when he had become under-secretary at the Department of Finance. She was opinionated, railing against what she saw as the unbearable English ladies who wanted to become Chinese, who wore their hair in chignons with ivory chopsticks, too-tight *cheongsams* to every event and employed local tutors so they could speak to the servants in their atrocious Cantonese. She did not understand such women and constantly warned Claire against becoming one of such a breed.

Amelia had taken Claire under her wing, introducing her to people, inviting her to lunch, but Claire was often uncomfortable in her company, listening to her sharp observations and often biting innuendo. Still, she clung to her as someone who could help her navigate this strange new world. She knew her mother would approve of someone like Amelia, even be impressed that Claire knew such people.

Outside, the thwack of a tennis ball punctuated the low buzz and tinkle of conversation and cocktails. Claire's group migrated towards a large tent pitched next to the courtyard.

'People come and play tennis?' Claire asked.

'Yes – in this weather, can you believe it?'

'I can't believe they have a tennis court,' said Claire with wonder.

'And I can't believe what you can't believe,' Amelia said archly.

Claire blushed. 'I've just never –'

'I know, darling,' Amelia said. 'Just a village girl.' She winked to take the sting out of her comment.

'You know what Penelope Davies did the other day?' Marjorie interrupted. 'She went to the temple at Wong Tai Sin with an interpreter, and had her fortune told. She said it was remarkable how much the old woman knew!'

'What fun,' Amelia said. 'I'll take Wing and try it out too. Claire, we should go!'

'Sounds fun,' Claire said.

'Did you hear about the child in Malaya who had hiccups for three months?' Marjorie was asking Martin, who had joined them with drinks in hand. 'The Briggs child. His father's the head of the Electricity over there. His mother almost went mad. They tried a witch doctor but no results. They didn't know whether to take him back to England or just trust in fate.'

'Can you imagine having hiccups for more than an hour?' Claire said. 'I'd go mad! That poor child.'

Martin knelt down to play with a small boy who had wandered over. 'Hallo,' he said. 'Who are you?'

'Martin wants children,' Claire said, *sotto voce*, to Amelia. Despite herself, she often found herself confiding to Amelia. She had no one else to talk to.

'All men do, darling,' Amelia said. 'You have to negotiate the number before you start popping them out or else they'll want to keep going. I got Angus down to two before we started.'

'Oh,' Claire said, startled. 'That seems so . . . unromantic.'

'What do you think married life is?' Amelia said. She cocked an eyebrow at Claire. Claire blushed, and excused herself to go to the powder room.

When she returned, Amelia had drifted away and was talking to a tall man Claire had never seen before. She waved her over. He was a man of around forty with a crude cane that looked as if it had been whittled by a child. He had sharp, handsome features and a shock of black hair, run through with strands of grey, ungroomed.

'Have you met Will Truesdale?' Amelia said.

'I haven't,' she said, as she put out her hand.

'Pleased to meet you,' he said. His hand was dry and cool, almost as if it were made of paper.

'He's been in Hong Kong for ages,' Amelia said. 'An old-timer, like us.'

'Quite the experts, we are,' he said. He suddenly looked alert. 'I like your scent,' he said. 'Jasmine, is it?'

'Yes. Thank you.'

'Newly arrived?'

'Yes, just a month.'

'Like it?'

'I never imagined living in the Orient, but here I am.'

'Oh, Claire, you should have had more imagination,' Amelia said, gesturing to a waiter for another drink.

Claire coloured again. Amelia was in rare form today.

'I'm delighted to meet someone who's not so jaded,' Will said. 'All you women are so worldly it quite tires me out.'

Amelia had turned away to take her drink and hadn't heard him. There was a pause, but Claire didn't mind it.

'It's Claire's birthday,' Amelia told Will, turning back. She smiled, brittle, red lipstick stained her front tooth. 'She's just a baby.'

'How nice,' he said. 'We need more babies around these parts.'

He suddenly reached out his hand and slowly tucked a strand of hair behind her ear. A possessive gesture, as if he had known her for a long time. 'Sorry,' he said. Amelia had not seen; she had been scanning the crowd.

'Sorry for what?' Amelia asked, turning back, distracted.

'Nothing,' they both said. Claire looked down at the floor. They were joined in their collusive denial; it suddenly seemed overwhelmingly intimate.

'What?' Amelia said impatiently. 'I can't hear a damn thing above this din.'

'I'm twenty-eight today,' Claire said, not knowing why.

'I'm forty-three.' He nodded. 'Very old.'

Claire couldn't tell if he was joking.

'I remember the celebration we had for you at Stanley,' Amelia said. 'What a fête.'

'Wasn't it?'

'You're still with Melody and Victor?' Amelia enquired of him.

'Yes,' he said. 'It suits me for now.'

'I'm sure it suits Victor just fine to have an Englishman chauffeuring him around,' she replied slyly.

'It seems to work for everyone involved,' Will said, not taking the bait.

Amelia leaned towards him confidentially. 'I hear there's been chatter about the Crown Collection and its disappearance during the war. Angus says it's starting to come to the boil. People have noticed. Have you heard anything?'

'I have,' he said.

'They want to ferret out the collaborators.'

'A bit late, don't you think?'

After a pause, when it became apparent that nothing more was forthcoming from Will, she spoke again: 'I hope the Chens are treating you well?'

'I can't complain,' he said.

'A bit odd, though, isn't it? You working over there?'

'Amelia,' he said. 'You're boring Claire.'

'Oh, no,' Claire protested. 'I'm just . . .'

'Well, you're boring me,' he said. 'And life is too short to be bored. Claire, have you been to the different corners of our fair colony? Which is your favourite?'

'Well, I have been exploring a little. Sheung Wan is lovely – I do like the markets – and I've been over to Kowloon, Tsim Sha Tsui on the Star Ferry, of course, and seen all the shops there. It's very lively, isn't it?'

'See, Amelia?' Will said. 'An Englishwoman who ventures outside of Central and the Peak. You would do well to learn from this newcomer.'

Amelia rolled her eyes. 'She'll grow tired of it soon enough. I've seen so many of these bright-eyed new arrivals, and they all end up having tea with me at the Helena May and complaining about their amahs.'

'Well, don't let Amelia's rosy attitude affect you too much, Claire,' Will said. 'At any rate, it was a pleasure to meet you. Best of luck in Hong Kong.' He nodded to them politely and left. She felt the heat of his body as he passed her.

Claire felt bereft. He had assumed they would not meet again. 'Odd man?' she said. It was more of a statement.

'You've no idea, dear,' Amelia said.

Claire peeked after him. He had floated over to the side of the tennis court, although he had some sort of limp, and was watching Peter Wickham and his son hit the ball at each other.

'He's also very serious now,' Amelia said. 'Can't have a proper conversation with him. He was quite sociable before the war, you know, you saw him at all the parties, had the most glamorous girl in town, quite high up at Asiatic Petrol, but he never really recovered after the victory. He's a chauffeur, now.' Her voice dropped. 'For the Chens, actually, do you know who they are?'

'Amelia!' Claire said. 'I give their daughter piano lessons! You helped me arrange it!'

'Oh dear. The memory goes first, they say. You've never run into him there?'

'Never,' Claire said. 'Although the Chens once suggested he might give me a lift home.'

'Poor Melody,' said Amelia. 'She's very *fragile*.' The word said delicately.

'Indeed,' Claire said, remembering the way Melody had sipped her drink, quickly, urgently.

'The thing with Will is . . .' Amelia hesitated. 'I'm quite certain he doesn't need to work at all.'

'How do you mean?' Claire asked.

'I just know certain things,' Amelia said mysteriously.

Claire didn't ask. She wouldn't give Amelia the satisfaction.

September 1941

Trudy is dressing for dinner while he watches from the bed. She has finished her mysterious bathing ritual, with its oils and unguents, and now she smells marvellous, like a valley in spring. She is sitting at her dressing-table in a long peach satin robe, wrapped silkily round her waist, applying fragrant creams to her face.

'Do you like this one?' She gets up and holds a long black dress in front of her.

'It's fine.' He can't concentrate on the clothes when her face is so vibrant.

'Or this one?' A knee-length dress the colour of orange sherbet.

'Fine.'

She pouts. Her skin gleams. 'You're so unhelpful.'

She tells him Manley Haverford is having a party, an end-of-summer party at his country house this weekend and that she wants to go. Manley is an old bigot who used to have a radio talk show before he married a rich but ugly Portuguese woman who conveniently died two years later whereupon he retired to live the life of a country squire in Saikung.

'Desperately,' she says. 'I want to go desperately.'

'You loathe Manley,' he says. 'You told me so last week.'

'I know,' she says. 'But his parties are fun and he's very generous with the drinks. Let's go and talk about how awful he is right in front of him. Can we go? Can we? Can we?' She wears him down. They will go.

So on Friday, late afternoon, he plays truant from work and they spend the twilight hours bathing in the ocean by Manley's house. To get there, they drive narrow, winding roads carved out of the green mountain, blue water on their right, verdant hillside on their left. His house is through a dilapidated wooden gate and at the end of a long driveway, beside the sea, with a porch that juts out, and rough stone steps leading down to the beach. He's had coolers filled with ice and drinks and sandwiches brought down to the sandy inlet. The still-hot sun and the water make them ravenous and they eat and eat and eat and curse their host for not bringing enough.

'Me?' he asks. 'I assumed I had invited civilized people, who ate three meals a day.'

Victor and Melody Chen, Trudy's cousins, wander down from the house, where they had been resting.

'What are we doing now?' Melody asks. Will likes her, thinks she's nice, when she's not with her husband.

A woman they have never met before, newly arrived from Singapore, suggests they play Charades. They all moan but acquiesce.

Trudy is one team's leader, the Singapore woman the other. The groups huddle together, write words on scraps of damp paper. They put them into the empty sandwich basket.

Trudy goes first. She looks at her paper, dimples. 'Easy peasy,' she says encouragingly to her group. She makes the film sign, one hand rotating an imaginary camera lever.

'Film!' shouts an American.

She puts up four fingers, then suddenly ducks her head, puts her arms in front of her and whooshes through the air.

'*Gone With the Wind*,' Will says. Trudy curtsies.

'Unfair,' says someone from the other team. 'Pet's advantage.'

Trudy comes over and plants a kiss on his forehead. 'Clever boy,' she says, and sinks down next to him.

Singapore gets up.

'She's your nemesis,' Will tells Trudy.

'Don't worry,' Trudy says. 'She's idiotic.'

The afternoon passes pleasantly, with them shouting insults and drinking and generally being stupid. Some people talk about the government and how it's organizing different Volunteer Corps.

'It's not volunteering,' Will says. 'It's mandatory. It's the Compulsory Service Act, for heaven's sake. Why don't they just call a spade a spade? Dowbiggin is being ridiculous about it.'

'Don't be such a grump,' Trudy says. 'Do your duty.'

'I guess so,' he says. 'Must fight the good fight, I suppose.' He thinks the organization is being handled in an absurd fashion.

'Is there one for cricketers?' someone asks, as if to prove his point.

'Why not?' somebody else says. 'You can make up one however you want.'

'I hardly think that's true,' Manley says. 'But I'm joining one that's training out here at weekends, on the Club grounds. Policemen, although I'd think they'd be rather busy if there was an attack.'

'Aren't you too old, Manley?' Trudy asks. 'Old and decrepit?'

'That's the wonderful thing, Trudy,' he says, with a forced smile. 'You can't fire a Volunteer. And at any rate the one here at the Club is convenient.'

'I'm sending Melody to America,' Victor Chen says suddenly. 'I don't want her to be in any danger.'

Melody smiles uneasily, but says nothing.

'The government is preparing,' says Jamie Biggs. 'They're storing food in warehouses in Tin Hau and securing British property.'

'Like the Crown Collection?' Victor asks. 'What are they going to do about that? It's part of the British heritage.'

'I'm sure all the arrangements have been made,' says Biggs.

'The food will go bad before anyone gets it,' says another man.

'Cynic,' says Trudy.

She stands up gracefully and goes towards the ocean. All this talk of war bores her. She thinks it will never happen. They watch her, rapt, as she plunges into the sea and comes up sleek and dripping – her slim body a vertical rebuke to the flatness of the horizon between the sky and sea. She walks up to Will and shakes her wet hair at him. Drops of water fall and sparkle. Then someone asks where the tennis rackets are. The spell is broken.

Over dinner, Trudy declares that she is going to be in charge of uniforms for the Volunteers. 'And Will can be the model,' she says, 'because he's a perfect male specimen.'

Colin Thorpe, who heads up the American office of a large pharmaceutical company, looks doubtful. 'Rather small and ugly, isn't he?' he says, although this is more a description of himself than of Will.

'Will!' Trudy cries. 'You've been insulted! Defend your honour!'

'I've better things to defend,' he says. And the table falls silent. He is always saying the wrong thing, puncturing the gaiety. 'Er, sorry,' he says. But they are already on to the next thing.

Trudy is describing the tailor who is going to make the uniforms. 'He's been our family tailor for ages and he can whip out a copy of a Paris dress in two days, one if you beg!'

'What's his name?'

'Haven't the foggiest,' she says easily. 'He's the Tailor. But I know where the shop is, or my driver does, and we're the best of friends. Do you fellows prefer orange or a very bright pink as colours?'

They decide on olive green ('So boring,' the women sigh) with orange stripes (a concession), and Trudy asks who is to measure the men.

They suggest her.

She accepts ('Isn't there something about dressing left?' she asks innocently), then says that Will can measure in her stead. Trudy's frivolity, Will has noticed, has boundaries.

Sophie Biggs is trying to interest everyone in moonlight picnics. 'They're ever so much fun,' she says. 'We take a steamboat out, with row boats, and when we reach the islands we row everyone ashore with the provisions and a guitar or an accordion or something.' Sophie is a large girl and Will wonders if she is a secret eater because she eats tiny portions when she is out. Now, she is poking her spoon in the vichyssoise.

Trudy sighs. 'It sounds like so much labour,' she says. 'Wouldn't it just be easier to have a picnic at Repulse Bay?'

Sophie looks at her reproachfully. 'But it's not the same,' she says. 'It's the journey.'

Sophie's husband claims to be in shipping, but Will thinks he's in Intelligence. When he tells Trudy this, she cries, 'That big lout? He couldn't detect his way out of a paper bag!' But Jamie Biggs is always listening, never talking, and he has a watchful air about him. If he's that obvious, Will supposes he's not very good. After Charles Pottinger left last year, someone had told Will that he was Intelligence. He hadn't been able to believe it. Charles was a big, florid man who drank a lot and seemed the very soul of indiscretion.

Edwina Storch, a large Englishwoman who is the headmistress of the good school in town, has brought her constant companion, Mary Winkle, and they sit at the end of the table, eating quietly, talking to no one but each other. Will has seen them before. They are always around, but never say much.

Over dessert – trifle – Jamie says that all Japanese residents have been sent secret letters about what to do in case of an invasion, and that the Japanese barber chap in the Gloucester Hotel has been spying. The government is about to issue another edict that all wives and children are to be sent away without exception, but only the white British, those of pure European extraction, get passage on the ships. 'Doesn't affect me.' Trudy shrugs, although she holds a British passport. Will knows that if she wanted, she could get on to a boat – her father always knows someone. 'What would I do in Australia?' she asks. 'I don't like anybody there. Besides, it's only for pure English – have you ever heard of anything so offensive?'

She changes the subject. 'What would happen,' she asks, 'if two guns were pointed at each other and then the triggers were pulled at the same time? Do you think the two people would get hurt or would the bullets destroy each other?'

There is a lively discussion about this that Trudy is soon bored with. 'For heaven's sake!' she cries. 'Isn't there something else we can talk about?' The group, chastised, turns to yet other subjects. Trudy is a social dictator and not at all benevolent. She tells someone recently arrived from the Congo that she can't imagine why anyone would go to a Godforsaken place like that when there are perfectly pleasant destinations, like London and Rome. The traveller actually looks chagrined. She tells Sophie Biggs's husband that he doesn't appreciate his wife, and then she tells Manley she loathes trifle. Yet, no one takes offence; everyone agrees with her. She is the most amiable rude person ever. People bask in her attention.

At the end of dinner, after coffee and liqueurs, Manley's houseboy brings in a big bowl of nuts and raisins. Manley pours brandy over it with a flourish and Trudy lights a match and tosses it in. The bowl is ablaze instantly, all blue and white flame. They try to pick out the treats without burning their fingers, a game they call Snapdragon.

Going to the bathroom later, Will glimpses Trudy and Victor talking heatedly in Cantonese in the drawing room. He hesitates, then continues on. When he returns, they are gone and Trudy is already back at the table, telling a bawdy joke.

After, they go to bed. Manley has given them a room next to his and they make love quietly. With Trudy, it is always as if she is drowning – she clutches at him and burrows her face into his shoulder with an intensity she would make fun of if she saw it. Sometimes the shape of her fingers is etched into his skin for hours afterwards. Later, Will wakes up to find Trudy whimpering, her face lumpy and alarming; he sees that her face is wet with tears.

'What's wrong?' he asks.

'Nothing.' A reflex.

'Did Victor upset you?' he asks.

'No, no, he wants to . . . My father . . .' She goes back to sleep. When he throws the blanket over her, her shoulders are as cold and limp as water. In the morning, she remembers nothing, and mocks him for his concern.

In the following weeks, the war encroaches – wives and children, the ones who had ignored the previous evacuation, leave on ships bound for Australia, Singapore. Trudy is obliged to make an appearance at the hospitals to prove she is a nurse. She undergoes training, declares herself hopeless, and switches to supplies instead. She finds the stockpiling of goods too amusing. 'If I had to eat the food they're storing, I'd shoot myself,' she says. 'It's all bully beef and awful things like that.'

The colony is filled with suddenly lonely men without wives; they gather at the Gripps, the Parisian Grill, clamour to be invited to dinner parties at the homes of those few whose wives remain. They form a club, the Bachelors' Club ('Why do the British so love to form clubs and societies?' Trudy asks. 'No, wait, don't say, it's too grim.') and petition the governor to bring back the women. Others, more intrepid, turn up suddenly with adopted Chinese 'daughters' or 'wards', dine with them and drink champagne, then disappear into the night. Will finds it amusing, Trudy less so. 'Wait until I get my hands on them,' she cries, while Will teases her about which Chinese hostess would soon get her claws into him.

'You're like a leper, darling,' she counters. 'You British men are going out of fashion. I might have to find myself a Japanese or German beau now.'

Later Will remembers this time so clearly, how it was all so funny and the war was so far away, yet talked about every day, how no one really thought about what might really happen.

September 1952

Claire was waiting for the bus after Locket's piano lesson when Will Truesdale drove up in the car. 'Would you like a lift?' he asked. 'I've just finished for the day.'

'Thank you, but I couldn't put you out,' she said.

'Not at all,' he said. 'The Chens don't mind if I take the car home for the night. Most employers want their cars left at home and the chauffeur to take public transport home, so it's no bother.'

Claire hesitated, then got into the car. It smelled of cigarettes and polished leather. 'It's very kind of you.'

'Did you have a good time at the Arbogasts' the other day?' he asked.

'It was a very nice party,' she said. She had learned not to be effusive, that it marked her as unsophisticated.

'Reggie's a good sort,' he said. 'It was nice to meet you there, too. There are too many of those women who add to the din but not to anything else. You shouldn't lose that quality of seeing everything new for what it is. All the women here . . .'

He drove well, she thought, steady on the steering-wheel, his movements calm and unhurried.

'You're not wearing the perfume you had on the other day,' he said.

'No,' she said, wary. 'That's for special occasions.'

'I was surprised that you had it on. Not many English wear it. It's more the fashionable Chinese women. They like its heaviness. English women like something lighter, more flowery.'

'Oh, I wasn't aware.' Claire's hand went unconsciously to her neck, where she usually dabbed it on.

'But it's lovely that you wear it,' he said.

'You seem to know a lot about women's scents.'

'I don't.' He glanced over at her, his eyes dark. 'I used to know someone who wore it.'

They rode in silence until they arrived at her building.

'You teach the girl,' he said, as she was reaching for the door, his voice suddenly urgent.

'Yes, Locket.' She said, taken aback.

'Is she a good student?' he asked. 'Diligent?'

'It's hard to say,' she said. 'Her parents don't give her much of a reason to do anything so she doesn't. Very typical at that age. Still, she's a nice enough girl.'

He nodded, his face unreadable in the dark interior of the car.

'Well, thank you for the lift,' she said. 'I'm most grateful.'

He raised a hand, then drove off into the gathering dusk.

And then a bun. A bun with sweetened chestnut paste. That was how they met again. She had been walking up Elgin Street to where there was a bus stop, when it started to pour. The rain – huge, startling plops – fell heavily and she was soaked through in a matter of seconds. Looking up at the sky, she saw it had turned a threatening grey. She ducked into a Chinese bakery to wait out the storm. Inside, she ordered tea and a chestnut bun, and as she turned to sit at a small, circular tables, she spotted Will Truesdale, deliberately eating a red bean pastry, staring at her.

'Hello,' she said. 'Caught in the rain, too?'

'Would you like a seat?'

She sat down. In the damp, he smelled of cigarettes and tea. A newspaper was spread in front of him, the crossword half finished. A fan blew at the pages so they ruffled upwards.

'It's coming down cats and dogs. And so sudden!'

'So, how are you?' he asked.

'Fine, thank you very much. I've just come from the Liggets', where I borrowed some patterns. Do you know Jasper and Helen? He's in the police.'

'Ligget the bigot?' He wrinkled his forehead.

She laughed, uncomfortable. His hand thrummed the table, though his body was relaxed. 'Is that what you call him?' she asked.

'Why not?'

He did the crossword as she ate her bun and sipped her tea. She was aware of her mouth chewing, swallowing. She sat up straight in her chair.

He hummed a tune, looked up. 'Hong Kong suits you,' he said.

She coloured, started to say something about being impertinent but her words came out muddled.

'Don't be coy,' he said. 'I think . . .' he started, as if he were telling her life story. 'I imagine you've always been pretty but you've never owned it, never used it to your advantage. You didn't know what to do about it and your mother never helped you. Perhaps she was jealous, perhaps she, too, was pretty in her youth but is bitter that beauty is so transient.'

'I haven't the slightest idea what you're talking about,' she said.

'I've known girls like you for years. You come over from England and don't know what to do with yourselves. You could be different. You should take the opportunity to become something else.'

She stared at him, then pushed the bun wrapper around on the table. It was slightly damp and stuck to the surface. She was aware of his gaze on her face.

'So,' he said. 'You must be very uncomfortable. My home is just up the way if you want to change into some dry things.'

'I wouldn't want to . . .'

'Do you want my jacket?'

He was looking at her so intently that she felt undressed. Was there anything more intimate than being truly seen? She looked away. 'No, I . . .'

'No bother at all,' he said quickly. 'Come along,' and she did, pulled helplessly by his suggestion.

They climbed the steps, now damp and glistening, the heat already beginning to evaporate the moisture. Her clothes clung to her, her blouse sodden and uncomfortable against her shoulder-blades. In the quiet after the rain, she could hear his breathing, slow and regular. He used his cane with expertise, hoisting himself up the stairs, whistling slightly under his breath.

'In good weather, there's a man who sells crickets made of grass stalks here.' He gestured to a street corner. 'I've bought dozens. They're the most amazing things, but they crumble when they dry up, crumble into nothing.'

'Sounds lovely,' Claire said. 'I'd like to see them.'

They went into his building, and walked up some grungy, industrial stairs. He stopped in front of a door. 'I never lock my door,' he said suddenly.

'I suppose it's safe enough in these parts,' she said.

Inside, his flat was sparsely furnished. She could see only a sofa, a chair, and a table on bare floor. When they stepped in, he took off his soaking shoes. 'The boss says I can't wear shoes in the house.'

Just then, a small, wiry woman of around forty came in. She was wearing the amah uniform of a black tunic over trousers.

'This is the boss, Ah Yik,' he said. 'Ah Yik, this is Mrs Pendleton.'

'So wet,' the little woman cried. 'Big rain.'

'Yes,' Will said. 'Big, big rain.' Then he spoke to her rapidly in Cantonese.

'Tea for Missee?' Ah Yik said.

'Yes, thank you,' he said.

The amah went into the kitchen.

They looked at each other, uncomfortable in their wet and rapidly cooling clothes.

'You are proficient in the local language,' she said, more as a statement than a question.

'I've been here more than a decade,' he said. 'It would be a real embarrassment if I couldn't meet them halfway by now, don't you think?' He took a tea towel off a hook and rubbed his head. 'I imagine you'd like to dry off,' he said.

'Yes, please.'

She sat down as he left the room. There was something strange about the room, which she couldn't place until she realized there was absolutely nothing decorative in the entire place. There were no paintings, no vases, no bric-a-brac. It was austere to the point of monkishness.

Will came back with a towel and a simple pink cotton dress. 'Is this appropriate?' he asked. 'I've a few other things.'

'I don't need to change,' she said. 'I'll just dry off and be on my way.'

'Oh, I think you should change,' he said. 'You'll be uncomfortable otherwise.'

'No, it's quite all right.'

He started to leave the room.

'Fine,' she said. 'Where should I . . .'

'Oh, anywhere,' he said. 'Anywhere you won't scandalize the boss, that is.'

'Of course.' She took the dress from him. 'It looks about the right size.'

'And there's a phone out here if you want to ring your husband and let him know where you are,' he said.

'Thank you,' she said. 'Martin's in Shanghai, actually.' And she went into the bathroom.

It was small but clean, with a frosted-glass window high above the lavatory. It was the wavy, pebbled kind, with chicken wire running through it. Next to that, a small fan was set into the wall with a string attached. It was humid, with the rain splattering outside, and the musty feel of a bathroom that hadn't got quite aired out enough after baths. Next to the bath, there was a low wooden stool with a steel basin on top. Claire leaned forward into the mirror. Her hair was messy, the fine blonde strands awry, and her face was flushed, still, with the exertion of climbing up the hill. She looked surprisingly alive, her lips red and plump, her skin glowing with the moisture. She undressed, dropping her soaked blouse to the floor, which sloped to a drain in the middle. She towelled herself and pulled the dress over her hips. It was snug, but manageable. Why did Will have a dress lying around? It was very good quality, with perfectly finished seams and careful needlework. She went out to where he was sipping from a Thermos of tea.

'Fits you well,' he said neutrally.

'Yes, thank you very much.'

All of a sudden, Claire couldn't bear it. She couldn't bear this man with his odd pauses and his slightly mocking tone.

'Something to eat, perhaps?' he said. 'Ah Yik makes a very good bowl of fried rice.'

'I think I'd better leave,' she said.

'Oh,' he said, taken aback. She took satisfaction from his surprise, as if she had won something. 'Of course, if you'd rather.'

She got up and left, putting her shoes on at the door while Will stayed in the living room. When she turned to say goodbye, she saw he was reading a book. This infuriated her. 'Well, goodbye, then,' she said. 'I'll have my amah return the dress. Thank you for your hospitality.'

'Goodbye,' he said. He didn't look up.

That night, after dinner, she couldn't relax. Her insides seemed too large for her outside, a queer sensation, as if all that she was feeling couldn't be contained inside her body. As Martin was still away she put on her street clothes and got on the bus to town, bumping over the roads, elbow out of the window, open to the warm night air. She disembarked in Wanchai, where there seemed to be the most activity. She wanted to be among people, not alone. The wet market was still open, Chinese people buying their cabbages and fish, pork hanging from hooks, sometimes a whole pig's head, red and bloody, dripping on to the street. This was the peculiarity of Hong Kong.

If she walked ten minutes towards Central, all would be civilized, large, quiet buildings in the European classical style, and wide, empty streets, yet here the frenetic activity, narrow alleys and smoky stalls were another world. All around her, people called to each other loudly, advertising their wares, a smudge-faced child playing in the street with a dirty bucket. A pregnant woman carrying vegetables under her arm jostled her and apologized, her movements heavy and clumsy. Claire stared after her, wondering how it felt to have a child inside you, moving around. A young couple, arms linked, sat down at a noodle stand and broke out loudly in laughter.

Next to her, a wizened elderly lady tugged at Claire's arm. Dressed in the grey cotton tunic and trousers that most of the local older women seemed to favour, she had a small basket of tangerines on her arm.

'You buy,' she said. She smelled like the white flower ointment the locals used to fend off everything from the common cold to cholera. One of her teeth was grey and chipped, the others antique yellow. The woman's brown face was a spider web of deeply etched lines.

'No, thank you,' said Claire. Her voice rang out like a bell. It seemed that its sound stilled the bustle around her for a moment.

The woman grew more insistent.

'You buy! Very good. Fresh today.' She pulled at Claire's arm again. Then she reached up and touched Claire's hair like a talisman. The local Chinese did that sometimes, and while it had been frightening the first time, Claire was used to it now.

'Good fortune,' said the old woman. 'Golden.'

'Thank you,' said Claire.

'You buy!' the woman repeated.

'I'm not looking for anything today, but thank you very much.' The hum around her resumed. Claire continued walking. The old woman followed her for a few yards, then shambled off to find more promising customers.

Why not buy a tangerine from an old lady? Claire thought suddenly. Why not? What would happen? She couldn't think why she had declined, as if her old English self, with its defences and prejudices, was dissolving in the foetid environment around her.

She turned, but the woman had already disappeared. She breathed deeply. The smells of the wet market entered her, intense and earthy. Around her, Hong Kong thrummed.

And then, suddenly, he was everywhere. She saw Will Truesdale waiting for the bus, at Kayamally's, queuing outside the cinema. And though he never saw her, she always lowered her head, willing him not to notice. And then she'd glance up, to see if he had. He had a way of seeming completely contained within himself, even when he was in a crowd. He never looked around, never tapped his feet, never looked at his watch. It seemed he never saw her.

When she went for Locket's lesson on Thursdays, she found herself looking for Will Truesdale. She heard the amahs laughing at his jokes in the kitchen, and she saw his jacket hanging in the hall, but his physical presence was elusive, as if he slipped in and out, avoiding her. She lingered at the end of her lesson, but she never saw him or the car.

Then they were at the beach the next weekend. She hardly knew how it had happened. She had come home. The phone rang. She picked it up.

'I've a friend with one of those municipal beach huts,' he said. 'Would you like to go bathing?' As if nothing had happened. As if she would know who it was by his voice.

'Bathing,' she said. 'Where?'

'On Big Wave Bay,' he said. 'It's a perk for the locals but they don't mind if we sign up as well. It's a lottery system and you get a cottage for the season. A group of us usually get together to do it and swap weekends. It's quite nice.'

She shut her eyes and saw him: Will, the difficult man, with his thin shoulders and grey eyes, his dark hair that fell untidily into his eyes, a man who stared at her so intently she felt quite transparent, a man who had just asked her to go bathing with him, unaccompanied. And she opened her eyes and said, yes, she would join him at the beach that Sunday.

Martin was away for three weeks and he had telegraphed from Shanghai to let her know he would be delayed for some time. He was on a tour of major Chinese cities to inspect their water facilities, which he expected to be very primitive.

And so, it was water. She wondered why she hadn't thought of it before. How it rendered everything changed. She was a different woman in a different sphere. And Will! The way he plunged in, without a thought, his limp gone, dissolved into the current. He was a fish, darting here and there, swimming out into the horizon, further than she would ever go.

They were the only Europeans at the beach. The water was still warm from the summer, the air just starting to crisp. The hut was a simple structure with wooden cupboards and woven straw mats. The sand was fine, speckled with black, and small, withered leaves. Families picnicked around them, chattering loudly, small children scrambling messily about. He wanted to go out to the floating diving docks, some two hundred yards out. When she said she couldn't, that it was too far, he said of course she could, and so she did. Out there, they climbed on to the rocking circle and sunned themselves like seals. He lay in the sun, eyes closed, as she watched surreptitiously, his ribs jutting out, his body pocked with unnamed scars of unknown origin. He wore short cotton trousers that were heavy with water. He wasn't the type to wear a bathing suit.

It was hot, hot. The sun hid behind clouds for brief moments, then blazed out again. There was no cover. She wished for a cold drink, a tree for shade, both of which seemed impossibly far away on the shore.

'We should have swum out with a Thermos of water,' she said.

'Next time,' he said, eyes still shut.

'Tell me your story,' she said, after allowing herself a minute to digest what that meant. She was still vibrating with the strangeness of the situation – that she was at the beach with a man, intentions unknown.

'I was born in Tasmania, of Scottish stock,' he said mockingly, as if he were starting an autobiography. He sat up and crossed his legs as if he were a *swami*.

'Why?' she said.

'My father was a missionary and we lived everywhere,' he said. 'I've only been to England once, and loathed it. My mother was a bit of a Bohemian and she had some money from her family so we were set in that way.'

Hong Kong was full of people like Will, wandering global voyagers who had never been to Piccadilly Circus. Claire had been just once, and there had been an old man in tattered clothes who would shout, 'Fornicators!' at everyone who passed.

'And how did you learn?' she asked.

'School, you mean? Taught at home – good basic education of the Bible and the classics.' He held up his hands so that they blocked the sky. 'It's all you need, really, isn't it?' His voice was sarcastic. 'Solid background for life.'

'So how did you come to be a chauffeur?'

'A couple I knew before the war, I used to live in their flat while they were abroad. They came back after, and found me this job with their cousins. I didn't know what else to do. No interest in going back to an office. And I've very few skills,' he said. 'But I do know Hong Kong like the back of my hand.'

'And how did you end up in Hong Kong?'

'My parents were in Africa, and then in India. When they retired to England, I stayed on as an assistant manager at a tea plantation, then got tired of that after three years and was on a ship to a variety of places and ended up in Hong Kong. Just picked it out of a hat, really. I came here, like everyone else, not knowing anything, and sort of took it from there.' He stopped. 'Of course, that's the story I tell all the ladies.'

She couldn't tell whether he was joking or not. 'Oh?'

They were still lying on the too-sunny floating dock, waves rocking them, sky an ethereal blue above.

'How was India?' Claire asked.

'Very complicated.'

'And Partition?'

'After I left, of course. They needed us out. But undoubtedly a mess in the interior. Trains carrying tens of thousands of corpses back and forth. Humans capable of doing the worst to each other.'

Claire winced. 'Why?' She had never heard anyone talk about historic events in such a personal way.

'Who knows?'

'And life there before all that?'

'Rather incredible. We'd carved out quite a world for ourselves, you know. Society's rather limited, of course. Women – our women – were in short supply.'

'You never married?'

'No,' he said. 'I never did.'

There was silence.

'Is the inquisition over?' he asked.

'I haven't decided,' she said.

He hadn't asked a single question about her life. They lay silently and let the sun beat down on them.

They went to eat, hot, salty chicken drumsticks from the Chinese vendor, who sold them bottles of juice as well. There were little stalls clustered around the small village where you could buy a woven mat to lay on the sand, a bathing-suit, a cold drink. Will watched her eat. A mangy dog ambled through the tables and chairs.

'I can't eat much,' he said. 'I'm all messed up inside from the war. I was a big chap before, if you can believe it.'

Her stomach leapt inside of her as he moved closer.

He took her hand, guided it to his mouth and took a small bite. His grip was firm and sandy. 'It comes up again, sometimes,' he said. 'Like bile.' He chewed slowly, grimaced.

After they ate, they walked back to the car. He leaned over to open the door for her. His limp was apparent. Human again. She turned to him, back against the door, and he pushed her shoulder back and kissed her, a fluid movement that seemed inevitable. She was encircled in his arms, his hands on the car. A physical kiss, one she felt intensely, his lips hard on hers – she felt as if she was drowning.

She told herself: This is Hong Kong. I am a woman, displaced. A woman a world away from who I am supposed to be.

He stood back and looked at her. He traced her profile with his finger. 'Should we go?' he asked.

'Do you like me?' she asked, on the car ride back, her hair full and thick from the sea salt. She didn't know where they were going.

'I haven't decided yet,' he said.

'Be good to me,' she said. It was a warning. She wanted to save herself.

'Of course,' he said, but there was no conviction in his voice.

After a few moments, he asked, 'Do you think you'll be teaching the girl for long?'

'I haven't any idea. She shows no enthusiasm but her parents seem keen that she learns to play.'

'You like her, though?'

'Well enough. I have no affinity with children.' She said this automatically; it was something her mother had always told her.

'You're too young. You're a child yourself,' he said.

'You like children?'

'Some children,' he said.

A few weeks later, she asked, 'Why me?'

'Why anyone?' he answered. 'Why is anyone with anyone?'

Desire, proximity, habit, chance. All these went through her mind, but she didn't say a word.

Then, the cruelty: 'I don't like to love,' he said. 'You should be forewarned. I don't believe in it. And you shouldn't either.'

She stared at him, the sting sharp, but she didn't change her expression. She knelt down, retrieved her clothes and went into the bathroom to dress. Claire often didn't speak when she was with

Will: she never knew what to say. She didn't want to give too much of herself when he gave so little, but when they were lying together in bed, she felt awful, sharing such intimacy with someone who seemed not to care. And then going home to Martin. With him, the private was mundane, a chore, some heavy breathing and shoving, not at all pleasurable or romantic. With Will, it was something else entirely: fraught and unexpected and excruciating. And like a drug. She had never known it could be like that. She closed her eyes and tried not to think of what her mother would say if she knew.

He would drive her home on Thursdays after the lesson. The amahs had started to talk, she knew it, from the way they would look at her and smirk. She ignored them, except when she asked them for tea. She had resorted to taking one sip, and then asking for more sugar or milk. It was petty, she knew, but the only way to redress the indignity of their sideways glances.

Today Will opened the car door with a flourish. 'Where to, madam?'

'Oh, shut up,' she said, climbing in. 'Let's go to your place.'

'Let's go out, do something,' he said. 'What about dinner on the water? There's a sampan restaurant I go to sometimes. They row you out, cook you a fish.'

'I have to have dinner at home,' she said. 'Martin's home tonight so I haven't much time.'

'Or let's go up to the Peak and look at the stars.'

'Were you even listening to me?' she said, exasperated. 'I don't know that I even have time to go to your flat today.'

'Whatever you want, darling,' he said. 'I'll just drive you home, then, and you can cook Martin a delicious meal.'

'Stop the car,' she said.

He drove up on to the side of the road and turned off the engine. 'As directed,' he said.

She was suddenly furious. 'You – you always do *whatever* I ask,' and then it seems like you're doing what you want to do.'

He looked at her with amusement. 'I haven't a clue what you're talking about,' he said.

'Oh, but you have,' she said. 'You know exactly what I'm talking about, but you're pretending . . . Oh, never mind.' She raised her hands in surrender. 'Just take me home,' she said. 'You've ruined it.'

There had been times when Claire felt she could become a different person. She sensed it in herself, when someone made a comment at dinner, and she thought of the perfect, acerbic reply, or even something racy, and she felt her mouth opening, her lungs taking in air so she could push out the words, but they never came. She swallowed the thought, and the person she could have become sank down again, weighted by the Claire who was already too evident in the world. She sensed it when she held a glass at a cocktail party and suddenly felt the urge to crush it in her hand. She never did. That hidden person ballooned and deflated so often, the elasticity of possibility slackened over time.

But then came Will. She could say to him all the things she thought, as long as it didn't have anything to do with them, and he didn't find any of it surprising. He didn't have an idea of what she should be like. She was a new person – one who could have an affair, one who could be ribald, or sarcastic, or clever, and he was never surprised. She was out of context with him. She was a new person. Sometimes she felt she was in love with the new person she could be, that this affair was an affair with a new Claire, and that Will was just the catalyst.

December 1941

The holidays are coming. Despite the rumblings of war, Hong Kong decks itself out with Christmas lights and decorations. Lane Crawford, store of a million gifts, advertises its genuine English crystal as the perfect present, costume parties are planned, the Drama Club puts on *Tea for Three*. The air is crisp, the moisture sucked out by the cool, and people walk briskly on the streets. The Wongs, a famous merchant family, are having a grand Diamond Jubilee Party at the Gripps to celebrate their sixtieth anniversary.

'The new governor's coming, that Young fellow,' Trudy says. 'And the governor of Macau, who's a great friend of Father's. I've three new dresses arriving today! A yellow silk chiffon to die for! And a grey crêpe-de-Chine, so elegant. Do you mind if I go with Dommie instead of you? You hate these things anyway, don't you?'

Will shrugs. 'Fine,' he says. 'Doesn't matter.'

Her eyes narrow. 'Nothing ever bothers you, does it?' she says. 'I used to like that but now I'm not so sure. Well, anyway, my father gave me something today. Something very special.' She motions him into her bedroom. 'He said he was going to give it to my mother for their tenth anniversary, but then, you know . . .' Her voice trails off. Trudy has always been unsentimental about her mother's disappearance, but today her voice catches.

'Darling Trudy,' he says, and pulls her close.

'No, I'm going to show you something,' she says. 'No time for hanky-panky.' She opens a drawer and pulls out a small black velvet box. 'Will you marry me?' she says jokingly, as she opens it and thrusts it towards him.

Inside is an enormous emerald. Will almost can't see the ring behind it. It glows and glows. 'Good Lord,' he says. 'That's quite a stone.'

'I love emeralds, although I should love jade, being Chinese,' Trudy says. 'Emeralds are so beautiful and so very fragile. Jade is so, hard. If I knocked this against a table – you know how clumsy I am – it might break. They're not durable like diamonds.' She plucks the ring out of the box and then suddenly throws it up into the air. Will's heart leaps inside him, like a small bird, and he wildly grabs for the jewel, catching it on its way down. He stares at the green gem in his hand, blood coursing wildly. It nestles in his palm like a cold insect.

'I knew you'd catch it,' Trudy says dispassionately. 'That's the best thing about you. You're . . . not dependable, exactly, but good in a fix, I suppose.'

Will hands the ring back to Trudy, angry now, and watches as she slips it on her slim finger.

'Beautiful, isn't it?' she says. 'It's the nicest thing I own.'

He walks out of the room.

On Saturday, there is another party, the Tin Hat Ball, to raise a hundred and sixty thousand pounds so that the people of Hong Kong can present a bomber squadron to England. Trudy begs him to go with her as, at the last one, the only dashing men were Americans and that 'wasn't right'.

'You are fickle,' he says but she ignores him.

In the ballroom at the Peninsula, Trudy is much in demand as usual. She is claimed three times in a row by a Canadian major. Will is at the Long Bar having a drink, talking idly to Angeline

Biddle, when Trudy comes up behind him and interlocks her fingers in front of his eyes. 'Did you miss me?' she says.

'You were gone?' he asks. He knows how to talk to her.

'What are you drinking?' Trudy asks Angeline.

'Ox's Blood,' she says. 'It's champagne mixed with sparkling burgundy and maybe some brandy.'

'Sounds dreadful,' Trudy says, seizing Will's whisky instead. She sips it. 'Don't the Canadians have the funniest names for their teams?'

'Regiments, Trudy,' he corrects.

'What are they, the Royal Guns or something?' says Angeline.

'No, they're the Royal Rifles and the Winnipeg Grenadiers. They've just come from Newfoundland to help protect us. They love Hong Kong.'

'I bet they do,' he says. 'I'm sure it seems like heaven.'

She pouts. 'You're not going to be all dull and jealous are you?' She adjusts the straps of her dress, distracted. 'Anyway, I'm spoken for in the next few dances. Angeline, you'll take care of my Will, won't you?'

Angeline and Will look at each other and shrug.

'Of course, darling,' Angeline says.

As soon as Trudy leaves, they drift away from each other. Will finds Angus Enderby leaning against a wall. Trudy's cousin Dominick wanders by, gives them a curt nod.

'Strange fellow,' says Angus. 'Can't figure him out.'

'Trudy says he's a girl.'

'Something more than that, though. Less innocent.' He pauses. 'You know there are fifth columnists infiltrating? They're supporting that Wong Chang Wai chap, who the Japanese installed in China. I've heard Dominick's been seen with that crowd. And Victor Chen, of course, thick as thieves with whoever can help him. Rumour has it that he had the Japanese consul over for dinner last week. Very hush-hush. Better watch himself. That's a dangerous game.'

'He's a survivor.'

'Yes,' Angus shrugs. 'Can't believe the war effort's been turned into a party. The new governor's a fool for coming.'

A stout woman is at the bar, with a thinner one, both sipping whisky, watching the dancing impassively.

'Do you know Edwina Storch?' Angus asks Will, nodding towards the pair.

'I've seen her. Not met them formally.'

'Headmistress of Essex, old timer. Grim, formidable. Been around for ever. And that's her friend, Mary Winkle.'

Will and Angus walk over to the women. Edwina inclines her head regally, a queen holding court. 'Hello, Angus. Merry Christmas.'

'Edwina, I wanted you to meet Will Truesdale, somewhat of a new arrival to these shores. And Will, this is Edwina Storch and Mary Winkle, Hong Kong institutions. They know where all the skeletons are buried.'

'Pleased to meet you,' says Will.

'I've seen you around,' Edwina says. 'You're with the Liang girl.'

'Yes,' Will says. He is not surprised by her bluntness. He has encountered this type before: the unapologetically rude Englishwoman who regards herself as an adventuress and desires nothing more than to intimidate.

'That didn't take you long.'

'No, it didn't, luckily,' he says lightly. 'She's been a wonderful introduction to Hong Kong.'

Edwina Storch harrumphs.

'That's a skewed sense of Hong Kong you're getting!'

Mary Winkle lays a small, reproachful hand on Edwina's arm. 'Now, now,' she whispers. 'Trudy has always been lovely, if misunderstood. I do like her so very much.'

Will smiles at her. 'She is lovely, isn't she?'

Edwina sips noisily at her glass. 'What's that you're drinking?' she asks Will.

'Single malt.'

'A man's drink. Since you're with Trudy, I thought you might be a champagne drinker.'

'Are you friendly with her?' he asks politely.

'Of course,' she says. 'In Hong Kong, everyone has to be friendly or life is very unpleasant.'

'Of course,' he says agreeably to the women and bows to them before taking his leave.

Angus joins him back at the bar. 'Something about that woman turns me into a schoolboy about to wet his trousers,' he says.

'And you keep going back for more,' Will says drily.

'That one likes her creature comforts,' Angus says. 'Always after me about civil salaries and what an outrage they are. Never met a headmistress more interested in money.'

The two men pull at their drinks.

'I heard the governor's told all the men in the Bachelors they were off their heads for wanting their wives back. His wife's still in Malaya, no?'

'Yes, but I don't know that that's any safer, do you?' Will says. 'How is Amelia?'

'Fine, but she's making noises about coming back. She's just in China, you know, refused absolutely to go to Australia. So, she's in Canton, and complaining mightily. I can hear the racket from here.' Angus looks gloomily at the dance-floor. 'Might let her come back just so I can get some peace.' He paused. 'Though that seems rather counter-intuitive, eh?'

'Everything to do with women seems counter-intuitive.'

'Trudy not leaving?' Angus asks.

'Refuses. Says there's nowhere to go. Which is sort of the truth for her, I think.'

'Pity,' says Angus. 'A lot of places could use her right now.'

'Yes, she'd charm everyone,' Will says.

'A formidable weapon, indeed,' Angus says.

'Did you see the paper today? Roosevelt sent Hirohito a cable.'

'Yes. We'll see how effective that is. What are they having you do at the office?'

'They sent round a memorandum a few weeks ago, saying that our Volunteer positions took precedence over company business, but we're supposed to register with them during fighting, if it breaks out. They've given us a number to call with our location. I don't know that they know what they're doing.'

They watch Trudy twirl round the dance-floor, laughing, ivory arms draped over her partner's shoulders. Afterwards, breathless and happy, she tells Will that her partner was the 'head of the whole thing. He's very important, and he seemed to like me very much, telling me all about the situation we're in. And it's terribly ironic,' she says. 'The dreariest of people are safe – the Germans, bless their stolid hearts, the Italians with their awful, funny ways. Hong Kong's going to be so dull, no parties worth going to at all.'

'So you're interested when he tells you about the war, are you?'

'Of course, darling. He knows what he's talking about.'

The orchestra is playing 'The Best Things In Life Are Free', and Trudy is complaining. 'He's horrible,' she says of the accompanist. 'I could get up right now and play better than that.' But she isn't given a chance because a short man with a megaphone strides through the ballroom and gets up on stage. The orchestra grinds to a halt.

'All those men who are connected to the American Steamships Line are ordered to report aboard ship as soon as possible. I repeat, all those connected with American Steamships Line are required to report on board right now.'

There is a long silence, then on the dance-floor, couples uncouple, at the bar, men stand up from their bar stools and pull down their shirt fronts. A few start to make their uncertain way to the door.

'I hate American accents,' Trudy says. 'They sound so stupid.' She seems to have forgotten her great love for Americans.

'Trudy,' Will says. 'This is serious. Do you understand?'

'It'll be fine, darling,' Trudy says. 'Who would bother with our small pocket of the world? It's just the alarmists.' She calls for more champagne.

Dominick comes by and whispers something in her ear. He stares at Will while he's doing it.

'Good evening, Dominick,' Will says.

'Hello,' is the laconic reply. Dominick is one of those queer Chinese who is more English than the English yet has no great love for them. Educated in the most precious way in England, he has come back to Hong Kong and is affronted by everything that is in the least bit crass, which is to say everything – the swill on the streets, the expectorating, illiterate throngs of coolies and fishmongers. A hothouse flower, he thrives only in the rarest of society circles, with damask napkins and clear, ringing crystal – Will would very much like to see him in a rubber apron ladling soup to butchers and their ilk in a street-market noodle shop, the kind with the bare electrical bulb hanging dangerously on a filament.

'Terrible news, isn't it?' Will says.

'This, too, will pass.' Dominick dismisses him with a slow wave of his marble-white palm. Will finds himself wondering if those hands have laboured at anything more arduous than the writing of a thank-you note on cream bond or the lifting of a champagne bowl. He watches the two of them, whispering together. They belong together (were it not for the accident of their family relations), but he supposes such a pairing would combust, their pale electricity extinguishing the other.

Dominick says suddenly, 'It's not all bad for Trudy and me, you know. The Japanese are closer to us than the English. At least they're Orientals.'

Will almost laughs and then realizes that Dominick is serious. 'But you're the least Oriental person I know,' he says mildly.

Dominick narrows his eyes. 'You've no idea what you're talking about,' he says.

Trudy intervenes: 'You're both talking nonsense. Don't talk about this beastly nationality matter – it makes me ill.' She brushes Will's hair back from his face. 'All I know is that the Japanese make me sick. They're very brutal people.'

'You should not say such things,' Dominick says. 'You should not.'

'Oh, bother!' Trudy says. 'Have another drink and shut up.'

It is the first time Will has seen Trudy irritated with Dominick. She wants to go shortly thereafter and they leave, but not before she gives Dominick a quick kiss on the cheek to let him know he's been forgiven.

On Sunday they wake and go to town for *dim sum*. There is an odd tension in the air, and the wet markets are filled with grim shoppers filling their bags. They go home to listen to the radio and eat a simple dinner. The amahs are flitting about, chattering non-stop, and Will has a headache. The office rings and says that work is suspended until further notice. That night, he and Trudy slip and slide in their sleep, waking each other in their restlessness, breathing loudly.

Monday, 8 December: the rude *brrring* of the telephone. Angeline wakes Trudy and Will with the news that her husband has just received word of a broadcast to all Japanese that war with Britain and the United States is imminent. The engineers have been ordered to blow up all bridges leading into the territory. Then, as they digest the news, still groggy from sleep, they hear the air-raid sirens, and then, terribly, from a distance, then closer, the whine of aircraft and the dull thud of bombs. The phone rings again. All Volunteers are to be in place by three in the afternoon. They turn on the radio and Will gets dressed as Trudy watches him from the bed. She is pale and quiet.

'It's madness for you to go out in this,' she says. 'How are you going to get to the office?'

'I'll drive,' he says.

'But you don't know what condition the roads are in. You might be hit by a bomb or someone might –'

'Trudy,' he says. 'I have to go. I can't just sit here.'

'Nonsense,' she says. 'And I don't want to be alone.'

'Let's not quarrel,' he says gently. 'Telephone Angeline. Then go over to her house. Have her send her boy to escort you. And I'll ring you there when I'm able. You should probably stock up on some food as well.'

He kisses her cool cheek and leaves.

In town, he drives past the King's Theatre. It still seems to be operating. *My Life with Caroline* is the feature and there are, astonishingly, a few people queuing for tickets.

When he reports to Headquarters, it's abuzz with activity, men jostling for space and supplies with a sense of urgency he has not seen before. Outside, it's eerily quiet but for the intermittent boom of bombs. He sits and waits for his assignment. There's a map over a desk with the colony marked out. A dotted line is drawn from Gin Drinkers Bay to Tide Cove with a fortress at Shingmun – the first line of defence. A concrete tunnel has been built south of the Jubilee Reservoir where soldiers can climb to pillboxes to fire. 'This should keep us for a while,' a man says, noticing Will studying the map. 'It's fairly difficult to breach, I'd say.' On the wall, someone has typed up excerpts from General Maltby's speech that morning: 'It is obvious to you all that the test for which we have been placed here will come in the near future. I expect each and every member of my force to stick it out unflinchingly, and that my force will become a great example of high-hearted courage to all the rest of the British Empire who are fighting to preserve truth, justice, and liberty for the world.'

Suddenly, over the radio, they hear Roosevelt's voice. 'Quiet, dammit,' someone shouts. The volume is turned up. Roosevelt announces the bombing of Pearl Harbor and a quiet shock descends upon the office.

Roosevelt has finished, and the radio buzzes before the announcer comes in: 'And that was President Roosevelt of the United States . . .'

'That's good for us,' a fellow says finally. 'Means the Americans are in it now, whether they like it or not.'

'It means the war has got much bigger,' says another, quietly.

November 1952

She was paranoid. She always had been. When she pushed open a door or picked up a wine glass, she made a point of smudging the slight map that her oils, finger whorls, and dust had created – as if Scotland Yard were hot on her trail. She didn't want to be leaving clues, fragments, parts of herself. When she ran her fingers through her hair, she kept the strands that slid out and disposed of them in a dustbin. Her nail parings were housed in a tissue and flushed down the lavatory.

This paranoia was beneficial, it turned out. Martin, distracted with work, with the workings of water, never noticed that her comings and goings had suddenly taken on a much more deliberate air. Must get Darjeeling at the shop, must visit St Stephen's hospital every Thursday, must have lunch with the girls every Wednesday. She limited their intimacy to the bare minimum. She could not think that she was that woman, that woman she had heard her mother and her friends talking about in the kitchen, that woman who went from man to man in a single day. The kind of woman who could be kicked out of the colony and sent home on a ship in disgrace.

The awful thing was, she didn't feel as bad as she thought she should. She had always thought of women who had lovers as immoral women who cared nothing about society and manners and the way things should be. And yet here she was, carrying on with a man who didn't even seem particularly to like her. And Martin was good. This was the inescapable fact. And he was good to her. Whether or not he loved her, she didn't know. He was certainly pleased to have a wife and a home and all of that taken care of, but she didn't know how much of that had to do with her as a person.

Sometimes, she felt he had married her, dropped her into a slot labelled 'wife', then gone on with his life. But she was sensible enough to see that she was the guilty one in this arrangement. Martin was guilty of nothing but benign neglect. She was taking advantage of a good man.

But any bad feeling she had about the situation was always drowned out by the sensation Will created in the pit of her stomach when he approached her, cut the space between them in half, and half again, coming at her with those hooded, sardonic eyes. It was narcotic, that feeling, and she couldn't go for long without it.

Claire was trying to become invisible, so that she would be all the more visible when she was with Will. She spoke less and less, didn't meet the other wives, never left the flat unless she had to. Her days revolved around him, when she could see him next, what she would say to him, how he would touch her. Sometimes he refused her. She would come over and lie in his bed, and he would roll over and go to sleep, saying he was tired, and she would be left alone, her hot breath coming in and out, her head spinning with frustration. She wanted to own him, for him to want to own her, but he trod lightly around her – he didn't want to leave a mark. She wanted to be branded, a red, raw wound.

At Will's she lay in bed and realized that someone in the flat above played the same song over and over again. It was a melancholy tune she didn't recognize, and the words were muffled through the ceiling. She never mentioned it to him, as if she wanted to keep it a secret, a knowledge she had, only for her, as if it were something of his that only she knew about.

When she bought him presents, it almost paralysed her. She had wanted to buy him a pair of slippers, but she thought the soles were rather slippery and had imagined an entire scene in which he wore them, then fell and cracked his head open, and she would be left, pale with regret and longing. So she didn't buy them, and bought him a new teapot instead. He handed it over to Ah Yik, barely noticing it.

Christmas was coming and she was filled with dread. This is what it's like to be Martin, she thought. Somewhat dim, simple, in love with someone who doesn't love you back. It made her miserable. Will had asked her not to telephone him during the holidays. It was a difficult time for him, he said. Memories. So she rang him during the day just to hear the phone ring. Sometimes he would answer, his voice tense and annoyed. Other times it would ring and ring and she would imagine the amah shaking her head, knowing, the way women know, who it was. Funny how that transcended culture.

Martin's superior, Bruce Comstock, had asked him to their beach club in Shek-O where they had hired a cabana for Saturday and so, that morning, they packed up towels and their bathing-suits, rolled down the windows in the company Morris and drove out to the end of the island.

The road was narrow and carved out of the hills. On their left was a wall of lush green mountain, almost steaming in the heat, and on their right, a glorious view of blue sea and sky. White boats bobbed on the water, looking for all the world like toys in an enormous bath.

'It feels like we're on the Italian coast, or what I'd imagine it to be like,' she said.

'Isn't it marvellous?' he said.

She reached into her bag, pulled out Melody Chen's scarf and tied it round her head.

'That new?' Martin asked.

'Yes,' she said easily. 'I bought it at one of those little carts on Upper Lascar Row. You know, where the curry shops and carpets are.'

'It looks good on you,' he said. They drove on.

The bathing club was simple and well-used. They met the Comstocks at the bar and had a drink before the ladies went to the locker room to change into their bathing costumes.

Minna Comstock was in her early fifties and formidable. She had two children away at university, and lived her life with vigorous energy. She played tennis twice a week and golf on Ladies' Day at Fanling. In the locker room, she stripped down to her underwear without embarrassment. Her body was firm but wrinkles hung from her bosom, her arms, her stomach. It seemed as if she had too much skin for the body she had.

'I bought a nice bathing-suit at Wing On,' Claire ventured. 'They have quite a lot of merchandise.'

'Wear British,' Mrs Comstock barked. 'The items here are cut for the Chinese frame and aren't suitable for us. Too small. I always bring things back from home leave, good marmalade and proper knives. Have you seen what they call a knife here? Barbaric implement called a chopper.' She hoisted a well-muscled leg on to a bench and started to oil it. 'Have some lotion,' she said, handing the slippery bottle to Claire. 'It'll protect you from the sun.' Mrs Comstock was brown in the oddest places – on her calves between her sock line and where her trousers must have ended, and on her arms between her shirt sleeves and where her golf gloves began.

'Thank you,' Claire said. She smoothed some cream on her face.

On the beach, the wooden cottages were covered with white cotton broadcloth, large and airy with hooks for hanging up robes and compartments for bags.

'We're number twenty-three,' Bruce said. 'You can put your belongings there while we bathe.' Inside, there were beach chairs and an icebox. Bruce surreptitiously made them gin and Schweppes ('Highway robbery what they charge you at the bar,' he whispered) and they sat down and sipped them.

'Isn't this nice?' Claire said. 'So relaxing.'

With a jolt of recognition, she suddenly spotted Locket running towards the sea in a white and red polka-dot bathing-suit. When she followed her path back, her eyes fell upon the Chens drinking cocktails on the club terrace with a group of people. Melody Chen had on a wide-brimmed straw hat and sunglasses, and looked like a film star.

'If you'll excuse us,' she said to the Comstocks. 'I've just seen some people I should say hello to.'

She took Martin to the Chens' table.

'Hello,' Victor Chen said, as she stood over him. He squinted at her. 'Oh, it's . . .' He paused. 'These are the Silvas,' he continued smoothly, gesturing to the couple sitting next to him. 'Michael is Hong Kong's foremost obstetrician. And this is Dave Bradley, with the NBC. He's from the United States, so he and Melody have been getting on a little too well for my taste.' He turned to the table. 'And this is Locket's piano teacher.' Claire nodded and smiled.

Mrs Chen gave a little shriek. 'Locket!' she cried, and was out of her chair and down to the beach where Locket was in danger of being enveloped by an enormous wave. The group watched her run to her child.

'My husband, Martin Pendleton,' Claire said.

'Of course,' Victor said immediately.

'Pleased to meet you,' Martin smiled, uncomfortable.

Melody Chen came back from scolding Locket. 'I wish they'd let the servants into the club. It's such a stupid rule,' she said. 'It's just exhausting not to have Pai with me. Oh, I mean Francesca.' She turned to Mrs Silva with a confidential air. 'Did I tell you what happened?' They started conversing in lowered tones. Claire couldn't decide whether to attend to Martin's conversation with Victor Chen, or his wife's conversation with her friend.

'... here with Bruce Comstock ...'

'... Austrian crystal figures my mother gave me ...'

'... very good banker ...'

'... everyone's trying out new girls from rural China but they're awful with meals, can't cook at all and their own food's inedible, you have to teach them every single thing ... I gave her a new name, of course, Francesca, because I want to go to Italy soon ...'

Claire stood there, caught in one of those moments when everyone is having a conversation and one is excluded. She felt ill at ease, as if she had been forgotten.

'What a beautiful headscarf,' Mrs Chen said to her suddenly. 'I have one that's a bit like it.' A strange expression glanced over her face.

'Thank you,' Claire said, with a calm she hadn't known she possessed. She had forgotten about the scarf. She patted her head casually, trying not to panic. 'Thank you very much.'

'Is it Hermès?' Melody Chen asked. 'I love the colours – orange and brown are my favourite. Autumn, you know.'

'Oh, no,' Claire said. 'I got it here, actually. It's just some inexpensive thing I got off a hawker. I can give you the exact location if you –'

'Well, it looks just as nice as the real thing,' Melody Chen interrupted. 'You tall women can pull anything off.' She sipped at her martini.

'Well,' Mr Chen said, in the ensuing lull, 'it was certainly nice to see you.'

***

Claire didn't sleep that night. She got up after Martin's breathing deepened, and walked barefoot over to the window. Beneath her feet, the lacquered wooden floor was smooth and cool, spotless from the mopping Yu Ling gave it every other day. Her body was still overheated from the sun she had received that day at the beach; her arms and legs felt as if the rays were still simmering beneath her skin. She cranked the window open slowly, the metal hinges creaking, and watched the pinpoints of light that were people with insomnia like herself. There was a breeze and the humid night air entered the room and cooled her.

Her head was abuzz. She hadn't been able to concentrate on anything since their encounter with the Chens. She was sure she had behaved oddly with the Comstocks – she had seen Minna give Bruce a look when she had knocked over her drink for the second time. She hadn't said anything to Martin because she hadn't the slightest idea what to say. 'Darling, I've been stealing from the Chens and I'm afraid I've been found out. I've stopped, though, don't worry.' He would think her quite mad. And perhaps she had been. She rested her head against the cool pane of the window. She didn't think Melody Chen had put two and two together. And she would never accuse Claire of stealing without concrete proof, would she? Claire gazed out at the dark night and wondered if it looked the same at home in England.

PART II

9 December 1941

So, this is war. Before, he would have called it driving. He's taking a lorry full of cable drums to Causeway Bay, with five or six Chinese workers squatting in the back. In the seat next to him is Kevin Evers, who apparently knows what to do with the cable, or what to tell the workers to do. It is now chaos back at Headquarters, phone and radio squawking endlessly. The airport was bombed just hours ago, with the loss of some twenty-five aircraft, and the tension is rising. Will has been told to deliver the drums and get back on the double. Evers is nervously jabbering away.

The roads at least are empty of vehicles, with hardly any traffic, although there are plenty of people still on the streets. A woman beats a man with a large burlap bag, striking him with her small hands, screaming, as he shakes her off and runs. Looting has begun.

And, hard to believe, a few days ago, he was at a party in a dinner jacket, sipping champagne and exchanging barbed jokes with Trudy and her crowd.

In Causeway Bay, he finds the building where he's to drop off the drums and they're unloading the lorry when the siren wails again. Everyone scurries inside. The whiz of air, and the loud reverberation of the explosion. The ground shudders. Evers breathes loudly next to him. When they ring Headquarters, they're told to stay as the bombing will probably intensify, park the lorry in a safe place, and billet at a flat on Montgomery Street. He writes down the number with a stubby pencil on a grimy piece of paper, smudged with oil: 140. It sounds familiar.

When they venture there, they ring the doorbell and find a frightened amah who lets them in and reaches into her tunic to unearth a wrinkled envelope. When they open it, they find a rather poignant note:

To Whoever You May Be,

Welcome to our home. We hope you will make yourselves comfortable in this difficult time. We are an English couple who moved to Hong Kong some seven years ago and enjoy it immensely, so we hope this is not the last chapter. We have moved as directed upwards, and hope that our flat provides you with safe shelter. In the spirit of wartime, we ask that you be courteous to our amah, mind the furniture, and refrain from smoking.

Sincerely, Edna and George Weatherly.

'Aaah,' says Will suddenly.

'What?' Evers asks, lighting a cigarette and giving Will one as well, for good measure.

'Nothing.' It's just that he knows them. He's met them before, and been here for a drink. This was when he first arrived, in the weeks before he met Trudy, before everything, as she would never know people like the Weatherlys. They were very good people, respectable, and coming to Hong Kong had been their great adventure. From a small village in the Cotswolds, they still had a wide-eyed wonder at the vastness of the world and marvelled that they had ended up in the Far East. He had met them at a small English shop in Causeway Bay, buying tea, a few weeks after he had arrived, and after striking up a conversation, they had invited him over for a drink. Nice people. He hadn't seen them since he'd started up with Trudy. Different speeds.

They toss a coin for the bed, and Will gets the floor.

'You could sleep in the old bird's bed.' Evers nods towards the small room the amah has at the back.

'I'm not that hard up,' Will says lightly. 'She's had a rough time of it, too, without me taking her room.'

'Just thinking of you, mate.' Evers shrugs. 'Do you think she could rustle up some supper?'

Will rummages in his pack. Trudy, still Chinese enough to be obsessed with food, had made sure he had some tins in his rucksack, although he had deemed it unnecessary. 'I have bully beef and some carrots.'

The amah is happy to have something to do. She holds up a cup of rice, cooks it with the meat and vegetable and then they eat, she taking a bowl to her room, and the two men in the dining alcove, with the radio turned on, disembodied voice crackling on with news of the war.

'The bridges at the northern frontier have been blown up to prevent the advance of Japanese troops . . .' Later, someone who was there will tell Will of the surreal scene – the British assiduously setting up their explosives in plain sight of the Japanese, who were just as diligently building another bridge to swing across once the destruction had happened, the two sides studiously ignoring the other, neither questioning the inevitability of what the other was doing, nor trying to stop it. 'Doesn't that just sum it all up?' this man, a policeman, said. 'Thoroughly demented.'

All through the night, the flat shudders and is lit with the fire of bombs. Will hears Evers, his rapid breathing, neither of them asleep.

In the morning, Evers washes himself thoroughly. 'Don't know the next time I'll be able to do this,' he says, drying himself with one of the Weatherlys' towels and tossing it into a corner. 'Do you think breakfast's in the offing?'

'Do you think of anything else but food?'

'What else is there to think about, mate? Times like these, you get to the basics – what you eat, where you shit, finding a place to sleep. It's what keeps you sane.'

They ring Headquarters to ask what they should do next. Nobody knows anything.

'Just stay there for now,' a voice barks at them. They hear clattering and men shouting. The line clicks off.

'Good to know they're on top of the situation,' Evers says.

'We're the civilians. I'm sure the top brass know what's going on.'

'One would hope so.'

They decide to go out. Montgomery Street is empty: it is primarily an enclave for European expatriates who have all fled to higher ground or to China. The few shops – a bakery, a cobbler – are closed and dark inside. The windows are already dirty from the soot and dirt flung up by the bombs, but through one, Will can see a rotting egg tart, its glistening yellow surface slowly invaded by green mould. A fly lands on it, legs twitching. An aeroplane whines overhead and Will flinches.

When they go back to the flat, the amah is gone, her room as empty as if she had never lived there.

'Nothing to do here,' Evers says. 'I think we should try to get back to HQ. It's going to drive me mad staying here doing nothing.'

They gather their belongings and pick their way in the gathering dusk through the streets. Refuse has started to build up on the kerbs and a low, persistent stench rises from the road. They see a car speed up as it approaches them, and in it a Chinese man averting his gaze. They are in sight of the lorry and Will is remarking that the doors are open when they hear it. Evers's head cocks up to the whining sound, and Will watches him watch the first bomb come down and destroy a building not fifty feet away. It is as if it is in slow motion. Evers yells, 'Watch out!' and dives for the ground.

Will follows, and feels the earth open up and fall below them, his body dealt an enormous blow, ears ringing and eyes stinging, and then, in the next moment of clarity, they are crawling towards the shelter of the lorry, the closest thing there is. In the back of his mind, as the ground is pounded and shaken by the intensifying chaos, Will notes that the lorry has been picked clean. The tyres are gone and the open doors reveal a missing steering-wheel. Evers is shouting something else, something about this being civilian territory and why are they bombing, but Will can't hear the rest because he is thinking that the tyres are missing and that it is hard to move forward with the ground shaking like this, and then all is white.

15 December 1941

When he wakes up, he is woozy and cold. Overhead, an enormous light is glaring down at him. The sheets are like ice on his swollen limbs. He is afraid to look at his body.

But here is relief. He is not dead. Then he remembers. Evers. But he doesn't remember. Every part of his body hurts so much, he feels as if his head is about to explode. He lifts the sheet. His left knee is swollen to the size of a small melon. Around the bandage flesh bulges, purple, black, livid, angry.

Jane Lessig, whom he has met at parties, comes by. She is dressed in white and in his woozy state, he thinks she looks like an angel.

'There you are,' she says. 'You had us worried, you know.'

'Water?'

'No water for you yet, doctor's orders.'

He doesn't think he's ever felt quite so awful in his life.

'I'm so embarrassed,' he tells her.

'What on earth for?' She cranks up his bed with a quizzical look.

'It was just a mishap,' he tries to explain. 'Nothing warlike about it.'

'You're talking nonsense.'

He tries again. 'Evers?'

'Don't worry about him,' she says, and walks quickly away.

He wanders in and out of consciousness.

He sees Trudy in a white dress, like a nurse, like a bride, like a shroud. She sponges his forehead. But her hair is blonde now. She is not Trudy.

'Listen,' whispers the wondrous Jane Lessig. 'You were not in the Volunteers. You're a civilian who was walking down the street and hit by debris from a bomb.' She doesn't want him to go to a POW camp. It's unclear who is going where but she thinks the civilians will be better off than the soldiers. He nods. He understands, then forgets. She says it to him every day, like an incantation that will save him.

Jane Lessig brings him a bowl of pudding.

When he gets up to look out of the window, the first time he has been up, he is surprised to find that he has a limp.

'I've a limp!' he says to Jane Lessig.

'Yes, you do,' she says. 'And a fine one at that.'

'I'm feeling much better,' he says. 'I think I could be discharged soon.'

'Do you now?' she says crisply. 'We'll leave that to the doctors, shall we?'

But he does feel better, and when Dr Whitley comes round, Will is dressed and ready to go. 'I don't think I'm doing much good here, do you?' he asks.

'Will,' Dr Whitley says. 'It's very different out there. Kowloon's besieged and we're trying to hold out here for as long as possible. There have been enormous casualties. Do you know where you could stay?'

'Could go to Trudy's?' he wonders.

'She's been here every day,' the doctor says. 'But I didn't let her come in. I thought it would be too upsetting for her. You're not at your most handsome. She said to tell you she's staying with Angeline and would be by later on today.'

'Oh,' Will says. 'Then I'll stay until she comes.'

The doctor gives him a peculiar look and nods. He's finished examining Will's knee.

When Trudy comes, she is different. He can't tell why and then he sees – she has no lipstick on, no jewellery, her clothes are drab, no colour of any sort. He mentions this to her, sort of an ice breaker to take away from the fact that he is injured, in a hospital, that the world is at war. It is odd to be shy with Trudy. He does not want to seem diminished in front of her.

'I don't want to attract any sort of attention,' she says. 'It's like walking on pins out there in case you run into a Jap. Father's gone to Macau. He asked me to go with him, but I didn't want to.' She walks over to the window. 'He's worried about me,' she says, looking down and fingering the cloth of her skirt. 'If they win, they'll be brutal beyond belief.'

'How did you get here?'

'I had Angeline's driver bring me. We're camping at her place on the Peak, although the whole Peak is supposed to have been evacuated by now. They think it's too exposed. But we've managed to stay undetected, and it's quiet up there. She has the dogs and her houseboy along with the amahs and the chauffeur so we have some protection.'

The upper class always do what they want, he thinks, inappropriately.

'It's nerve-racking, like playing poker,' she says. 'You never know when you're going to be stopped, and people are turning against each other. Old Mr Enderby was roughed up by some Sikhs because they said he looked at them oddly. That lovely old man.' She stops suddenly. 'How are you feeling? Here I am going on about the outside and you're all . . .' Her voice trails.

'Evers is dead,' he says. 'But you didn't know him. He was with me when the bomb got us.'

Trudy looks at him, blank. 'You're right,' she says. 'I didn't know him.'

'I want all the news,' he says. 'Do you have any?'

'Angeline says that we're not doing very well. Apparently they expected the Japs from the south, by the sea, but they came from the north instead and just breezed right through the defences there. And it's really awful outside.' Her voice hiccups. 'I saw a dead baby on a pile of rubbish this morning as I came here. It's all around, the rubbish and the corpses, I mean, and they're burning it so it smells like what I imagine hell smells like. And I saw a woman being beaten with bamboo poles and then dragged off by her hair. She was half being dragged, half crawling along, and screaming like the end of the world. Her skin was coming off in ribbons. You're supposed to wear sanitary pads so that . . . you know . . . if a soldier tries to . . . Well, you know. The locals and the Japanese are looting anything that's not locked down, and thieving and generally being impossible. They're all over the place in Kowloon, running amok. We're thinking about moving out to one of the hotels, just so we're more in the middle of things, and we can see people and get more information. The Gloucester is packed to the rafters but my old friend Delia Ho has a room at the Repulse Bay and says we can have it because she's leaving to go to China. We can share it with Angeline, don't you think? And, apparently, the American Club has cots out and people are staying there as well. They have a lot of supplies, I suppose. Americans always do. Everyone wants to be with other people.'

'I suppose that's a good idea,' Will says.

'Dommie says it's only a matter of time before the Japanese have the whole island.'

'That's hopeful.'

'I don't think he really cares.' Trudy laughs shrilly. 'He's just waiting to see what side he should join. He's learning Japanese at a fast clip.'

'You know what a dangerous thing he's doing. It's not a matter for laughter.'

'Oh, bother!' Trudy comes and sits down next to him. 'Your injury has quite done away with your sense of humour. Dommie is a survivor, just like you and me, and he'll be fine. When can you leave?'

'I think soon. And they're eager to be rid of me. There are people with far more serious injuries, I imagine.'

'But can you walk and all that?'

'I'll be fine,' he says shortly. 'Don't worry about me.'

Dr Whitley discharges him with reluctance. 'If it weren't for Trudy,' he says, wrapping fresh bandages around Will's abdomen and knee, 'I would never let you go. I know she'll take care of you.'

Trudy is sitting at the foot of the bed. 'And the fact that you have too few beds,' she rejoins. 'Will here is taking up valuable space. I'm on your side, Doctor. I was a nurse for two weeks. Remember?'

The doctor laughs. 'Of course. How could I forget?' He becomes serious. 'Trudy, you must change the bandages daily, and you must cleanse the skin and the wounds with a solution of water and peroxide that I'll have the nurse make up for you. No matter if Will says he doesn't need it, you must do it without exception.'

Trudy nods. 'I'll be a model of reliability and efficiency,' she says.

Once at Angeline's, she puts him to bed although he feels fine. Their room is messy, with her clothes spilling out of a suitcase on to the floor and her toiletries scattered on the windowsills, the bathroom basin, the bed. There are model aeroplanes strung from the ceiling and a wooden desk piled high with schoolboy mysteries.

'Whose room is this?'

'It's Giles's. He's my godson – did you know?'

'I've never met him.'

'He's always away at school and now he'll stay with Frederick's family in England until this all settles down.'

'Oh,' he says. The room is streaked with dusty light from the window.

'I'm not an invalid, you know,' he adds. 'I could probably walk to Central and back.'

'Don't be ridiculous,' she says. 'You're to take it easy.'

But he is better, and she sees it, and soon they venture out, to see empty roads, closed shops, people scurrying from place to place, not looking anywhere but the ground.

'There's been an incredible amount of looting,' she says. 'And the government is rationing rice. It's been rather amazing. I was walking down Gloucester Road and I saw police firing their guns into the air to disperse a crowd, and I wondered, Where do those bullets go? When they come down, if they hit someone, won't they kill them?'

'Trudy, darling. You always think of things nobody else thinks of.'

'And probably for good reason,' she says. 'I'm rather an idiot about everything.'

They walk further.

'It doesn't feel like our town any more, does it?'

'It's too dreary.' They link arms and go home where Angeline is crying in the cellar. The amahs have made a small meal of rice and Chinese vegetables, dotted with salted pork. They eat, and drink weak tea, feeling the invisible constraints of the reality around them.

The next few days are Spartan and regulated, lived as if they might be the last, heightened with the surreal. They eat to sustain themselves, listen to the radio for the latest news, and go to the distribution centre for supplies, which are given out sporadically and randomly. One day it's bread and jam, another it's bananas, and then it's flashlights. They take what they can get and go to the black market for the rest as, between them, Trudy and Angeline have a lot of cash. At the black market in town, the atmosphere is tense, the buyers irate at the prices and shouting insults at the vendors, a few having the grace to look awkward behind their tables of random goods – the tins of potted meat, the small bags of sugar, the cooking utensils. The price of rice is at an all-time high, and it is as precious as gold.

The ground shakes intermittently and the night is lit by fire. They see piles of dead bodies and weeping women beside them. Dominick calls in with provisions he's got hold of somehow, and they have the delicacy not to ask. He tells them to stay at Angeline's for as long as possible. They have not been bothered and that is a good sign. There are a few other families holding the fort at their homes as well. Will's injury makes it impossible for him to go anywhere too far. Angeline's driver manages to get hold of the newspaper most days, and the news is grim – the Japanese advancing inexorably and surprisingly fast.

'I can't believe they still get the paper out every day,' Angeline says. She has not bathed in days, and is starting to smell more than musty. She has not heard from her husband. He had last sent a message a week ago when he was fighting for the Volunteers on Mount Nicholson.

'Should we go to the Repulse Bay?' Trudy asks.

'I feel odd not doing anything,' Will says. 'I feel like other men are fighting and I'm sitting around, doing nothing.'

'You're injured, you imbecile,' Trudy says. 'You'd be more of a hindrance than a help. You're slowing me down and I'm only putting up with it because you're a warm body to sleep next to at night. I assure you that others will not feel that way.'

The next day they wake up to find the servants have vanished. Trudy is entirely unsurprised. 'A clean get-away. I'm surprised the dogs haven't deserted us.' She starts washing the dishes that were left in the basin. He rises to help her. 'You sit down,' she orders. 'They lasted longer than I thought. Angeline's always been a beastly employer although she pays twice the going rate.'

'What happened to Ah Lok and Mei Sing?' Will asks, remembering Trudy's amahs suddenly.

'I told them they should leave, and they wouldn't, so I locked them out of the flat until they went away. There was lots of crying and wailing – you know them. They have relatives I'm sure they'd rather be with.'

'You're their family, Trudy.'

'But I'm not, really. And it's more dangerous for them to be with me. They're not going to be bothered once they're part of the crowd out there. I'm the one who's going to get attention, hanging about with all you foreigners.'

'It must have been very hard to make them leave,' he says, reaching for her hand.

She shakes him away. 'It's fine, Will. Please don't be sentimental right now. I couldn't stand it.'

'What day is it?' he asks.

'Almost Christmas. The twentieth, I think.' She looks wistful. 'The parties should be in full swing by now.' Then, 'Will.'

'Trudy.'

'I've some things I've had to hide, but I want you to know where, because if something happens, you should go and get them.'

'Like?'

'I've a lot of money that my father gave me before he went to Macau, and my jewellery too. Altogether, it's worth a lot . . . more than enough to live on for ages.'

'I don't need it, if that's what you're implying. I'll be fine with what I have.'

'And I hired a box at the bank, the main one. And I've put down your name and Dominick's as people who can access it. But the thing is you'll both have to sign for it, unless one is dead, so you have to get along. There's a key. It's in the plant pot that used to be outside my bedroom window in the flat. I've brought it in, and it's just filled with earth. The key's at the bottom, so you'll have to dig it out. But if there's no key, you can still get to my things – it will just take a bit longer. Legal things, you know.'

'Right,' he says.

'You must remember,' she says. 'You really must.'

Angeline emerges from her bedroom in a dressing-gown and they explain about the missing servants. She collapses into a chair. 'I don't understand,' she says again and again. 'They've been with me for years.' Quickly, she becomes practical. 'Did they take anything?'

They hadn't thought to look. They go to the pantry and see their fast-dwindling supplies, rice, a few potatoes and onions, flour, sugar, a few soft apples, untouched.

'Servants get a raw deal,' Will says. 'They're always the last thanked and the first accused.'

'This is survival,' Angeline says. 'I'm surprised they didn't take anything. I would have, and not had a single qualm.'

'Let's all have a drink,' Trudy says.

'That's the most sensible thing you've said all week.' Will goes to get a bottle of Scotch – they are not in danger of running out of that any time soon. They pour glasses, turn on the radio, and the announcer is reading a message from Churchill. 'The eyes of the world are upon you. We expect you to resist to the end. The honour of the Empire is in your hands.'

'We're being abandoned,' Trudy says. 'They're not doing anything to help us. What do Churchill and the goddamned British Empire expect us to do?' Her eyes look hard and glassy, but Will sees they are filmed with tears.

Every day leaflets fall from the sky, Japanese planes whirring overhead and letting loose propaganda, all over the colony, telling the Chinese and the Indians not to fight, to join with the Japanese in a

'Greater Far Eastern Co-prosperity Sphere'. They've been collecting them as they fall on the ground, stacking them in piles, and Trudy wakes up on Christmas Day to declare a project: they will use them as wallpaper. In their dressing-gowns, they put Christmas carols on the gramophone, make hot toddies and – in a fit of wild, Yuletide indulgence – use all the flour for pancakes, then paste the leaflets on the living-room wall – a grimly ironic decoration. One has a draw-ing of a Chinese woman sitting on the lap of a fat Englishman, and says in Chinese, 'The English have been raping your women for years, stop it now,' or something to that effect, or so Trudy says.

'Hmm . . .' she says. 'Isn't this a drawing of you and me?' She sits on his lap, puts her arms round his neck, and bats her eyelids. 'Please, sah, you buy drink for me?'

'It's of me and Frederick, you idiot,' says Angeline. 'Look at how fat the man is.' It's the first time she's mentioned her husband in days.

Another leaflet has two Orientals facing each other and shaking hands. 'Japanese and Chinese are brothers. Do not struggle and join our side,' translates Angeline.

'They seem to have forgotten Nanking,' Trudy says. 'They weren't so fraternal then, were they?'

'I feel . . . oppressed,' says Angeline. 'I think we should turn Will in, don't you, darling?'

'I think that fellow's Dominick.' Will points to one of the Chinese figures.

'Don't joke about him.' Trudy pouts. 'Why do you think we have so much food? Dommie's taking care of us, and I don't mind how he does it.'

'Point taken but not agreed with,' Will says. 'Why are those damn leaflets so obvious and inflammatory?'

They hear a car motoring up the driveway and tense their shoul-ders. Trudy runs to the window and tentatively lifts the curtain.

'It's Dommie!' she shouts, with relief, and goes to open the door.

'Speak of the devil.' Will sits down.

Dominick enters and unwraps a scarf from round his neck.

'Merry Christmas and all that,' he says, languid even in the midst of war.

'And to you,' Will says.

'I've brought a few provisions to make it feel extra holiday-ish.' He brandishes a basket from which he extracts the *South China Morning Post*, a tin of pressed duck, a bag of rice, a loaf of bread, two jars of strawberry jam and a fruit cake. The women clap their hands like pleased children. 'Can you make anything with this, Trudy?' He sprawls in a chair, elegant limbs splayed out, the hunter having provided for his women.

'I'm hopeless in the kitchen, you know that.' Trudy grabs the newspaper.

' "Day of good cheer," ' she reads. 'That's the headline. "Hong Kong is observing the strangest and most sober Christmas in its century-old history." '

'It's as if Hong Kong didn't exist before the English got here,' Dominick interrupts.

'Shut up, I'm reading,' Trudy says. ' "Such modest celebrations as are arranged today will be subdued . . . There was a pleasant interlude at the Parisian Grill shortly before it closed last night when a Volunteer pianist, in for a spot of food before going back to his post, played some well-known favourites in which all present joined with gusto." ' She looks up. 'People are at the Grill and I'm not? That's a travesty if ever I heard one. I've been isolated up here on the Peak and people have been going out? Have you been going out, Dommie? And how dare you not take me with you?'

'Trudy. It's not good for women to be out, these days. You should be tucked away, safe, at home. Now, mend my trousers and make us some lunch.'

She throws the paper at his head.

'What's the news?' Will asks.

'Not good for England,' Dominick says easily. 'They're outnumbered and outclassed. There are just so many Japanese and they've been properly trained. They're on the island already, swarming everywhere. They landed the night of the eighteenth. The English are depending on soldiers who haven't been trained on the terrain and don't know what to do. The chain of command is not being well executed. And malaria's rampant.'

Will notices Dominick is careful not to say 'we' or 'our'. 'So we're not doing well.'

'No,' Dominick says evenly. 'You're not doing well at all. I think it's only a matter of time. The governor's a fool, rejected an offer of cease-fire with some absurd British proclamation of superiority. Has his head in the sand. I've been getting news from our cousin, Victor, who always knows what's going on with these things. He's still at home.'

'Do you want pancakes?' Trudy interrupts.

'No, thanks,' Dominick says. 'I can't stay long.'

'What are you doing with your time, these days?' Angeline asks. 'Besides taking care of us, I mean.'

'You can't imagine what's going on,' he says. 'You're in a cosy little bunker here. It's horrific out there. I'm just trying to keep on top of the situation.' His face is bland and smooth, eyes like black coal. Will wonders if it would be right to call a man beautiful.

'If we hear of a surrender, we'll leave, since I assume they'll be looting up here on the Peak first thing,' Will says.

'And if you see any uniforms at all, you should be out of here like a shot.'

'Is there anything else we should be doing?' Angeline asks.

'No, not really. You have money, I assume. If it gets really bad, I suppose a hospital is the safest place. You know where they are. They've turned the Britannic Mineral Water Works factory over in

Kowloon into a temporary shelter as well. But then you'd have to get over the harbour. Stay on this side, actually. There's some Japanese custom that when they win a battle, the soldiers get three days to run wild and do whatever they wish so that's the most dangerous time, obviously. Try to stay indoors at all times.' Dominick pauses, and looks at Will. 'By the way, I've got a Christmas present for you.'

He goes to the car and comes back with a cane, a beautiful one, made of polished walnut with a brass tip. 'I'm afraid I didn't have time to wrap it. But I thought you might find it useful.' He smiles crookedly and hands it to Will. 'There you are, old chap.'

'Thank you,' Will says. He takes it and hangs it on the arm of the chair he's sitting on.

'What about me?' Trudy says. 'Nothing for me?'

'That fell into my lap,' Dominick says. 'I saw it on the black market and I had just enough money for it. Didn't ask for much. I guess the market for canes isn't so good in wartime.'

'Funny, that. I'd have thought they'd be popular, what with the war creating all those cripples and everything,' Will says.

'One might think, yes.'

Trudy stops the exchange. 'But the doctor says that Will is going to be as good as new, so he won't need it in a few weeks, will you, Will? We'll use it as a poker for the fire, then.'

After Dominick leaves, they sit, the air somehow gone from the room. It feels colder, the evening approaching.

'Turn on the gramophone,' Angeline says. 'I want to hear music and dance, and feel normal.'

'And drinks!' Trudy cries. 'It's Christmas and we should be having drinks.'

She fetches clean glasses, lights candles, then puts the duck and bread and jam out on the table, and it tastes marvellous, their Christmas supper, with the drink warming their cheeks and stomachs.

They carry on in this way, Trudy and Angeline dancing, carols playing, Will applauding, pouring more drinks. They drink and dance in the chilly drawing room of Angeline's grand old house, the twilight encroaching, glasses in hand, tippling until they are all quite drunk and they stumble up to their rooms and collapse. Trudy is sweet with Will in bed, her hands and mouth moving over him until he forgets the dull throb of his knee and the spinning of the ceiling. That is the Christmas of 1941, a wistful, melancholy, waiting kind of day he will remember for ever.

In the morning, Angeline knocks on their door. Will opens it, groggy, his mouth feeling like cloth. For some reason, she leaves her hand suspended in the air, frozen mid-knock.

'Morning,' he says. She looks at him, her face pale and hung-over.

'Happy Boxing Day,' she says. 'It's finished. I just heard on the radio. We've surrendered.'

26 December 1941

Trudy is frantic to find Dominick. 'He will know what to do,' she says over and over.

'We'll stay here until we can't any more,' Will says, trying to calm her. 'It'll be fine in the long run. The Japanese cannot win against England, and America, Holland and China. It's just going to take a little while.'

'Would you mind if I went into town and looked for him? Or maybe I should try to find Victor,' she says, ignoring him. 'I don't think you should go.'

'I'd slow you down, I know.' He cannot calm her. 'How are you going to find them? It'll be impossible. Just stay and see. It will all be fine, you will see.'

She whirls on him, her face unrecognizable. 'And in the meantime?' She almost spits it out. 'What do you suggest we do in the meantime while the Japs are swarming over the town, doing whatever they like to whomever they like? They're going to be all over the place, like filthy little ants. What do you think America and Holland and jolly old England are going to do then? Are you going to help me? With your leg the way it is? We have to . . .'

He hesitates, then takes her shoulder with one hand and slaps her face with the other. 'You need to settle down,' he said. 'You're hysterical.'

She sinks to the floor, weeping. 'Will,' she says, through her hands. 'Oh, Will. What are we going to do?'

He gets up with difficulty and kneels down on the floor with her. 'Darling Trudy,' he says. 'I will take care of you, even with my terrible, gimpy leg. I swear.'

Later, after he has put her into a bath, and fetched her a drink, there is a knock at the door. With the women upstairs, he goes to answer it, first looking outside to see who it is. A sandy-haired man in uniform is standing by the door.

'Who is it?' he shouts.

'Please, sir, it's Ned Young – from Canada. With the Winnipeg Grenadiers.'

He opens the door. 'Come in. Are you all right? Are you alone? What the devil are you doing out here?'

'Yes, sir. I was on a van being transported with the others, as POWs, you know, and I managed to jump off and just walked and knocked on doors that looked safe.'

Inside, the man is revealed to be a boy, so young that acne still pocks his skin. His trousers are soiled and he smells to high heaven.

'Have you had anything to eat?'

'Not in the past few days, sir.' He looks ravenous and polite at the same time.

'Here, sit down here in the dining room. I'll get you something to eat.' He finds a plate and puts out some bread and the remaining duck from last night. There's a beer and he opens it, pours a glass of water as well. The boy falls on the food, shoving it into his mouth.

'There's more. Don't worry,' Will says. 'You'll get your fill.'

'It was awful out there,' the boy says. His mouth is full and he begins to weep. 'It was awful. We were in the mountains, in trenches.'

'Don't talk. Just eat and try to relax.'

The boy goes on, as if Will hadn't spoken: 'I saw my buddy's guts come out. He was alive. He was talking to me, and his guts were outside. Then I smelled him. He was cooking, his guts were cooking and it smelled like food. I saw a woman with her head blown off and her child sitting next to her, naked, with shit running down his backside, flies buzzing. We had to leave him. They wouldn't let us take the child. I've never seen such things. We were in Jamaica just a month ago, training, eating bananas. They told us we wouldn't see any action here.' He weeps and weeps but keeps eating. 'And I didn't have water for days. I just wanted to die, but I jumped off that truck 'cause I seen what those Japs do. They're not human, what they do to other people. They're not human. I saw them rip a baby out of a pregnant woman. I saw them chop off heads and put them on fenceposts.'

Angeline walks into the room. 'What on earth?'

The boy stands up, still crying, still eating. 'Hello, ma'am. I'm Ned, Ned Young, from Winnipeg.'

'I see,' Angeline says, and sits down. For once Will appreciates her cut-and-dried sophistication, so needling in peacetime. 'Ned Young, where were you? Did you see any of the Volunteers?'

'We've lost. We've surrendered. I haven't seen anyone but Japs. They're so well equipped. They have mountain shoes, and belts with food concentrate, and maps. We didn't have any of that. They gave us rum for breakfast. They just dropped us here weeks ago and told us we'd have time to train.'

'What did you see in town?' They want information. He wants balm.

'There're riots, and dead people. Everything smells so bad, you want to die too. It's thick out there, the smell, and people are scared, but the scoundrels are out, stealing, burning. They're taking advantage before the Japs get everything.'

'Why don't you rest, Ned?' Will says, realizing he is not able to tell them anything useful. 'You bathe and rest. There's a bed upstairs and we'll wake you if anything happens.'

116

Angeline takes him up. When she comes back down, Will feels the need to be outside for some air. The young boy has brought with him a tantalizing glimpse of the outside world.

'I'm going out,' he says. 'My leg feels better and I need to know what's going on. It's driving me mad, being cooped up in here all this time.'

'Fine,' Angeline says. 'Just don't go too far. When Trudy wakes up, she'll be wanting you.'

Outside, the sky is still blue, and there are birds singing faintly. Save the occasional plume of smoke, it is quiet and lovely up here on the wide, well-paved roads and green manicured hedges of the Peak. From a cliffside fence, he can see Hong Kong spread out before him, the harbour glistening, the sky gleaming. It is so still outside, he can hear himself breathing.

'One of those moments,' he says, before realizing he has said it out loud.

He comes back to find Trudy and Angeline in the kitchen pouring all the bottles of Scotch down the sink.

'Don't worry,' Angeline says. 'We got blotto first. And we saved some for you, and our new friend, young Ned Young.'

'Only thing worse than a Jap is a drunk Jap, right?' he says. 'Keep the empty bottles. They might come in useful.'

'We've been thinking, Will,' Trudy says, 'and we agree that the best thing to do now is stay here since we don't know that anywhere else will be any safer, but we think that you and Ned should be hidden. Since it's so very obvious you're not Chinese, you know. Unless, of course, you're needed to rescue us, but Angeline and I could pretend to be servants and they might leave us alone.'

Will cocks his head. 'Really? That has rich comic possibility, certainly, but I don't know if that's the thing to do.'

'I know it sounds mad, but where would we go? What do you think we should do?'

'We could go into town and see what other people are doing.'

'But we might not have anywhere to sleep or anything to eat.'

'Well,' Will says, 'let's do this. We'll take the car early tomorrow morning and we'll go down to Central and see what's going on there. Then we can come back up.'

'All of us?'

'Ned should stay, since he's had a rough time, but you and Angeline can come if you want.'

The next morning, they pile into the car, Ned as well, as he had not wanted to be left alone. He is freshly bathed and absurdly attired in some of Frederick's clothes, the sumptuous weave of the shirt glowing under his childish face, his torso swimming in trousers cut to Frederick's not inconsiderable girth, cinched inefficiently by an alligator belt.

The road winds down the mountain, and as they round this curve or that, they catch a glimpse of the harbour and Central, looking eerily similar, but without cars. As they enter town, they are quiet, looking at the empty buildings, the barren streets.

'Let's go to the Gloucester,' Trudy says. 'There should be people there.'

They park and walk down Connaught Road. Ned touches Will's hand and motions to the side. Between two buildings, a man's body lies crumpled, blood streaking his clothes. They pass silently.

'It's so quiet,' Trudy whispers.

'No cars or people anywhere,' Will says.

But inside the Gloucester, it is bustling, with more people than they've ever seen in the lobby of that elegant hotel. They are sleeping on sofas, on the marble floor, the potted plants all moved tidily to one side, forming a verdant fringe to this strange refugee camp.

Uniformed hotel boys are scurrying around with cups of coffee on silver trays, trying to serve the unorthodox guests as best as they can.

'There's Delia Ho!' Trudy cries. 'I thought she'd gone to China. And there's Anson and Carol. And Edwina Storch with Mary. The whole world's here!'

People throng round the new arrivals, asking where they've been, what they've seen.

'Can't help you,' Angeline says. 'We've been hiding out at home.'

'Undisturbed?' asks an American.

'Quite,' says Trudy. 'But eating like dogs. Is there any food here?'

There isn't much, unfortunately, the hotel trying their best to supply their guests with what remains in their cellar. Trudy sits down to share a rice pudding with Delia, spooning some into Will's mouth, then, seeing Ned off in a corner, beckons him over to have some as well.

'The coffee is atrocious,' she says. 'They've gone to well water.'

'What's going on?' Will asks Dick Gubbins, an American businessman who, even before all this, always knew what was going on.

'I've been at the American Club, came here to see if I could find out anything. They're starting to rampage through town, celebrating their victory. Mitzy, that old bird with the antiques store on Carnarvon Road, was stabbed by a drunken soldier for not handing over her purse fast enough, or something.' His voice drops. 'And you know what happened at the hospital.'

'I don't.'

'Awful stuff. They're just animals, sometimes. The nuns were violated, the other nurses too, doctors bayoneted trying to defend them. They're not supposed to touch hospital workers, obviously, but tell that to a bloodthirsty mob. Drew McNamara's over there, trying to clean the whole mess up and see that those responsible are apprehended, but everything's so chaotic now. Under the Hague

Convention, police are supposed to be able to keep order, the old Hong Kong police, but I haven't seen much of them. It's complete madness out there, I tell you. The Japanese are using some of the British constables to stand guard outside their consulate. I don't think they understand the concept of irony.

'The Chinese and the Indians should be able to move freely. Trudy's cousin, that Victor Chen, is doing a good job acting as go-between, trying to lessen the violence and looting. The neutral Europeans should be all right, but it's touchy there. The Japs have asked for prostitutes, but they're already swarming all over the Wanchai brothels. Hopefully, that'll get some of their energy out. If you get a drunk or crazy one, they'll swing at your head with a sword and not care if they cut your head off. They're demanding money and watches and jewellery from anyone they meet on the street. There's supposed to be a victory parade on the twenty-ninth.'

'Any word on what they're planning to do with us?'

'No. But if you can get to China, I would. I'm trying to arrange passage now for me and some of my men.'

'I don't know why Trudy doesn't go.'

'And you should as well, my friend. Nothing for you here. Listen, best of luck, and we'll have a drink when this is over, okay? Call me if you're ever in New York.' They shake hands and Gubbins leaves, trailing almost palpable clouds of American prosperity and assurance.

Trudy comes over. 'You remember Sophie Biggs and her husband? We saw them at Manley's party,' she tells him. 'Well, her husband knows some Japanese and spoke some to a few soldiers in the street and they thought he was being disrespectful and shot him in the knee. And he was lucky, Sophie says. He's not in good shape because the hospitals have been bombed and are operating at the barest of levels. Delia says they're setting up checkpoints soon, so we're not going to be able to get around without passes. Should we go back and get our things? Should we stay up there or come back down here? It is rather more convivial down here in town. I was going a bit stir crazy up there.'

'I think it would be nice if we moved into town, yes. But there's no room here. We shouldn't sleep on the floor here when we have perfectly good beds at Angeline's. We should conserve our strength to prepare for whatever might be ahead. Who knows when we'll get to sleep well again?'

'So, you think we should stay at Angeline's?'

'I just don't know where we'd stay in town. I'm not going to stay here.' He gestures around. 'This is a riot waiting to happen. I think it's going to get ugly, and I don't mean with the Japanese.'

'So cynical. Isn't that my job?' But she doesn't disagree. 'Isn't it funny?' she says. 'We're at war but most of what we've done is wait for something to happen.'

'We don't want anything to happen, Trudy. We want everything to remain boring and uneventful.'

'But you know what I mean. We just sit at home and look at each other. Is that what war is? I wonder what Vivien Leigh is doing right at this very moment.'

He slaps her lightly on the bottom. 'She's fast asleep,' he says.

Edwina Storch comes over with Mary Winkle. 'How are you, my dear?' she says to Trudy.

'All right, darling. How are you all faring?'

'Can't complain, but trying to work out the new order and how to go about things.'

'It's like quicksand, isn't it?' Trudy says.

'You're a survivor, though,' says Edwina, with an odd cast in her voice.

Trudy pauses. 'As are you,' she says lightly. 'I'm sure we'll all be raising a glass of champagne to each other when this is all over.'

'I certainly hope so,' says Edwina. 'You're at home?'

'No, at Angeline's,' says Trudy. 'Don't know if that's the best place, but that's where we are for now.'

'Well, be well,' Edwina says, 'I'm sure we'll see each other soon.'

'I certainly hope so,' says Trudy.

When the women leave, Trudy makes a face at Will, sticking out her tongue.

They gather up Ned and Angeline, Trudy kissing everyone in sight, and stop off at a newly sprung-up market to buy rice, *choisam* and rambutans at an exorbitant price and drive home carefully, avoiding the main roads, feeling like some strange, new orphaned family.

The electricity finally goes out on New Year's Eve. Will has been making quick, urgent drives to town to get information and supplies, trying to avoid running into any Japanese. He's been successful for the most part, with the exception of one day when he was in the car with Ned, leaving town with a sack of rice, melon seeds and some tins of bully beef, feeling rather victorious at his successful scavenging. A Japanese soldier appeared suddenly on the road ahead of them and waved down their car. Will's stomach had plummeted into the seat.

'Don't say anything,' he warned Ned. The soldier had them open the boot. He looked at the rice, then motioned them out of the car. Gesturing with his rifle, he told them to empty their pockets and take off their wristwatches. 'American?' he asked.

'English.'

The man laughed. He looked around twenty-two, with a wide, naïve face.

'We win!' He pushed up his sleeve to reveal five wristwatches, lined up on his pale arm.

There was no reply to that, so when he had their money, and watches, the rice and beef, Will and Ned got into the car silently and went home. They had felt lucky.

And then on New Year's Eve, Will wakes up and turns on the switch, only to find the electricity is cut. The telephone works intermittently.

Trudy rallies against the silence that greets these announcements. 'Who needs all those gadgets?' she says. 'They're more work anyway. And everyone looks better by candlelight.' She pauses. 'I think we should have a party, a real New Year's Eve party, and invite all our fellow campers who are up here with us on the Peak. I'll see what we have and we can do pot luck.'

The Millers live down the road, a fashionable American family of six who are hunkering down with their six or seven servants – two or three amahs, a baby amah, a cook, houseboy and gardener. They call in every once in a while to share information and for human contact. Trudy goes with Will to invite them and insists they bring everyone, including the servants and the baby.

'They can stay in the kitchen and be part of it. You don't want to leave them alone – they might not be there when you get back!'

The bemused Millers agree to come, bring whatever they can spare, and to spread the word.

On the way home, Trudy says, 'There's that story of the village with the soup. Do you know it?'

'No,' Will says. 'Village?'

'There was a village with a chief who wanted to throw a big party with a communal soup. He asked everyone to bring something for the soup – meat or a vegetable or something good, you know. But everyone thought that everyone else would bring something so they just brought a stone, believing no one would notice. And in the end, tragic as it is, the soup was not delicious, or something like that.' She stops. 'I don't know why I told you that just now. Except that the people in that village were definitely not Chinese, having so little respect for food.'

'You're afraid the Millers will bring rocks to our party?'

'No, idiot,' she says. 'I'm afraid people aren't honourable.'

But of course the party is a wild success. Though dress isn't specified, people come in their finest, a sort of last gasp to the world as they know it. They gather together at Angeline's house, like moths to a flame, bringing surprising delicacies from secret cellars – a case of champagne ('Why not?' the giver reasons. 'Better to drink it now than have some Jap bathing in it later.'), five freshly slaughtered chickens, sardines, a small sack of rice, watercress, cheese, bananas. And this still being Hong Kong, people have brought their servants to prepare and serve it all.

'A veritable feast,' Trudy says, looking at the table.

'The proverbial groaning board,' says Will.

'I wouldn't go that far, darling.' She kisses him on the cheek. 'Doesn't it feel like we're on holiday? You don't need to go to work, I don't need to pretend to do anything with my time. Anything goes.'

Young Ned Young, a little more comfortable with his situation now, pulls Will aside. 'That Trudy is something else,' he says. 'Where'd you find her? I never met anyone like her, for sure.'

Men in dinner jackets and women in evening gowns are lounging in chairs, on the floor, drinking beer and tea out of odd containers – jam jars and tins – eating crackers and sardines. There's no music, so people offer to sing and play the piano. The instrument is terribly out of tune, but the music is sweet and the voices lovely.

Close to midnight, they gather round the biggest candle in the living room and count down.

'Ten, nine,' they start, before Trudy interrupts.

'Let's prolong this. Let's count down from fifty instead. Do we really have anything better to do?' People are agreeable and start again.

'Fifty, forty-nine, forty-eight . . .' And then something odd happens. Somewhere between thirty-four and thirty-three, the mood changes and it seems as if they are counting towards something rather important. They are chanting and their voices gather force and purpose, so that as they count down into the twenties and into the teens and the single digits, they become louder and braver, until they get to 'five, four, three, two . . . one' and burst into cheers, hug one another and feel, for a moment, as if something has been salvaged. Women wipe away tears and men clap each other on the back.

'Happy New Year, my darling,' Trudy says, kissing Will. 'May this be the worst New Year's Eve we ever experience.'

To the room she lifts her glass. 'It's time,' she says, 'to bury the silver and put away the sheets. It will be over, but we don't know when.'

At the end, guests leave in the small hours, or stay, strewn among the many sofas and chairs, scared to go outside, but wanting to get home. Trudy ministers to them, providing water and soothing words, until they muster the courage to pull themselves together, expel the effects of drink, and lurch into the night, one eye cocked towards the sky for enemy aircraft.

4 January 1942

On the fourth day of the new year, Trudy comes in with a leaflet in her hand. 'They're collecting people,' she announces, and reads from it.

' "Since the Japanese occupation of Hong Kong on Christmas Day, enemy aliens have been allowed free movement in practically all urban districts of the colony" – very generous of them, isn't it? Then there's something about generals and army orders, and then it says, "All enemy civilians" – that does make you sound dangerous, Will – "all enemy civilians shall assemble at the Murray Parade Ground on 5 January," you are allowed to carry personal effects, and the care of your house is your own responsibility. Enemies include British, Americans, Dutch, Panamanians and whoever else has been disagreeable enough to make war with our conquerors.' She looks up. 'I think I'm off scot-free.'

'Are you?'

'Well, I'm none of those categories, certainly. And I've secreted my British passport somewhere very safe so no one need know about it. And I don't think a dislike of origami qualifies me as warring against the Japanese. But we'll have to get you there, I suppose, unless you want to go elsewhere?' She wrinkles her brow. 'China? Some people are arranging passage.'

'No, I think staying in Hong Kong will be better. They'll have to do things in a way that is accountable. If they gather us together, they have to register us and let our governments know, I would imagine.' He shrugs his shoulders. 'But we should decide what to do with Ned.'

Over a sparse lunch of rice and salted cabbage, they decide to clean the Canadian up and register him as British.

'Pretend you lost your passport – a fire when a bomb hit your home or something. Your accent is a problem, though,' Trudy says. 'Do you think the Japanese will notice?'

'I could pretend to be American,' he says earnestly.

'But we don't know any Americans to take you under their wing. Better you stick with Will and keep your mouth shut.'

Trudy says again that she will not register. 'Angeline, you could go with Will and Ned, since Frederick is English. You're counted as English then. You have your marriage certificate somewhere, don't you? I'll be fine out here without you. So many family friends have offered to take me in, I won't be alone.' Trudy strokes her friend's arm.

'I'll stay here with you, I think. Don't you?'

'Why can't you pretend you're in government and not go?' Trudy asks Will. 'Colonial staff are exempt from the order.'

'Darling,' he says, 'there are ways of verifying these things. It would be worse if I lied and was found out.'

'But you won't be allowed to come back then, will you? They're not going to write down your name, give you a pat on the back, and send you on your way?'

'Realistically, they're going to keep us all in a group. So I assume there will be some sort of collective living for a while, as they decide what they're going to do with us. I've heard of mass exchanges between governments, so they might exchange us for Japanese who are living in our countries. But it might take a rather long time to get all that sorted out, so we should really have a plan of how to keep in contact.'

After lunch, Will and Trudy go upstairs to pack a suitcase. 'What will you need? A toothbrush.' She hands him a new one. 'Tooth powder. Surely those are necessities. A comb – can't have you looking dishevelled. On the other hand, perhaps we don't want you looking too handsome and getting yourself and all the ladies into trouble.'

'Will you come with me?' he says. This is what he has wanted to ask all morning. The thought of leaving her makes him short of breath. He has seen her every day for months, not gone more than a few hours without smelling her skin, her hair. He finds other women grotesque now – they are too large, too loud, too slow. One afternoon, a short while after he had first arrived in Hong Kong, he and Simonds had sat at their desks and watched, mesmerized, as one is by the mundane, as their office lady, Miss Tsai, boiled water and poured it into a Thermos. Miss Tsai was thin and wore metal spectacles. Her shoulders, which she covered with the same grey cardigan every day, were so small they looked as brittle as a bird's bones. Her hair was cropped short and often shone with grease. Simonds had turned to him – this was before Trudy – and said, 'I don't understand how some men find Chinese women attractive. They have no sex, so spindly.' Will wishes Simonds had met Trudy, the languorous slip of her. He had shipped out a little after Will had first met Trudy, still professing his desire to find a buxom young Englishwoman with whom to form a family. He'd probably found her by now. But Will suspects he would find his English lass too rosy, too exuberant, next to the rapier-sharp silhouette that is Trudy.

She stops at his question, but only for a moment, then continues packing. 'Why on earth would I cage myself up if I had a choice?'

'You don't know what it's going to be like out here,' he says. 'At least in there, you'll get three squares a day and a bed.' He cannot bring himself simply to ask her to come to be with him.

Finished with his suitcase, she begins to pack some of her own clothes. 'I'd rather take my chances out here,' she says. 'You don't know what it's going to be like in the camps. The Japs can be brutal. And it'll be good for you to have someone on the outside. I'll bring you parcels and news of the outside. The Lusitano Club is taking all Portuguese, half-breeds like me too, and they have decent sleeping quarters. If things get bad, I'll just go there. And Dommie will take care of me.'

'We could marry,' he says. 'I'll take care of you better.'

She looks up. He is frightened by her face, wilfully blank. 'You don't know what will happen out here,' he repeats. 'At least we'll be together.'

She goes on folding her sweaters. Her hands are quick and sure. 'Do you know what the Chinese think of the English?' she says a moment later, as if he hadn't said anything of importance.

'Not really, but I hope Dominick isn't representative.'

Trudy laughs. 'Well, a bit, although there's more to that situation than meets the eye. Don't be too harsh about him. He has his reasons. But many Chinese think the English are rude and arrogant and think too much of their own heritage when ours is so much older and richer. And they're terribly stingy. I've never seen an Englishman pick up the bill for dinner, when even the poorest Chinese would be ashamed to let someone else pay if it were his invitation. It's odd, don't you think? I like our way so much better. We Chinese are not stupid. We know that most of the Englishmen here live in a way they could never afford in their own country, and they're living here like kings because their money happens to buy a lot more of our labour than our own money does. So they think they're the lords here and we're the serfs. But it doesn't change the fact that back at home they could never have the lavish life they have here. They're living on borrowed money, under assumed identities. You're not very English, Will. You're generous to a fault, very gracious and humble. I'm so glad you're not like most of your countrymen.'

'I say,' he says, 'I don't know if this is what we should be talking about. I mean, this is quite a moment.'

'I know, I know,' she says impatiently, as if he's missing the point. 'I just meant that a lot of the locals don't really care what happens to the British. But at the same time, they don't really care about the Japanese either. Everyone just wants to live their life, make a little money, make a little love, die with some food in their stomach. That's all.'

Trudy's points always take a while to sink in because they're unexpected, as if spoken from the mouth of a child, and then Will always realizes how very shrewd she is. And how practical. He watches her pack an evening dress and, after a moment's hesitation, a matching shawl. 'Have you seen my silver evening shoes?' she asks.

'Never knew you had any,' he says. He doesn't ask why she might think she would need evening clothes in a time of war.

'I always look forward,' Trudy says suddenly. 'Never back. I hate photographs, diaries, clippings. What's the point? I don't understand how people can keep diaries – horrid things.'

He is surprised by her vehemence. 'I've always kept a journal of my travels.'

'That's different, more of a travelogue, I would think.'

'Well, my impressions, certainly. And the people I meet.'

'I certainly hope I'm not in this journal of yours.'

'You would be disappointed,' he says after a pause.

'People can be so loathsome, don't you think?' she says. 'If we aren't together in the future, please don't think of me with hatred.

Think of me kindly or forget me. I always try to do that. Think with kindness and don't judge. And know the entire story.'

'What on earth are you saying? Don't make such absurd leaps.' He feels as if she's punched him in the stomach, cannot feign nonchalance but cannot say either, 'Don't leave me.'

'If you love me, you know exactly who I am.'

'Trudy, you are not this person. You are not.'

'And you are not stupid, my love.' She hands him his suitcase. 'There. All set for your grand adventure.'

At the Parade Ground, he notes with chagrin that others seem to have brought all of their belongings, stuffed into enormous suitcases, filled to bursting and tied shut with thick string. Some practical joker has brought his golf clubs. There are people sitting on their luggage, drinking from Thermoses, looking lost. There are also, curiously, Chinese people with all their belongings tied up in pink and red cloths, slung over their shoulders, squatting in the shade.

Will has money tucked into his trousers, and a few gold rings and bracelets Trudy has forced on him. 'Gold is good, people will always take it,' her voice ringing in his ears. He has only his small satchel, with the few essential items she had packed. Ned has some of Frederick's clothes Angeline has given him, ill-fitting as they are – the young Canadian bringing out the maternal side of both the women.

Trudy had stopped just long enough for them to get out of the car and give him a light kiss, and then she had spun away quickly. A goodbye made of nothing. He stands there for a moment, Ned shuffling awkwardly near him, then picks up his case, slightly embarrassed that the young man has seen their bloodless farewell. He spots the Trotters, the Arbogasts. He goes over to see Hugh Trotter and introduces him to Ned, explaining his situation.

'This is quite bad,' Hugh says, not caring about the travails of the young Canadian. 'I hear that over at the bank, they're burning unsigned notes so they don't get into the wrong hands.'

'Yes,' Will says. 'This is not good at all.'

'You know, two days ago, they declared a new government for Chinese civilians – they're calling it the Civil Department of the Japanese Army and they're trying to sort things out, get the gas, water and electricity operating smoothly again. They want everyone to get back into the flow, open their shops, resume their jobs. All except us, of course. We're enemy prisoners now.'

'Then why are the Chinese here?' Will looks around at the locals. 'Surely they can't be registering everyone in the colony.'

'No, it's a mix-up. The Japanese didn't realize that the Chinese here regard themselves as British nationals, so a lot of them have turned up, and there's confusion as to what to do with them. I think they only want the *gweilos*, to put it bluntly. I would imagine the Chinese will go home today.'

Will notices children playing – what are they doing here? They should have been sent away months ago. Hugh follows his gaze.

'Yes, and, of course, the children. Damn fools, the parents,' he says. 'Sentimental. Didn't want to send their families away to safety. Like ostriches, they were. I hope the conditions are half decent.'

'Well, one hopes, yes.'

'And you heard Millicent Potter went blind from shock?'

'No, I hadn't,' Will said.

'Her child died in her arms, shrapnel from a bomb, and she was holding him, and her husband said that all of a sudden she couldn't see. It comes and goes apparently, but it's been gone for a while.'

'Awful.'

'And Trudy?' Hugh asks. 'I assume she's not involved in all this?'

'Yes, she's Portuguese and Chinese, so both good things to be at the moment.'

'It'll be good to have someone on the outside. She can help you get things and deal with messages. We have our amah and houseboy tailing us at the moment. I've given them more money than they'll see in a lifetime so I hope they don't run off with it. But what could we do?' Hugh gives a wintry smile. 'Ironic, isn't it?'

Reggie Arbogast joins them. 'The situation is bad right now. They're winning in the Philippines and all over Malaya and Burma. They're gaining too much momentum.'

A Japanese soldier rides up on a horse. 'Line!' he shouts. 'One line. No Chinese.'

The crowd hesitates, moves in an amorphous mass, like a jellyfish, Will thinks, if he were watching from the sky. They ripple and lap, an uncertain sea creature.

'One line! No Chinese!' shouts the soldier again, this time louder. He canters the horse around, waving a sword in the air. The Orientals pick themselves up and move to one side, a gradual sifting of the races.

'It's like he's herding us,' Hugh says to Will. 'We're cattle.'

Will takes account of the clothes he is wearing – a sturdy pair of cotton trousers, two shirts, a sweater, and a jacket. He's suddenly aware that they might have to last him for a long time. He's glad he wore a heavy belt. Somehow, he thinks the strong leather and metal will come in useful.

The soldier swings round and leaves. The crowd is silent. A woman sits down on her suitcase and begins to cry. 'Buck up,' her husband says. 'This is just the beginning.'

They divide them into nationalities and march them in single file. Will watches the Americans walk away, with the Dutch and the

Belgians. The British are made to wait until the end. The Japanese seem to have some special prejudice against them.

They walk for hours, on almost unrecognizable roads with burning piles of rubbish outside charred buildings and the overpowering stench of rotting bodies and human waste. The mothers and children march with the men, babies crying. The roads are lined with locals, silently watching the unlikely spectacle of Western people being led away under the rule of the Oriental. Some spit in their path but most just stare. Will sees relief in their faces, relief that they are not the victims, at least this time. There is also pity in some of the older ones. One brave soul in the procession tries to strike up a rendition of 'Rule Britannia', but the melody fades under the implacable gaze of a soldier who slows his steps until he is menacingly abreast of the singer. And there is the silence again, broken only by the tramping of feet and the heavy breathing of the conquered.

They are herded into the Nam Ping Hotel, which has clearly been used as a brothel in the recent past. The lobby is dingy, with peeling red paint and garish gold Chinese characters painted on signs.

First, they are told to take off all their watches and jewellery and put them into a large sack. Then a Japanese soldier jerks his gun up the stairs to indicate they should go up.

The rooms are tiny, and things get ugly, with people rushing to claim their space until they realize that, no matter how quick they are, they will have to squeeze four or five into a room. The stucco walls are bubbled with moisture and decay, and flakes of ceiling fall at the slightest tremor. Iron beds with wafer-thin mattresses and *mintoi*, the Chinese quilt, with large, copper-coloured stains. Large cockroaches scurry around, alarmed at the sudden invasion, and the floor is wet and unpleasant. It is chaos, with people demanding lavatory paper, towels, clean water, not knowing that no one is there to supply them. Some don't seem to realize the days of amahs and chauffeurs are gone. The lavatories block almost immediately and the hallways are filled with an unspeakable odour. Will and Hugh organize teams to clean. Some men refuse. Will tells the others not to worry, that there will be plenty of work to go round soon, and that everyone will do their share. The Japanese provide no guidance – some look amused at the chaos, and others are simply oblivious, putting their feet up and having Chinese children run errands for them, fetching them beer and cuttlefish.

There is no food the first night. They go to bed hungry, rooms alive with the sound of whimpering children and the laboured breathing of their parents. Will tucks his hands into his armpits, hears young Ned's snore – a strange, interrupted, barking sound – and wonders what Trudy is doing.

And so he finds out. Not tooth powder but food. Food is the luxury. The Japanese hand out a watery vat of rice the next evening, with too few chipped bowls and spoons. There is some putrid boiled meat, a few rotting vegetables swimming in brown water. Some women refuse to eat it. The following day everyone takes their share. They find Chinese willing to fetch food for coins tossed from the balcony, but this is an unreliable proposition at best as some disappear with the money, never to be seen again. Those lucky enough to have their amahs or houseboys on their tail throw down money and receive fish and vegetables in return.

There is a lieutenant in charge of the hotel, Ueki, a small man with round glasses and a moustache. He is impossible to read, as Will finds out when he is elected to meet with a supervisor about the living conditions and the food. It is an odd meeting, tense and excessively polite.

Ueki has commandeered the hotel manager's office behind the reception desk and is sitting at a metal desk with an open bottle of whisky and a lit cigarette smouldering in an ashtray. Smoke hangs thick in the air, despite the fan that circles slowly overhead.

Will bows because it seems the right thing to do. Ueki inclines his head slightly.

'I have a few matters to bring to your attention,' Will says.

'Speak,' says the man.

'The lavatories need to be cleaned, and we need supplies for that. Can you provide us with brushes and cleaning powders? Also, a plunger would be helpful.'

'I will see what I can do.'

'And Mrs Aitken is eight months pregnant and quite uncomfortable. Could we find a bed for her? She's in a bed with two other people right now. Everyone else is doubled or tripled up as well.' Except the corpulent secretary from Australia who refuses to give up her bed, but that's another matter.

'Fine,' Ueki waves off the request, so Will is not sure if he means yes or no.

'And the food . . .' Will hesitates.

'Yes?'

'The food is inadequate.'

The short lieutenant studies Will. 'Do you want smoke?' He offers a slim silver case, probably freshly looted from some friend of Trudy's.

Will takes one and leans over so that the Ueki can light it.

'Do you know where I learned the English?'

'No, but it's very good.' Will tells himself he's not currying favour, not being obsequious, just honest.

'English missionary came to Japan, taught me for three years.'

'There are lots of missionaries doing good works out there,' Will says, idiotically, it seems to him.

'He was good man. For him, I will try to help you.'

Will thanks him, and then sits for a moment before he realizes he has been dismissed. Getting up, he says thank you again.

Nothing comes of the meeting.

It is in this unlikely place, this old brothel, that those detained find themselves pooling information and tales of what had happened in the days before their imprisonment. Since they have nothing but time, they gather to exchange stories, trying to piece together a coherent history of the final, chaotic period before the surrender.

Regina Arbogast, a delicate-faced socialite who had arrived at the Parade Ground in a rickshaw with seven trunks, six of which she was forced to let her servants take home, is full of stories of atrocity that happened not to her but to friends of friends of people she knew. She is full of opinions and appropriated outrage.

'The Chinese got the brunt of it, really. They're defenceless, without a proper government to protect them. They've been under our protection for so long, they don't know what to do. All the girls have been raped, but the Japanese are afraid to touch the English. They know it will come round in the end.'

Regina had been staying at her friend May Gibbons's house, where they were living in fairly high style until some Chinese gangsters came in and tied them up while they looted their house. She talks incessantly about the jewellery she lost and how she'll never be able to replace it. Her husband, a successful importer and businessman, finally blows up after she has gone on for a particularly long time. 'For God's sake, Regina, just shut up and give us some peace. I'll buy you all the jewels in China after all this is over.'

She looks at her husband balefully and whispers to her friend, Patricia Watson, about how beleaguered she has been and how Reggie has been just impossible throughout. Patricia smiles and looks satisfied. She still had her valuables as she had placed them on the floor in front of her at the hotel: the Japanese had refused to bend down to pick them up, and had not bothered to ask her to do it.

A young woman, Mary Cox, says her husband was grabbed by Japanese soldiers and made to clean up after bodies had been dragged along the street, shedding body parts like animals. They had to clear all the bodies before they got into the water supply and spread disease. He had come home soaked with blood and covered with bits of decaying flesh and wept before falling on to the sofa, exhausted. He was gone the next morning. She hasn't seen him since. She has a two-year-old boy, Tobias, who trails her, one hand always on some part of his mother, the other holding a toy aeroplane. He hasn't spoken since Christmas, she says. Another man, gaunt with worry, says he had been walking with his wife down Carnarvon Street, and some soldiers had seized her. They held him at gunpoint while they took her away. He hasn't seen her either. 'And yet,' he says, 'I used to think the Japanese were the most peaceful, serene people, with their cherry-blossom paintings and the elaborate tea ceremony. How can they be so brutal?'

'A soldier is only one part of a country,' Hugh says, 'certainly not representative of an entire people. And wartime makes different animals of us all.'

'How can you say that?' Regina Arbogast cries. 'They are each as brutal as the last, as far as I'm concerned. You would never see a British soldier behave the way these men have behaved to us.'

'You are, of course, right, my dear,' Hugh says, ending the conversation.

The next day, Mickey Wallace comes into the lobby where some of them are sitting listlessly. He is bleeding from the ears, his eyes already starting to swell blue and shut. He had been on the roof, looking down, when some Japanese soldiers saw him. They stormed up to him and beat him bloody because nobody is to look down on the Japanese. Only they are allowed to look down on others. This, their enemies' peculiar preoccupation with placement and particularly with height, because of their generally smaller stature, becomes ingrained in all of the prisoners: many years after the war is over, they will still check automatically who is standing where, on which step or in what position.

And the random cruelty makes them all wary. A soldier, drunk and angry about his gambling losses, strikes a small child on the way to his post. The little boy has a fractured nose and loses three teeth. A more senior Japanese spirits him away with his mother, and they are never seen again. Evidence gone. On his way up the stairs, Will looks down at the alley between the hotel and the adjacent building. He sees a body covered with a blanket, a shock of fair hair, too high up for him to identify who it is. When he goes down, the body is gone. He wonders if he imagined it, knows he did not. Another day Trotter comes to him, says *sotto voce,* 'I wonder if I'm going mad. I was on the balcony having a smoke, and in an alley between buildings, I could have sworn I saw a man beheaded by two others.' His voice trembles but his face is calm. 'I saw the spurt of blood, the man falling down from his knees, hands tied behind his back. I could have sworn I saw it.' How can one stand it? 'And then I left. I didn't want to see the clean-up.' How does one stay sane?

There are small insults in addition to the large. A plague of the most enormous mosquitoes Will has ever seen, caused by inadequate drainage. His body is spotted with their bites, red, raised and angry. When he swats at them, they explode into red bursts of blood, gorged on their many victims. Pests crawl into the thin mattresses, which they try, unsuccessfully, to combat by immersing the iron bed legs in bowls filled with camphor and water. Weevils in the rice. Warm, foetid water that they have to hold their noses to drink. The diarrhoea that comes from drinking it, until they gather together some tins and boil it first. Then the burned tongues from drinking the newly sterilized water as fast as it comes off the flame, because they are so thirsty.

And they can look out of the dirty windows to the sight of Japanese soldiers, drunk and vomiting on the pavements, held up by Chinese prostitutes as they celebrate their victory. Sometimes an unfortunate coolie is dragged in to clean up the mess, but more often it is left to rot in the street. Will thanks God it is not high summer when the stench would intensify ten times as quickly.

He does not remember what it is like to smell fresh air. Instead, urine, faeces, the thick, cloying smell of human waste, clings to his nostrils. His skin, his hair, his fingers are infused with the smell of shit, no matter how thoroughly he washes. His hands have known the slick inside of a lavatory bowl, trying to get the foul mixture of vomit, urine and shit to flush through its own thickness. The drainage systems are no match for five hundred rapidly sickening refugees – and that is what they are, regardless of whether they were bankers or barristers before – fed with pest-ridden rice and tainted water. The guards are cruel, save one. He is a young boy, dressed in a soldier's uniform with a wide, placid face, and he smiles constantly, apologetically. He drops his eyes when his colleagues hit the prisoners or poke at them with their bayonets. He speaks a halting English, but only when there are none of his compatriots nearby.

Trudy never comes, although others' loved ones find a way to come, leave messages. He finds himself mentioning her to everyone, including her in the conversations, as if the mere incantation of her name will keep her alive. Her jasmine scent, a mere memory. He shifts constantly in bed, unused to the tight, narrow quarters of a space without a companion, her slight warmth. He is not angry with her, yet. Who knows what is going on outside?

Ned is going mad. The young soldier is far from home, far from any love or comfort he might know. He has stopped talking and eats very little. His face is wan and swollen. Will tries to get him to move around a bit every day but as time passes he withdraws a little more.

And yet for most life settles down quickly. Human beings tend towards routine. It is as if they have been displaced refugees for months, although it has only been a week. Businessmen shuffle around with vests falling out of their trousers, their natty suits packed away. Socialites do the washing alongside schoolteachers and shop proprietors. A black market springs up. As some have a lot of money, Arbogast and Trotter arrange a fund so that everyone will get some food. People contribute what they can, and then they arrange to buy Russian black bread for six Hong Kong dollars a half-pound, pow-dered milk, soy beans, carrots, sometimes butter, which they spread sparingly on their bread and eat slowly, savouring the precious fat in their mouths. Young Chinese boys smuggle in the food, but must get past the Japanese guards, who know what's going on, but take what they want from the meagre supplies. 'Tax,' says one, every time, laughing at his inane joke. That guard takes almost half.

'I do think,' Trotter's wife says fretfully to Will, 'that it is so spread out that no one gets to enjoy it. Don't you think it would be a better idea to have a lottery of some sort so that someone could enjoy a proper meal for once?'

Will shrugs. He's not about to get into it with her. He does notice, though, that she is as plump as ever. Some women volunteer to do the cooking – one is Mary, the woman with Tobias, the mute child, who hasn't seen her husband. She is sweet and quiet, and does not take the opportunity of being in the kitchen to help herself to more food for her and her son, although Will would not have blamed her if she had. The cook girls, as they call themselves, come up with startling dishes: broccoli black bread sandwiches with oyster sauce, watered-down condensed milk stews with plums bobbing about, eggy greens. They have managed to get a stove from the outside, and in the evenings they huddle around the blue flame, where their dinner is cooking.

If they steer clear of the guards, they are generally left alone, as the guards are too busy drinking and finding women or things to steal. There are always rumours about where they are to be relocated. Some think they will be repatriated immediately. Others, more realistic, hope for a more comfortable place to wait out the war. But they, too, think it will be over in a matter of weeks or days.

21 January 1942

Finally, after two and a half weeks, the order comes. Dr Selwyn-Clarke, the director of Medical Services, has persuaded the Japanese to move the civilians to the empty Stanley Prison on the southern tip of the island, where he believes the fresh air and proximity to the ocean will lessen the outbreak of infectious disease. Excited, the women gather their belongings and make the beds, filthy as they are – habit dies hard even in wartime. Men try to get more information from the guards and are rebuffed. Will gets Ned out of bed and makes sure he is counted.

Lined up outside the hotel, they are packed into large lorries that rumble into life and the children peer through the slats in the back and shout as they pass various landmarks. The children have come to be a blessing, although it is hard on them. They make games out of nothing, play jacks with pebbles and run around shrieking. Women sit on their bags in the back of the lorry, flesh trembling with the uneven road, society matrons looking as haggard as the governesses and nurses next to them.

Soon, buildings give way to trees as they drive through Aberdeen and into the South Side, where the sea meets the mountains and a lonely, winding road takes them to Stanley peninsula. It is quiet here, and seemingly untouched by the violence of the past few weeks.

The vehicles drive through a large gate and into a compound with large three-storey concrete buildings, hastily painted with large A, B, C marks. Soldiers jerk their guns to indicate everyone should disembark. They are grouped by nationality, lined up to be counted and registered – name, age, nationality, family or single – an exercise that will grow all too numbingly familiar over the coming weeks and months: 60 Dutch. 290 Americans. 2325 British. The rest odds and ends: Belgians, White Russians, foreign wives, even Akiko Maartens, a Japanese woman who married a Dutchman and refuses to leave him. The guards spit at her and leer, knowing she's one of them, voicing what Will can only assume are outrageous vulgarities, but she ignores them as she waits in line with her husband for their room assignment. She never speaks a word of Japanese, but her bowing and mannerisms give her away immediately.

All the enemy nationals have been assembled at Stanley for internment. Will sees faces from that day in the Murray Parade Ground. Everyone says to each other, 'I heard you were dead,' smiling and relieved that they are not. Will spots Mary Winkle, the smaller friend of Edwina Storch, looking bewildered. Her constant companion seems not to be with her. The Americans and Dutch have been sequestered in different hotels from the British, the Belgians in their consular office, since they are so few in number. From what Will can glean in hurried asides, their experience has been much the same: they are all dirty and hungry. He asks after Dick Gubbins, the American businessman he saw at the Gloucester, and no one has heard anything about him. Hopefully, he's made it across the border into free China.

The Americans have been assigned the best building and pull together rapidly to organize everything, arranging to have furniture delivered, sorting out rooming and distribution of supplies, building a store. They are cheerful and productive, as if at a picnic. They seem already to have a government of sorts running, from when they were in the hotels. The first evening, they are seen sitting out-side in the twilight, in languorous poses on makeshift chairs, laugh-ing, talking, drinking glasses of weak tea.

'The Americans may have the best building,' a man Will recognizes vaguely says, ushering people through the door of the building he's been directed to, D, 'but there's not a lot we can do about it. They all have private bathrooms in their quarters. They seem to have found favour with the Japanese – maybe the governments have some understanding. And our police have the next best one but they won't give it up for the women and children. They got here a few days ago and they've taken all the good spots. In my opinion, they should be in the POW camp in Sham Shui Po, but they've ended up here with us civilians.'

Will just nods. He is too tired to care. He and Ned go up the stairs and in through a door. 'You can't sleep here, it's our room,' someone snarls from a corner.

'Fine,' he says, and they keep going until they find an empty room and put down their cases.

They are divided up, and the fractions get smaller, the more people stream in. Eventually there are thirty-five people per former prison-guard flat, fifty in the bungalows, six or seven people to a room. Many rooms have no furniture at all. Some people rush to mark out the prison-guard flats because they are larger and a little better furnished, but it turns out they are more crowded in the end. There are two or sometimes three married couples per room, and a lot of families in the administrative buildings. The singles in the cells have actually fared better, excepting the bathroom situation, which is: a hundred people to a lavatory. Will finds himself in an old prison cell, two yards square, with Ned and one other, Johnnie Sandler, a playboy who was always at the Gripps in a dinner jacket, always with a blonde and a Chinese beauty on either arm. Amazingly, he still radiates style, despite the soiled trousers and already fraying shirt. Unselfish, he's the first to help, rearranging beds, moving bags. It's surprising how true personalities shine through after a few weeks of hardship. The missionaries and the police are the worst. They steal food, don't pull their weight with the work and complain all the time.

The first day, after people have established their places, everyone congregates in the large central yard, sitting on the ground. All fear that they are missing something, a meal, a handout, information. Hugh Trotter gathers the British together and explains the need for a more formal government and some sort of order. Will has talked to him about it, and found Hugh thinking the same thing.

'Why don't we nominate Hugh as the head of things?' Will says. After a pause, people murmur their assent. 'All in favour say aye.' Will looks around. A loud round of ayes. 'Any noes?' Silence. At least in this, their first foray into group politics, there is harmony. That's something.

Hugh elects other people to head sub-committees. They settle on housing and sanitation, work rotas, food, health, and grievances, with others to come as needed. Will is selected to head up housing, to mediate in any disagreements stemming from accommodation.

Sleep is elusive the first night, as they try to get used to the new surroundings; those lucky enough to have beds shift around, unused to the strange creaks. Will is on the floor, which is filthy, with his case as a pillow and various articles of clothing as blankets. The stone is cold, even after he puts more clothing down as a mat; he is unable to doze for more than ten minutes at a time. It is a relief when the sun begins to stream through the window and he can stop the charade of sleep.

They come down to posted signs that say all rooms will be inspected for contraband in the afternoon. Most scamper back upstairs to squirrel away their belongings, hoping they will not catch the eye of the guards.

'I don't have anything worth taking,' Will tells Ned, 'and I don't think you do either,' so they continue to the dining hall.

At the appointed hour, Will, Ned and Johnnie watch as a chubby soldier rifles through their things. He holds up a particularly fine cotton shirt, Johnnie's, of course, and shakes it insolently, while rattling off something in Japanese to his companion.

'He's going to the ball in that,' Johnnie says. The soldier whirls round and barks something – clearly that they are to be silent. He flings the shirt on to the dirty floor.

In the end, they come off better than most. They have given up a few gold cufflinks ('Thought they might come in handy for bartering,' Johnnie shrugs), a little box of tools Johnnie had smuggled in, with pliers, a hammer, and scissors, and a wool hat.

'You did such an atrocious job of packing, they didn't want anything of yours,' Johnnie observes to his roommates, after the men have gone. 'Congratulations!'

'It's lucky few of us are their size,' Will says. 'Otherwise I think we'd be going around starkers.'

'They can take the women's clothes. They'd look quite fetching in a nice poplin garden dress, I think.'

They gather in the hallways and compare what's been confiscated. Some are beside themselves at the loss of family heirlooms, others happy that they managed to hide their valuables away.

'Did you stick them up your bum, then?' asks Harry Overbye, an unpleasant sort who is smug because he has a Chinese girl on the outside – he's sure she'll provide for him. He has a wife he sent back to England some months before, and then he acquired the girlfriend. He is ignored.

'While we're here,' Will says, 'I'm organizing a cleaning rota to make our conditions more pleasant. I'll put a notice up when I can get hold of cleaning supplies, and I expect everyone will want to pitch in and help keep our temporary home as clean as possible.'

Overbye snorts, but there are general noises of assent from the others.

'Good,' he says. 'It's not the Ritz but it'll have to do for now.'

'That's an understatement if ever I heard one,' Johnnie says.

Will is getting very worried about Ned. He speaks only when spoken to, and then only in one- or two-word replies. He says he feels all right, but he is wasting away, hair thin and matted, eyes dull. He sleeps all day and shows little interest in food.

'Shock,' says Dr McAllister, when Will asks him. 'He's had such a shock, he can't process anything. Who knows if he'll come out of it? This is certainly not the ideal situation for convalescence.' Asked for a tonic, or anything, he throws up his hands. 'I have nothing! Not even an aspirin! I've put in a request with Selwyn-Clarke and the authorities here for some basic medicines and supplies, but they've yet to reply. Just keep an eye on him. Unfortunately that's about all we can do at the moment.'

At dinner time, they gather in the dining hall where the separation of countries is again evident. A tall, rangy American businessman, Bill Schott, has been elected camp representative to the Japanese by the Japanese, and he stands up to address everyone.

'The Japanese have decided that we are to man the kitchens and cook our own meals. These will be coveted jobs, so we will rotate them so that everyone gets a chance to serve.' He doesn't say why the jobs will be so desirable, but everyone can see that proximity to food is only a positive thing. 'We will also be assigned what I'll call housekeeping duties, not only our private rooms, which should be kept clean and which will be inspected on a regular basis, but also sweeping the courtyard and other duties as they see fit. I have been assured that these tasks and our conditions will be in keeping with the Geneva Convention, although, technically, Japan is not bound by it. They signed the agreement but never ratified it. They say they are agreeing to it for the sake of goodwill. We will be given adequate food, as per the Convention, which I believe is some 2400 calories a day. I have enquired as to mail and contact with the outside world and we are to receive letters and parcels on set days of the week. Obviously, we will not know whether that is reliable, but they have said they are willing to do it. Our governments are to be notified of our presence here and of the living conditions and we are to have Red Cross representatives come periodically to make inspections. In the best case, of course, there will be arrangements for repatriation and there will be some sort of exchange of citizens between countries.'

He pauses. 'Obviously, it is unclear when all this will come to pass. We are, it is important to remember, in a war that is still very much going on. It could be weeks, it could be months. In the meantime, I hope we can all live together in harmony and try to help each other as much as possible. If anyone has any complaints or comments, please come to me and I will try to make our views known to the camp supervisors, but I'm afraid we are not operating from a position of great power. At any rate, I wish everyone well as we go forth from here. Let's make our countries proud.'

He sits down. There is an exhalation of breath, as everyone digests what he has said. And then hands pop up in the air. Schott stands up again to take questions.

'Do we have any idea how long we're to stay here?'

'None at all, unfortunately.'

'Are we allowed to have money? Or can we get money from the outside?' asks a Dutch man.

Schott laughs. He is very rich himself, and has already acquired a great many comforts for the American faction, which have all been diligently and enviously noted by the others.

'I imagine you're allowed to have whatever you want, if you can keep it a secret, or if you want to share it with them. I don't know. This is one of those murky areas you don't want to get into officially. Just use your common sense.'

'Can we write letters to the outside?' Hugh Trotter asks.

'I don't think so. Or if we did, I think the people we wrote them to would never receive them or get such censored letters that they would be rendered useless – an exercise in futility, I suspect. I will certainly ask, but it seems unlikely. I'll try to catch Ohta, the camp commandant, in a good mood, and ask him then.'

The questions fly fast and furious, mostly routine matters, prisoners worried about their daily comforts. Will starts to eat.

'What about me?' Ned says suddenly to the table. It's the first time he's spoken all day.

'What do you mean?'

'I'm registered as British, but there's no British Ned Young. It's going to be all messed up. No one at home is going to know I'm here. Where are all the Canadians?'

'I think your compatriots are at the POW internment camp at Sham Shui Po. It is odd there are no other Canadian civilians, but perhaps they went home before all this erupted. I think you're better off here than with the troops. And I'm sure Britain has enough Ned Youngs or Edward Youngs – it's a common enough name – that they'll take you in first, and you can sort it out from there. It will be asking for trouble to get you back with your colleagues.'

'No, no,' he says. 'It's all messed up. It's all messed up now. I've done it for myself, haven't I? No one knows I'm here. Nobody. My mother won't know I'm alive or anything.'

'It's all right. You're here and you're alive. That's the important thing. Don't worry too much about registration and things like that.'

'That's easy for you to say,' the young Canadian snaps. 'You're all proper and accounted for. I'm alone here.' He stands up and walks out.

'He needs to have a moment,' Johnnie says. 'Let him go. He'll be all right.'

Will looks after Ned's receding figure. 'It's hard for him. I don't think he's eighteen yet. He's here, halfway across the world, all by himself, with no hope.'

'Join the club,' Johnnie says. 'It's misery all round at Camp Stanley. And it's only the second day.'

After dinner, Will and Johnnie go back to their room. On Will's bed there is a neatly wrapped package, with a note. It's unsigned but it's apparent that it's from Ned.

'I wish you the best. Don't worry and thank you for everything.' He has left the majority of his borrowed clothing.

'How on earth does he think he's going to get out of here?' Johnnie sits down on the bed.

'Lord knows. He didn't want to incriminate himself or us, I suppose, with this rather cryptic note. I'm thinking the worst. He has no idea of the terrain out here, or even in town, no friends, no Chinese language, nothing. Even if he gets out of the camp boundaries, he's a blind man. And he's left all his clothes . . .' His voice trails off.

'Not the sign of a sane man, certainly,' Johnnie offers.

'No.' Will crumples up the note and puts it into his pocket.

In the morning, some people are talking over breakfast about how they heard gunshots in the middle of the night, towards the southern wall of the camp.

The next week February dawns and it is cold. Hong Kong is a sub-tropical clime so there is no heating as a rule and the winter is always an insidious, creeping cold that surprises you in the middle of the night or when you're outside for too long. No sign of Trudy. It's now been more than three weeks since he's seen her. It's getting to be more than disheartening – it's embarrassing now as people ask after her. Amahs, houseboys, local girlfriends, and spouses who are still on the outside for one reason or another come to try and see the internees but the camp is still working out visiting rules and they are turned away with their parcels. Still, the visitors are allowed to leave word that they've been.

Will concentrates instead on winterizing the buildings. Beds have been provided, with some semblance of coverings, but the temperature plummets at night. He's never thought of the cold in Hong Kong as anything more than brisk but he realizes now that that was with a proper winter coat and well-insulated walls. Everyone is hunched over, trying to conserve body heat, sleeping with all their clothes on, shivering in the bathrooms, not taking baths. When Will brushes his teeth, the silver water feels like ice. He puts in an official request for more blankets and winter coats, especially for the children, who are running around in their parents' extra clothing, hems and sleeves trailing on the floor. He organizes a patching team who go around plugging holes in the walls with a crude mix of mud and leaves. But all of this does little to alleviate the creeping misery of unrelenting discomfort that clouds their days.

Trudy, when she comes, is unexpected. A guard plucks Will from the lunch queue and takes him to the office of Ohta, the camp commandant.

Expecting a response to his blankets and coats request, Will is taken aback when he is told he has a visitor. They have not been allowed in yet. But, of course, rules have never really applied to Trudy.

Ohta, a portly man with greasy skin and smudged wire spectacles, gestures that Will is to sit down. He is attired in a Japanese version of a safari suit.

'You have a visitor.'

'Is that so?'

'We have not yet allowed any visitors.'

'I'm aware of that. But I don't know anything about it.'

Ohta eyes Will over his desk. 'You want drink?'

'Please.' Will knows to accept.

Ohta gestures to the soldier by the door and barks something in Japanese. Whisky is poured into small, dusty glasses.

'*Kampai!*' He lifts up his glass with one hand, and drains it, tossing his head back with a grunt. Will follows suit, with less vigour. Ohta shakes his head as if to throw off cobwebs. 'Good!' He pours more.

'Your visitor – your wife?'

'I have no idea who my visitor is.'

'Woman, Chinese.'

'Trudy Liang?'

'Yes. Miss Liang is here to see you.'

'Oh, good.' Will's heart is beating fast. 'Thank you very much.'

'I told her only one time she can come on no Visitor's Day. Special for her.'

'Well, she is special, isn't she?'

Ohta stares at him. 'No one special now. Everyone same, prisoner or not Japanese. Same!'

'Yes, of course.' Mercurial, he thinks. 'Well, I think she's special because she is to me.' Lame.

Ohta gets up. 'Wait in room here.'

After a few minutes, during which Will sips his whisky, enjoying the warm burn in his throat, trying to calm his nerves, the guard gestures for him to come. They go into a small room with a table and five chairs, where Trudy is sitting, looking uncomfortable. She is thin, her clothes serviceable. Her hair is pulled back into a chignon, face colourless without make-up. Still, somehow, she radiates privilege. 'Darling,' she says. 'I've missed you so much.'

He doesn't say anything about her absence, just asks her what she's been doing, forfeiting the right to rebuke her for her neglect. 'Frederick is dead, so I've been with Angeline, but she hasn't really spoken for weeks. I keep telling her she has to cope for Giles's sake, but she doesn't seem to listen. She wants to bring him back here but what kind of place is this to be responsible for a child? She doesn't want to go to England where she doesn't have any family but Frederick's, not that she could go now anyway, and his family was against the marriage in the first place, so it's a rather difficult situation. So that's what I've been doing. Besides trying to get a foothold in the new world out there.'

'You're all right for food and all that? Dominick's taking care of you?'

'The Japanese are so odd,' she says, ignoring him. 'They have this extraordinary custom of defecating in every room of every house they loot. Isn't that awful? Marjorie Winters's house was completely soiled – she found it when she went up to get some supplies. The odour! The whole city smells of waste. That's one Japanese custom I'm not enraptured by. So extraordinary. They have that beautiful tea ceremony and all that lovely gardening, and then they go and do something like that. And, of course, all the women are in a tizzy about rape. You're not supposed to go anywhere alone. I brought a driver.'

'Ned is gone. I think he tried to escape but I'm quite sure he was shot in the attempt. He was going rather mad.'

Trudy's face falls. 'Don't tell me such awful things, darling. I can't stand it as it is. Can we talk about something else? Something else entirely, something quite trivial in comparison. Like how I'm scrabbling all the time. It's terribly unbecoming. At least here you don't have to do that. You just stand in a queue and get food handed to you.'

'You have quite a good idea of what goes on here, have you?' It's the first time he's been sharp with her and she takes note.

'Is there anything you need that you think I might be able to get for you outside?'

'It's scant hunting out there too, isn't it?'

'Yes, but I could get Dommie on to it. We have food but it's rather expensive. I could weep when I think of the Japanese bombing the godowns. There was so much food in them, and they incinerated it. They said you could smell it burning miles away. Makes me ravenous just thinking of it. At least there's no chance I'll get plump if this goes on. You don't like plump women, do you, Will? No chance of me getting that way.' She chatters on. 'Conditions in Sham Shui Po and Argyle are supposed to be hideous,' she says. 'They're coming down very hard on the uniformed. You're lucky you're here. That Jane woman at the hospital saved you, I think. Very clever of her.'

'Do you think I should be there?' he asks, hard. 'Do you think I'm a coward for being here?'

'Are you mad?' she says, with genuine astonishment. 'Of course, I don't.'

How quickly he has lost the ability to gauge what she thinks, he realizes.

'Do you remember what it was like just three months ago?' she asks. 'Conder's Bar, the Gloucester, the Gripps, the parties. Can you believe it was just a few lousy months ago?'

'No,' he says. 'Have you any news of what's going on out there? We've no way of getting any reliable information and it's driving us mad.'

'Carole Lombard died in a plane crash, that's the biggest news.' She winces at his reaction. 'Not appropriate? All right, reality, then.

It's grim all round, darling. I don't know much but I'll try to find out for you. The paper now is all Japanese propaganda and says everything is going swimmingly. We can get rice at one of fourteen depots, so that's usually our main task. We send the maids to one, and we go to another, and hope one of us is lucky. But that's not so grand in the way of news, is it? What else? In the days just after you left, they were in a democratic mood so they were encouraging one and all to go to the old colonial bastions. You could walk into the Peninsula and see labourers squatting on the chairs, having tea! They came with the cash they made from looting to see how the other half lived. It was just beyond! It's difficult to get reliable information – the paper just says that the Japanese are conquering everything in sight and it's hard to read between the lines.'

She pauses. 'Dommie's doing fine, fraternizing with the Japanese. He seems to think he's one of them. He's in business with Victor now, a bit shady, but what isn't, these days? When I go to visit him in his offices – he has offices in Central – he always opens a bottle of champagne. The whole thing makes me quite ill but I drink it anyway. And I see some of Victor. He's the one who got me in here. Had a word with someone he does business with.'

'Dominick's never had a job before and now he's a businessman?'

'War does strange things to people. I think this might be the best thing to happen to him. He's rather found himself.' She laughs, an odd laugh.

'He should be careful. At the end of all this, he's going to have to account for himself. And Victor too.'

'Dommie doesn't think that way. He's always lived in the present – you know him. Victor is another story. I'm sure he's covering his tracks well.'

'But you should warn Dominick that he should think ahead this time. And tell him to be careful of Victor.'

She waves her hand impatiently. 'So I've been summoned by a Japanese,' she says. 'A man named Otsubo who lives in the Regent Suite and is in the gendarmerie, which I'm told is a good thing to have on your side. They're the military police. He wears a special chrysanthemum pin on his collar, which signifies gendarme-ness. I think he might want me to teach him English. Do you think I should do it?'

'Not you too,' Will says. 'Are you going to be best friends with the enemy?'

'I resent that,' she says. 'You know me.'

'I do, darling, and I love you despite it.'

'Very funny, my idiot.'

How are they back to this already? This needling, their sophisticated parrying, from a time when such things mattered.

'Do you think it's safe?' he says, after a moment.

'Well, I'm taking Angeline with me. She'll be my chaperone so don't worry.' She pauses. 'It's the funniest thing, I've had a phrase running through my head all week – plutocrats and oligarchs – and I haven't the slightest idea what it means. It must have been something I heard somewhere. You're clever – what does it mean exactly?'

'Plutocrats are the ruling class,' he says, 'and oligarchs are governments ruled by a few. I suppose they mean the same thing, really. Why do you think you've had that on your mind?'

'Haven't a clue,' she says, dismissing it as quickly as she brought it up. 'So I'll be a tutor. He's very important, apparently, head of the gendarmerie. And he lives at the Matsubara – I mean the Hong Kong Hotel. They've renamed everything, you know. The Peninsula's the Toa now. Maybe I'll get some special privileges and then we'll be on Easy Street.'

'Yes, maybe,' he says. He notices, but is not suitably appreciative of, the 'we'. He wishes she would go. He is tired. But when she gets up to leave, he feels bereft. 'I'll see you again?'

'Of course, I'll bring things too, what I'm able to scrape together, if you think it would be helpful. Maybe next week if they're less irritating about the visiting hours.' And she's out the door, elegant even in her reduced circumstances. He smells her jasmine perfume in the sweep of air she's left behind.

There are five guards assigned to their building. They patrol the adjacent grounds, do random inspections, and make their presence felt. Most leave the prisoners alone but one, Fujimoto, a skinny fellow who smells like rancid fish, is particularly cruel and delights in making the men sweep the yard or do a hundred jumping jacks when they are so tired and weak they can barely stand up. Fujimoto has it in for Johnnie, for some reason, and whenever he sees him, he will stop him and make him clean the lavatories or dig holes in the garden, senseless, brutal tasks that just reveal the hardness of the man. But he is mild compared to the men who are assigned to investigate covert activities. Word of a shortwave radio gets out and the three men who are supposed to have the components are dragged off to a distant room. Only one comes back, and he is barely alive, bones broken and one eye almost gouged out. He dies later in the makeshift infirmary. 'They let him come back alive as a warning,' says Trotter. 'That much is clear.'

Lack of food makes them tired. The promised 2400 calories turn out to be more like five hundred per person – a large bowl of rice is supposed to feed a roomful of adults for the whole day. Sometimes, there is a protein, conger eel or red mullet, but it is often spoiled and melts away to oil when cooked. Still, they eat it hungrily, their bodies ravenous for any fat or flavour. People are sick constantly, pellagra, dysentery; wounds never heal, teeth rot, fingernails don't grow. Will's eyelids are hooded and his limbs leaden. All he wants to do is lie in bed, especially in the late afternoon when time drags. He forces himself to get up and find tasks to do. Many sleep the days away but he can't bring himself to join them. 'Doesn't it seem as if we should be getting something out of this time?' he asks Johnnie. 'When people ask what we did, I don't think the answer should be slumber.'

'Such a good man,' Johnnie says. 'Industrious little bee.' But he is also the first to help Will, and never complains.

The next week, Trudy is allowed to visit again, and others are allowed in as well. She is ebullient. The head of the gendarmerie says she is to come twice a week to teach him English at the hotel where he is quartered.

'The food there! You wouldn't believe it!' Her voice lowers to a whisper. 'I eat enough to last me until the next visit. And he's had me up to the house he's requisitioned on the Peak, the old Baylor place. He has it as a sort of weekend home. The old staff are still there and were so thrilled to see me! An odd scene, though. When I got there, he was practising archery on the lawn and had someone bring me a glass of champagne. It's as if he were mimicking the life of an English aristocrat. One can almost believe life's back to normal when it's like that. And he just wants to chat, get his conversational English up to par. Of course, he's pumping me for information too, thinks I'm an idiot, but who cares when you're eating bananas and fresh fish and all the rice you can manage? Can you believe I've become such a peasant about food? Anyway, Otsubo is obsessed with lining his pockets. He thinks I will help him, unknowingly, or knowingly. It's a time-honoured tradition of war, I suppose, the officers getting rich off the conquered.'

'And you and Angeline go to teach this man?'

'He told me to drop her, says he doesn't need two teachers, but I bring her back loads of food. Told him I'm staying with her so I should. He wants me to teach him Western table manners. Isn't that a scream? He wants to know the whole thing, fish knives, dessert spoons. He can't pronounce "etiquette" since I've brought it into his life, but he means to be a master of it. We had lobster the other night and he wanted to know the proper way to eat it. I just smashed away at it merrily and he thought I was joking.'

'So, now you're having lobster dinners with this man?'

'Oh, it's not what you think – Dommie was there too. They're best friends. It's really quite sickening. I'm just in it for the free food. I brought you some too, darling, look.' She glances behind her to make sure the guard isn't watching, and spills out of a duffel bag some fruit, tins of meat and a small quantity of rice. 'I slipped the guard who checks the bag some cigarettes at the door so he didn't bother me but I don't want this one to be getting any ideas. Don't go being noble and sharing this with everyone. I want you to have it, not little Oliver or Priscilla, no matter how gaunt and adorable their little faces are. It's for you, and I wouldn't give it to you if I thought it was going elsewhere. You have to develop a thick skin, Will, it's wartime.'

'What makes you think I don't have one?'

'You're too good, that's your problem. People like you have trouble surviving in times like these.'

'But you're having dinners with this man,' he says again.

'Yes,' she says patiently, as if he's mentally impaired. 'It's not the sort of situation where I can tell him to bugger off. I have to keep on his good side.'

'But surely you can do that without having these inappropriate –'

She cuts him off. 'You've no idea what it's like outside. It's quite the norm. We have to get along with these beastly people until we prevail. Have a plum and shut up.'

When he doesn't take it immediately, she snatches it back petulantly and takes a bite. Juice trickles out of her mouth, and Will thinks suddenly that she looks like an animal.

* * *

When it rains, it is difficult to rouse oneself. On a cold, damp Tuesday, Will lies in his bed, thin mattress hard against his body, and listens to the rain splatter rhythmically on the roof. He's not sad, just immobile. The grey wall opposite is marked with water leaking in, and a pool is forming on the concrete floor. It's become a routine faster than he would have thought, internees shuffling around, arguing about food distribution, pilfering, work duties.

There is no damn colour here in camp. Their clothes have long faded to grey, the food is an indistinct muddy brown on the plate, the buildings concrete. He longs for red, magenta, sunflower yellow, a vibrant green. The only relief from grey and brown is the sky, occasionally a glorious bell-clear blue, and the sea, a choppy turquoise. Sometimes he sits at the fence and just stares out. It is absurdly beautiful still, the horizon and the water and the clouds. Dr Selwyn-Clarke chose the site because he thought the seaside location would reduce cholera outbreaks and other infectious diseases. Unfortunately, it is not the infectious diseases that are the issue, but the lack of vitamins and proper nutrition.

Johnnie walks in, soaked from the rain.

'Lovely day.' He sits down heavily on his bed.

'Can you believe we're here?' An inane response is all Will is capable of.

'Rather be home, that's for sure.' He brightens. 'There's a rumour that Red Cross parcels have arrived. They might distribute them after dinner.'

'What's in a Red Cross parcel?'

'Food, man! Chocolate sometimes. Diversions. The children have been talking about it all day. I might have to wrestle a little girl for hers.'

In the afternoon, Will hears little Willie Endicott, shouting as he runs through the camp as fast as his spindly legs will carry him.

'The parcels are here! The parcels!' Looking out of the window, Will can see that Willie's arms are covered with mosquito bites, which he has scratched until they are red and runny, making his mother worry herself to death because of malaria. She has plastered the welts with valuable toothpaste. He runs, the toothpaste-speckled boy, shouting his message, delirious with the notion of food.

The line is tense as everyone waits. When it comes to their turn, the guard hands them a soft brown paper packet. They retire to their room in high excitement to open it.

'Feels like Christmas!'

Will is finding the package hard to open. His fingernails are as soft as the paper. Finally he is able to undo the knots. They store the string carefully – nothing is ever discarded these days – and gaze in grateful wonder at the inside.

'It looks as if a scientist packed this!' Johnnie exclaims.

There are six chocolate bars, slightly mouldy, but no matter, a large tin of McVitie's biscuits, coffee, tea, a good amount of sugar and powdered milk, some knitted socks and a scarf. These ordinary items look as valuable as gold coins. There is also a bonus: a tiny chess set and, hidden discreetly within, a small piece of paper with rounded, girlish handwriting.

Johnnie reads it aloud, the scarf tied comically around his head like a turban:

'Our thoughts and prayers are with you. Keep your spirits up and good WILL prevail. My name is Sharon and I would love to correspond with you if you are able. I have blonde hair, blue eyes and people say a ready smile.'

'Lovely penmanship,' says Johnnie, sniffing the paper. 'Nice sense of balance, just enough so that the censors wouldn't get her, yet unambiguous. And, look, she's written her address.'

'Delightful,' says Will drily. 'Sharon from Sussex, our saviour.'

'I'm going to look her up when I get home,' says Johnnie, tucking her note into his shirt pocket. 'She seems like the kind of girl I should settle down with.'

'What about me?'

'You already have a sweetheart. Don't be piggy. Sharon's mine.' Johnnie shoves an entire bar of chocolate into his mouth.

'Do you know how to play chess?' Will begins to assemble the pieces.

'Is there any money in it?'

'No, but there is your mental well-being to consider. Our brains are beginning to rot in here.' Johnnie is his first friend, Will realizes. He hasn't made any in the colony, didn't have to, with Trudy. It feels good.

The next morning, Will sees the little boy from the hotel, Tobias, squatting alone outside the washroom with his aeroplane. 'Did you enjoy your chocolate?' he asks. There's no answer. 'Where's your mother?'

The boy just stares at him, his face pale, his fair hair lank and matted. He works the plane round his hand, smoothly. It's become part of his anatomy.

'Is your mother not feeling well?'

The boy starts to cry.

'It's all right. If she's in there she'll be out in a minute.'

Just then the door bangs open with a crash. Fujimoto steps out, buttoning his trousers. Will steps back instinctively but the man ignores him and walks away.

'I suppose she's not. Do you want to come and find her with me?' Will extends a hand. Tobias looks down at the floor and shakes his head vigorously.

'Listen . . .' And then the door opens again. Mary Cox comes out. He blinks.

Her hand goes to her mouth when she sees Will. She turns away. 'Come on, darling,' she says to Tobias. 'Let's go and have supper.' She brushes past Will and scuttles down the hall, dragging the child with her. Then she turns and stares at him, her face hardening into something unapologetic, fierce.

So that's how it goes, he thinks. That's the beginning of how it all changes. We become survivors or not.

He tells Johnnie about Mary Cox.

'That was only a matter of time, though, wasn't it? Market economy springs up everywhere. People work out what they have to sell and what they want to buy.'

'Bloodless of you.'

'This war has been bloody enough without me getting sentimental. And you too, old man. Don't go soft on us. It won't do anyone any good.'

But Will is unable to get the image of Tobias waiting outside the washroom out of his mind.

At dinner time, they walk outside to find that a scandal of another sort has erupted. Regina Arbogast has accused one of the mothers of stealing chocolate and biscuits from her Red Cross package and is demanding a trial. Hugh Trotter is trying to explain to her that the legal system they have set up is meant for more serious matters, such as mistreatment by the guards, or stealing from the communal kitchen, but she refuses to listen.

'You and your filthy children are eating more than their share! They should have been sent home to England months ago. They shouldn't be here at all, taking food from others! They shouldn't be here at all.'

The woman looks ambushed. 'Regina,' she starts. 'I didn't take your food but you have a family too. How can you talk about children like that?'

'My children were properly brought up, not like yours. They're like animals! And mine are in England where they belong!'

'But yours are grown. I couldn't send Sandy and Margaret away. They're too young to be separated from their mother.'

'You should have gone with them!'

'You shouldn't be here either then,' the mother says finally. 'It should all be just the men. All the women and children are supposed to be gone. So you're draining us of resources as well.'

'What rubbish!' Regina looks as if she is ready to strike her. 'Your family has always taken advantage of situations. Reggie's done business with your husband and always said he was a common man, a slippery sort, always getting around things.'

'Just a minute,' Hugh Trotter interjects. He has wisely tried to keep on the sidelines, but this venture into the personal cannot be ignored. 'Let's keep to the matter at hand.'

'The *matter at hand*, Hugh,' Regina says slowly, as if he is mentally challenged, 'is that this woman has taken some of my personal belongings and you are refusing to treat it as a serious matter.'

'For God's sake, Regina.' Hugh throws up his hands. 'We're bloody refugees here. None of us owns anything at the moment. They were parcels for refugees. Can't you be a little more generous? We're all in the same boat.'

'Don't you dare swear at me!' Her voice is high-pitched now. 'We are not in the same boat! I will never be in the same boat as that woman. She is something else quite entirely.'

The Americans are watching from afar, aghast. Sometimes Will feels traitorous, the way he admires the Americans, or not so much admires them as feels like one of them. Despite her professed love for Americans, Trudy never really liked them – Will thinks they're too democratic for her taste. She likes a little delineation between the classes. Here, though, the Americans' system is so clearly superior to anything any other group has. Even in these surroundings, they radiate plenty and wealth. Bill Schott is autocratic, certainly, but he gets things done efficiently and quickly and has managed to acquire a great many things for his people, mostly at his own expense, it is surmised, but still. Those in the British camp who have the wherewithal to help others rarely do, preferring to hoard what they have for fear of darker days ahead. The Americans share what they have, although because they are fewer and not so strapped, it must be easier.

Regina Arbogast stamps her foot like a child and cries out, 'This is impossible! There are no standards at all! I'll have to take matters into my own hands.' She walks off in a huff.

'A little diversion is always welcome,' observes Johnnie. 'She's quite a pistol, that one. We're going to have to watch her.'

Rice, rice, rice. After some two months, it's all anyone talks about. They have become absurdly creative with it – grinding it into flour, boiling it for gruel and water, trying to stretch it as far as possible. Food is the main topic. For one glorious week, there is pork on the ration lorry every day, until the story gets out that a pig farm had been shut down for disease and they are being fed the carcasses. Still, most boil it well and continue to eat it. Beggars can't be choosers.

The internees make tea out of dried bark, and dry grass on sheets, which they shred and roll into cigarettes. They have lost so much weight, men's faces gaunt, women looking decades older. Some suffer excruciating pain in their feet, the result of malnutrition, and cannot walk.

Some people are cracking under the pressure. Reggie Arbogast comes to Will to ask him to talk to his wife, who has stopped speaking to anyone, but apparently she has always had a soft spot for Will, a feeling he had certainly not known existed, and did not reciprocate to any degree. Still, he agrees to go and visit her.

Knocking on the door, he goes in to find a surreal picture – Regina Arbogast sitting on her bed dressed in a crimson evening gown, her hair put up in a messy chignon, wisps escaping. Her eyes are smudged with black. Looking closer, he realizes it is charcoal. Her lips are messily slathered with lipstick, the crimson bleeding past her lips and on to the skin.

'Mrs Arbogast,' he starts.

She jumps, but continues to sit, looking like a grotesque marionette.

'Regina,' he says. 'You must get out. The sun is glorious today.'

She looks at him. 'Will,' she says finally. There is lipstick on her teeth.

'Yes, Regina? The fresh air will do you good if you go outside.'

'Will. You have always been a good man. I have admired you. You came to Hong Kong and were not polluted by it, like so many others.'

'Thank you, Regina. I don't know –'

'But others are poisoned by it. It's too easy here, life. As many servants as you want, lives subsidized by the government or your company. Everything is provided. You become weak.'

'Regina, these are not good things to dwell on. Keep your mind exercised. I think some of the women are talking about putting on a show, a play. You should get involved with them . . .'

'Paaah!' She spits on the floor. 'Stupid cows!'

He sits, not wanting to provoke her further.

'They are stupid, absurd women, who think a few clever lines will make us forget we're here, in this tragedy of a situation. I despise them.'

And they you, Will thinks, but doesn't say. 'What would you like to do?' he asks.

She looks at him incredulously. 'What the bloody hell do you think I'd like to do? Get out of here and go home to England!'

Regina Arbogast seems to have been transformed into a dock worker.

'Language, Regina,' says Reggie, who's just come through the door. His eyes are dull and sunken. The doctor has told him he needs vitamin C but there is no citrus to be had anywhere.

'Oh, shut up, Reggie.'

Will stands to leave.

'No, you stay,' Regina orders. 'Reggie can do whatever he wants. I really don't give a fig any more. I have things I want to tell you, Will, because I think you deserve to know.'

'Regina, I don't think Will –'

'Reggie!'

Reggie Arbogast looks at Will helplessly, as if to say, See what I'm dealing with? And then leaves.

Will looks longingly at the door, then turns back. 'Regina?'

'Will, I had high hopes for you when you arrived.' She said it like the high priestess of society she had always styled herself to be. 'Reggie knew about you from work and always spoke so highly of you. I wanted to ask you to dinner many times.' Regina Arbogast's dinner parties had been sought-after invitations in Hong Kong for their lavish style, elaborate themes and restrictive guest lists, for those who had cared about such things.

Trudy had laughed at everything Regina did. 'So fussy! So pretentious!' she said. 'You know she was a Manchester shopgirl before she married Reggie? All of her airs are very recent indeed. I heard he used to be a very nice man before he met her.'

'That's very good of you, Regina.'

'But then you took up with that Liang woman. Did you know about her past? She got her claws into you straight away. She knows what she's doing, that's for sure, that one. She took you off the market before anyone else even knew you had arrived. You know what they call her, don't you? The Queen of Hong Kong!' She laughed. 'It's preposterous! With her queer half-breed customs and way of thinking she's above everything. Forgive me, but she's insufferable. I suppose love makes you blind.'

Will doesn't know why Regina is talking to him as if he were one of her fellow society matrons and they were gossiping over tea at the Peninsula. 'I don't know that this is the right time or place for this,' he starts.

'Listen. I have a point. You think I don't but I do.' Regina Arbogast leans forward. 'Reggie met with the governor when he arrived. Governor Young had a secret meeting the first week. The day of the Tin Hat Ball. Young wanted to get to know some key people in the colony and ask their advice. He didn't know a thing about how it ran. He knew the war was getting close to Hong Kong but he didn't want it to get out and alarm the general public, the nincompoop. So, at this meeting . . .' Regina sits back. 'Do I have your attention now?'

Will looks at her, exasperated and compelled at the same time. 'Regina.'

Satisfied, she leans over again. 'At this meeting it was discussed, among other things, what was to happen to the Crown Collection at the governor's mansion. As you may know, it contains some priceless pieces, mostly Chinese antiquities that are sensitive because the Chinese think they were stolen, ancient texts and vases, things like that, which were excavated. Reggie said they were centuries old, some of them. It was decided that the Collection would be hidden away and the location would be divulged to three people in three very different situations so that, no matter what happened, at least one would . . . survive.'

Despite himself, Will is listening, intrigued.

'And, of course, Reggie was one of the three.' Regina permits herself a congratulatory smile. 'And then he told me about it. But he hasn't told me where it is. Or who the others are.' Her smile disappears. 'He's always been irritatingly honourable about that sort of stuff. He values country over anything, something bred into him by his family. I really think he would give me up if it came to that.

Maybe the children? I suppose he was a good choice, then.'

She gets up and shuffles towards the door.

'I don't have any proper shoes here, and no one has been able to find me any. All I have are these terrible slippers that look as if they belong in a fish market.'

'Regina, why did you tell me this?'

She smiles coyly. It is a grotesque thing. 'I have a feeling, Will. I know things are going on outside, and I know that many secrets and plots are in motion. I just wanted you to know.' She reaches over and clasps his hand in both of hers. They are dry and reptilian. 'Consider it a gift from me.'

Trudy turns up the next week in a well-tailored suit and a hat, clutching the most enormous parcel he's ever seen. 'The outside is so queer,' she says, pulling off her gloves and sitting down. 'There is the oddest society of people you've ever seen, a motley crew if I ever saw one. All the Russians we loathed before are everywhere, and they are even more unbearable. They think they're somebody now that everybody is gone. They're worse than the Swiss with their self-righteousness. I was at dinner with the doctor – you know Dr Selwyn-Clarke, he's the official medical adviser to the new Japanese governor who's arrived, Isogai – and Sir Vandeleur Grayburn who's still as delicious as ever, although terribly down about everything that's going on, and this Russian girl, I don't know if you remember her but her name's Tatiana, always out and about town before, but out in that bad way, drinking a little too much, a little too forward, you know, and she said the rudest thing to him, the doctor, and she is married now to a Chinese man who is in bed with the Kempeitei so now she's bulletproof, or so she thinks . . . Of course she didn't bring him to dinner. I think she just married him as an insurance policy. I'm going to shoot her myself when this is all over.'

'Where was the dinner?'

'At the Selwyn-Clarkes', but you know they had to do it so hush-hush. He had to pretend it was a planning meeting, for supplies and things, which it partly was, but they had guards outside, listening, so it was hardly a casual event. And do you know who's dead? Crumley, the American who was always at the Grill. I remember the day he came in and told us how he had opened his mouth while he was at a picnic in Shek-O and a butterfly flew in and he swallowed it, and now he's dead. Swallowed butterfly or not. That's what I think about sometimes, you know.' She speeds up, talking about this and that, nonsense about people.

'Otsubo adores me now and gives me anything I ask for. Look at all I was able to bring you! Ham and coffee, sugar and powdered milk. I've unearthed more of that strawberry jam that seems to be everywhere. Honey, even. You do have cause to be jealous now, darling.' But she looks worse than ever, gaunt, with cracked, dry lips and hair scraped back into an untidy bun. Her blouse is very large on her, the collar gaping up behind her neck, as if she's sinking into it.

'I've been trying to think what kind of man he is, and I think I've got it. He's the kind of person who, when you say something, and he doesn't understand, will ask you to repeat it, then again and again until he understands, whereas most people would politely pretend to grasp it after the second or third explanation. He's unrelenting, and has no interest in social graces. I suppose that's why he's done so well for himself in his career – meticulous and all that.'

'Are you eating? You look like you're eating nothing.'

'I took Otsubo to Macau and fed him those "beans" – you know, the baby mice that the uninitiated think are beans. He loved them. And they say the Chinese will eat anything.'

'I don't care about that. But you look like death warmed over.' He grabs her hand. 'I don't care if he's mad about you and you have to do things you don't want to do. I just want you to be all right.'

She laughs abruptly. 'And how do you know I don't want to do them?' she asks. 'What if I'm a willing participant?'

She thrusts a parcel towards him. 'Here,' she says. 'More food.'

'Come into the camp,' he says. 'I'll take care of you.'

'Will, darling,' she cups his face in her hands. 'It's too late. I like it on the outside. I've finally got a foothold on the situation, however tenuous.'

The door opens and Edwina Storch comes in with a large parcel.

'Hello,' Trudy says. 'Are you here to see Mary?'

'Yes,' says Edwina. 'Hello, Will. How are you?'

'I'm fine, thank you. Mary is as well as can be expected in here. Her good spirits and courage are a boon to the community.'

'Yes, she's very good,' Edwina says. 'What a horrid situation.' She takes in Trudy's parcel with a discerning eye. 'You've acquired a large ration of the jam, Trudy. And coffee! You must know someone very important indeed.'

Mary Winkle enters and the two women embrace, one large, one small. They go into another room.

Trudy looks at the closing door. 'I see her all the time now,' she says. She pauses. 'But I think I like her.'

Will takes her hand. She looks so lost.

'Do you know my best quality?' she asks.

'Of your many good ones, I couldn't say, my darling.'

'I see the best in people. I fall in love with people when I see a window into their beings, their shining moments. I've fallen in love with so many people but the trouble is I fall out of love so quickly too. I see the worst in them just as easily.

'Do you know I fell in love with you straight away? That day at the Trotters' I noticed you because you were new, of course, and then you sat down at the piano, and you played a few notes, but you played them so well, with no self-consciousness, and no idea that anyone might be listening. It was in that room off the garden and you were the only one there. I was passing through on the way to the bathroom and saw you. I fell in love with you there and then, and so I spilled my drink all over myself so I could meet you.'

'Darling Trudy,' he says.

She stands up. 'I can't bear it,' she says in a rush. 'I just can't.' And then she turns to leave. 'Eat what I've brought you,' she calls out behind her, as the door swings shut with a clang. 'You need to be strong.' Her voice fades as she walks away.

'Johnnie, I have to get out of here.'

He says it that night, after they have gone to bed, and he can hear his companion's breath just deepening into sleep. It stops, then starts again.

'You do?'

'I'm losing her.'

'I see.'

'Will you help me?'

'Of course.'

But he hadn't needed to ask. Of course, Trudy had another way.

'I've got you a week's furlough. Otsubo got me a pass that says you're to do some work for him. Isn't that wonderful?'

'What kind of work?'

She looks at him as if he's completely missed the point.

'No idea. Some kind of clerical work that you and only you, the inimitable Will Truesdale, are qualified to do. Proper accounting. Plant watering. Japanese flattering. Does it matter? You're coming out! Aren't you thrilled? There's gratitude for you!'

'What do I have to do?'

'Are you a complete idiot? Nothing!' she cries. 'Absolutely nothing. I thought it would be nice for you to get out and see what's going on outside. No one else has this kind of opportunity, you know.'

'Well, thank you,' he says. 'I do appreciate it.'

'You'll find out what life outside is like, what my life has become.'

'Perhaps you'll do an exchange,' he says. 'Come in here for a fortnight.'

'*Peut-être*,' she says. Maybe. She always speaks French when she wants to change the subject.

So, the next Monday, Will is waiting by the sentry's bungalow. He has been treated rather well over the past week. Ohta came to see him with a copy of the exit pass, fishing for information.

'Otsubo has sent for you,' he had said.

'Yes.' Will nodded.

'He is head of gendarmerie.'

'Yes.'

'You have important skill?'

'Yes.'

Ohta stood for a moment, waiting for Will to elaborate. When he didn't, he threw the pass on to the floor and said he should wait by the gate on Monday. By then Will had noticed the guards were more polite and that he was not subject to taunts and searches.

Trudy arrives in a convertible and insists on driving, although she is alarmingly bad, screeching the gears and turning far too wide. 'This is what happens when you have a driver all your life,' she says with a shrug when Will finally demands she pull over so he can take the wheel.

'You look well,' he says, glancing at her. She's in a spring dress, now that the weather is warmer, and a wide-brimmed yellow straw hat.

'I found my old tailor, and he whipped up a few things for me. He desperately needs the work and I have events I'm supposed to look nice for.'

He doesn't ask.

She takes him to the Peninsula. 'It's the Toa now, remember,' she says.

Trudy is greeted with smiles and bows as she sweeps through the formerly grand lobby, which is now filled with soldiers, steel tables and other grim army-issue furniture.

'Otsubo has a suite of rooms here so Dommie and I stay in them. He's requisitioned a place up on Barker Road for himself. It's better here than the rat-hole we have outside. We're lucky. You wouldn't believe how people are living, two or three families in a flat. Rather appalling, but I suppose it's wartime. My old place has been requisitioned for some middling soldier. Insulting, isn't it? I thought it was quite nice, myself.'

'How's your father?'

'Fine,' she says abruptly. 'He's fine.'

'What are you doing for funds?' Now that he is outside, he is thinking of matters he has not had to worry about for weeks.

'We're allowed to withdraw a little money every week, but it's sensitive. Not large amounts, obviously. In any case, you don't want to make them wonder too much. Everything's fluid, in a bad way. There are no rules, and even if there were, they could be changed at any moment.'

'Do you have to fend for yourself? Isn't Otsubo the magic trump card?'

Trudy considers. Her mouth draws into a bow. Will resists the urge to kiss her small, self-preserving face.

'Mmm . . . I wouldn't put it like that because he's rather mercurial. He does favours and then regrets them. He gives and wants to take away. And he has to be persuaded rather strongly not to. Not a generous man. Powerful men usually aren't. Here we are.' She opens a door into a room that is a veritable palace compared to his quarters back at Stanley. A suite with large windows overlooking the blue sea, dotted with boats, plush carpet, thick silk draperies and fans that swing lazily round and round.

'Welcome to the Pen!' Trudy curtsies.

'Look at this,' he says, sitting on the bed. 'A bed made up with actual linen! Curtains to draw against the sun! And I'll wager there's even paper in the bathroom.'

'You would be right. And now do you want to thank me, you ingrate? It's been complaint and suspicion ever since I cooked this up. Thank me.'

The reunion is sweet, the late-afternoon sun slanting through the window, the flat horizon of the sea and the boats floating in the harbour, and Trudy, right here, right next to him. He has thought of her for so long, missed the feel of her skin, and the smell of her breath, that he moves as if he's in a dream. She is quiet, more than usual, but seems skittish. They are both too sapped, too thirsty ever to be quenched by something as mundane as the physical.

'Tell me the truth.' She sits up afterwards, clutching the sheet. 'Is there a hussy you have in Stanley? Some American vixen who's stolen your heart? Surely you can't have been celibate all this time, someone as voracious as you. What else do you have to amuse you in that dreary camp?'

'I'm only voracious with you, you know.' He doesn't ask her the same question, feels any answer would be unbearable. If he can keep some small part of her for himself, it might be all right. 'Don't worry about those things, and I won't either.' He extends this olive branch so that their time together might be enjoyed.

She relaxes and curls into him.

'It's been horrible,' she says. 'The Japanese are rounding up Chinese who are . . . sympathetic, shall we say?, or pretend that they are, for business purposes, and holding these absurd dinners where their policies are toasted with champagne and they're lionized as if they've made an enormous contribution to society. All quite surreal. Victor Chen is hot and heavy with the Japanese, of course, and trying to do business with them every which way. I'm worried about Dommie. Victor is just using him.

'We went to one of these dinners, and an old family friend of ours, David Ho, stood up and offered a toast to Pan-Asian superiority. Now, mind you, he was married to an Australian woman, and devoted to her, but she died a few years ago, and he remarried, lucky for him, to a Chinese. He's such a coward. I wouldn't have believed it if I hadn't seen it with my own eyes. He has children at school in Australia. Don't know how he'll be able to look them in the eye now. They're the funniest dinners. They have them in the ballroom at the Gloucester and try to make them fancy but they are just the worst functions you've ever seen. Propaganda films, bad alcohol and hypocrites. Nothing worse.'

'So why do you go?'

She gets out of bed, her body a long rebuke. 'I'd forgotten what it was like to have my conscience with me always. Sometimes, Will, you have to do things you don't want to. We can't all live in perfect harmony with our integrity.'

He hears her turn on the water. She has always loved baths, and used to spend so much time in them she would emerge with her glossy skin pruny and her face glowing with the heat.

'How's the water here?' he calls out, by way of apology. Their time is too short to be beset by old complaints.

'Not bad, as these things go. Nothing worse than a lukewarm bath, don't you think? Do you want to join me?'

She pours in Badedas, bubbling the water hot and steamy. The green, limey scent rises in the heat. Together, they slip and slide, washing each other while careful not to probe too deeply, keeping everything on the surface, their mood as fragile as the bubbles in the bath.

Outside is strange – an odd approximation of free society. Pinched faces, suspicious shoulders, everyone trying to blend in and look inconspicuous. The opposite of normal – Americans speaking softly, British being humble, Chinese shy. Everything is hushed, except for Trudy and Dominick, who joins them for lunch. He meets them in the lobby at the hotel, kisses Trudy on both cheeks and nods slightly to Will.

'Hello, darling,' he says to Trudy, handing her a large envelope filled with papers. 'This is from Victor. He sends his love.'

Trudy blanches. 'Love, is it?'

As they leave the hotel, Trudy and Dominick walk down the street as if they own it, laughing loudly and wearing flamboyant, obviously expensive clothes.

'If you behave as though you're bulletproof, most people will assume you are, darling,' Trudy assures Will. 'Believe me, I've tested this theory extensively.' She pulls out a worn blue booklet covered with stamps. 'And this helps enormously, of course. It's from Otsubo and it tells whatever foot soldier stops me that he'd better treat me with kid gloves or there'll be hell to pay. Usually, when they see his stamp, they sort of freeze, then shove it back at me as if it's on fire, and they bow and scrape to an embarrassing extent. I'm quite addicted to it.'

'And Dommie?'

'He has one with his patron's stamp. All the best people have one, you know.' Her laughter is brittle.

'And what does Otsubo think of you getting me out of the camp? Does he know?'

'Well, he arranged it for me. I don't think he's the jealous type, to be honest. I'm sure you won't be spending much time together. Do you want Cantonese food? I'm in the mood for noodles, actually.'

'Chinese?'

'Yes, the other food is unbearable, these days, since there's no one proper to cook it.'

'Have you ever missed a meal?'

'Darling, if you miss a meal, the light quite goes out of the day. All Chinese know that. I wouldn't unless things were absolutely desperate. Dommie knows this little place where they serve the most amazing rice noodles with broth they steep all day long. Of course, it's better at two in the morning since it's been cooking all day but nowadays you're viewed suspiciously if you're out late without one of our great leaders.'

'How is the Grill? Still working?'

'Oh, we still go. It's rather jolly, actually. And not all Japanese. There are groups of Americans and British on the outside, and it's not done to ask why. The Japanese don't seem to bother them, and there are all sorts of other people, you know, Swiss Red Cross, the occasional German. I tell you, Hong Kong right now is the most *interesting* mix of people. The war just shook out all the people and what remained behind in the sieve is diverse, should we say. There's this woman, Jinx Beckett, who's an American. I don't know her story or why she's not in Stanley with you as I'm sure she isn't an important banker or government official. I'm sure you'll meet her – she's absolutely everywhere, and poky too, nosing around in all sorts of things. And there are still parties. We still go to the Gripps for dancing but they stop the music every once in a while and project these hilarious propaganda films on to the ballroom walls. It's all about pan-Asiatic superiority, don't you know? They don't seem to understand that they're screening for a bunch of non-Asiatics. Screaming irony.'

Will sees a newsstand, for him, a startling sight. 'I'd love a newspaper. How is the English broadsheet these days?'

'Run by a Swede under the careful watch of the Japanese,' says Dominick. 'Result as you would expect. Piffle. I expect you'd like one.'

'I would,' Will says and takes the *Standard* and the *News*. Trudy pays for them.

'It's propaganda,' whispers Trudy. 'They print whatever they're told to.'

'Subtlety, my darling,' Dominick says, shushing her. Suddenly he relaxes and turns to Will. 'So, how is it being on the outside?' They have only exchanged the barest of civil greetings. 'And is it as atrocious on the inside as they say? Of course, the paper claims that you are being treated as if you were honoured guests at the Ritz.'

'Certainly not ideal. But it seems rather fraught out here as well. Everyone tiptoeing around.'

'Is it true that Asbury's in there, doing his own washing like a common rickshaw boy?' A famously haughty banker, whom Will has indeed seen poking around in the dirt, trying to establish a garden, and hanging up his vests to dry, as his wife is in bed most days.

'He is, but he's holding his own. Surprising the dignity that withstands any circumstance.'

'Yes, we're not our own men any more, are we?' Dominick looks around. 'But some are more so than others.'

Will says nothing.

'It's better to be a free person, though, isn't it?' asks Trudy. 'We have to mind our manners out here but there's no one telling us what to do or when to eat. Services are all coming back. Food prices were going up and down but they seem to have stabilized. We can withdraw small amounts of money. Public transport is working, as is the post, in a way, and people are starting to settle, although it's still a hard life. You do still run across the occasional corpse in the street, which is unpleasant. And the Japanese work the coolies quite hard, harder than any

Chinese I've seen. They're sending them back to China in droves as well. I think they aim to reduce the population by half.'

'Nothing is easy these days, is it?' Dominick says. 'Ah, here's the noodle shop.'

After lunch, Dominick goes to work, 'Such as it is,' he remarks, languid as always, and Trudy and Will go shopping. Trudy frequents the markets in search of treasures.

'I've seen things that I recognize from friends' houses!' she says, rifling through a table of pilfered goods. 'The ormolu clock from the Hos', and that extraordinary dagger that used to hang above the mantelpiece at the Chens'. I wanted to buy them but didn't have enough money. Those . . .' her voice drops ' . . . filthy rats just took away everything they could carry, and then the locals came, and picked every house clean. Enough to make you weep, seeing those ships set out for Japan filled to the brim with all the lovely things our friends had collected. Cars and furniture and jewellery! Many a soldier's wife is giving tea parties with someone else's Wedgwood.'

'Is there food we can buy that I can take back to the camp?'

'Depends on the day and what they've been able to find. Sometimes there's powdered milk, sometimes there's crates of mustard. We'll see.' She pauses. 'It's sort of freeing, this paring down to the necessities. It seems so frivolous to have thought about dresses and picnics.'

'You and Dominick seem to have your meals and lodging reasonably well sorted out,' he says, striving for a tone without judgement.

'Yes, we do,' she replies carelessly. 'But it could all be taken away tomorrow so we must enjoy it while we can.'

She cuts down Pottinger Street and into a small alley. 'There's a small shop here where you can get some amazing things.'

'What's in demand?'

'Food, mostly. Some people have started speculating in gold and such. We'll go to the market after this.'

A bell jingles as Trudy pushes open the door. Inside, it is dark and pungent with the smell of teakwood and the waxy oil used to polish it. A curio shop, with scratched, smudgy glass counters filled with Oriental peculiarities. Trudy speaks in Cantonese to the woman, who scurries to the back, cloth slippers swishing on the floor.

'What are we looking for here?'

'Oh, I'm just doing an errand for my master. You know.'

'How mysterious,' he says.

The woman comes back with a man, small, with a bent back, dressed in black silk. He seems irritated. Trudy speaks rapidly again, her small hands outlining a large rectangle in the air. The man shrugs and shakes his head. Trudy's voice turns shrill. She ends with a sharp outburst and turns to leave.

Outside, the sun is shining, an abrupt change from the dark gloom of the shop.

'So, food?' he asks. She'll tell him when she's ready.

'Yes, food,' she says, taking his arm, an implicit gesture of thanks. 'Sometimes I think you might be Chinese too.'

The wet market seems the same as ever – wizened old ladies with wide-brimmed coolie hats, dressed in black smocks, bent over their wares, calling out to potential customers. Here a basket of greens, there, soy bean curds resting in a container of milky water, with yellow sprouts. He remembers the smell, the slightly brackish scent of dirt and water still clinging to the vegetables. He used to come with Trudy at weekends, her mother having told her that she was never to become too grand to go to the market for her own food. 'At least, every once in a while,' she said. 'Not all the time, of course. And you won't catch anyone we know here. But I don't mind. It's kind of elemental, isn't it? Deciding which onion you want, or what fish you're going to eat and asking them to clean it for you.'

'How is it that there isn't a shortage?' he asks, as she bends over to inspect some radishes.

'There is, but these are available for exorbitant prices. All the peasants from the outlying territories come into town now because they know they'll make five or six times what they'd get out there. They come out with ten watermelons or a bag of water-cress. It's good for the soul to see how basic life can be. Grow something on the land, dig it up, sell it for some money, buy something you need.'

Afterwards, when they have procured some tinned foods, vege-tables and cigarettes for Will to take back to Stanley, Trudy takes him for a drive around the Peak to see all the bombed houses and ruined roads. Every wall is crumbling, bricks falling to the road.

'Can you believe what the bombs did? They're starting to rebuild, though. They have slave labour – or the Volunteer Corps from China, as they call it – and they're patching up the roads and trying to salvage the homes. Some have been taken over by the Japanese military and look quite nice.'

They pass a house where a dozen coolies are painting the exterior white.

'The King of Thailand has an elephant that they trained to paint.'

'That's one of your outlandish stories.'

'No, I'm serious. Father said he saw it himself.'

'They made the elephant paint the palace?'

'Certainly not! I'm sure he just did the rough outbuildings and barns and things like that.'

'Of course, darling.' They've stopped at an overlook where tourists used to come to look over Hong Kong harbour.

'Should we get out?'

There is a wobbly iron fence, pebbles and dirt underneath, wind with the metallic smell of lingering winter. She leans into him, hair blowing wild, as they look out on to the green sea, the white, stocky buildings crowding the shore and the harbour.

'It looks so peaceful now, doesn't it?' Trudy says musingly. 'The water in Hong Kong is a different colour from anywhere else in the world – kind of a bottle green. I think it's the mountains reflected in it.' She pauses. 'It was red with blood just a few months ago. There are boats and bodies at the bottom of the sea, thick on it, I'm sure. It was shocking how quickly things looked normal again, how nature swallows up the aberrations.'

'What happened to Angeline's house?'

'She's managed to hang on to it, although I don't know why she doesn't come into town. This place is filled with Japanese Army officials who have taken over the houses and I don't see how it can be safe for her here. We have lunch when we can, Dominick, Angeline and I. Try to pretend things are normal.'

'She's all right, though?'

'Not really. None of us are.'

They return to the hotel where Trudy starts to pack his newly accumulated things into his suitcase. 'You'll be popular when you get back.'

'We have to figure out a way to get supplies into the camps. The children need vitamins and protein.'

The phone rings.

'Victor,' says Trudy, when she picks it up. Her voice is even. 'Yes, I did get it. Dommie gave it to me.' She pauses. 'I know. I'm trying.' Another pause. 'I'll be in touch when I can, but please don't call me about this again.' She hangs up the phone with a bang.

'Everything all right?' Will asks.

'Watch me be frugal, Will,' Trudy says instead, ignoring his question. She starts to brew coffee on a small hotplate. 'This is my third go-around with these grounds. Have you ever seen anything so industrious? Aren't you proud of me?'

They sip the hot, bitter drink without milk or sugar.

'Oh, I forgot. There's something I wanted you to see.' She goes to the bedside table and pulls out a folded newspaper. 'This editorial was in that ridiculous paper on Valentine's Day. Dommie wants me to frame it.' She reads, ' "The Eurasian is a problem in all British colonies. The term is applied loosely to the offspring of all mixed marriages and to their children, etc. etc. That Britain and some other of the Occidental Powers chose to victimize the Eurasian rather than accept him and make use of his qualities is astonishing to students of the question. The Eurasian could be of great help to these Powers, contributing valuable liaison between the ruling nation and the native population." ' She looks up. 'Want to hear more?'

'Can I see that?' She gives it to him. He scans it. A column of coarse intelligence.

'The funny thing is, I was talking about being Eurasian to Otsubo about a week before it came out.'

'Really?'

'Yes, really. Isn't that interesting? I was telling him how when I was young, the other children would laugh and point at me, and on the streets some Europeans would take my photograph as if I were some animal at the zoo.'

'It must have been difficult, but those people are just ignorant.'

'Turn the page,' she orders, gesturing to the paper.

'More of your influence?'

'No, just another example of the absurdities we're subjected to every day. Do you see that piece about the houseflies, there? If you catch two taels of houseflies, you are entitled to a catty of rice if you take it to a District Bureau. And I've seen people carrying around these bundles of flies. The Japanese are even more bizarre than the English. I've never imagined such a thing.'

Suddenly, she turns to him. 'Did you know I was eight when my mother disappeared? And eight is supposed to be such a lucky number for the Chinese. I've always wondered if it was because I was only half Chinese. And half of eight is four, which is a terrible number. You know, it means death.'

'What do you remember of her?'

'Bits and pieces. She didn't go out much because she didn't fit in. She wasn't English, so the English wouldn't have anything to do with her, and the Chinese *taitais* certainly didn't like her. And she wasn't strong enough or confident enough to do anything about it. So she had very few friends and she was at home a lot, dressed beautifully with nothing to do but gossip with the servants. I suspect even they looked down on her. My father loved her, married her despite family disapproval, but he was so busy he didn't have much time for her. She took me to the Botanical Gardens every once in a while, and to tea at the Gloucester. She wore gloves and a pillbox hat, and straight skirts. She wanted me to be dressed properly as well. She was very beautiful. But I think she was sad.'

'You've never talked about her before.'

She pauses. 'I remember she told me about her childhood. She was very poor. She was funny about it, too. She refused to eat soup, because to her that meant poverty. She had grown up in a house where they threw whatever little they had into a pot of water, sprinkled it liberally with salt and called it a meal. She didn't want me to grow up oblivious to our good fortune, but at the same time, I think she liked the way the rich felt bulletproof – not her, obviously, but I think she liked that I might feel that way, but worried at the same time that it wouldn't last. And she was right, wasn't she? I'm not bulletproof. I've come a long way in the world, but the world has changed and I'm not sure any more of what I am or what I can do.'

After love, they lie on the bed. She shifts away, suddenly shy, and stares at the ceiling. Words burst forth from her, unbidden, a confessional fountain.

'I've always known, my love, that I was a chameleon. I was a terrible daughter because my father let me be one. He didn't know what to do with me, feeling so guilty that I didn't have a mother. And I was a good daughter when my mother was here. Because she couldn't imagine anything else. And then when I was older, I was a different person every year, depending on who I was with. If I was with a scoundrel, I became the type of woman who would be with a scoundrel. If I was with an artist, I became a muse. And when I was with you, I was – for the first time, I'm sure people have told you – a decent human being. All Hong Kong wondered why someone like you would bother with someone like me. You know that, don't you?'

She props herself up on an elbow, bronze hair falling across her shoulders. 'But now circumstances have changed, and I have reverted to form and become a woman who is with somebody because it suits her situation and for no other reason than that simple and venal one. I'm no different from that Russian girl, Tatiana, the one I pretend to despise. We're more sisters than anything else. We recognize each other. I'm sure no one is surprised. Do you understand?'

'Melodrama,' he says. 'You're being absurd.' She is quiet, one hand nervously pulling her hair back from her face, the other fluttering at her mouth.

'Don't ever say I didn't tell you. You must know that I told you.' The phone rings.

Trudy picks it up and her mouth draws into a tense line. 'Yes, of course . . . Of course. I'll see to it.' She hangs up and turns to him, face unreadable. 'As it turns out, Otsubo is interested in meeting you. *Intéressant, non*?'

'Is it?'

'I don't know what his intentions are. But we have to do as we're told, don't we? You don't mind? It's not as if we have much choice in the matter. Dommie will be there too.'

* * *

So that evening, after another silent, hot soaking bath and having got dressed in silence – Trudy had brought out some of Will's old clothes and they had laughed to see how they hung loose on him, one spot of forced gaiety in a tense afternoon – they are seated in a small room of a restaurant in Tsim Sha Tsui, contemplating nuts in a small porcelain dish embellished with red dragons as Trudy quaffs champagne at a rapid clip. Will lights a cigarette.

'This place any good?'

'Not much to look at but currently the best seafood in town.' They had seen the tin buckets in front upon arriving, large, lazy fish swimming inside, oblivious to their fate.

'He likes Chinese food?'

'Seems to be acquiring a taste for it.' Her nails clatter on the table as she drums her fingers. 'Dommie's late, the fool. Why does he do this all the time?'

'You eat with him often?'

'Every night.'

'Why are there so many seats? Who else is coming?'

'They travel in packs, darling. He wouldn't dream of being seen without his entire coterie of yes-men and sycophants.'

'And he is, of course, late.'

Just then the door opens and a string of men is ushered in. It is immediately clear who Otsubo is as the others wait inside the room until he has entered, and then for him to choose his seat.

'Otsubo-san,' Trudy says gaily, standing up. 'You're late as always.' She looks lovely tonight, dressed in a sleek tomato-red silk tunic dress and hair swept back into a chignon.

Time to sing for supper. Will stands up. ' Very nice to meet you. I'm Will Truesdale.'

'Otsubo,' the man says gruffly, and gestures to them to sit. 'Mr Chan not here?'

'He'll be here soon. It's a difficult time to get around.' Trudy sits between Otsubo and Will.

The man is stocky and short, in a well-cut suit of tropical-weight wool. His hair is cut close, military style, so the oily surface of his scalp shines through. His eyes, porcine and bulbous, sunken in a puffy, smooth face. In short, an unattractive man. Next to him, Trudy looks like a gaudy, gorgeous flamingo.

His men sit at the table, anonymous in their multitude. They talk among themselves, but quietly, so that Otsubo need not raise his voice to be heard. He orders cognac.

'Otsubo's acquiring Chinese tastes,' Trudy says. 'He loves XO now.'

'Some things Chinese are good,' Otsubo says. 'At least they are Asiatic.'

There is a silence.

'What should we eat?' Trudy asks into the void. 'Abalone? Shark's fin? Would you like me to do the honours?'

Otsubo nods and she orders rapidly in Cantonese. She speaks everything well – Cantonese, Shanghainese, Mandarin, French, English. Some of the men watch her, their faces unreadable. She must be a complete mystery to them, probably straight from the Japanese countryside, pressed into service for their country, to come to this place, where the language and customs are different, where a woman like Trudy flits around like a flamboyant butterfly. They drink beer, straight from the bottles, and smoke ceaselessly. They are not offered cognac.

Dominick enters hastily.

'Otsubo-san,' he bows, 'so sorry. Urgent matters held my attention.' Will has never seen Dominick in this ruffled state.

'You are late again,' Otsubo says. 'Bad manners for business and society too.'

'I know, I know. My masters at Harrow were always berating me for it.'

Trudy will tell him later, the Japanese love that Dominick was at the best schools in England, they want to know all the details and that Dominick indulges them at every chance. 'They hate it but they love it too. Isn't that always the case?'

He presents a box to Otsubo. 'A gesture of my appreciation for everything you've done for me, and for Hong Kong.'

Otsubo grunts thanks but does not take the box. Dominick, so obviously unused to gruffness, takes a step back, recovers and slides smoothly into a chair.

'Maybe later then,' he says to Will, a collusive greeting that implies they are made of finer stuff than this Japanese man.

Will turns away, unwilling to be allied with Dominick, unwilling to be as stupid as he. Trudy pours more tea.

'Mr Truesdale,' says Otsubo in English. Then he speaks through his translator.

'How are you finding the camp?' The translator is a young, slender man with spectacles. His accent is almost unnoticeable.

Will hesitates. How honest to be? 'It's liveable but, unfortunately, despite the best efforts of the camp officers, there are often shortages of food and medicines and, as there are also women and children in the camp, we feel this need acutely.'

Otsubo listens and nods. He replies. 'We will look into the matter.' The translator looks nervous.

The first dish is served. Chinese style, it is a cold jellyfish hors d'oeuvre. Will has learned from Trudy that a proper Chinese meal unfolds in a certain way. First, a cold dish, like pig's feet over jellyfish vermicelli, then a warm one, perhaps sesame-crusted prawns, a shark's fin or winter melon soup, a signature dish such as Peking Duck, a meat – sweet and sour pork or braised beef with *choisam*, a fish, a vegetable, finishing always with noodles or fried rice, depending on the region. Chinese don't take to heavy desserts, enjoying a cold coconut-milk dish or, if especially peckish, apple dumplings fried in hot oil then immediately crisped in ice water.

Otsubo takes the first portion, then spins the lazy susan to his men. Trudy pretends not to notice the slight. She serves Will and Dominick before taking her share, a minute serving of amber tentacles covered with mustard sauce.

After chewing laboriously, Otsubo speaks again. 'There are many illustrious people in the camps, are there not? Leaders of society and business?'

'I suppose there are. But we're all reduced to the same circumstances now, really. Nobody has more than anyone else.'

'It must be curious for them to be in such a place. Quite difficult to come down so far in life.'

'I imagine it is.'

Trudy has been uncharacteristically quiet. 'Like poor Hugh,' she interjects finally. 'I can't believe that lovely man has to wash his own socks. I don't think he'd ever made himself a ham sandwich before this.'

They eat the jellyfish. It is cold and rubbery.

Otsubo speaks again.

'And there is a man named Reggie Arbogast?' asks the translator. 'A businessman? With ties to government?'

'Yes, Reggie is one of the interned.'

Otsubo looks at Will thoughtfully. 'Is he a friend of yours?' he asks through the translator.

'Friend is too strong a word. We are acquaintances but our mutual experience has made us more intimate, no doubt about it.'

'Have more drink.' The translator fills Will's glass with whisky.

'Thank you.' He raises his glass to Otsubo.

'Whisky good.' The man speaks for himself.

'Yes, very good.'

'Drink. Tonight you are free.'

'Not so bad.' Will holds the door open for Trudy. The evening air is crisp and clean after the smoky, warm room.

'Yes,' Trudy says. She seems happy, relieved the evening is over and her pass has not been revoked. 'Better than expected.'

'He's an interesting . . .'

A car stops in front of them, and a window rolls down. A pudgy hand emerges and waves Trudy in. She looks sick, then gives Will a quick kiss and climbs into the car. 'I'll see you later, darling,' she says. 'Don't wait up.'

Early in the morning, around three a.m., while he is sleeping restlessly, the door opens quietly and Trudy stealthily pads her way to the bathroom. He turns on the bedside light, listens to the water running and waits for her to come out from her ablutions. When she slides into bed, he sees the enormous yellow bruise starting to form around her left eye. Something about her demeanour warns him not to fuss.

'That's quite a shiner you have there,' he says.

'He's surprising, that one,' she says, and reaches to turn off the lamp, plunging them into grey, a wakeful twilight where they listen to each other breathing.

After a few long minutes, when he is about to drift into sleep despite himself, seduced by the utter luxury of the soft bedding and the now unfamiliar warmth of another, she murmurs, 'You know when I said surprising? I meant a surprising lover. You knew that, right? He's not a bad man. Really.'

At that moment, lying there with the moonlight glinting off her shiny hair and smooth, glossy skin, he thinks she looks like a scorpion. He cannot let it go. He sits up. She looks at him, quizzical.

'Trudy.' He stops to consider how to say it. 'I need you to know there is a limit.' He raises her chin towards him. 'There is a limit to how sophisticated I can be.'

'Oh.'

'I'm not the person you want me to be. Not right now.'

'I should be careful. I should take care.' She says it penitently. 'I'm sorry, darling. I'm drunk. Don't let's quarrel.'

'Yes.'

She sits up and turns on the light. 'Sleep is not something I can do right now. Should we talk? Should we try to become who we were before all this happened, just for a moment?'

'That's impossible.' He pulls her to him, her head nestled in his shoulder. She smells of cigarettes and liquor. He tells her so.

'I smell like a whore.' She moves still closer to him. 'I told you Frederick died but I didn't tell you how.'

'No,' he agrees. 'You didn't.'

'Well, he was able to get back to Hong Kong. His whole regiment had been slaughtered and since he was the head, or whatever his title was, they allowed him his life and let him walk back, escorted. They let him come back, but they made him carry . . .' She falters. 'They made him collect the ears of all of his fellow soldiers, and he had to put them in a little bag and carry it. They said his hands were soaked in blood and the bag was drenched. And the smell . . . I keep thinking about it, over and over . . . , and how it must have smelt awful and how it must have been slippery and how he must have been so tired . . .

'And then the hunger and the famine, before they could re-establish some of the markets. The rumours, the horrible, horrible rumours. Pets disappeared. Even . . .' a hiccup '. . . even babies, they said.'

'Trudy, there's no end to the misery if you keep thinking about it.'

'And that dinner I told you about, the one where the local swells were trying to get on with the new order, where my family friend who had married an Australian denounced the white races, you remember that one? The one Victor organized?'

'Yes, I do.'

'I didn't tell you but at that dinner, we were all trying to sit there in our smart clothes without feeling too hypocritical, without feeling as if we were giving up too much of ourselves, and hoping we could still look at ourselves in the mirror at the end of it, and then at some point in the evening – there had been quite a lot of drinking – Dominick said something stupid. I don't even remember what it was, but it was silly and clever, you know, like him.'

'I do know,' he says.

'And then the man who hosted the dinner, Ito, the head of the economic department of the Gunseicho, whose table it was, he just stood up, walked over, and he walked very deliberately, and the crowd sort of hushed because he had this sense of, I don't know, I suppose you'd call it purpose, and he walked right up to Dommie – we had been seated at one of the best tables, his table – and he stood in front of Dommie and he slapped him across the face. He slapped him really hard.'

She works the sheet through her hands over and over.

'And that sound, you know, it sounded like a gunshot, because everyone had been watching, and it got very quiet, there might have even been a gasp from everybody, I don't remember, and Dommie sat there, with his cheek going red, and then he tried to gather him-self, he just sort of looked away, and then he picked up his cham-pagne glass, and took a sip. And then the whole room took a collective sigh, and we tried to pick up where things had stopped. And Victor, that bloodless leech, didn't do a thing about it.

'But it was as if the whole room had been slapped. And Dommie, you know, he tries to be a cool customer, but his hands shook the whole night after. I know you think he's dreadful and soulless, but you don't know him. You do not know him. I've known him all my

194

life and he's fragile, and can break at any minute, and I want to protect him and save him from himself if I can. He is my only family out here. We are looking out for each other. He can be a terrible person, but there are reasons for that, you know. Not like Victor, who's hateful because he only thinks of himself and money. Dommie hates himself, so he can be awful.' She pauses. 'I've never told anyone this, but Dominick was never quite right. There was a scandal when he was younger, around twelve, something about him and the maids. He made them . . . do things, and he did things to them, and they were found out. Someone walked in on them. So his parents were dreadfully embarrassed and they got rid of the maids, young girls from China, paid them off, and sent him to England when he was really too young. They were never really cut out to be parents. I think he was a mistake. And although he had done these terrible things, he was still so young. And he went, and he didn't speak very good English at the time, and he stuck out with his odd clothes and his funny accent. And then, somehow, it got out at the school what he had done, and the older boys . . . they made him do the same things. They made him . . . you know. You know what it's like in those schools. He told me this one night when he was dreadfully drunk. I don't know that he even remembers telling me. But we've always been like brother and sister. So, after that, I don't think he was ever quite the same. How could you be? And that's why he hates the English, for the most part, although he is so damn English in so many ways. It's very complicated. And in the end, I think, we're all just trying to survive, aren't we?'

'Sometimes there are things more important than survival.' It sounds self-important but he cannot help himself. He wants to warn her, not for himself but for her own sake. And to defend a horror like Dominick! She's blinded by misguided loyalty.

'Tell that to someone who's about to go to the guillotine,' she retorts hotly. 'Tell that to someone who's about to be shot. I'm sure all they're thinking about is how to get out of the situation. I'm sure survival is quite important to them at that moment. You might even say the only thing. You might have the luxury of pondering the dignity of the soul, but – never mind.' She stops. 'I can't explain it to you, or justify it to you, or anything, so what's the point?'

'I'm sorry you feel you have to justify yourself to me.'

She waves her hands above her slowly, like small satellites. 'This night feels like forever. I feel like Scheherazade trying to prolong the night.'

'Do you think I'm going to kill you come morning?'

'Everything changes when the light comes, doesn't it?'

Later, he will wonder what exactly she meant.

They go to sleep, or an approximation of it, each careful not to disturb the other.

In the morning, over coffee, she offers her feet to him to be rubbed.

'Everything seems better in the morning, don't you think?' Her peace offering. She pours cream into her cup and spills some into the saucer. Her hands are shaking a little.

'*Mon amour*,' she begins.

'Yes?'

'*Une question pour toi.*'

'Yes?'

'The good general is interested in me for many reasons,' she begins. 'One of which is that I'm rather pretty. But, as you know, Hong Kong is filled with pretty women, so his interest in me has lasted the time it has because he is also very interested in assuring his future while he's here. An ambitious man, Otsubo. And he thinks I should be able to help him. And, being a man of large appetite, he is not content with the occasional wristwatch and women's trinket – his sights are set much higher. He'd take land if his government would let him, but it won't, and he's getting rather frustrated.' She pauses. 'There are those in Tokyo who are particularly interested in the Crown Collection of Hong Kong. It's supposed to contain many priceless Chinese pieces, centuries old, inestimable in their value, politically sensitive, of course. And they have not been found. It's thought they were secreted away before the war began here. The Chinese want their heritage back, the Japanese want them for their value, and the English think the Collection belongs to them. It's very confusing.

'To cut a long story short, Otsubo thinks that a few of the men in Stanley are privy to information that would help him locate these pieces. In particular, he has an idea that Reggie Arbogast knows where they are. I think Otsubo would be handsomely rewarded for locating these items and getting them back to Japan. You know, it's been a complete madhouse over here, with the looting and the ransacking and things turning up in the markets, museum pieces selling for two cents or worthless rubbish being shipped off to the homeland as if it's of value. No one really knows what's going on, but he's determined to find these pieces. He's had me look through the pawnshops and talk to people, but nothing. So, that is why he allowed you out of the camp and wanted to have dinner with you and talk to you.'

'But why would he think I'd know anything about it?'

'He's heard that you're well liked in camp. You've been elected head of something or other, haven't you?'

'What's that got to do with it?'

'Do you know anything?'

The abrupt question takes him by surprise. 'Do you wish I did?'

'Does that mean you do?'

He stands up. The parrying is sickening to him. 'Trudy, we're not at war with each other.'

'No, but we might be at cross-purposes. Will, I need something from you now.'

'Everything I have is yours.' It sounds false, even to him, metallic in his mouth, as he watches her desperate, dissembling face. What does she inspire in him now? Still love? Or pity?

'So, you'll help us?'

What could he do? She hadn't asked for herself. She asked for them. She was lost already.

PART III

2 May 1953

Miss Edwina Storch, an institution in Hong Kong, hosted occasional ladies' lunches at her home in the New Territories. She was the headmistress emeritus of a well-regarded primary school in Pokfulam and a renowned expert on Chinese porcelain – an old China hand who had retired to the New Territories. She lived famously in an old house with Alsatians, chickens, an elderly married Chinese couple in service, and another English spinster – her lifelong companion, Miss Winkle. They sometimes came for lunch at the Ladies' Recreation Club, where Claire had seen them holding court among the other expatriate women, and she had seen Miss Winkle wrestling carnations into submission at Mrs Beazley's flower-arranging class at the Duddell Street YWCA. Miss Winkle was small and slight, with frail bird-bones, and Miss Storch was large and heavy, with thick calves that ended in a straight line at her feet. They both wore knee-length skirts and white-cotton buttoned blouses with Peter Pan collars, and often took slow constitutionals around the countryside with their sensible shoes and large dogs. Miss Storch's invitations were rarely turned down, for some reason that Claire had not been able to glean. So, when her invitation arrived in the mail, heavy cream bond with a gold crest – rather much for a retired schoolmistress, she thought – she accepted with curiosity.

Claire drove up to a white wooden gate. She had to get out of the car to open it and drive through, then get out to close it again, with a little hook that had been haphazardly screwed into the wood. Somehow she didn't dare leave it open, although she knew some twenty people had been invited for lunch. She drove up a dusty road, past gracious old trees, one with a wooden swing attached to a large branch, to the house itself, a rambling stone structure that seemed on the verge of falling down. There was a porch, with a screen door slightly ajar, but she walked round the house to the back garden where she could hear music and voices.

Alongside the house there was a drinks table set up with a bucket of ice and various mismatched glasses, a large punch bowl and small egg-salad sandwiches that were already attracting flies. Five other people had already arrived, none of whom Claire recognized. Then Miss Storch came over to greet her, walking slowly with a cane.

Miss Storch was one of those people so comfortable with herself that everything she did seemed unsurprising. If she served you wine in a teacup, it would seem the most natural thing in the world, and that anyone who thought otherwise was hopelessly bourgeois. Her lunch was, Claire would discover, rabbit pie, tomato soup and sandwiches, and ice cream on a stained tablecloth in a weathered old tent outside in the garden. At each chipped place setting was a carved camphorwood fan, to stir the hot and humid air. Women stood around, fanning themselves as they sipped warm lemonade and ate cocktail sausages and pineapple speared on cocktail sticks.

'So nice to meet you,' Miss Storch said. 'I've been meaning to have you over.'

'The pleasure's mine, Miss Storch,' Claire said. 'I've heard wonderful things about you.'

'Edwina, please, and call Miss Winkle Mary. I'm giving you permission right now.'

'That's very kind.' Claire was aware of Miss Storch's intelligent, razor-sharp gaze. Beads of perspiration trickled between her breasts. 'Do you give these lunches often? I've heard of them, of course, but didn't know if they were . . .' She trailed off, unable to come up with the words to complete the sentence.

'Mary and I live so far out, although this is the way we choose to live. We like people, and it's hard to see them out here, so we came upon this idea, to have regular lunch parties, and people seem to enjoy them, luckily, so they make the effort to come. We've invited almost everyone here, a few governors, the occasional peer, many travellers in from England.'

'And you've been in Hong Kong long?'

'Longer than you would believe, child.'

'Oh!' A large Dobermann had come up and nosed her hand.

'That's Marmaduke, the dear,' said Miss Storch affectionately. 'He keeps us safe and eats his weight in scraps every day.'

'Do you have more dogs?'

'We have seven, but most of them are out on the prowl. They'll come home for dinner. We adopted them after the war when so many animals were looking for homes. We couldn't bear to say no, and we ended up with far too many. There are eight budgerigars in the house, with three cats who would love to eat them, and I think there's a terrapin somewhere in the kitchen as well.'

'Were you here during the war?'

'Of course, through all the madness and its aftermath.' Miss Storch adjusted her spectacles. They were steaming up in the heat. Her eyes bulged behind them, her skin red and fleshy.

'A friend of mine –' Claire stopped.

'Yes?' Miss Storch prompted.

'A friend was here as well. But I've just realized how stupid that must sound. There must be thousands of people who went through that experience. I'm sorry.' Claire ducked, a sort of apologetic curtsy, and left abruptly. Marmaduke trotted behind her hopefully, then went off to find better prospects. Her heart was beating so hard, it felt as if it might burst through her chest. She walked in a daze until she came to a chair and sat down heavily. She had no idea what had come over her, what strange combination of the heat, Miss Storch's intent gaze, and her own preoccupation with Will had conspired to make this moment into something that felt so momentous.

She got up to fetch a fan from the table and cooled herself. When she glanced back, Miss Storch was busy with someone else, and didn't look at all put out by Claire's strange reaction.

She sat and cooled off. Gradually, she started to take in her surroundings. There was a large, graceful oak tree and an expansive lawn rolling down to a view of the mountains.

'Doesn't feel like Hong Kong, does it?' said a voice behind her.

Claire jumped.

'So sorry, I didn't mean to startle you.'

She turned to see a little woman with spectacles hanging round her neck. 'Mary Winkle.'

'Yes, of course. I'm Claire Pendleton. Thank you for having me today.'

'It's our pleasure. We like to see people so we try to entice them out with a good meal.'

A small Chinese woman came by and waited expectantly.

'Would you like a drink? You can tell Ah Chau what you'd like.'

'Some of that lemonade would be lovely.'

'Lemonade, please,' Miss Winkle said loudly. Ah Chau nodded and left. 'She's been rather deaf since the war. The Japanese knocked her about a bit.'

'How sad,' Claire said, ' but so good of you to keep her on.'

'She's a member of the family now. When I was at Stanley, she came with provisions every single week, and I know her own family didn't have enough to eat. And she stayed with Edwina, who was on the outside.'

'All these stories I keep hearing. It's extraordinary.'

'Well, it wasn't comfortable back in England either, I'd imagine.'

'We were quite sheltered. The food was a bit short but otherwise not too bad. I remember the air-raid sirens and running to the shelter with my mother.'

'Of course. And the dropping feeling in your stomach when you heard them.'

'Yes. Like a bad dream, as they say.'

A bell tinkled, the signal for lunch.

'It looks like it's time to eat.'

They walked over to the tent.

At lunch, Claire watched Edwina Storch take one of the tomatoes that were piled in the centre of a table and eat it as if it were an apple, with utter disregard for the red, staining juice as it dribbled on to her white blouse.

Miss Storch noticed her stare. 'Delicious, child. Have one. They're as sweet as sugar, grown in my garden. We made the soup with them too, to use up the last of them.'

'No, thank you,' she said. 'But how wonderful to think you can grow your own vegetables in Hong Kong.'

'Oh, I couldn't live anywhere else. I've been utterly spoiled. If I went back to England, they'd say I'd gone native, and they'd be absolutely right.'

'Do you think you will ever return?' There was something about the older lady that invited intimacy.

'I don't know what I'd return to. I haven't any real family any more, and the family I've made is here.'

Claire sipped the cold tomato soup. She grew bold. 'May I ask you something impertinent?'

'If I can choose not to answer it,' Miss Storch said.

'How do you decide who to invite to your luncheons? We've never met before, and although I was so pleased to come, I don't know how you even knew who I was to extend the invitation.'

Miss Storch laughed, pleased. 'A good hostess always thinks of the whole. What a bore to see the same people over and over again. You need a mix of nationalities, professions, personalities. As you know, Hong Kong can become tiresome as the community is so small. And one must amuse oneself as one gets old, don't you think?'

A Chinese woman with an American accent spoke to Miss Storch. 'I've heard you have a museum-quality collection of Song porcelain from Shan-xi. Do you ever show people?'

'Sometimes,' Miss Storch said, with a smile.

The Chinese woman waited expectantly. Miss Storch's smile grew wider.

The red-haired woman on the left of Miss Storch spoke up in the pause. She had been talking importantly on women's suffrage and the plight of immigrants throughout the meal. 'Have you heard? The government is forming a commission to rout out all the Japanese sympathizers once and for all. They're sick of those scoundrels trying to blend in and pretend they weren't part of the evil.'

'Well,' said Miss Storch, 'that's a strong word. There were certainly those who were opportunistic. But most people were simply trying to find any sort of work and put food on the table. I think the ones who most need to be prosecuted are those who had no such worries but simply wanted to profit enormously and didn't care whom they hurt along the way. Greed and dishonesty are always around, whether there is war or not.'

'They'll have to answer to a higher authority,' said the redhead, with a certain pleasure.

'It's difficult to prove anything, what with the lack of documentation during that time,' said another woman, plumpish. 'They never did find out what happened to the Crown Collection.'

'I suppose they will rely on witnesses and first-person accounts,' Miss Storch said.

'Why now?' Claire asked. 'It's been ages since the surrender.'

'Well, it's not anything official, but there have been a few events that make this particularly timely. The obvious people, Sakai, the Japanese commander-in-chief, and Colonel Tanaka, have been executed or imprisoned, but I think there's an emphasis on finding the local civilians who were a little too enthusiastic in befriending their new masters and who are pretending that nothing of the sort happened. I do think old grudges are being dredged up.'

'So you've heard of this?' said the red-haired woman.

'I have been told that something like this may happen, because I may be of some help to those in charge.' Miss Storch stood up. 'Who wants to come and see my new Crosley?' she said. 'They delivered it last week. It doesn't spoil the butter and defrosts automatically.' It was clear the conversation was over.

Women were lingering over lemon tea and Tcachenko's cream cake when Miss Winkle was suddenly standing at Claire's shoulder.

'Claire, would you play for us? We've heard what a talented pianist you are.'

She flushed. 'Hardly talented,' she demurred. 'I teach, but rarely play for myself any more.'

'You're teaching Locket Chen, are you not?'

'Yes, she's been studying with me for a few months.'

'How do you find her? And her parents, Victor and Melody?'

'I haven't had the pleasure of getting to know them more intimately as they're rarely at home when I'm there.'

'Yes, they're busy, I'd imagine.'

'You know them?' Claire asked.

'Know them?' Miss Winkle said, with an odd cast in her voice. 'Yes, I should say we know them. And Edwina knows Mr Chen very well indeed.'

'Well,' Claire said, 'I'll give them your regards if you wish.' She sipped her tea. Thankfully, the idea of her playing for the party was not resurrected. Miss Winkle was called away on some issue with the biscuits and she was free to gather up her scarf and handbag and say her farewells.

5 May 1953

'People have always expected me to be bad and thoughtless and shallow, and I do my best to accommodate their expectations. I sink to their expectations, one might say. I think it's the ultimate suggestibility of most of us. We are social beings. We live in a social world with other people and so we wish to be as they see us, even if it is detrimental to ourselves.' She laughs, lifting her face towards his. Her eyes, her skin, they glow, distracting him. 'What do you think?'

He woke with a start, then exhaled heavily in the hot air, slowly noticed the fan moving sluggishly overhead as consciousness surfaced. Perspiration covered his body and the bed linen was soaked. Her voice was as clear as a bell in his head, her sharp, vivid outline moving against a dark background. He had forgotten how much she loved her own pronouncements, how she would philosophize over a cold drink, how she was startlingly insightful at the oddest times.

She was waiting for him, expecting him to save her.

What would become his story now? he wondered. And there was Claire, who had grown important to him despite himself, in whom he saw his undeveloped self, nascent, with her silly prejudices, cherished ignorance and, surprisingly, her moments of clarity. Her naïveté was a salve to his battered expectations. Wasn't love always some form of narcissism after all? She came unbidden to his dreams too, battling with the other woman, the one who haunted him day and night. Claire, with her blonde and familiar femininity, English rose to Trudy's exotic scorpion.

The black night beyond the window was velvet and welcome in its anonymity. He got up and opened the windows. Hong Kong's warm, intimate smell came into the room, redolent of human bodies and the ever-present sea, even at this elevation. It was never crisp here, just moist and close, though not always unpleasant. The darkness enveloped him. A lone light winked in the distance – a boat? A fellow insomniac?

He heard her voice again. It sounded more desperate now, more shrill.

He knew it was time to act.

7 May 1953

Coronation fever had hit Hong Kong. The imperially slim Elizabeth and her handsome prince had seized the imagination of expatriates and locals alike, and all through town there were placards declaring coronation sales, tailors advertised coronation gowns, and special coins and stamps were being processed to mark the occasion. Society matrons were planning their coronation parties and teas, and all the hotels were booked up for balls. Claire found herself waiting for the newspaper delivery every morning so she could read about all the details and preparations.

She had always been fascinated by the princesses, had read the scandalous book by their nanny, Marion Crawford, and devoured the details of their private lives. And now the princess was queen!

In Hong Kong itself there would be grand parades and decorations. Both the *South China Morning Post* and the *Standard* devoted much of their front pages to the impending event. There was to be an illuminated fountain in Statue Square with a royal blue maypole topped by a crown, four lions to symbolize the United Kingdom and four braziers to represent the flame of Commonwealth unity. It was to be guarded day and night by Her Majesty's personal representatives. There was also a Coronation Garden in Kowloon, planted with blue hydrangeas and red and white water-lilies, in the pattern of the Union flag. The newspapers also dealt with the mundane. The

Building Authority had warned that verandas and balconies should be sufficiently buttressed if property owners felt they might be filled to capacity with revellers.

Claire read carefully about the arrangements the Post Office was making so that the high demand for commemorative stamps would be adequately handled. There would be counters dedicated to selling the stamps, and more counters would be added. She planned to go to the Des Voeux Road branch to get hers. She had also put aside money for commemorative plates with an image of the Queen stamped on them.

Will laughed at her when she told him of her excitement. 'Why on earth do you care about a woman getting a crown because she happened to be born into a certain family? And because her uncle fell in love with someone that others find objectionable?'

Claire was shocked. 'You sound like a Communist, Will,' she warned. 'I wouldn't go around airing that sort of idea.'

'Sometimes you're such a ninny,' he said, but his voice was kind. 'You are the silliest woman I care to know.' And he kissed her forehead gently.

They had been together for some eight months. Long enough to have a rhythm, but new enough that her palms still tingled, new enough for her still to check her reflection in any available surface before she was to meet him. Martin's steady hours gave them time together, but it was Will's work that confounded Claire.

'They never use you,' she said. 'They have two others, local Chinese. Why did they hire you?'

'I'm useful in my own way,' he said. And refused to elaborate.

But his lack of work meant they could spend afternoons together in his small flat, having sent Ah Yik on yet another errand. How to deal with the small woman was one of Claire's regular ordeals. Her illicit status ate at her, making it difficult for her to look Ah Yik in the eye. She worried ceaselessly about what to say, or what not to say, or whether to even acknowledge her presence. When asked his opinion, Will claimed not to care, even more maddening than usual.

'It doesn't matter,' he said. 'She's the soul of discretion and loyal to a fault.'

'That's not what I'm worried about,' Claire said.

'You're worried about her opinion?' he needled.

'I find it uncomfortable, Will,' she said. 'That's all.'

'I understand. But she doesn't care at all what we do. She's seen much worse.'

'And how is that?'

'She's been with me for years.'

'Are you saying –' She stopped. 'Never mind.' She didn't want to know what he meant.

'Why do you care about the Queen?' he asked suddenly.

'She's our Queen,' she said. 'What do you mean, why do I care? Why would I not care?'

'You believe in Empire?'

'Of course,' she said, although she didn't know exactly what he was talking about.

He propped himself up on an elbow, interested now. 'Now, what about this. Do you think the Queen cares about you?'

'What? You're asking such queer questions, Will. Sometimes I don't understand you at all.'

'I just want to know if you think the Queen takes an interest in your well-being.'

'She has many subjects but I'm sure she wishes the best for all of us.'

'And you owe her your loyalty, and regard yourself as her subject.'

'I do, yes.' She shook her head. 'Why are you being so obstinate? These are the things we hold dear as British subjects, and it is not so uncommon to think this way.'

Will smiled, a lazy smile. 'I just think that the lovely Elizabeth doesn't care for you as much as you seem to think she does.'

'You're incorrigible,' she said. 'Let's not talk about it any more. It's putting me in a bad mood. You're a terrible person and you make me angry.'

He laughed. He liked it when she scolded him.

But Will was erratic. His temper flared at the oddest things.

She had locked the door after them once, and having heard the click, he had turned round with real anger in his face. 'I told you,' he said. 'I never lock my door. Please unlock it.'

She had, feeling chastised, her face blooming with embarrassment.

Later, she tried to bring it up. 'Why did you get so angry when I locked your door? It seems so silly.'

'It's a long story,' he said. 'But please don't ever do it again.' He offered no apology or further explanation.

She tiptoed around him, but then he would pull her into bed or kiss her, and she would feel that all the uncertainty and humiliation and guilt was worth it.

And there was this, too. Claire wanted a baby.

It had happened all of a sudden. After years of regarding the mewling creatures as nothing more than nuisances, something had shifted inside her, and every particle of her yearned for a child, an infant to hold and smell and embrace. She longed for her belly to swell and expand, to feel the mysterious knocks from within, to walk around knowing that she was nurturing a child inside her.

She saw babies everywhere, strapped to the backs of Chinese women in cloth sacks, tow-headed infants playing on the lawn at the Ladies' Recreation Club. She felt bereft, unwomanly, as if something vital had been torn from her. She recorded her menstrual cycles and wept when blood stained her underwear. When acquaintances told her they were expecting, her stomach dropped, as if from the want.

And, of course, it would be Will's baby. The thought of having Martin's child was, while not entirely repulsive, foreign to her, as if it were hardly a possibility. Martin had receded so far from her life as she lived it that she was always faintly surprised when she woke up next to him. His smell seemed foreign, his skin too clammy and corporeal. She resisted his advances, and he good-naturedly acquiesced, which made her despise him – and herself. Had she always been this cruel? Martin simply worked harder, spent more time at the office, and made it easy for her. What had made him like that? What had made her like this?

8 May 1953

A chance arose to get to know the Chens better. Not that Claire felt she wanted to.

It had been an odd circumstance. Locket's mother had come into the room after the lesson, looking rather harried. There was something about her that was different, these days. She spent most of her time locked up in her room, it seemed, as she was now almost always at home when Claire came for Locket's lesson. And she had lost so much weight she was gaunt.

She started when she saw Claire. 'Oh, Mrs Pendleton,' she said. 'How are you?'

'Fine, thank you.' Claire started to put away her things. It was the end of the hour. Locket had scampered off as soon as Claire had leaned back from the piano.

'I say,' Mrs Chen began, 'you wouldn't be free for dinner tonight, would you? You and your husband? I know it's terribly short notice.'

Claire didn't know what to say. Her mouth opened but nothing came out.

'It would be lovely to have you. Victor and I are having a dinner party, you see. . . .'

And then Claire did see. It was a last-minute invitation. Someone had dropped out and they needed to make up numbers.

'I'm afraid –'

'Oh, please say you'll come,' Mrs Chen cried. 'It's a nice group of people. Government officials as well, so I would think Mr Pendleton would be interested.' She dangled this before Claire.

'Well . . .' she said. She knew Martin would want to go.

'It's settled, then. It's at the Golden Lotus, a Cantonese restaurant in Central, at eight. We have a private room.'

'Thank you so much for the invitation,' Claire had said.

'Do you think they'll expect us to eat caterpillars or chicken's feet?' Martin asked at home when told about their sudden plans.

'Who knows?' Claire said. 'I won't eat anything like that.' She watched Martin wet his comb and draw it through his hair.

'What shirt should I wear?' he asked.

'I don't know why we're going to this dinner, I really don't,' she said, but Martin had already left the room to rummage through his shirts. She stared at her face in the mirror. She looked drawn. She powdered her nose and pinched her cheeks for colour.

The dinner did not go well. It was difficult to have a conversation with people who talked on a scale Claire was unused to. And they talked about themselves so much!

She and Martin had arrived on time, so they were the first other than the Chens, who were standing in a corner with drinks.

'Oh, I'm so glad you could make it,' Melody Chen said, coming towards them. Her gaunt body was enclosed in a fantastic outfit of green silk chiffon with bell sleeves, emerald chandelier earrings, and on one hand she wore the most enormous emerald ring Claire had ever seen. She couldn't take her eyes off the stone.

'Melody,' Claire said, feeling the unfamiliar name on her tongue. She had thought about what she was going to call Mrs Chen and decided on the way to the restaurant it would be appropriate for her to call her by her first name since it was a social occasion.

'Melody, this is my husband Martin. You met briefly at the beach club.'

Martin and Victor Chen shook hands.

'I understand you're in water,' Mr Chen said. He took Martin over to get a drink from the barman.

'Your dress is lovely,' Mrs Chen said, of the simple shift Claire had also worn to the Arbogasts' party on the Peak, ages ago, when she had first met Will. 'I adore white, so fresh.' She seemed sincere. Her once-pretty face reminded Claire of a bony chicken, the flesh thin but sagging.

They were perfectly pleasant – ideal hosts, entertaining and engaging, introducing them to everyone else, yet Claire felt more and more uncomfortable as the night progressed.

She was seated next to a Mr Anson Ho, who operated textile factories in Shanghai and was setting up new ones in Hong Kong. He made it very clear that the scale was large, and that the British had had nothing to do with his success. 'Chinese are very entrepreneurial,' he kept saying. 'We will find a way to make money anywhere. The old government did not give enough chances to the local population. The British are very arrogant but they need to realize it is a new age now. The Chinese in Hong Kong need to govern themselves.' He had a red, bulbous nose that suggested too many nights of cognac. He drank his wine roughly, swirling it around in large circles, gulping it down. She nodded and smiled.

Martin was seated away from her, and was talking to an attractive Brazilian woman. He had drunk a fair amount and his gestures were becoming more animated. Around the table they spoke of Red China, the Koreas, 'Rhee is playing with fire,' and what was going on in Burma. Opposite Claire was Belle, a woman from America, a journalist, she said, and she declared the harbour in Hong Kong to be inferior to those in Sydney and Rio. Belle smoked theatrically and asked Claire's opinion about the harbour matter. Claire wiped her mouth with her napkin and excused herself to go to the powder room.

There, she found Melody Chen washing her hands nervously, wringing them again and again in the water, looking at herself in the mirror. She started when Claire came in. The ring rested on the basin.

'That's a beautiful stone,' Claire said. 'I've never seen anything like it.'

'I have to take it off before I wash my hands,' Melody said, drying them. 'Emeralds are very fragile and I'm afraid I'll do something to it. It keeps slipping off my fingers too.' She picked it up gingerly and put it back on. 'Such a bother!'

'You've lost such a lot of weight,' Claire said. 'Are you all right?'

'Fine, yes, fine,' Mrs Chen said, not meeting her eye. 'I must take better care of myself. Victor says I run around too much.'

Claire didn't move although she was blocking the way to the door.

'Are you having a good time?' The Chinese woman stepped around her. 'Victor and I were so glad you could join us at such short notice. We're delighted with Locket's progress – you've been a real boon to her musical education.' She held the door open for a moment. 'It's a nice evening, isn't it?' The door closed behind her.

Claire took one of the cloths carefully folded on the shelf and wiped all the moisture off the basin. It looked pristine again.

When she returned to the table, people were reminiscing about the war and its aftermath.

'What I found extraordinary,' Melody Chen was saying, 'was how, after the war, Hong Kong was so friendly, and there was so much good feeling towards all and sundry when everyone was coming across the border. Now, of course, if someone manages to get here, they're no longer greeted with such enthusiasm. There are just too many of them, and too many sad stories. Our sympathy has a time limit. You know Betty Liu had some six relatives staying with her for a year? She finally managed to pack them off to Canada but it took some doing. She had to hire three more maids!'

'That must have made for a busy Arrivals and Departures column,' Belle said, speaking of the much-read column in the *Post* that reported those leaving Hong Kong by aircraft, and those who had arrived and were staying at the Gloucester Hotel.

'It's like the tide. The Chinese come and go between China and Hong Kong depending on what turn history takes,' said Victor. 'But nothing ever changes too much.'

'Where were you?' Belle asked Melody. 'Were you here when the Japanese were?'

'Oh, no,' she said. 'Victor saw what was coming long before it did, and he packed me off to California to stay with my college roommate, who lives in Bel-Air. I was pregnant at the time.'

'Very clever of him,' Belle said. 'But he's always been clever.'

Everyone seemed to have a history, as if they had all grown up together, although they hailed from all corners of the world. Their language was the same.

'Yes, I'm very lucky,' Mrs Chen said. 'Victor has always thought ahead.' Her face was still as she said it. There was a slight pause.

'Well!' said her husband. 'My prescient self thinks we should play games. Isn't that what you English love to do at dinner parties?' He directed this question to Claire. 'I'm always being forced to play charades and act like a horse. For some reason, that's viewed as entertainment by your countrymen.'

Claire opened her mouth but nothing came out. Everyone waited for her rejoinder. All she could think of, absurdly, was the phrase, 'The Communists are coming, the Communists are coming.' It ran through her mind like a jaunty little ditty.

'You're a fine one to talk, Victor,' Belle said finally, rescuing her. 'I've seen you crack a monkey's head open and eat the brains, thinking that's a fine way to spend the evening.'

'Well said!' exclaimed a Frenchman. 'A good defence is always a good offence!'

As the conversation drifted on, the tension successfully defused by the others, Claire sat quietly, trying to tamp down the flush of pure panic that had enveloped her when everyone's attention had been mercilessly focused on her for that brief moment. She wished desperately for the evening to be over, even as she felt Melody Chen's eyes, not unsympathetic, on her, and managed a wan smile.

When she and Martin got home, he garrulous with wine, she silent, they washed, put on their nightclothes and went to bed.

'Did you find there were a lot of awkward moments tonight?' she asked.

'I didn't notice, no,' he said.

She wanted to beat him then, for his dumb, unknowing nature, beat her fists against his stolid chest.

He laid a questioning hand on her shoulder. She turned away and he fell quiet.

'Claire,' he started, a few minutes later.

'Martin, I'm exhausted.' She cut him off. 'Please.'

He was silent. Then he settled into the sheets and pulled up the blanket. After a pause, a gentle 'Goodnight, dear'.

She didn't know whom she hated more at that instant: Martin or herself.

The next day she told Will about the ring, how beautiful it was. A strange look came over his face. 'It's unforgettable,' he said. 'I've seen it before.'

'Are emeralds very costly?'

'Some might say that that one is without price,' he said.

'Has she had it long?'

He laughed, a short, violent sound. 'You women and your baubles. All the same.' And refused to be drawn further.

'I was at Edwina Storch's for lunch the other day,' she told him finally. 'Do you know her?'

A shadow passed over his face. They were lying in bed together.

'I've known her for a while. She's been in the colony just about longer than anybody else. She's pleasant enough, I suppose, although she managed to keep herself out of Stanley during the war under very murky circumstances. A survivor, to be sure.' He paused. 'Did you enjoy yourself? The din at those hen parties must be as loud as blazes, what with everyone chattering away about their latest frock.'

'Is that what you think we do? Talk about dresses and how to make jam?'

'Isn't it?'

'I'll have you know,' she said, 'we have very serious discussions about politics and reparations for war.'

'And amahs,' he said, biting her shoulder. 'And where to find the best leg of lamb, and how to entertain your –'

She covered his mouth with hers. 'Do shut up, darling,' she murmured, thrilling to the notion of being a woman who would say such a thing.

Afterwards, she turned to him. 'There was something interesting. Someone said they were going to be digging up all the people who had collaborated with the Japanese during the war and prosecuting them. Do you know anyone who did such a thing?'

'What is it with you today?' he asked. 'I feel like I'm being interrogated. Where does this sudden curiosity come from?'

'Don't be silly,' she said. 'I just want to know. They say war does awful things to people, and I wanted to know if you knew anyone who had really done terrible things and got away with it.'

'No,' he said. 'I don't, and I'm glad of it.'

'Must be awful to live with secrets like that.'

'It must be,' he said. 'I imagine you'd want to die sometimes.' He paused. 'I need to go to Macau to take care of a few matters. Would you think about going with me? Do you think you could make up an excuse to get out for a night?'

This Will, suddenly shy, touched her. It was so rare he asked something of her. He was usually not very kind to her.

Claire couldn't rest the night before the trip to Macau. She had coasted on the edge of sleep for most of the night, and when she finally got out of bed, she felt light-headed and silvery with exhaustion. She had told Martin the Ladies Auxiliary was going bird-watching in the New Territories and making a trip of it at a member's weekend house out in Sai Kung.

When she met Will at the terminus, she felt him look at her and imagined he found her sallow. When he wasn't looking, she pinched her cheeks and bit her lips to bring the colour back.

They walked to the pier where the ferry would take them to Macau. There was a crowd forming around the entrance. Policemen were preventing people going on to the dock. Will went to ask what was going on. He came back while Claire waited by the ticket office, nervous she would see someone she knew.

'Very unfortunate. A man has jumped off the pier. Apparently he had just lost his job as a cook. He's being taken to the hospital now, but he's dead.'

'How awful.'

'Yes. It's all being cleared up now, and they'll be resuming the service soon.'

The sea was green and brackish. When she stepped on to the gangplank, she could see rubbish floating on the water below. Someone died there today, she thought, and could not reconcile the momentous thought with the dirty surface that had paper and orange peel floating on it.

Once on the boat, her seasickness and apprehension merged and she was unable to speak. She sat trying to focus on one spot on the faraway horizon. Two weathered men in singlets and grimy trousers clambered around the deck, winding and unwinding thick rope around various posts, and pushed the boat off the dock, chattering loudly all the while. Their skin had the texture of brown leather and their teeth were yellow and cracked.

Around them were locals, a couple with a baby, the woman exhausted-looking, the baby wailing. Claire's stomach flipped and she looked away. The baby cried on and on, sickened by the waves. A man dressed in a vest read a newspaper. The front page carried a photograph of two English sappers who had been lately much in the news for murdering a local woman. They had been sentenced to death yesterday, the first Europeans since the war to attract such a punishment.

'Their faces are so young,' she said to Will.

'They're getting what they deserve,' he said. 'Too much of the old attitude. They think they can treat the locals like animals. It's a different world now.'

'The woman was an amah at the barracks.' Claire was not sure if she meant it as innocently as she said it. She had been with Will long enough to know she had thrown down a challenge.

'And?' Will said. It was the first time he had been sharp with her.

Later, he told her a story. A family had asked their amah to follow them while they were interned during the war. She was to bring them extra food and supplies to Stanley camp, which she did, in a large picnic basket. She had been with them for sixteen years, from when she was a young girl, and the family had been very kind to her, so when they were interned, she was determined to show them her loyalty. The amah brought food faithfully, every week, until one week she had not appeared. The day after she was to have come, the family received the same picnic basket. Inside, was a small hand, wrapped in dirty towels. 'They thought it a joke. Of course,' he said, 'the truly sadistic Japanese were the exception, but they were all we could think about and all we ever remember. We never knew what happened, whether she had offended someone or done something wrong or was just in the wrong place at the wrong time.'

The story was his apology. He didn't owe her one. This was how she knew of his affection.

At Macau Station there was a portrait of the governor, Commodore Esparteiro, with a moustache and a white hat, waiting to greet the visitors.

'He looks very distinguished,' Claire said.

They stepped outside Passport Control to instant chaos. Clamouring men pressed up against the steel fences, waving their hands, shouting.

'Taxi, taxi.'

'Car, car, drive you.'

Will went off to the side and negotiated with one quickly, in Cantonese. When he spoke the language of the locals, the unfamiliar sounds coming from his familiar mouth, she felt her insides tighten, something more than desire. The driver looked at her, understood. He leered, showing brown, chipped teeth. She looked away and let Will put his arm round her, he instinctively knowing what had just transpired.

'Let's go now,' she said, grateful for his protection.

'Almost done,' he said, and finished the bargaining.

In the taxi, it was unbearably hot. Will rolled down the windows. As it picked up speed, the wind was filled with particles that hit her face but it seemed churlish to complain at the beginning of their romantic escapade.

Here I am, she thought, a woman on an illicit holiday in the Far

East with her lover. She looked out at the people on the street. They didn't know. Her secret was safe with them, their blank Oriental faces, their busy lives unencumbered with her transgressions.

They got out of the taxi at the Hotel Lusitania, off the Largo de Senado.

'This is the centre of town,' Will said. 'And that over there is São Paolo, the white stone façade of an old Jesuit church. It's just the front that's left.'

'Was it the war?'

'No, a fire in the 1800s. We'll go there later. You can still see all the reliefs and carvings. Quite beautiful.'

The lobby was shabby but grand. Will seemed to know his way around.

'Have you been here often?'

'I used to come a fair amount,' he said. 'But not in the recent past.'

They were shown up to their room by a very young Chinese bell-boy, and when the door closed behind him, they looked at each other, shy.

'You look different here,' she said.

'Yes,' he said.

In the waning light of the day, sun streaking through the dusty window, they reacquainted themselves with each other, their displaced bodies somehow new, somehow more thrilling.

Afterwards he said, 'It's almost as if we're an old married couple, coming away to a new place together.'

'It's nice,' she said. His tenderness was new and it unnerved her.

'It is.'

'What is it you have to do here?' she asked.

'I have to pay my respects to someone,' he said.

'Am I to come?'

226

'If you wish.' He twirled her hair round his fingers. 'It doesn't matter.'

They took a taxi to a cemetery. Will paid the driver and got out. Paint peeled off a dilapidated, vacant guardhouse. A large tin sign with garish red Chinese characters teetered precariously above it.

'A cemetery!' she said. 'You know how to treat a girl on holiday.'

'Do you know anything about how the Chinese bury their dead?' he said, ignoring her.

'No,' she said. 'Is it very different from our way?'

'Yes.' He consulted a map on the wall and traced his finger along a route. 'Here we go.'

The air seemed thicker here. Claire didn't want to breathe in, for fear that the essences of the dead would enter her. She had grown more superstitious despite herself during her time in Hong Kong. In the cemetery, there were tombstones – smallish grey stones with English and Chinese characters interspersed – and paths intricately cut among the graves with rough stone steps leading up the hill.

She read the tombstones as they passed.

' "Here lies William Walpole, brother of Henry." No other family, I suppose. He died in 1936 at the age of forty-three. And this one, "Margaret Potter, beloved". I like that. I think I'd want something simple on my tombstone, wouldn't you?'

Will spoke as if she had not said anything. 'It was very difficult after the war, you know, to catalogue the dead. For the most part, they did mass graves. But it was very hard on the families. Not having the body of their loved ones to bury.'

'The ceremony is what comforts, a little, at least, I would think.'

'Yes, these rituals came about for a reason. People need something to focus on, to focus their grief on, and to keep busy. All over the world, rituals are part of death. It makes you hopeful for humans, that they have something in common.'

'In civilized times,' Claire said. 'People are different when lives are at stake, not death.'

Will looked up, surprised.

'Yes,' he said. 'In civilized times. At other times, all bets are off.' He grinned. 'My savage mistress,' he said. 'You are magnificent today.'

'Can I ask who we're looking for?'

'An old friend,' he said.

They stopped at the top.

'Chinese like their graveyards to be built on hills. They think it's more auspicious and, class-conscious society that they are, they are consistent even in death: the top of the heap is still the top of the heap, as it were.'

The gravestones had given way to small structures, some quite elaborate, with turrets and gates and carved doors, resembling houses or temples. Some had porcelain urns underneath.

'Do those contain ashes or bones?' she asked.

'Bones,' Will said. 'The skull is laid on top.'

He was looking carefully at each little house as he passed. Suddenly he stopped. 'Here we are,' he said.

It was whitewashed stucco, and had a wooden door with an iron knocker in the shape of a dragon. Above the door was a sign with gold characters.

'We didn't bring anything,' Claire said.

'We're not here to give,' Will said. 'We're here to take.'

He pushed the door open and stood outside. He seemed to be waiting for something.

'Will!' Claire said, scandalized. 'You're disturbing the dead!'

'I'm quieting them,' he said, and went inside.

12 May 1953

What she remembered later of Macau was vague. The heat, of course, a good Portuguese restaurant with wooden benches and crumbling plaster walls, hot, crusty bread, carafes of red wine, something called African chicken and the *dan taat*, the glossy yellow egg tarts. ' "You say pataca, I say potato," ' he sang to her, changed in this little colony. The cemetery, coming back to the hotel, and Will on edge throughout. The interior of the little shrine had been cool and dark, but with the pungent odour of incense. They had knocked up flurries of dust when they entered.

'This is where Dominick is,' he had said.

'Who is Dominick?'

'A man who was, I think, misunderstood. Not least by me. At any rate, that's what I think when I'm being my most charitable self. But a sad story. In the end, his family didn't want anything to do with him, so he is buried here by himself, not with his family in Hong Kong. He wasn't from Macau but this is where he ended up. An unwilling exile.'

'Did he die during the war?'

'Something like that. Maybe because of the war?' Will raised his voice in a question. 'Who knows? It wasn't that simple.' He ran his fingers along the dusty altar. 'In the end, it doesn't matter, though, does it? Here he lies, and all he's done and all he did is forgotten by most.'

Then he spat on the coffin.

He had taken something from the little mausoleum, something he put in his pocket so casually she dared not ask what it was. But after that they did nothing else unusual: they ate good meals, napped, had champagne at the hotel bar, walked around and looked at Macau, so she assumed that was what he had come for. He reverted to his old sarcastic self. They came back to Hong Kong and he did not mention what had happened at the cemetery again.

13 May 1953

She went to the Chens' the next week and found Locket missing.

'She gone somewhere!' cried one of the servants. 'Don't know!' But she didn't seem very concerned.

She sat in the room for half an hour then went to the lavatory. As she washed her hands, she saw Melody Chen through the sheer curtain. She was sitting outside in the garden, writing a letter and weeping. Quietly, Claire gathered her things and left.

The next week, Yu Ling brought the newspaper to the breakfast table. The main story of the day was the Queen's honours list. Victor Tsing Yee Chen.

'Look, Martin,' she said. 'Victor Chen's got himself an OBE.'

'Really?' Martin said, impressed. 'They're not handing those out by the boatload.'

'Yes.' She scanned the column. 'Did you know his grandfather was instrumental in opening up trade between China and the world?'

'Well, you'll have to congratulate him for me when you go to their house next. Is today your lesson day?'

'It is, but I rarely see him,' she said. 'There's usually no one in the house except the child and the servants.'

'Well, I'm sure it's a proud day for him.'

'I never knew they gave such things to foreigners,' she said.

But when she went to the Chens', she ended up losing her temper with Locket. It had been a terrible lesson.

'Locket, if you don't practise, you'll never improve,' she said, as she stood up and put on her jacket. Her head was throbbing from the discordant pounding Locket had produced. There had been long silences as Locket strained to read the notes she had clearly not looked at since the last lesson.

'Yes, Mrs Pendleton,' Locket said, as she pushed herself back from the piano.

'And it's a waste of my time and yours for you to have a lesson and then not touch the piano until the next lesson.'

Locket giggled and covered her mouth. She had the irritating Oriental habit of laughing nervously when in uncomfortable situations.

'I don't know if it's worth my trying to teach you.' Claire was getting more and more agitated. The girl had stumbled over the simplest exercises and had no instinctive ability to read music. And she with a Steinway!

'I'm sorry, Mrs Pendleton.' Locket was already by the door.

'And it's extremely rude of you to stand by the door as if you were waiting for me to leave.'

Victor Chen poked his head in. 'What's going on here?' His voice was not friendly.

'I haven't been practising, Baba,' said Locket. 'And Mrs Pendleton was telling me I should.'

'But what was the talk about manners?'

Claire's mouth opened but nothing came out.

'Mrs Pendleton said it's rude of me to stand by the door,' Locket said.

'She did, did she?' He looked at Claire. 'You think it's rude for Locket to stand by the door?'

'I do,' she said finally. 'I feel as if I'm being rushed out.'

'Locket, you can go to your room now. I'm sure you have studying to do,' he said, without looking at his daughter. She ducked out gratefully.

'Did you enjoy yourself at dinner the other night?' he said from the doorway, apropos nothing. 'The company was good?'

She nodded. Then she remembered. 'Congratulations,' she said. 'On the OBE. Your family must be very proud.'

Victor Chen walked right into the room and up to Claire as if he hadn't heard her. He put his head close to hers, as if he were about to tell her a secret. She flinched even before he spoke. 'I hear you're spending time with Truesdale,' he whispered. He put his hand behind her head and drew it closer, gently, intimately. 'Is it love?'

The violence in his voice was almost palpable. She started back, stumbling a little on the edge of the carpet, then grabbed blindly for her bag.

'Do give him my regards,' Victor Chen called, as she backed out of the room. 'And be sure to ask him if he's going to come back to work any time soon. We haven't seen him lately.'

She ran out the room and out the door, into the sudden heat.

'And ask him about Trudy!' Victor Chen's voice filled the hallways of his house. 'I'm sure you should know about that.' He laughed, a loud, bitter gasp.

She walked quickly down the path, past her bus stop, past the other buildings, in a panic. Her head was filled with a hot white noise that slowly diminished as she got further away. Almost imperceptibly, the sounds of the day, cars passing by, the occasional bird call, began to filter through and she slowed her pace. She was drenched in perspiration and her blouse was stuck to her back. She pulled it loose and tried to air her body. The heat roared up her back and exploded in her head.

'Claire?'

The voice came from a distance.

'Claire?'

'Will?' she said, struggling through the dark.

'It's Martin,' said her husband. 'Who's Will?'

'Martin,' she said. 'Where am I?' It was now too bright to see. Her head throbbed at the sudden change from black to white.

'You're at home now. The Chens' amah found you on the street and brought you home. Yu Ling rang me at the office. You woke up, had some water, and went back to sleep.'

'Did I faint?'

'Must have. How do you feel? You're white as a ghost.'

She shut her eyes. 'Awful.' She remembered. 'Oh! Victor . . .' she started, then shut her mouth.

'Victor Chen?' asked Martin.

'. . . was so kind,' she said. 'I saw him at the end of the lesson.'

'Well, that's good,' Martin said. 'Did you congratulate him?'

'I forgot,' she said. 'I only saw him for a moment.'

'Oh.' He paused. 'Well, I'll let you get some rest. Do you want anything?'

'No, I should be fine. Just need a moment.'

'The thing is . . .' he lingered '. . . there's this project . . .'

'Go,' she said. 'No good you hanging around here. I'm feeling better already.'

He pressed his lips to her forehead. 'Darling,' he said, and left.

The next day, Melody Chen rang as Claire was about to leave the house. 'I heard you fainted outside our home,' she said. 'I just wanted to make sure you're all right.'

'That's very kind,' Claire said. Then she didn't know what else to say.

'So, is everything all right?' Melody repeated.

'Oh, yes,' she said. 'Sorry. I didn't . . .' she trailed off. She remembered Victor Chen's breath hot on her face. She remembered seeing Melody weeping through the lavatory window.

'And you're feeling better now?' Melody asked into the silence.

'Yes.' Claire remembered the dinner. 'And thank you so much for inviting us to the other evening. We had a very nice time.'

'Oh, of course.' Melody Chen clearly had no idea what she was talking about. She had already forgotten the dinner. 'I'm so pleased.'

The conversation had started and stopped so many times Claire felt disoriented. 'Well, thank you very much for calling. It was very kind of you. I was just on my way out.'

'Of course,' Melody said. 'I'm glad you're feeling better.'

She was meeting Will at the Botanical Gardens above Central, a steep, winding maze of tropical flora and animals. She had called him for an emergency rendezvous, but he had sounded unconcerned with her urgency.

'I just had a call from Melody Chen,' she said, when she saw him waiting for her on the corner.

'Hello to you, too.' He snaked an arm round her and kissed her hard on the mouth. Possessive. She looked round instinctively. The animals lazed inside their cages, too hot to move.

'The monkeys don't know you're married,' he said.

Sometimes she hated his nonchalance.

'Melody Chen rang me,' she repeated.

'Something about little Locket? A situation with the Steinway?' he asked, not really interested.

'Something like that,' she said. Suddenly, she was afraid of what Will would do if he found out what Victor Chen had said to her. Or maybe she was afraid of what he would not do.

'Let's go back to my place,' he said lazily, turning away, sure she would follow. And her insides folded, as always, and she did exactly that.

The sound of water splashing, Will humming a song in the bath, the door slightly ajar, a humid milky-sweet fragrance escaping the bathroom. Claire sat at his desk, heart pounding. She opened the drawer to his desk quietly. A bank book. She opened it – a modest balance. Some letters, tied together with red postal string, names and addresses she did not recognize. London postmarks, scribbled writing. Some stamps, a pen, a book of matches from the Gripps. And then a photograph. Four people, in evening dress, laughing, with cigarettes and drinks in hand, at a party: a picture of privilege. Will, Melody Chen, and another man and woman, both Asian or Eurasian, Will the only European. The woman who was not Melody (Trudy?) was very striking; she dominated the photograph, although she was slight, in a close-fitting short dress, with her vivid face and short hair that somehow emphasized her femininity. It was hard to tell who was with whom; they were all linked together familiarly. Claire traced Will's face with her finger. He looked so boyish, so innocent, his face all smooth cheeks and bright eyes above his dinner jacket, bow tie loosened and hanging.

Will came into the room, wrapped in a towel, rubbing his head with another. He stopped when he saw her in front of the open drawer. 'What are you doing rummaging through my things?' he said.

She couldn't read his tone. She decided to be unapologetic. 'What's this?' She held up the photograph.

'A picture,' he said.

'I can see that. It's of you and Melody and some other people.'

'Yes,' he said. 'It is.'

'Did you used to see her socially? Who are the others?' She tried hard to make her tone conversational.

'Sometimes, Claire, you can be so provincial.' He let out an exasperated whistle. 'But yes, I'll say it for you. I used to see Melody at parties, not just in the back seat of the car I drive.'

'But it's so strange,' Claire said. 'What happened?'

'Do you feel my fall in social status? Does it bother you?' he said. He was mocking her, mean.

'I just want to know about you!' she cried. 'Why must you make everything so ugly?'

'There's a lot, Claire,' he said, 'that you don't want to know.'

'How can you be so sure?'

'Claire,' he said, 'just stick to pilfering from the Chens and leave the rest alone.'

She felt immolated from within. Her face stung with a blush that rose so quickly she felt almost faint. She hadn't been sure he had known. She had stopped stealing long ago but he knew how to turn the knife. She slapped him, hard. He didn't move. As she got her clothes on and left, he stood still, watching her. The silence between them was so long it waxed and waned in its intensity, then felt ridiculous. The other questions – *who is the other woman? Why does Victor Chen care?* – were so big she could not bring herself to ask them. She closed the door behind her quietly. Slamming it would have seemed childish. She hated him, did she not?

On the street, she didn't know where to go. She hailed a taxi to go into town. It was still bright daylight and in Central everyone seemed to have a purpose to their walk. She got out on Queen's Road and wandered among the frame shops and jewellery stores. She stopped in front of a window. The display glittered at her, necklaces and rings and bracelets, even a small diamond tiara. The Chinese were quite showy with their jewels. In the reflection from the glass, her face floated in front of her, an Englishwoman, attractive but wan. Someone whose lover had been cruel, someone who didn't know what to do about it. She tried to position her face so that a diamond necklace would be reflected around her neck. She crouched, to make it the right height.

Then she stood up, straightened her blouse and walked to the Star Ferry where she would wait for the bus that would take her home to Martin.

20 May 1953

When Claire went to the Chens the next Thursday, she noted a driver sleeping on a bench in the garden, newspaper over his head, the maids chattering gaily as they washed the windows, and breathed a sigh of relief that Victor Chen was apparently not at home.

'Missee all right? Fall down!' the maid who had answered the door asked.

'Yes, thank you very much.' She noticed for the first time how this servant had a generous face, with bright, wide eyes and a pleasant mouth. 'It's very kind of you to ask.'

The woman smiled uncertainly and led her to the piano room, where Locket was waiting.

'I heard you had an accident last week, Mrs Pendleton. Are you all right?' Locket was leaning over a tray of biscuits, crumbling one into her mouth. 'Would you like some lemonade?'

'That's very kind of you, Locket. I'm feeling much better, thank you.' The little girl was finally learning some manners, she thought.

'Mummy said you must be expecting!' Locket giggled. 'And Daddy laughed and laughed.'

Claire's back stiffened. 'Locket, have you practised?' she said, with frost in her voice.

Locket looked up, startled at the sudden change. 'I had a rehearsal on Monday for *The Mikado . . .*'

'Never mind,' Claire said. 'Let's just begin.'

After the lesson, Melody Chen appeared and asked Claire to stay for a cup of tea to talk about Locket's progress. She took Claire to the living room and excused herself to go see about the maids.

The Chens had a mantelpiece full of photographs in silver frames. Very English, Claire had thought when she first saw them, except the photographs were filled with Orientals. She got up to look at them more closely. Mostly Victor and Melody, with various family members and older people, a few of Locket by herself, and then a woman in a swimsuit at the beach, holding a cigarette and sticking her tongue out at the camera. It looked like a picture from a fashion magazine, and as Claire peered closer, she got a shock as she realized it was the same woman in the photograph at Will's house. She was Eurasian, whippet-thin, very glamorous, with a flowered bathing cap. Her face stuck out, angular and attractive.

'That's my cousin, Trudy,' said Melody, coming up from behind with a small glass of water.

'She's very beautiful,' said Claire, careful not to sound too eager.

'Not beautiful,' Melody said immediately. 'Not beautiful. She was half Portuguese, so Eurasian, you know, and the Europeans always found her attractive. But Chinese don't like half-breeds, really.' Claire noted the casual slur, was surprised by it. Melody was usually so refined.

'But everyone, absolutely everyone, noticed her. She was very famous in Hong Kong. Some might say infamous. She brought her terrier to a dinner party once as her companion. Had him in a bow tie. She sat him on a seat and everything, until he urinated on it. Betty Wong was livid!'

'Well, she looks as if she knows how to have a good time.'

'Yes. I always think that if she were still around, she'd have been the first woman in the colony to wear a bikini, and she'd have worn it to a picnic at the governor's house or something wildly inappropriate like that. She was that type of girl. Scandalous, but she got away with it usually. Fearless.'

'Is she not?' Claire asked delicately. 'Around any more, I mean.'

Melody looked away, sipped her water, grimaced. 'No, not any more. She was a casualty of war, I guess you would say.'

'It's difficult to believe,' Claire said, looking at the photograph. 'She seems so full of life.'

'Almost to bursting,' Melody said. 'Her father was my father's cousin, so she was my second cousin.'

'Were you close?'

'Oh, in a way,' Melody said. 'I think she probably found me quite boring. We were very different. And we had a lot of cousins running around Hong Kong. We're a big family. She was close to another cousin of ours – Dominick – but he died during the war too. I would say they were best friends. They were quite well known, the two of them. The Terrible Two.'

'And . . .' Claire didn't know where to begin. But it didn't matter. Melody Chen was in the mood to talk.

'And she gave me this beautiful emerald ring, which I always wear on special occasions because it's so spectacular.' She stretched out her hand as if she had it on.

'I saw it at the dinner party you gave. It's really something. That was very generous of her.'

'I like to have something to remember her by,' said Melody. 'Isn't that what family's all about?' The servants came in with a silver salver of drinks.

'Tea?'

'Yes, please, with lots of milk.'

Melody poured her a cup, but didn't have any herself. She sipped at her small glass.

'Victor treats me like some fragile flower,' she said suddenly. 'But I'm not as weak as he thinks I am. You know, he shipped me off to California. I kept asking him questions. I think I was irritating to him.'

'I'm sure you were no such thing,' said Claire.

'And I came back, and everything had changed,' she said faintly.

The afternoon stretched on, with Melody Chen talking in circles, as if she had all the time in the world to chat with her daughter's piano teacher. She had not mentioned Locket or her progress, even once.

'Have you ever thought back about someone who died?' Melody asked. 'How it was when they were alive? Sometimes, when I think about Trudy and Dominick, I feel as if I saw a black spot hanging over their heads, as if they were marked and I just couldn't fully see it at the time. I feel like they were doomed from the beginning, that they had this spectre hanging over them.' Melody stopped, and her eyes became glossy, wet.

'I still can't believe Trudy's dead. Her father married a Portuguese woman, and she was so peculiar. Do you know she disappeared when Trudy was a child? They put it about that she had been abducted but my mother always thought she got tired of the whole thing and just got on a boat for America.

'Her father was related to my family. Who knew he would have such a head for business? I think he did better than anyone, actually.'

'Is he still alive?' Claire asked.

'Of course not,' Melody said. 'He died along with all the other wretched detritus of the war, those who were not on the right side of things, who refused to play along.'

Claire nodded.

242

'So someone close to you died?' Melody asked again. 'I know it's a silly question after the war but, still, some haven't been touched. Some were lucky.'

'Yes,' said Claire. 'Not anybody close, though.' An uncle, met once, a picture of him at her eighth birthday party. Various acquaintances during the war. The closest had been a girl from primary school, who had gone on holiday to Wales and drowned. The school had given everyone a day off, and when the students came back, many had black ribbons tied round their arms. Claire had not known they would do that and had felt excluded, as if everyone had known something to which she had not been privy.

'Do you know Reggie and Regina Arbogast?' asked Melody, switching subjects again.

'I've been to their house but I wouldn't say I know them,' said Claire. She was trying to keep up with the odd, meandering conversation.

'They're having a coronation party. They're having two, actually. The first is a bit smaller, more intimate, and they're listening to the coronation on the radio. Then they're having the reels flown in from England, and they're going to have a television-watching party for a larger group. I think that one is more of a cocktail party. It should be fun. Do you have plans for the coronation?'

'Not as yet,' Claire said.

'I'm putting something together so you and Will must come,' Melody said suddenly.

'You mean Martin,' said Claire, taken aback.

'Of course,' Melody said smoothly. 'So sorry.'

'Of course,' repeated Claire.

Melody seemed to be waiting for something else. The afternoon light had dissipated and Claire could no longer see the motes of dust floating on the rays of sunlight that had streamed through the window. 'I think it's late,' she said. It had been the oddest, most disjointed afternoon she had ever experienced. 'I should be going.'

At that moment, Will came through the door.

'You!' Melody called to him, in a wavering voice. 'You're stirring everything up!' Her tone was light, but for the first time Claire understood, the knowledge blooming in her head like a rapidly spreading ink stain: the Chens were afraid of Will. They had taken him on to keep him close, had paid him money for a job he didn't do because they had no choice. She saw her lover through a new lens. He was the benevolent one. He was the dispenser of their destiny.

'I need to see Victor,' he said, without acknowledging Claire.

'He's not here,' Melody said.

'Is he expected back soon?'

'Don't patronize me, Will,' Melody said abruptly. 'We've known each other long enough.'

'You have nothing to do with this, Mrs Chen.'

'Oh, stop the charade, Will,' Melody cried. 'The Mrs and the Mr and the sir, and the "Where would you like to go today?" Were you laughing at us the entire time? And what you've done. And poor, poor Trudy.'

Now Claire grasped that Melody was quite drunk, and that she had been drinking a spirit, not what Claire had assumed was water.

'Don't mention her, Melody. You have no right ever to say her name again.'

'And you? You have one?' The Chinese woman's voice grew shrill. 'As if you have any right at all! The woman you pretended to love!'

Will was white with anger. 'Melody,' he said. 'That is utter rubbish.' He controlled himself with difficulty. 'This is not for you to do. You stay out of it.'

'Will,' Melody said, 'this is spinning out of control. Victor is furious. You have to stop what you're doing. I'm telling you as someone who was once your friend. You have to stop it.'

'It's too late, Melody,' Will said. 'There's nothing I can do now.'

While they spoke, Claire let herself out, quietly, and stood in a corner of the driveway, heart pounding, waiting.

When Will walked out, he looked angry, his hands shoved deep into his pockets.

'Who is Trudy?' she asked, stepping forward.

He started.

'Not now,' he said. 'Not now, Claire. Come with me. Let's go for a bathe.'

20 May 1953

The sharks were back. They had been sighted off Stanley Beach and Shek-O as well. A local man had been dipping his hands in the water while on a diving platform in South Bay and had had a finger nipped off. He had sat in blind panic waving his hand about and screaming until a woman on the beach had heard his cries and they had sent a boat out to get him.

Claire and Will liked to bathe at Shek-O but they could only go in the early morning or in the late afternoon during the week, when it was unlikely that anyone they knew would see them. On this day, they drove in silence to Will's flat and picked up some bathing things, drove to the beach and parked the car. They were in luck. The beach was empty.

The sand in Hong Kong was gritty. Will had told her of beaches in India where the sand was like sifted flour, so fine you could almost inhale it. But at Shek-O, when the tide went out, there were pools filled with hermit crabs, and in the past, they had caught them and Claire had brought them home and put them into a bowl with sea water until they had started to smell foetid.

'You are a mermaid,' Will said, finally breaking the silence. He was sitting on the straw mat they had unfurled on the beach, watching her as she undressed.

She still became tongue-tied in his company, unable to respond to his teasing. She folded her clothes and put them into her basket. He stood up.

'Let's swim to the dock,' she said, then remembered. 'Do you think there are sharks around?'

'The unfortunate man from last week would say it's a certainty,' he said, getting up.

'Should we bathe, then? I've been longing to all day.'

'How adventurous are you feeling?' he asked. They were both facing the water, she slightly behind him.

'Never very, but it's so hot.' She put her hands flat on his back. He had taken off his shirt and it was already slick with perspiration. 'Do you ever get used to it? The heat?'

'No, you just live in it.' He reached behind and took her hands off his back. He did things like that a lot, gestures that felt like rebukes, ways to keep a distance between them. She pretended not to notice and moved away, walked into the water up to her knees.

'And the water's never cold here either, is it?' she called back to him. 'More like a bath.'

'Yes, Claire,' he said. 'Hong Kong is not England.'

She looked towards the horizon. The day had had a jerky quality – things happening that were out of control, that she didn't know how to react to or how to feel about. 'Why so rude?' she said, but he didn't hear her, or pretended not to.

He plunged into the water. 'Last one there loses.'

'Wait,' she called. 'I don't –' but he was already in the waves, swimming a fast crawl towards the diving platform. She hesitated but, watching him grow smaller and smaller, she knew she would have to follow.

'Damn you, Will Truesdale,' she said.

The water had two levels – the warm layer above, heated by the sun, and somewhere below her waist, the chill of the deep. She tried to swim in the warm part, frightened by the cold but her legs sometimes sank into it.

She did a leisurely breaststroke and tried not to think of sharks. Ahead of her Will pulled himself up on to the diving platform. His body glistened in the sun. His was an older body, but still lean. He evoked desire in her, so strange when her body was surrounded by water. She swam on, pushing away the panic, the desire.

By the time she got to the platform, she was furious. 'I told you I didn't want to swim out here.'

'You didn't.'

'Only because you were so far out already you couldn't hear me.' She sat away from him, on the bobbing disc. 'You gave me no choice.'

'Don't be angry, kitten.'

She didn't answer, just twisted her hair into a ponytail and squeezed the water out. The drops puddled on the wood and disappeared into a large dark stain.

'Do you remember the first time we were on a platform?' He was trying to make amends. 'Doesn't it seem so long ago?'

On the beach, a local couple appeared, laid out a blanket and put up an umbrella.

'It does, yes,' she allowed. Then, 'You should know I can go. You could lose me.'

He nodded, understanding, capitulating for the moment. 'You don't need me any more, Claire, if you ever did.'

'Yes,' she said.

They sat together peaceably now, the pressure let out. The weather was perfect, the sun slowly sinking towards the horizon, a cool breeze coming off the water.

'Will,' she said. 'What's going on?'

When he didn't answer, she said, 'You know what I'm talking about. Everyone is behaving so oddly, and you're at the heart of it.'

He lay down and shut his eyes.

'You know, the most absurd things happened during the war,' he said. 'Do you know that while we were interned, the Japanese administration presented us with a bill for accommodation and food. Can you imagine? And we couldn't very well throw it back in their faces, so we had to tell them we would write promissory notes that would be honoured by our government after the war. They wanted us to pay for the rotten vegetables and cup of rice we got every week.'

'But now?' she asked.

'I'm getting there,' he said, with an edge to his voice. 'Just listen.' He began again.

'And so we danced with them, our captors, although it was always a fine line between being good and being proud. We always hoped. There were small things like growing the vegetables in the garden in a V so that when they sprouted it would be a nice surprise and an encouragement. Childish, you know. One never gets used to being a prisoner, although we got used to our daily routine.

'And people were petty, of course. And others were unbelievably kind and generous. You had all sorts of behavior. The Japs too. There were good ones and bad ones.'

'There was a woman,' Claire said. 'Trudy.'

'Yes. Trudy.' He stopped. 'Trudy. I think you would have liked her.'

'We are different,' Claire said. She didn't know why, as she said it, but she felt that she was being kind to Will.

Will snorted. 'Yes, you are. That's an understatement. But you would have liked her, I know.'

'You were with her.'

He hesitated. 'Yes.'

'And . . .'

'No longer. She's gone,' he said.

'How?'

'I failed her,' he said. 'She wanted me to come out and live on the outside with her. She was on the outside because she wasn't British. She got me a pass. But I refused.'

'You didn't want to leave the people inside the camp?' Claire asked.

'Yes,' he said. 'That was part of it. I was helpful inside the camp and could get things done. Certainly no one wanted me to leave. But –' He stopped.

'Yes?' Claire prompted.

'But I think I was afraid too,' he said softly. 'If I went outside, it was a whole new world and I'd have had to learn the new rules. I would have had to start as a beginner, disadvantaged, get my bearings all over again.

'I was tired,' he said simply. 'And I didn't want more change. It was hard in the camp, but if you obeyed the rules, you weren't bothered. Outside it was chaos. Trudy had things snatched from her hands as she walked down the street – once it was food and the boy crammed some bread into his mouth as he ran. He was starving and couldn't run properly. He had no shoes and no shirt. I think all he had were the trousers he had on. There was starvation and desperation and misery. She told me about it. There was no filter. It was real.'

He looked at Claire.

'And she died,' Claire said, almost without knowing it.

'Yes, she died.'

'How?'

'Some would say by the hand of her benefactor,' he said. 'A man who gave her many things, and took them away when he chose to. If I had been outside with her, he would have controlled me too.'

A mosquito buzzed between them, floating in the damp air.

'He made her do awful things. He found out she was smuggling messages into the camp with the food, so he made her bring tainted food the next time. Not enough to kill, just sicken, and there was nothing in the way of medical supplies, so people suffered. That's the kind of bastard he was. I had to tell her the next time she came, and her face just crumpled. She hadn't known. I believe that still. She hadn't known but she couldn't do anything. She didn't know if he would do it again, or if the food would be all right the next time, and we were in such desperate need that we just took it and ate it.'

'How do you know he did it?' Claire asked. 'Maybe it was just a mistake.'

'Oh, yes,' Will said. 'We knew. He asked her after she returned how her friends were doing, and laughed in her face. She only told me that afterwards.'

'And Victor?'

'Victor Chen.' He laughed. 'Oh, yes, my esteemed employer.'

'But what?' she asked. 'What of him?'

'What of Victor Chen?' Will said. 'What of Victor Chen? How to begin?'

Suddenly he slapped Claire's arm.

'Got it,' he said, lifting up his hand to show a bloodied black spot, a tangle of tiny insect legs and antennae. 'Damn bloodsuckers.'

He leaned over and rinsed his hands in the sea. He lifted them up. Drops of water sparkled and dripped from his fingers. He looked at them contemplatively. 'Victor Chen murdered Trudy,' he said.

10 April 1943

'A grateful Otsubo is what I want,' Trudy is saying. 'If he's grateful, who knows what he'll do? Maybe he'll get you repatriated! But you can't leave. I don't want to live in England.'

She never asks him again, not directly. She whispers, implies, ingratiates. She dangles rewards before him and then, finally, hatefully, hints at what may befall her if she does not come through for the man. 'He wants one big payday, you know,' she says. 'He's a simple man. He wants to go back to his country, buy some land and build a cottage for himself and his family. He wants to bring his parents out, take care of them. He's really a family man.'

As she outlines this outlandish idea, he nods, pretends to listen, possibly agree.

'And he's getting a wee bit impatient, but I think he's getting close. He's found out that Reggie Arbogast is indeed one of the people who was entrusted with the location. So you should know that. He has eyes and ears everywhere and I think they're making progress. But he does get frustrated . . .' She trails off. 'And when he's frustrated . . .'

Three weeks later, another trip out. 'I'm working on getting it weekly for you. Do you like it?' she says, when she picks him up. 'All the bankers are outside and I don't see why you shouldn't be.

They're putting them up at the Luk Kwok and they escort them to the office every day. I don't think they're getting better rations than us, but who knows?'

He gets into the driver's seat. 'Have you seen Angeline? How is she doing?'

Trudy looks up at the sky. 'Angeline,' she starts. 'Angeline seems to have suffered a crisis of conscience – is that what you call it?'

'What happened?' He starts the car.

'She has decided that I'm not a person she wishes to associate with. Can you imagine?' She smiles tightly. 'The godmother of her child!'

'Did she give you a reason?'

'No,' she says. 'I went to visit her in Kowloon and her maid told me she wasn't at home. She was funny about it, though, and when I walked away I looked up and saw Angeline at the window. She wasn't even trying to hide. She stared straight at me and then drew the curtains. Very grim.'

'You are presuming . . .'

'Oh no, darling,' she says. 'I know Angeline very well and she doesn't need to say anything to me for me to know exactly what she's thinking. I'm just hoping you won't come to the same conclusion. I'm going to become a pariah. I can see it now.'

He bursts with his own confession. 'Trudy, I haven't asked.'

She knows immediately what he is talking about. 'Maybe the right time hasn't come up,' she says.

He cannot lie to her. 'I won't ask,' he says. 'It just seems wrong.'

'Oh! You won't even try!' A choked sound comes from her throat. 'Wrong! Well, I can see that.'

'And why would Arbogast tell me anyway?' he finishes lamely. 'We aren't friends.'

She doesn't speak again until they're at the Toa. 'Here we are,' she says. 'Are you hungry?'

Always the Chinese with their damn food, he thinks. 'No,' he says, getting out of the car. 'Are you?'

'Otsubo wants us to meet him for lunch,' she says. 'He's waiting upstairs.'

'And when were you going to tell me this?' he says. 'When I sit myself down on his lap?'

'Will!' she cries. 'This is serious. Dominick has promised Otsubo he will get the information and that I will help him. I wouldn't ask you if it weren't important, but . . .'

'Trudy, I can't help you,' he says. 'I cannot.'

'Will,' she says. 'If you knew what was at stake . . .'

But her mouth is set. She knows this man. The question is how well she can manage the other.

By the time they get to the room, she has shaken off her bad temper. Her moodiness is like a cloak she can put on and take off at will.

'If I lose my pass because of this, you'll be the first to pay,' she says lightly. She pushes the door open. 'Otsubo-san! The valiant Will Truesdale is here to tell us of the wonderful resort-like conditions in Stanley. Was it *coq au vin* for dinner last night? And I hear you have entertainment now. The Stanley Players?' And she's off, bubbling with vivacious energy, going round the room, dispensing kisses and quixotic pronouncements, clinking ice in highballs, as if she hasn't a care in the world, as if she hadn't fixed him with a long, pleading look just before they entered.

Dominick joins them for lunch, and Will notices the way Otsubo looks at him with barely disguised contempt, and yet, now his hand lingers on Dominick's shoulder longer than necessary, he allows Dominick to serve him food, and Dominick treats him with a servility that sickens Will. So that's how it goes, he thinks. The sophisticate becomes the dog and the soldier becomes the master. Brute force trumps all in the end, doesn't it?

But this is not what concerns him. What's been eating at him since they alighted from the car and made their way to Trudy's suite is something else entirely.

What is making him uneasy is his own unwillingness to compromise and where it might be coming from – the niggling feeling that he cannot shake off: that he is calling his reluctance integrity, but what it might be is simply cowardice.

2 May 1943

Arbogast is screaming. Will cannot stand to hear it, cannot stand not to hear it. He is frozen, wants to clap his hands over his ears, wants to scream himself. Around Will, the adults are pale and silent, mothers rushing the children away.

Usually, the guards take the unfortunate suspects away to a far-off house where they are made to sign their confessions, written long before they start to talk. But Arbogast! They had come silently, grimly, filled with purpose – two men – seized him under his arms and dragged him to Ohta's office, next to the officers mess. He had gone quietly, but then the screaming started.

It has been three days since Will returned from outside and he has made it a point to avoid Arbogast, as if even coming close to the man will transmit his secret to him – a secret he has no intention of learning if he can help it.

He doesn't want to know anything about Arbogast. If he is the type of man to keep a secret to the end, if he is the kind of man who will value his family more than his country, or if he is the kind of man who will take a deal to better his circumstances. He wants to know nothing. Instead, he tries to ignore him – the once proud man with his swollen beri-beri feet, dragging around the camp, complaining about his wife and his dysentery.

The door opens and Arbogast is brought out, bucking. Strange how violence is not as vivid in real life. There are only a few streaks of blood. Mostly the impression is that he is wet. The water torture. They take him to the outskirts now. He is still screaming but his voice is fraying with the exertion. Will's own throat hurts from the tearing sounds coming from Arbogast's mouth.

So this is the man he reveals himself to be, Will thinks suddenly, inappropriately, bloodlessly – a man who screams when he is in danger. He hopes he himself will be silent. But one never knows.

Johnnie is at his side, suddenly. They watch the man being dragged off again.

'That poor devil,' he says. 'I wonder what they think he's done.'

'Does it matter?' Will asks.

'Not at all.' Johnnie glances at Will. 'What a cynic you've become.'

The next day, Arbogast is brought by two soldiers to his room and dumped unceremoniously on his bed, where Regina has a fit, falling and having hysterics on the floor while her husband lies, nearly unconscious, above her. His right hand is gone, the stump of his wrist wrapped in bloody rags.

Some sensible women drag Regina away and ply her with tea while the doctor is summoned. He shakes his head, powerless without any equipment, any medicine. 'What can I do?' he says. 'He will live or die. That is all.'

They leave him there, with the powerless doctor, his face swollen blue beyond recognition, blood from the wound soaking through layers of ripped sheets. In the morning, the other residents of D Block will complain they could get no sleep because of the man's moaning. Arbogast, the rich businessman, has been reduced to this, and the others have been reduced to that.

The secret must be out now, Will thinks. And that should be that.

27 May 1953

Victor Chen was in a panic. Even Claire could see that, hidden away in the piano room. He was streaming from room to room, shouting at the servants, shouting at Melody, picking up the phone and banging it down again.

For the sake of the child, she tried to keep the lesson going but it was almost impossible. After a door slammed for the third time, she reached over and shut the instruction book. 'Well, Locket, what do you say?' she said.

'About what, Mrs Pendleton?'

For the first time, Claire felt sorry for Locket. What must it be like to live in a house like this, with parents like Melody and Victor? The child's face was heartbreakingly smooth, the Oriental skin almost glossy, her eyes curious hazel orbs. Claire reached over and tucked a loose strand behind Locket's ear. The maternal gesture surprised her almost as much as it did the girl herself, who gave a quick, shy smile.

'Shall we finish a little early?'

'All right, Mrs Pendleton.' Locket got up quickly, bumping into the piano and spilling the glass of water that had been sitting on top. 'Oops.' She giggled. 'Mummy says I'm very clumsy.'

'You must try to be more careful,' Claire said. 'All children are careless.'

'Mummy says I give her a headache,' Locket said more sombrely. 'I'm not to disturb her in the afternoons any more. That's why she's arranged so many lessons.'

'I'm sure she wants you to grow up to be an accomplished lady with many interests.' Claire patted her head.

'We're having a party!' Locket brightened. 'For the Queen's coronation. Daddy got an honour from the Queen, you know.'

'Yes, I heard. You must be very proud.'

'I'm getting a new dress. It's a tangerine silk taffeta with guipure lace,' Locket recited carefully. 'Mummy had the lace flown in from France and it's the only piece in Hong Kong.'

'That sounds lovely, Locket.'

The girl beamed, then looked uncertain. 'Of course,' she faltered, confessed, 'it's just the leftover bits from Mummy's dress. She had some extra so she gave them to me so I could have them on mine.'

'I'm sure you'll both look lovely,' Claire said.

The reason Victor Chen was in such a state, Claire surmised, was what had appeared in the paper today. It had been relegated to page seven, pushed back by the relentless, breathless coverage of Princess Elizabeth and the latest details of her procession to Westminster Abbey, but it was still there – a small column about the formation of a War Crimes Committee, to be headed by a Sir Reginald Lythgoe, based on new information that had come to light. Will had pointed it out to her earlier in the afternoon.

'It's bloody unfathomable!' she heard Victor shout into the phone. 'It's a witch hunt. The war's been over for a decade and they want to dredge up this rubbish. You tell Davies I won't forget this. It's pure anti-Chinese sentiment. They can't stand to see someone do well, and the OBE was just the last ... That wretched old woman was playing Chopin on the Government House piano the entire war, drinking Scotch and dining on veal under my protection! She has no right –'

Someone shut a door so his voice was muffled.

Locket smiled. 'So I can go?'

'Yes,' Claire said. 'Run along.'

Claire let herself out quietly, without running into Melody or Victor. She had an appointment with Edwina Storch.

The old woman had rung last week, asking if they could meet for a cup of tea. They decided on the Librarians' Auxiliary in Mid-Levels, and Claire had arranged to meet her today.

The bus stopped outside the building on Tregunter Path and Claire got out. Miss Storch was just entering the clubhouse. Claire stopped to watch her. She had on a pink hat, beneath which her salt-and-pepper bun was just visible. Her bottom was wide and encased in a matching pink cotton skirt that went to the knee. Varicose veins trailed down her thick calves, and as she walked with her cane, she swayed ever so slightly from side to side. She stopped to catch her breath outside the door, then stepped up and went inside.

Behind her, Claire waited, then walked to the door and pushed it open. Inside, it was dark and cool, fans swaying as they turned, and heavy damask curtains shielding the furniture against the bright sun outside. Claire squinted, trying to make out the shapes in the room.

'Hello,' said Edwina Storch. Claire jumped. Miss Storch had taken off her spectacles and was rubbing them with the hem of her jacket. 'They steam up in this humidity, you know.'

'Hello, Miss Storch,' she said. 'I was behind you on the path but it was just too hot to rush.'

The old woman did not reiterate her invitation to Claire to address her by her first name. 'Yes, it's terrible out there, isn't it?' she said, pulling out a white handkerchief and wiping her forehead. 'Does something to the character but I haven't pinned it down yet.

It's something that people who live here over twenty years develop but I can't put a name to it.'

'The heat?' Claire said.

'Yes. Most of your day is spent trying to avoid it. And the endlessness of it. Always at war with the elements, instead of in harmony with them. That's us, the British colonials, battling against our circumstances, always.' Miss Storch peered at Claire, who was reminded of the first time she had met her and the gaze that had almost made her faint. 'Shall we sit?'

'Certainly.'

Claire was unsure as to why Edwina Storch had rung her. The old woman moved slowly, and was treated with great respect by the staff.

'Lovely to see you again, Miss Storch,' said the manager, who had come out to greet them. 'So nice that you can come into town and see us.'

'Do you know Mrs Maxwell?' Edwina Storch asked Claire. 'She's been here almost as long as I have.'

They shook hands and were escorted into the dining room – more of the heavy damask curtains, a mix of old good tables and new chairs, too shiny.

'We have your favourite currant scones today,' Mrs Maxwell said. 'And the good Chinese oolong.'

'Splendid,' Edwina Storch said, as she lowered herself carefully into a chair. 'You're too kind, Harriet.'

'It's very pleasant here,' Claire said. 'It's my first time.'

'Not too bad,' Edwina said. 'During the war, I spent a few nights here.'

'Yes?' Claire said.

The waitress came over and poured water for them into faded, scratched glasses.

'There's something sad about the Eurasian, isn't there?' Edwina Storch said, looking after the girl as she left. 'Something incomplete, something wanting in them. I always feel they're searching for something to make them whole.'

'Do you think so?' Claire said politely. 'I find them very attractive, actually, with their beautiful skin and golden eyes and hair. When I first was in Hong Kong, I did find them odd-looking but now I think they're just splendid.'

'Hmph,' snorted the old woman. 'You're young and romantic. The children feel dreadful because they're not accepted by either race.'

Claire had not thought Miss Storch would be so narrow-minded when her own lifestyle was not at all conventional.

As if she could sense what Claire was thinking, Miss Storch drew herself up slightly. 'Mary and I have always led our lives with good Christian values!' she said. 'We love all of God's creatures, even the less fortunate.'

'Of course,' said Claire.

The Eurasian girl came over again with a pot of tea. She set down the cups and put a strainer on each of them. Her eyes were downcast, steady on the table.

'I'll pour,' said Miss Storch, dismissing her.

'You don't think she's attractive?' Claire asked. She felt an obstinate urge to pursue the matter.

'Claire,' Miss Storch said, 'I do not. She is unfortunate. She is lucky to have a respectable job because I am sure that her father left her mother after he had had his fun with her. You know, that's how most of these situations are.' She poured the hot tea into Claire's cup. Claire lifted up the milk jug.

'You don't pour milk into this sort of tea!' Miss Storch barked. Claire's hand froze, suspended in the air. 'It must be drunk unadulterated. Put that milk down. I don't know why they even give us milk.'

Claire paused, then poured milk into her tea. 'I prefer my tea with milk,' she said.

Miss Storch stared at her, then took off her spectacles and started rubbing them again. 'So you've got some spunk,' she said, inspecting her glasses. 'Glad to see that.'

Claire was silent.

'You're going to need it,' Edwina Storch said. 'There's a pretty kettle of fish going on and, from what I understand, you are in the middle of it.'

'I don't understand,' she said.

'Oh, I think you understand more than you let on.' Miss Storch sipped her tea, grimaced. 'Too strong. They let it steep too long.'

'I'll call for hot water,' Claire said, and raised her hand.

'Don't bother. I've more important things to talk about.' She sighed. 'You have a fondness for the Eurasian race.'

'Hardly,' Claire protested. 'I just –'

'And I'm sure you know of Trudy Liang.' She peered intently at Claire over her glasses. 'She was one of the better-known Eurasians in Hong Kong when she was alive. She was from a very wealthy family and therefore escaped much of the prejudice that comes from being mixed.' Edwina Storch said this with a complete lack of irony. 'You know who I'm talking about?'

'Yes,' Claire allowed. 'I have heard of her.'

'And that whole business during the war. She was out of the camps because she was Portuguese and Chinese, and I was out of the camps because I had a Finnish mother. If you were persuasive in the early days these things could happen. It was very confusing and the rules changed every day.' Her eyes shifted, became wistful. 'Of course, I couldn't get Mary out, but I was able to provide for her when I was outside, and brought her packages and all that. It was for the best.

'You know, Claire,' she said suddenly. 'You have a face for

263

listening. People must always confide in you. Do you find that to be so?'

'Not really,' Claire demurred. She thought that Edwina Storch's face resembled a large, fleshy reptile's now. It had shrewdness, opportunism and greed written all over it.

'You know about Trudy and Will Truesdale, then?'

'I've just heard stories, like everyone else,' Claire said. 'But it has nothing to do with me.'

'It doesn't!' Miss Storch gave a harsh chuckle. 'Oh, I imagine you would like everyone to believe that. But, yes, the two of them were thick as thieves. Everyone thought they would marry. If you ask me, he got the thin end of the wedge. He could have done much better. But no, he was with her, and then the war happened, and a lot more.' She paused. 'I'm sure you're wondering why I asked you here today, and why I asked you to lunch the other week. I wanted to get a good look at you, at your face. But it's a long story. You should eat while I talk.'

She looked suddenly very serious. 'You must rise to the occasion,' she said. 'And you must be strong. Now is the time for you to make a difference.'

In the late-afternoon light, the door to the Librarians' Auxiliary opened. Claire stood, blinking even in the fading light. She was saying goodbye to Edwina Storch.

'Thank you very much for the tea,' she said.

'You're very welcome, my dear,' said Miss Storch. 'I hope I have been enlightening.'

'Yes,' Claire started. Then, 'No. Actually – I don't know.' She stumbled over her words.

'That's not the way, dear,' Miss Storch said. There was exasperation in her voice.

'But, Miss Storch,' Claire said hurriedly. 'Miss Storch. I do feel – There is something I would like to say. When I met you at your garden party some weeks ago, you said I reminded you of yourself when you were young. I just want to tell you that I think that is not right. You and I are as different as can be.' Then she turned and walked away quickly, not looking back.

The sun was setting and Claire could not imagine that it had been an ordinary day outside before she had entered the dark rooms and an afternoon of storytelling by a vicious old woman with an axe to wield.

1943

There was a baby.

   There was a man with eleven fingers. Now ten. Now eleven again. The finger always grew back, taking one year exactly. A good measure of time.

   There were good men.

   There were bad men.

   There were dead men.

   There was a woman, disappeared.

   There was a baby.

Trudy, her slim figure enveloped in looser and looser tunics. Her face growing rounder, her skin mottled with the mask of pregnancy. When had he noticed? It came upon him, like so many revelations, when he was about to drift off to sleep, after another weekend outside. He jerked, realized: *a baby.* He could not sleep after that, turning on his thin mattress, restless and wild, his mind aflame.

She had not told him. He had not noticed. It had been so gradual.

His thoughts like an old woman's. What sort of world is this to bring a child into? How was she going to have a baby during a war? And then the other thought, the one he pushed down, but which kept surfacing.

Did those things even matter any more at a time like this?

Then one day, another weekend, Trudy saying abruptly, 'I always knew I'd be one of those women who grew enormous during pregnancy.' The first time she had acknowledged her condition. She had said it gamely, over a breakfast of noodles and roast pork, shovelling the long noodles into her mouth like a street hawker, not caring what she looked like. If she had told him a few weeks earlier, before he had noticed for himself, he would have been more generous, said it suited her, but he kept quiet. His small, petty revenge. But against what, whom? Not the woman. The war. The unfairness of it all.

And then it grew obvious, suddenly, in that way women look pregnant overnight. Her growth accelerated. She was still small, but her belly swelled and spilled out of whatever loose dress she was wearing. It looked like a tumour to him. He was ashamed he felt that way.

She never said anything else about it.

There was a man with eleven fingers.

Dominick. His face grown sharp with his newly acquired cunning, his body gone soft with indulgence. Trudy, saying *sotto voce*, 'Dominick has changed. He's with that odious Victor Chen all the time. They're trying to get my father to join in on some Macau company they're setting up that's doing a lot of trading with the Japanese. I don't want my father involved in any of that – he's not well – but Dommie won't listen. He's gone over to Victor's side.' And in that statement, her profound disappointment. Her best friend, gone. Loneliness. Will was inside the camp. Dominick was changed. Trudy didn't have anyone any more.

There were good men.

When Will went back to camp, after the first trip out, eager faces greeted him, hungry for news and hope. He distributed what he had brought – the guards left him alone now, as news had spread that he had a connection outside – and went back to his room.

Johnnie Sandler appeared at the doorway. 'You prefer to be alone?'

'No, it's all right.' He waved him in.

'So, how was your leave? Lots of jealous people back here at home base, you know. The news spread like wildfire. You're either a scoundrel or a hero. Opinion's divided.'

'Johnnie . . .' He didn't know where to begin.

'Anyone still out there that we know?'

'Yes, but . . . They say that two hundred Chinese die every day on the streets. Brutally. Anonymously. Half the hospitals are still closed.'

Johnnie studied his face. 'You look a bit shell-shocked. Is anything else going on?'

'Too much, my friend. Too much.'

'Trudy doing all right out there?'

Will nodded. 'You don't know her well, do you?'

'As well as I knew you, I suppose.'

'And what did you think of her?'

Johnnie hesitated. 'That's a rum thing to ask. She's your girl.'

'No, really. I want to know.'

'I liked her. What I knew of her. There was always the noise about her, I know, but I've learned that most of that was just that – noise. She seems a good sort, just had a lot of attention on her all the time, and I thought that must be hard.'

'Very diplomatic,' Will said.

Johnnie grinned. 'What do you expect, old man?'

'Why did you never find someone? I always saw you with a few girls, never one, never for a long time.'

'Never found anyone who'd have me,' Johnnie said lightly. 'Once they'd spent enough time with me, they were off like a rocket.'

They sat together for a while. Johnnie brought out some home-made cigarettes. 'The good stuff, rolled from native Stanley grass.' He offered one to Will.

Will shook his head. 'What am I thinking?' He produced two packets of Red Sun cigarettes from his bag under the bed. 'I brought these back for you. Japanese, of course, but the real thing, nonetheless. I don't know if your scruples will allow it.'

Johnnie laughed with delight. 'That's very good of you, sit!'

They smoked for a while, enjoying the small pleasure of nicotine.

'There's a few men in Block C who've rigged up another shortwave,' Johnnie said. 'They haven't found anything interesting to listen to yet, but they're trying.'

'Trudy's got in with a bad sort,' Will said.

Johnnie looked at him. 'I'd thought as much.'

'She's in over her head, although of course she doesn't think so. She thinks she's doing well, surviving, keeping in with those she thinks will be helpful.'

'What does she need?'

'It's not what she needs. They're asking her for things. Asking her for things that might compromise others.'

'That's dangerous,' Johnnie said simply. 'She should watch out, and you too.'

'Yes,' Will said. 'We will.'

'It's almost time for supper,' Johnnie said, standing up. 'Our brilliant cooks have invented a new dish that is startlingly good. Banana peel fried in peanut oil. If you close your eyes, it tastes like mushrooms. I can't get enough of it.'

'Sounds good,' Will said. He was glad to stop talking about Trudy.

There were bad men.

Victor Chen, embracing Reggie Arbogast, both in Western dress, the blue tropical-wool suit, red tie. He had thrown a cocktail party for select Stanley survivors after the release. Not the riffraff, of course, but the doctors and the barristers and the company heads. He commiserated with them about what the war had done to them and their countries, and plied them with champagne.

And imagine this. Governor Mark Young coming back from his arrest in Malaya to the site of his humiliation and that of his country. The war is over. Every effort is made to glorify his triumphant return. An RAF Dakota, escorted by Beaufighters and Corsairs of 721 Squadron. A dramatic landing at Kai Tak. Motorcycle escort back to the Peninsula Hotel, and then the ceremony. Guns, uniforms, pomp. He shakes the hand of community leaders, is welcomed back with speeches. And see Victor Chen there, reading a speech of his own, about Hong Kong's fortitude and greatness of spirit.

Otsubo, reading documents in the dark, a table lamp illuminating only a small circle on the desk. His lips moving as he reads, Trudy and Dominick sitting next to each other on a bench in the office. They do not talk or look at each other. They wait for his signal.

There were dead men.

Was it his imagination? The sound of a man screaming. Will sat up in bed and tried to listen. The sound of the sea came in through the open window, but he did not hear anything else. A child cried out in its sleep. A mother shushed, drowsy.

In the morning, passing by, he discovered Johnnie gone from his room. The room was ripped apart, although the man was fastidious. The mattress lay half off the bed, sheets rumpled.

They brought Will to the interrogation rooms on the east side.

Johnnie, his eyes open, his shirt ripped and dirty. He lay on the floor of the room, a blanket thrown carelessly over him, with only a stool and a bare electric bulb. They had let Will in to see him, a warning, he supposed.

'He didn't talk,' they said. 'So this.'

'He didn't know anything,' Will said.

'You say,' they said.

'He didn't,' Will said.

'Do you?' they asked.

Dominick.

He screamed and begged and wheedled. Was prodded with the tip of a bayonet. His cheek scratched so blood beaded. Then a little finger broken with a mallet. Then all of the others. A week in the hole.

Denied everything. Confessed to everything.

Scratch the surface of a man. See what appears.

Wan Kee Liang, Trudy's father.

Dead in his mansion on the Praia Grande, body wasted away, urine soaking the sheets. A neglected corpse, not found for days.

There was a woman, disappeared.

Trudy clattering up the stairs of the gendarmerie headquarters on Des Voeux Road, stomach swollen, about to give birth.

Looking back to blow a kiss to Edwina Storch, who had accompanied her. Her eyes wistful, not condemning. We are condemned to repeat the past. Trudy's mother, gone. Trudy, gone.

10 May 1943

Edwina Storch was outside by suspect means, people whispered. She had parlayed a dead Finnish mother into a Free National passport and revoked her English citizenship. Mary Winkle had been corralled and sent to Stanley and Edwina sent her provisions as often as she could.

Spotting her on the street, Trudy went over to say hello. She had always had a soft spot for the idea of Edwina, although she had heard odd stories about her tenure at Glenealy Primary. She had apparently wielded her authority with a bit too much enthusiasm and not enough oversight. There had also been a story about a boy who had ended up in hospital after a too-vigorous disciplinary action, but that had been hushed up. He had been Eurasian, the father an English civil servant, the mother a local Chinese mistress, preferred but not legitimate. He hadn't returned to the school.

'You're out too?'

'Yes, thanks to my dear departed mother. Finland.'

'Any way you can. It's dreadful everywhere, though, isn't it?'

'Yes, but your relative Victor Chen has been very helpful to me. He has the magic touch and can procure anything!'

Trudy's face darkened. 'For the right price, I'm sure. I'm glad he's been helpful to someone.'

'You're cousins, aren't you?'

'Not exactly. I'm related to his wife, Melody. She's in California. She's going to have the baby there.'

Edwina's eyes flickered down to Trudy's swollen belly. 'That works out well, I suppose.' She lowered her voice. 'Until everything here is sorted out, I mean.'

'Yes, well,' Trudy said. 'I suppose it will be sorted out, won't it?'

'Of course,' said the headmistress.

'Well,' Trudy said, 'I hope I'll see you again soon in this strange new world of ours. I'm just on my way to meet Dominick for lunch.'

'Give him my best. And, yes, we will all get by.'

Trudy watched Edwina Storch walk away, with an odd look on her lovely face.

28 May 1953

In the late afternoon sun, Will grunted and moved in bed, his sleep disturbed. His head was damp, perspiring in the midday heat. Claire clapped her hands to see if she could rouse him, but Will just shifted again, whimpered.

She looked at his face, damp with sweat, his mouth moving almost imperceptibly in his sleep, and felt pity for him, for the first time.

'Touch me,' she says. Her voice is desperate. 'I want to feel real again.'

He embraces her, holding her as tightly as he can.

'You don't know what he made me do,' she says, muffled, into his shoulder. 'You don't know.'

'It's all right,' he says. 'Don't worry.'

'It's not all right!' she cries. 'It's not. You don't know. If you knew, you'd never want to see me again, never touch me again. You could never look at me straight in the face.' She draws back and looks at him, searches his eyes.

He is quiet. She winces. 'I knew it,' she says. 'I knew it. What did I expect?'

'I don't know what you need from me,' he says.

'This is why I loved you so much,' she says. 'Not only because you were so good and you didn't need anyone and I thought I might be able to make you need me, but because –' and she's crying, this Trudy he's never seen, this Trudy who's as fragile as gossamer and doesn't care who sees it. 'Because no one has ever loved me. They loved my money or the way I looked, or even the way I talked, because it made them think they knew what sort of woman I was. Or my father, he loved me because he had to. My mother loved me but then she left. No one loved me for me, or thought I was more than a good distraction at a party. It's the most trite thing in the world, isn't it? But you loved me. You liked the person I was. I really felt that. And it was a revelation to me. But then, after Otsubo and after I asked you to get me the information, I saw that you changed. Or that your feelings changed. You didn't love me in the same way any more. I was changed in your eyes. I wasn't that person you loved, no matter what.' She wipes her eyes. They are red and swollen.

'Oh, I must look awful,' she says suddenly, the old Trudy surfacing for a moment. 'So when that happened,' she takes a deep breath, 'when that happened, Will, it all snapped into place.

'I had been playing at being this person I am when I'm with you, and all it took was a few weeks' separation . . .'

'And a war,' he says. He doesn't know where the words are coming from, where this mechanically speaking person has sprung from.

'Yes, a few weeks' separation and a few well-equipped, menacing Japanese, and *poof*, I was back to being the old Trudy, who cared only about herself and her very malleable morals. And it felt right. It felt awful, but it felt right. I'm not who you think I am. I told you that before you left to go to the Parade Ground, and I wanted you to understand what I was saying. Did you? Did you?'

'I can't be the one to absolve you, Trudy.'

She slaps him.

His hand goes up to his cheek, like a woman.

'I want to kill you sometimes,' she said slowly. 'You and your so-called morals.'

She turns and tries to leave. He catches her elbow.

'Even that,' she says, 'is so false. It's not worthy of you. Be a man and show what you really feel for me.' She stares at him. He cannot move. 'I thought so.'

She turns back to the door.

'Thank you, Will,' she says quietly, with the back of her head to him. 'I know where I stand. Thank you for releasing me.'

She has always been too strong for him.

The way we hurt the ones we love.

The nightmares. The visions.

Men with their tongues burned, knees crushed, eyes gouged out, piled in heaps on the side of the road to Stanley, mothers covering their children's eyes.

Girls in rooms with blank faces, torn dresses, bloody chunks of hair torn from their scalps, bruised legs slick with men's fluids.

A door opened, a girl found tied to a desk, almost mute.

A body, sewn in hessian, arms crossed, tipped into the sea, making barely a splash as it sinks into the dark.

Ah Lok brushing Trudy's hair in front of her dressing-table. Methodical strokes, the glossy strands, the sound of bombs outside. Trudy applying lipstick. Her jasmine scent.

Dominick's refined head, in front of Otsubo's legs. His eyes meeting Will's, opening wide in panic, then deadening to grey. He didn't stop, just closed his eyes. Will, leaping back instinctively, yet knowing not to slam the door, having the presence of mind to conceal his intrusion.

A baby, born in the middle of the night, given away to an indifferent nurse, never seen by its sedated mother.

A young woman, just back from California, still puffy from childbirth, with empty eyes, arms filled with another's child.

277

2 June 1953

A good evening party always gave off a glow. Drinks were refilled quickly, the food was abundant, the servants silent and efficient, and the guests all secure in the knowledge that they had been chosen to attend, that many others had been excluded and might wish to be there in their place.

The Chens' coronation party gave off such a glow, even as Claire and Martin approached the front door.

Candles set in sand in small pots lit the driveway up to the house. Uniformed men whisked away the cars. Music tinkled in the background: the Chens had hired a string quartet, installed in the foyer, three sweaty Chinese men in dinner jackets and a tiny woman with a violin tucked under her chin. Their arms sawed back and forth, making the music seem more labour than art.

The hostess at the door, holding a glass of champagne, an apparition in a dress seemingly made of silver.

'Hello, hello,' trilled Melody. 'How lovely to see you all. Sceptres for everyone.' She gestured to a bowl filled with wands. 'We're all queen today.'

'You're so wicked!' rasped a rapier-thin blonde. 'Another day, another party. I've seen you, what, three times already this week? At the Garden Park, at Maisie's lunch, and at that little Italian in Causeway Bay? Who were you with, you minx? That was a very handsome man.'

'A cousin, of course.' Melody winked. 'Family's very important to me.'

'What nonsense we all talk!' said the blonde, and swept inside.

Martin and Claire stood together, waiting.

'Claire!' Melody said. 'I'm so glad you could come.'

'Thank you so very much for asking us,' Martin said.

Claire could see he was uncomfortable and was suddenly irritated with him for it. 'Nice to see you, Melody,' she said. 'What a lovely party.'

Martin went to fetch drinks and Claire stood in the sitting room she had been in so often before. It was alive, different, filled with people, talking, laughing, leaning towards each other confidentially.

'I don't know a soul,' Martin said, when he returned. 'Makes you wonder why they invited the piano teacher and her husband.'

'Martin!' Claire said. 'You don't need to feel like that.'

But Martin was right. The other guests at the party all knew each other and were not receptive to newcomers. Claire and Martin smiled and sipped their drinks in the corner, ignored.

Martin gave up and went out to the garden to look at the flowers and the view of the harbour. Claire stood by herself for a moment, then went to inspect the photographs on the mantelpiece.

Trudy was still there, in her swimsuit, laughing at the camera.

There was a group of four, talking about their last trip to London, the type with feathered hats and silk suits. Claire listened to their conversation, nursing her drink.

'But it was beastly. Service there is horrible after you've been in the Far East. You can't imagine what they serve you for dinner, cold and awful, and they're not in the least apologetic about it. The idea of service is dead in England. Grim, grim, grim. Much prefer it here where they take some pride in it.'

'And Poppy's in London now, isn't she? I wouldn't be surprised if she were at Westminster Abbey now.'

'Oh, she's horrible. I'm sure she's tried everything to get herself in. I suppose we'll have to hear about it when she comes back.'

Claire cleared her throat. One of the women, a buxom redhead, glanced over her shoulder, and continued talking.

From her position, Claire could see the two men facing her, and the two women with their backs to her. They were all English. She had expected the Chens to invite more locals.

'Is Su May coming today?' the redhead asked the other, a younger blonde with a bob. The men left to refresh their drinks.

'I don't think so. I think she and Melody had a falling-out.'

'Really? Do tell!'

'The usual. You know,' the blonde's voice dropped, 'Melody is just impossible, these days, so forgetful and rude. You know, I threw a lunch for the Garden Club on Thursday, and she didn't let me know if she was able to come, never appeared and then never said anything about it! I don't know what's going on with her.'

'The OBE's gone to her head!'

Even lower. 'Isn't it funny how the most local people are the most anglophile?'

'I know, darling. Look around! We could be in Mayfair!'

'But you know, it's unusual for locals to host anything at home. I think this is the first Chinese house I've been in since I arrived here.'

'Victor is good at hedging his bets. He's having another party tomorrow, for an entirely different crew, but at the club, with mah-jong afterwards and everything.'

'His own kind.'

'I don't know how Melody puts up with that man. He's the most obvious, venal person Charles has ever dealt with, he says.'

'But, you know, I've wondered. They say, *opium* . . .'

The two women stopped talking as another woman passed by and said hello. They swooped and rustled and pecked at each other like birds.

'Lavinia!'

'Maude!'

'Harriet!'

Claire slipped away.

Later, she found herself talking to Annabel, a frosted champagne-blonde American from Atlanta, Georgia, who was in Hong Kong for her husband, Peter, who was with the State Department.

'What's your story, darlin'?' Annabel asked. Her eyes were bright with alcohol, her hair in a beehive.

'I am here with my husband, who's with the Water Department,' Claire said.

'All these departments!' Annabel hooted. 'The state! Water! Make sure it's in the pipes!'

'Er, yes,' Claire said. She never knew how to talk to Americans, who were so informal, or what to say to their odd exclamations.

'And what do you do to pass the time? Do you have children?'

'No,' Claire said. 'Do you?'

'I have four, all under five. I keep popping them out and Peter's ready to strangle me. I tell him, "I wasn't the only one involved here, you know!" At least in Hong Kong, we have all the amahs. Back home, it's not like this.'

'Have you been long in Hong Kong?' Claire asked politely.

'Three years. Had Jack here, thank God he was a Caesarean . . .' the woman chattered on and on, buoyed by her own effervescence, and Claire listened, glad to have an excuse to stand quietly and not look awkward.

Martin found her later, waiting by the cloakroom. 'Hello,' he said. 'Ready to leave soon?'

She shrugged. 'I'll be back in a moment.' She ducked into the cloakroom and splashed water on her face. She felt as if she was waiting for something to happen.

* * *

Later, she heard the redhead and the blonde, Maude and Lavinia, discuss her.

'Who was that woman lurking around?'

'I think I heard Melody say she's the piano teacher.'

'Really?'

'Pretty, though, don't you think?'

'In a wan, blonde sort of way, I suppose.'

The sound of a light slap. 'You're such a bitch!' Laughter.

'It's that skin, you know. Drives men wild.'

'Yes, it just goes, though. It's wasted on the young.'

A sudden commotion near the door. A maid had fainted in the heat. The houseboy was summoned and carried her out.

'Bloody hot,' a man in a boater said.

'Always,' rejoined another. 'Haven't you heard?'

Into this senseless conversation, Will strode, unexpected. He stopped in front of them, the first people he saw.

'Did you hear?' he said, with shock on his face. His voice was not loud but everyone heard him. 'Reggie Arbogast's shot himself.'

The two men gaped.

'The man who had the parties on the Peak?' Claire cried, before she could help it. In her simple mind, she still imagined that money might buy happiness. A few people turned to stare at her; most were still in shock.

The buzz rose audibly, immediate.

'His poor wife.'

Sotto voce: 'Regina? I wonder he didn't shoot her instead.'

'The children?'

'All back in England. They'll send a telegram, of course. What a tragedy.'

'When I saw him at Fanling, he seemed rather down at the club-house, drinking. Rather the worse for wear after I finished my round.'

But Will was there for a reason. He looked around the room for Victor and walked over to him. 'You bastard,' he said, and swung at the man. 'You let him think all this time he was the one who broke.'

The room quieted immediately.

Victor Chen staggered back but did not fall. He came up, holding his jaw and tried to smile. 'Now, Will, you come here for the first time in days, then take a swing at me? You've been quite the absent driver.'

'You're despicable.'

Around them, people were spellbound, unable to move, even though manners dictated they should leave. A few, more decorous than the others, inched towards the door.

'You're behind all of this. You brokered the damn Crown Collection back to the Chinese government under the guise of patriotism, didn't you? You didn't care who suffered, just that you enriched yourself and got in with the new people. And you know what your Chinese government did with it? They probably smashed it to shards, as representative of bourgeois values!' His voice rose.

'The Chinese have the right to their own history,' Victor said stiffly. 'It should never have been taken from them in the first place.'

'You are such a hypocrite,' Will continued, as if he hadn't heard. 'When you were reading history at Cambridge, you were all for jolly old England, punting and strawberries, but when it suited your purpose here, you became the model Chinese, currying favour with the Nationalists, the Communists, whoever would receive you. You don't know whether you're coming or going, old man.' He stepped closer to Victor, menacing.

'I wouldn't expect you to understand, Will,' Victor said, adjusting his shirt. 'You least of all. You come to Hong Kong, find your little nest of cronies and your half-breed filly, and all's right with the world. Bloody British on their moral high horse. They poisoned half of China with opium for their own gain.'

'It doesn't matter any more, Victor. You're doomed.'

'You've always been dramatic, Will,' Victor said. 'Just like Trudy. Sentimental too. Those qualities are luxuries, I assure you.'

Will stood still for a moment. 'You aren't worth it,' he said finally. 'You will never be worth anything.'

Suddenly Melody was beside him. 'Will,' she pleaded, 'we're not enemies here. We loved the same people. We all had tragedies during the war. Can't you forgive, just a little?' She looked at him, but he didn't move. She shifted, then for some reason changed direction towards Claire, and appealed to her. 'Surely you must understand, Claire. Life is so complicated and we make decisions that are difficult.'

Claire, caught off-guard, was exposed. Martin was there. The whole world was there. The women who had been talking about her stared; she was reborn in their eyes – someone worth seeing.

Now she was being unveiled in front of the world as somehow connected to their hosts, and to Will, a part of this puzzle. She was unused to the attention. She remembered the moment at the Chens' dinner party when everyone had stared at her, waiting for her witty rejoinder, a sign that she belonged with them – a response that had never come. She thought of the feeling she often experienced when she was with Will – when she was someone else entirely, the other Claire who had never had a chance to surface, a Claire who had opinions and said things that people listened to, someone who was visible. She thought of all these things, and looked back at the sea of faces as they waited for her to answer Melody.

First, she nodded, as unobtrusively as possible. She blushed, looked down. Edwina Storch's pale, sweaty face rose in her mind. *You must rise to the occasion.* Yes, but in a different way from what the old woman had imagined.

Claire looked up from the floor, raised her eyes. 'Melody, we all make choices but we have to stand by them and acknowledge responsibility if we find ourselves on the wrong end.' Her voice quavered but the attention of every person in the room was on her.

She felt Martin staring at her, bewildered. She couldn't look at him. She focused instead on what she was saying. 'I don't know what's going on here, but I do know that Will is telling you something important.'

She wanted to be generous, she wanted to understand. The Queen, being crowned in England on this very day, surely would expect it of her. She wanted so badly to be merciful and kind, and to touch Melody gently on the shoulder and tell her it would be all right, that things would work out, that she herself would make sure of it.

Claire was thinking of all of these things, feeling the warm glow of benevolence.

But then Melody's face twitched.

It was quick, but Claire saw it. This woman, Melody was thinking, is my daughter's piano teacher! She is someone I hired to teach Locket how to strike some black and white keys on a musical instrument. She is simple, English, not someone from whom I need to ask favours.

And then it was gone, erased by the woman's innate practicality. But it was too late. Claire had seen it already. The heat rose from Claire's chest to her head. She was the one who didn't need anything from anyone. She turned to her lover. 'Will,' she said, emboldened. 'I know you don't –'

'This doesn't concern you, Claire,' he interrupted.

He was barely seeing her. But she knew him well now. 'I know,' she said. 'But Melody has a point.' She knew this would inflame him further.

'Don't be absurd. You have no idea what's going on.'

'But –'

'Out,' he said, pointing to the door.

Part of her thrilled to Will's command of the situation. He was owning her, finally. She heard a faint 'I say', that sounded as if it had come from her husband. She closed her eyes. She couldn't see Martin now, couldn't see his bewildered, humiliated face, and have to sort out how that made her feel. She felt the dull throb of the blood coursing through her head and the weight of all those eyes on her, and she opened her own, looked at the blurry sea of faces, and then she thought about what she should do and everything seemed to be happening in slow motion, as if she were under water. She blinked, and everything was still blurred. A maid cried out from the kitchen, unaware of the drama going on at the party, she heard glasses clink as they were assembled on a tray by another unsuspecting servant, a fly buzzed terribly near her ear, and she saw a red-headed woman slowly, slowly, sweep her hand through her hair, all the while looking at her. All this took place as if it were in a room far away from her, enclosed in glass.

In the end, she stood up a little straighter, took a deep breath, and then she did the only thing she could think of doing at that moment, that particular instant: she just walked away. It was cowardly and messy and left much to be dealt with later, but her heart felt full and tender and she didn't see that she had any choice. She walked away from the gaping women and the perplexed men, and went directly to the door and put her hand on the knob. She hesitated, she didn't know why, and then she turned the door handle – she remembered always the cool metal in her palm – and she walked out. She didn't look at Martin. She couldn't. She didn't even look at Will. She walked outside, to a new and unknown life.

3 July 1953

Later, she heard what had happened. Women who had never acknowledged her presence rang her up or stopped her in town, ostensibly to ask how she was or to tell her what had happened after she had left, but really to find out her connection to the situation.

'They said he went out on the tennis court and put the gun in his mouth. Very messy. And you know, he only had the one hand. The hook, of course. Quite tricky. The amah found him. Had to be taken to hospital herself with the shock. They always want to be a part of it, don't they?'

'Poor Regina,' said Claire. She remembered the party she had been to, the one at which she had met Will, with the Pimm's and the boy and his father hitting the ball back and forth in their tennis whites. She tried to imagine Reggie Arbogast sprawled on the grass, blood running out of his mouth. 'Does anyone know why? Other than what was said?'

'He'd not been himself,' they would say. 'Blamed himself for letting the Collection disappear. And couldn't stand all the fuss with the coronation, the patriotism. Made him feel awful. And I think he felt he was in some way responsible for the death of Trudy Liang.' A pause. 'And did you *know* Trudy? Or Dominick?'

'No,' she would say. 'They were gone before I even arrived. I found out only recently who they were.'

'Dominick was just terrible. He went through women like they were used handkerchiefs, although they say he liked both sides, if you know what I mean . . .'

Claire would wait patiently.

'And the Chens? They were just livid about how Will ruined their party. I can't believe you just left, darling, it was so dramatic! Melody was in hysterics, Victor tried to be cool, and Will, well, he controlled himself and left not long after you, all of us gaping like fools in his wake. I'd never seen anything like it. What a scandal! Were you close?'

'I don't know much about that,' Claire would say. 'You see, I was teaching Locket but didn't have much contact with the Chens. They'd always been kind to me, though.'

'Oh.' A sigh, down the telephone line, disappointed. 'Well, they're really quite something.' A pause. 'And are you . . . all right?'

'As well as can be expected,' she would say, or something of the sort.

'And . . .' only a few of them could bring themselves to say it '. . . and Martin?'

And she would not answer, and the deepening silence would embarrass them into hurriedly filling it with small-talk and fervent wishes to see her soon, to have tea, or to go for a walk.

They rang off shortly afterwards and never called again. She wondered at their transparency.

The government wrapped up its investigation into the disappearance of the Crown Collection. Reggie Arbogast was posthumously honoured for his services to the British Empire. Regina Arbogast sold the big house on the Peak to a Shanghainese merchant looking to relocate to Hong Kong and set sail for England. Victor Chen was not officially mentioned.

5 July 1953

From a distance she saw him approaching, a spindly figure with a cane. Hard to imagine this man was the enigma who had ignited such desire in her a mere two weeks ago.

But then he came close, his pale, narrow face, his untidy hair, and he spoke, and she felt his pull all over again.

'Claire,' he said, kissing her cheek. 'Sit down.' Almost avuncular. She felt rebuffed. He always set the tone of their meetings.

They sat on a bench overlooking the harbour. They were on the Peak, where they had arranged to meet, thinking they would not run into anyone they knew, for different reasons than before, and they had been right. They were alone in the twilight hour. The warm wind blew, not unpleasantly.

'I came here with Trudy sometimes,' he said. 'That iron railing was there when I was here with her. I touched it then and I can touch it now, but the circumstances are so different. I'm so different. Do you ever think about that?'

He was a different man, as if a great weight had been lifted off his shoulders. She could feel his lightness. 'Will,' she started.

'And what will you do?' he said, as if she had not spoken.

'I don't know,' she said. 'I've been in touch with my parents but they don't seem too eager to take me in. Something about the cost and my father's pension. I don't have a job, or any means of getting one. So I don't know.' She said this simply, not to suggest obligation on his part.

'I see,' he said.

'And you?' she asked.

'I don't know either,' he said. 'It seems impossible to stay here, and it seems impossible to leave.'

'Yes,' she said.

'So here we are,' he said. 'Two people without places to go.'

'Do you think I should continue with Locket?'

'They haven't said anything?'

'We haven't spoken since the party.'

'Well,' he considered, 'if they haven't told you to stop, I would go. But then,' he grinned, 'I'm perverse.'

'What was it you took from the grave in Macau?' She had been wondering.

'Oh,' he said. 'Trudy had a deposit box at the bank and she had always told me that Dominick or I could gain access to it. After she died, I had a letter from her solicitors telling me I could pick up the key after the war when she had been declared legally dead. She had told me about another key to the same box before the war but I had never tried to find it. And when I received it from the solicitors, I didn't know where to put it. So I hid it in Dominick's grave. Thought no one would ever go there. And it felt right. A little dramatic, but right. And I was always looking for what felt right.'

'What was in the box?'

'Some bank books, financial papers. But what she wanted me to have were the documents, the letters, the things that showed what she had done for Otsubo during the war, and what others had done.'

'Others including Victor Chen?'

'Yes,' he said simply.

'And what did you do with the contents of the box?'

'I had them sent to the right people. Anonymously.'

'But Victor knew it was you.'

'He knew I was the only one that might have access to that sort of information.'

'Are you in any trouble?'

'I don't think so,' he said. 'But I've been wrong before.'

They sat together, strangely comfortable.

'The thing is,' he said, 'Victor Chen was not entirely wrong. The British government didn't, doesn't, have the right to own all those irreplaceable Chinese artefacts. They stole them in the first place, although they would dispute the verb. But the way Victor went about it . . .' He shook his head. 'That man only knows one way to do things.

'And I didn't abandon Trudy, not totally. Otsubo stopped signing me out of the camp when he realized I wasn't giving him anything. But there was never a particular reason for me not to get out. Trudy would have got me out altogether if I'd wanted her to. That's one of my deepest regrets. That it just kind of . . . fizzled out. She deserved better than that. And I don't know, really, what happened to her. I don't know. I suppose I could find out. There are only too many people who would be delighted to tell me all about it. Including Victor.'

'But what could you have done?'

'Anything but what I did,' he said. 'Anything but the nonsense I did in camp – form committees, campaign for hot water or more sheets!' His voice rose, grew violent. 'I was a coward, a coward. I didn't do anything to help her. The woman I loved. I did nothing. Hid behind what I pretended was honour.'

'Did Trudy ever . . .' Claire couldn't finish the question.

'She never said anything. She never reproached or challenged me. She was always who she said she was. She never pretended to be anything else. That was the beauty of her.'

He straightened his back.

'She behaved as if she believed me when I said I couldn't help her. But she was so clever – she saw the real situation. Yet she didn't say anything. She forgave me.'

He stood up, walked over to a tree and absently snapped off a leaf. He split it in half, then half again, scattering the pieces on the ground.

'Hong Kong is always so damn green,' he said. 'Don't you wish for some absence of colour sometimes? Some English grey, a touch of fog?'

Claire nodded. He was unravelling, slowly, and she wanted to give him some room.

He continued: 'Sometimes I hate her for that. That she let me be a coward. It was cruel, in the end.' Trudy would have despised a man who wept, he knew. 'I have this image,' he said slowly. 'This image of Trudy running around outside, frantic, not knowing what to do, not having a centre, just desperate. I feel like she was desperate. But she didn't come to me for help. Not after the first time. When I said no, she never asked again.'

Claire reached for his hand, resting on the top of his cane. He didn't yield and she settled for placing her hand on top of his.

'And she wouldn't have had anyone to confide in. She was totally alone. And I made her that way.'

The air was damp with the ever-present Hong Kong humidity. A drop of perspiration slowly wended its way down Claire's back. She willed him to look at her, to acknowledge she was there, a part of this, but he stared out at the harbour, his eyes blank. Slowly, she realized: his new lightness was not just relief at the passing of his burden. There was emptiness there too.

He sees Trudy, waving on the steps of the Toa as he gets into the car that will drive him back to Stanley. She has a wistful look on her face, her amber hair lit from behind, the setting sun sinking into the Hong Kong horizon. Pregnant madonna. She blows him a kiss, suddenly winks. He hates how she does that – always turns a serious moment into a joke. But this is how she lives, how she survives. This is the animal she is. She had warned him.

Arbogast broke, she had told him, and he had nodded. 'Yes, I saw him afterwards,' he said.

'But you know,' she says, her voice slightly panicked, 'it wasn't the correct information. Otsubo is furious. But there was evidence that it was there. An old storage building in Mong Kok. Someone else got to it first.'

'How did Otsubo find out that Arbogast would know where it was?' he asks.

She hesitates. 'I think Victor,' she says finally. 'Although I have nothing to back that up. He has a finger in every pie, that man.'

'Be careful,' he says.

'I know.' She nods. 'Otsubo's tired of me now, anyway. I think we've run our course.'

'What does that mean for you?' he asks, careful to mask his relief.

She laughs. 'Oh, nothing good, I'm afraid. Just that I'm under his thumb as much as ever but I can no longer coddle him out of his bad moods.'

'Do you want to come into the camp now?'

'Again, with the camp! You cannot cage this bird, my love. I've grown used to dark, dangerous freedom and all its attendant humiliations.'

'But you could –'

'I am in the process of lining up another . . . sponsor,' she says slowly. 'Or one is being lined up for me. So don't you worry.'

Tears spring to his eyes, hot, unexpected. He feels he might die if she sees them.

'I should go,' he says.

'Yes.'

He turns away. She catches his arm, studies his face. 'Every time I say goodbye to you, I wonder if it's *au revoir* or *adieu*. You know what I mean?'

He nods.

'You've too much power over me,' she says lightly. 'I have to pretend that it doesn't matter, that you don't matter. How did that happen?'

He looks at her, his love, her face ruddy with pregnancy, slender ankles swollen, this woman, a survivor, six months with an unwanted child, and finds he cannot forgive her this last transgression. It is easier to brand her a villain and go back to camp, play the victim, lick his wounds. This is what he does. There is no glory in it, but there is survival. And, he realizes, that is what they are playing at now.

27 May 1953

Edwina Storch had told her everything, sure that she would pass on the information to Will.

Edwina's voice in her head, the old woman pouring tea in the dark club.

'Trudy redoubled her efforts to be indispensable to Otsubo. She knew what kind of asset she had in him. I knew Otsubo because he had been of some help to me in getting my pass, and I kept in touch and tried to help him in whatever small matters I could.' She had peered at Claire over her spectacles. 'You understand, I was not collaborating with the enemy. I thought I would be of better use to England and everyone else here if I kept abreast of the situation, and there was no reason to alienate the man.' She took off her glasses and polished them.

'And when Trudy started to prove herself really indispensable to Otsubo – you know the girl knew everything about Hong Kong and all the skeletons in the closet – her cousin, Dominick, whom I never liked, started to get jealous. It was as if they were both vying for Otsubo's favour, and there was only room for one. Dominick was a terrible person. I don't know if you know anything about him but he was just awful. A sadistic, small man who always felt that life owed him everything. They were both Otsubo's flunkeys and ran around getting him meetings with Chinese leaders and keeping him informed about everything that went on in the Chinese community, and even in the small European community that was still outside. Dominick made some money buying and selling necessities. He would buy cheaply through his sources and charge exorbitant rates to the local market. Most distasteful. He'd also try to get information on who was helping whom and report back to Otsubo. Needless to say, this made him less than popular with their old crowd, but he was certainly the best fed. Dominick was more open about it than Trudy. People stopped talking to him.'

Claire interrupted: 'Did you have to do any work? How did you survive?'

Edwina pursed her lips. 'I've always preferred not to dwell on the unpleasantness of the past.'

Claire almost laughed aloud, but saw that the other woman was unaware of the enormous irony of what she was saying.

'There was all this business of the Japanese in Hong Kong trying to enrich themselves. It's quite common after a victory but there was a lot of chatter about the Crown Collection, which included some extremely rare and priceless porcelain. Otsubo found out I knew a bit about the subject and called me in to get some information. I told him what little I knew.'

Edwina's eyes sparkled. 'Actually, I knew quite a bit more than I let on but didn't think it was an opportune time.' She paused. 'What if I were to tell you, Claire, that the governor had just flown into Hong Kong on the eve of the war.' She sat very still, as if in a trance. 'He was stepping into a very tricky situation and he knew it. He had just been sworn in and was taking over a colony that was, from most intelligence reports, going to be conquered in short order. He had orders from London, one of which was to secure the Crown Collection, stored in Government House. His strategy –'

She laughed, interrupting herself. 'Interesting story, isn't it? Politicians are so stupid. No sense at all. His strategy was to tell three different people where he would send it so that it would survive the war. Communications to London were already compromised so he had to think of another way.' She looked at Claire. 'I was one of the three.'

'What an honour,' Claire murmured. She imagined the scene: Edwina Storch summoned to Government House, given tea, scones, a cordial reception from a man who had little knowledge of his new territory, still settling into his private quarters, getting to know the servants, his enormous task, Edwina condescending as only a woman of her age and experience could be. How did she get away with it for so long and without challenge?

'They knew I had been a long time in Hong Kong and knew a great deal about the people, the history, the place, which I do of course,' Edwina mused. 'And the other two? Well, I found out who they were. We weren't supposed to know, but this kind of information gets round. The governor was nervous and told a few others our identities. As chatter grew, it all came to light. One was Reggie Arbogast. Do you know him?'

Claire nodded. 'Slightly.'

'He turned a bit queer after the war.' Her mouth grew set, grim. An unforgiving expression settled on her face. 'And a silly cow of a wife, Regina.'

'And the third?' Claire couldn't help asking.

Edwina looked surprised. 'I thought you would have guessed. The third was Victor Chen.'

April 1942

When it rains in Hong Kong, the world stops. The deluge is so overwhelming, so strong, that the city disappears under a sheet of grey water and people vanish like panicked rats, scurrying into doorways, shops, restaurants. Inside, they shake off the water, ordering coffee or browsing through dresses while they wait for the rain to stop.

Trudy and Victor Chen sit inside Chez Sophie, a small French restaurant in Causeway Bay and watch the downpour.

'It never seems clean here, even after the rain,' Trudy says. 'The water washes the grime off the streets but it's back two instants later. Hong Kong is just *dirty*. Always has been. Can't live anywhere else, though. This filthy city is home.' She rubs the arm of her chair, red velvet, the fabric shiny from constant use. 'I've always loved this restaurant,' she says. 'When I was a child, Father used to bring me here each week for Sunday lunch, and I'd buy a new dress to wear.'

Victor harrumphs. 'Every week?' he says. 'You were spoiled, weren't you?'

'Spoiled?' she asks. 'Don't worry, Victor. I'm sure this war will beat every last shred of privilege out of me.'

'People will show their true colours.'

'They already are, Victor, dear cousin, and people are already commenting on it. I've heard people call us collaborators. Isn't that what you call those who get too close to the conquerers?'

'Collaborator is a dirty word, Trudy. I'd be careful how you use it.' Victor sips cognac, his face reddening.

Trudy lounges in her chair, sleek in a tan wool skirt and ivory blouse. A half-empty coffee cup sits in front of her. 'But that's what we are, aren't we, Victor?' Trudy asks, needling him. 'Isn't that what they call people like us?'

'Don't be naïve,' he snaps. 'You're teaching English and etiquette. You're basically a governess to the good general, educating him in the ways of the Western world that he is so interested in, despite himself. And I am merely doing my best to provide a smooth transition so that our people do not have to suffer. Never say something so stupid again. Not everything is black and white. Should we spite ourselves and alienate the very people who might help us through this difficult time? Trudy, you are no longer a child.'

'But Otsubo is so . . .'

'You do not have to concern yourself with him other than to give him English lessons and try to satisfy his requests.' His face turns shrewd. 'I would say you should comply with every request, no matter what it is or how veiled.'

'He is a pig,' she says quietly. The waiter comes and silently refills her cup. She adds sugar and milk, takes a sip.

Victor studies her face. 'You've changed,' he says. 'Is it the Englishman? Has he inculcated you with his timeless values, the right way to do things, honour and all the other rubbish the English are so good at spewing? And yet, when it comes to their responsibilities, they always find a reason why they can't fulfil them, and they always sound so good when they do. They've refined it to an art. They sound good and do nothing.'

'Who don't you hate, Victor?' She thinks privately that his speech is undermined by his Oxford accent.

'You are more Chinese than anything else, Trudy. You will always be viewed as foreign in any other country. You belong in Hong Kong.'

He lights a cigarette, doesn't offer her one. She knows he's always disapproved of her smoking in public. He thinks women should be demure and quiet when outside the home.

'These are going to be currency too, now, you know,' he says, inspecting the lit tip. 'Things are going to be different, and getting a foothold in the new world will be like building foundations on quicksand. You have to be adaptable.'

Trudy puts her hands on the table and leans forward. If she could, she would bare her teeth and hiss. 'I'm busy, Victor. Why did you want to see me?'

'I just want to be sure we're on the same side,' he says. 'Being as we're family and all.'

Trudy laughs. 'You've never felt so familial before, I'm sure.' She hesitates. 'Maybe I'll go into Stanley instead. Will said –'

'Don't be idiotic, Trudy. You can accomplish more out here than you can in a prison. And make no mistake, that's what it is in there, a prison. Why would you give it up?'

'But Will . . .'

Victor laughs. 'I didn't know you were so sentimental, my dear. And, of course, there's the matter of your father.'

Trudy tenses. 'What of him?'

'I didn't want to say anything but . . . he's not well.'

Trudy's face doesn't move. 'He's never said anything to me.'

Victor looks at her as if she were stupid. 'And you think he would?'

'I don't believe you.'

Victor waves his hand. 'It doesn't matter to me in the least.' He catches himself. 'Of course, I'm concerned for his welfare and I thought you had a right to know.'

In the restaurant, the pianist comes in and sits down. He starts to practise. Trudy and Victor sit across from each other, each unwilling to make the next move.

'Debussy,' Trudy says.

'Yes.'

They sit, two chess players, looking at anything but each other. Victor smokes his cigarette down to the stub and crushes it out in the crystal ashtray. He speaks first, oblique.

'Player's Navy Cut are already hard to get. The Japanese are bringing in their own brands, Rising Sun and low-grade tobacco like that. It's going to be all about transport and access to imports. The channels will get narrower. Some goods will be expensive.'

Trudy looks up. 'Goods like, say, medicine, you mean?'

'Well, of course. That's just one example. Good-quality medicine. American and British pharmaceutical companies are certainly not going to be shipping to conquered territories. At least, not legally. People will have to be clever.'

'You've always been clever, Victor. And criminally unsubtle.'

He throws up his hands. 'I've always been called something. But I'm just trying to make sure you understand the entire situation. *Food* is going to be in very short supply. It's not just a matter of silk stockings and good port.'

Trudy stands up. 'Excuse me, I must powder my nose.' She walks gracefully over to the ladies' and the door closes silently behind her.

Victor waits, tapping his cigarette packet on the tablecloth.

When she emerges, she is fresh-faced, with a new coat of lipstick, woman's armour.

'People will think we're in love, Victor. This illicit meeting in an out of the way restaurant.' She smiles at him.

'Having an affair?'

'You don't find me appealing?'

301

Victor considers her teasing more seriously than he should. 'You're like a sister to me, Trudy. Melody has always been very fond of you. She asked me to take care of you while she was gone, make sure you were all right.'

'That's funny. She told me to go to Macau, be with my father.'

'He does need someone to take care of him.'

'He has Leung.' Her father's devoted houseboy, with him for forty years. 'He'll take better care of him than I ever could.'

'Didn't you hear?'

Trudy's face falls. 'No, what?'

'Leung was knifed in the lung. Seems he was trying to prevent some Japanese private from taking your father's Rolex. It was touch and go for a while, but then he died. These soldiers know just where to put the knife.'

'Father would have told me,' Trudy says. 'He would have contacted me.'

'You know how it is with your father,' Victor says soothingly. 'He doesn't want to be a burden to you. But don't worry, Trudy. I took care of it. I have a woman from Shanghai living with your father, cooking and taking care of him. He didn't want you to worry. I didn't want you to worry. I only brought it up because . . . '

There is a long pause. Trudy looks up and smiles at Victor, brittle. She reaches slowly across the table for the cigarettes and takes one. Victor does not offer a light so she goes into her handbag and gets out a lighter. Her hands are shaking. She inhales deeply and blows the smoke at Victor.

'Otsubo,' she says. 'He adores me. Thinks I'm some exotic flower.'

'I know,' Victor says. 'You should make sure that lasts.' He looks at her searchingly with narrowed eyes, then turns away, satisfied. 'I'm having a garden party next week,' he says. 'You will be the hostess. We are family, so people won't talk. Bring Otsubo and tell him to invite whoever he wants.'

Trudy nods, so slight a movement it is almost unnoticeable.

'I think we've finished here,' Victor says. 'But one more thing, Trudy. When you decide to do something, you should do it all the way. There's nothing worse than indecision, or ambivalence. That's the kind of thing that endangers lives. But you're a smart girl – you know what I'm talking about.' He tosses some banknotes on the table and walks out.

27 May 1953

Claire sat in the library with the retired headmistress, stunned.

'Victor Chen?' she asked. 'He was one of the three? Why didn't he just –'

'Oh,' Edwina said. 'He didn't want to sell the information too cheaply. Nothing if not a good businessman, that fellow. Very misinformed about him, the government was. I could have told them he'd sell his own mother if the price was right. They thought it would be good to have a Chinese person in the know, in case the British were all imprisoned or killed. And they thought he was loyal to Britain because he had been educated there. He found out that I knew and that Reggie knew, but Reggie was in Stanley and he knew he'd never say anything. Me, he didn't know so well. So he invited me over a few times. I've never been so lavishly entertained and skilfully interrogated about my intentions. But I knew better. We played cat-and-mouse for a while and he always kept tabs on me.'

'Did Trudy know about this?'

'I don't think so, or she wouldn't have run around so hard, trying to procure the information. I think Victor took pleasure in seeing her work so diligently to get something he already had. And Dominick too. The two of them were something to see. Victor watched them for a while, and then I think he decided they were getting a little too influential and decided to do something about it. He was really the one pulling the strings. They were just his puppets.'

Edwina paused.

'Would you care for a scone?' she asked. 'They're the best in Hong Kong. Made by a Mr Wong – I trained him myself. He's the best Chinese English baker in the colony.'

'No, thank you,' Claire said.

Edwina broke off a piece, spread jam on it and popped it into her mouth.

'Mm,' she said. 'I've lived here so long but still can't get by without my tea and scones.

'So, Victor Chen started to get irritated with the way Trudy and Dominick were carrying on. They were being rather conspicuous and too cosy in their relationship with Otsubo. It was quite unseemly. So, he started to sow a little unrest between them. He wanted them more under his thumb than Otsubo's. He also included Dominick in his business, which was flourishing. He was supplying Japanese troops in Guangzhou with petrol and basic supplies and making an absolute fortune. What Dominick had been doing before was small beer and he told him so. He had factories and enormous resources behind him. Then he told Dominick that Trudy was going behind his back and trying to get the information without him and, of course, Dominick believed him. So Dominick started to do things that would undermine Trudy. He told Otsubo that Trudy knew where the Crown Collection was but just wasn't telling him. Victor was only too happy to back this up.'

'Did Dominick know that Victor knew?'

'No,' scoffed Edwina. 'Victor didn't tell anyone. I was the only one who knew. But you know, the funny thing is . . .' Edwina's eyes looked faraway '. . . it was very odd. It was as if Trudy knew what was going on but she didn't do anything about it. She had already given up. It was as if she didn't care any more and was just going through the motions.'

Someone opened the door and looked in. Edwina Storch didn't look up. The door closed silently.

'And so Otsubo decided that Trudy was too much trouble and he'd grown tired of her. He'd moved on to Dominick at any rate. They were lovers as well. He liked anything and everything, that man. He was insatiable. A real pig. So he used this as an excuse to get rid of her. And he asked me to help. But the odd thing was that nothing he did seemed to faze her. She was untouchable and it drove him crazy. After she fell pregnant, he told her he was giving her to his lieutenant, that he was done with her, but she went quietly. She did everything he said and didn't give him any satisfaction. I think he wanted her to suffer. So he passed her round – she was an heiress, you understand, had been given the best of everything from birth, knew everyone. I don't know why she did it. She just did not care any more.' For the first time, Edwina Storch seemed saddened.

'So how did she die?' Claire asked.

'Dominick had told Otsubo that Trudy knew where the Crown Collection was. Trudy denied it. Otsubo thought she might confide in me because I was English so he asked me to bump into her, as it were, so that we could rekindle our acquaintance. It was easy because he knew where she was all the time. So, Trudy and I bumped into each other regularly.'

'Did you feel any scruples about doing this for such a man?' Claire asked.

'Not at all,' Edwina said instantly. 'You have to understand, Claire, that no one was a saint in any of this. Otsubo was the enemy but Trudy, Dominick, Victor, they were all getting into bed with him, so as far as I was concerned, they were all the enemy. They didn't have anyone's interest at heart except their own.'

'It was almost your patriotic duty,' Claire said quietly.

'Yes,' Edwina seized on this idea. 'I thought this was one way I could help my country. I knew Victor Chen would give up the Crown Collection at some point. It was just at what price. And I thought if I kept an eye on it, I might be of some help in tracking it down. So, what I did was . . . I told Otsubo that Trudy did know.'

'What?' Claire's mouth hung open. 'But . . .'

Edwina stiffened. 'I thought it was the best approach. The man had to be led down the wrong path so he wouldn't find the right one.'

'But you assured her death by telling this to Otsubo.' It was out before she could smother the thought.

'So simple,' Edwina said, 'so black and white for you, is it? The truth is, my dear, that Trudy was doomed from the start. The way she was behaving. She wouldn't have lasted another month. So, Otsubo had two sources telling him that Trudy knew but was keeping it from him. He asked me to escort her to his office. It was very odd the way he wanted to handle it. Must be Japanese. Odd people, you know. She knew something wasn't right because she went there all the time and didn't need me to escort her, but she was very polite. When I arrived at her door, she let me in and we sat down for tea. We had a nice chat. And then we walked over together and she went into the building by herself. I told her he was expecting her. And that was it. No one ever saw her again.'

The room seemed colder. Claire folded her arms across her chest. 'So . . .' The thought hung in the air.

'No, my dear,' said Edwina. 'The Japanese are quite unsentimental about that sort of thing and don't leave witnesses. I think they may have let her have the baby but I don't know what happened after that.'

'And Dominick, her cousin?'

Edwina shook her head. 'That one was never going to come to a good end. He got in over his head. He was used by everyone. Victor installed him at a company he had formed called Macau Supplies.

He made sure Dominick's name was on all the legal papers so he could keep his hands clean. But it didn't matter. I think Dominick got greedy, started skimming, and the Japanese found out. It was never clear what happened to him either but at least there was a body. He turned up in a canal in the seedy part of town. All of his fingers had been cut off, save one – an eleventh he had, apparently a birth defect.'

'Oh.' Claire exhaled slowly. It was so much to take in. 'And whatever did happen to the Crown Collection?'

'Well, you can never let it be said that Victor Chen isn't clever. He had an inkling that the secret might leak, either through me or Arbogast, so he had the Collection taken away and stored somewhere else. And then he intimated to Otsubo that he had found out Arbogast knew where it was. So he manipulated the situation masterfully. He had Otsubo owing him a favour then, you see. And Arbogast never knew. They took his hand. He was lucky they didn't do more. So Arbogast broke, as many men would have under that sort of . . . duress, and when Otsubo sent his men, the Collection was no longer there. Arbogast had some rough days after that as well, but Victor Chen got off scot-free. Arbogast never knew whether he had given it up or not. I think that was worse than the torture.' Edwina's face turned contemplative. 'Funny what the mind can do to you. He did very well for himself after the war, and did a lot for the less fortunate, but he was never happy. Felt he had failed his country, you see, and he was the sort of man that the notion would always haunt him.

'Anyway, later, Victor sensed the tide turning in the war and he thought it might be more advantageous to give it back to the Chinese and bank a few favours from them. So he put the Collection on a train to China. A gift from a loyal citizen. I didn't know until afterwards.'

'And that was the end of it. And you never told anyone?'

'No,' Edwina said. 'Victor made it abundantly clear it was to my advantage to keep silent.'

Claire thought of Edwina's comfortable life, her large estate in the New Territories, all apparently paid for on a headmistress's civil pension. 'Who knew?' she asked.

'I've no idea, my dear. Victor plays his cards close to his chest.'

'How much of this does Will know?'

Edwina smiled. 'Well, you'd have to ask him, wouldn't you?'

'And why are you telling me? I have nothing to do with this story.'

'You are . . . close to Will, are you not?' asked Edwina.

'I know him,' Claire allowed.

'Don't be coy,' Edwina snapped. 'He listens to you?'

'Not at all.' Of this she was sure.

'Well, I think you'd be surprised. You're the first person in years with whom he's deigned to spend time. I think he needs a little push to do the right thing. A woman knows the right thing to say. It's our instinct.'

'I don't know that I understand what you're saying.' Claire was deliberately obtuse.

Edwina slapped her palms on the table. 'That man!' she cried. 'That man, Victor Chen, parades around Hong Kong as if he owns it. He hobnobs with anyone of any importance – you know he was chosen to host a party for Princess Margaret when she visited? And who is he? Some jumped-up Chinese in a Savile Row suit! A collaborator. An opportunist.' She said this, almost spitting. 'He pretends to be better than everyone! It's nauseating and I won't have it.'

Her outburst rang out, incongruous, against the heavy damask curtains.

'He snubbed Mary in town the other week. He's forgotten old friends in his haste to get to the top. Well, he'll learn.' She looked at Claire. 'He is an awful person who doesn't deserve any of what he has.'

'It's hard to say who does deserve the good in life,' Claire said. She felt as if she were placating a large, angry animal.

'He thinks the past can be buried. But it has a way of surfacing, again and again.'

'And the baby? Trudy's baby?' Claire asked. An innocent, perhaps the only, in all of this.

'I don't know, my dear. I suppose it was taken care of.' She paused. 'Yes. That was the end. I think about that last afternoon with Trudy quite a lot, how remote she was, how removed. She didn't care if she lived or died after Will abandoned her. I always thought that Will Truesdale broke her heart. And how about that? Who knew that the remarkable Trudy Liang had a heart to break?'

5 July 1953

'And now,' Claire said, 'what of us?'

She and Will had sat in silence for long minutes, looking out at the water, the boats streaming silently through the harbour, passing each other smoothly, like toys in a child's bath. It started to drizzle slightly. It had taken great effort to ask and she could not bring herself to look at him. She put her hands in her lap and cupped them together primly.

'You don't need me,' he said slowly. 'I've said it before and it's truer than ever. I'm a liability now.'

Her first reaction: automatic withdrawal. Then she realized that with Will's new release came uncertainty: he had lived too long with his secrets and now that they had been poured out, he would be feeling empty.

'I don't need you,' she echoed his words. How porous he seemed, always slipping from her grasp. Even in their most intimate moments, in bed, his face hovering over hers, intense with passion, he was never fully there. Now she understood why: he had always been with another.

Another unbidden memory: Will, lifting the strands of her hair as she lay beneath him, letting the fine gold slip through his fingers, his face oddly distant. 'Gold,' he had said. 'I love hair the colour of metal: gold, bronze, even silver. The gold and bronze will turn silver, eventually, yes?' It was the closest he had ever come to saying the word *love* to her. It stung suddenly. She had turned away, buried her face in the pillow. In bed, she was always shy with him, afraid that she would say something she would regret later.

'You deserve better, you know,' she said, trying to save something, she didn't know what. 'You can live your life without always regretting.'

'You're trying to be kind but you don't understand,' he said.

'It's not kindness,' she said.

He didn't reply.

'You're always telling me to be strong, but you're never strong yourself. When we first met, you told me I should take the opportunity to become something else, to transcend what I had been given. But you can't do that yourself. You're mired in the past and determined to be unhappy.' She had never seen so clearly before. Anger swept through her – unexpected – clarifying even more. 'You cannot let go, and you're sinking. And you pretended to be so strong!' It was as if she had been duped, taken under false pretences. The man she had loved was a mere shell. And she felt something more, unwelcome: pity, fatal to passion.

'And I told you to go. Don't bother with me,' he said, also angry now. He just wanted to be left alone.

But she wouldn't leave him without trying to salvage something. 'Why did you come to me?' she asked. 'You changed my life. You didn't like me, you said. What was it? Were you bored?' She shot the last word at him, an accusatory arrow.

'You were pure,' he said. 'You weren't like the others. You had your prejudices and silly ideas, but you were open, willing to change. And I hadn't minded being alone. But you came along . . .'

'And you were the great opener of my eyes, the wise and –'

'That's not fair,' he said. 'That is beneath you. I never looked at another woman after Trudy until I met you. But it felt wrong, as if

I was betraying Trudy, whom I had betrayed in so many ways already.'

'You're wasting your life,' she said. Rain had wet his hair so it hung in jagged spikes down his forehead. He made no effort to wipe away the water running down his face. He looked so defeated.

She was cruel, finally. 'You're a coward.'

How could he be the man she had changed her life for? It seemed inconceivable.

'And you are simple,' he said fiercely. 'And naïve. To think that you can just leave the past behind, like shutting a door.'

'You won't even look at me!' she cried. 'You won't give me even that. You've always been mean with your attention, so measured.' She looked down at herself. She had dressed with care this morning, mindful of the impression she wanted to make: quiet, not reproachful, confident. This had translated into a knee-length, navy cotton-voile dress with covered buttons down the front, a few decorative pleats: tailored, not fussy. Her freshly washed hair was held back with a navy satin band. She tamped down the word that kept rising to the surface of her consciousness: *fool, fool.*

'I am telling you that it doesn't need to be like this,' she said. Her mother's voice suddenly in her head: 'Chasing a man, are you? Shame!' Her face turned scarlet despite herself. She waved a hand in the air, almost unconsciously, to dismiss her mother's presence.

'Do you know,' he asked fiercely, 'do you know what it's like to see your life unravel because of something you failed to do?' He stood up. 'It haunts you like nothing else.'

'So you give up,' she said, in a low voice.

'Sometimes,' he said, 'you don't have a choice in how you lead your life. Please stop before I say more things that I'll regret later.'

'You should know about regret,' she said. 'It's what you have made your life about.'

They sat, furious now, their anger running clear through them, like a solvent. It washed away their short past and allowed them to wipe it clean.

He got up and walked away. She didn't call after him.

12 July 1953

The next week, Claire went to the Chens' to resign. She went at the usual lesson time and was shown to the sitting room where Melody was by herself.

'Are you all right?' she asked. The Chinese woman was sitting very still on the edge of the sofa with a cup of tea cooling in front of her.

'No,' she said. 'Something's terribly wrong. There's been a misunderstanding. Everyone's got the wrong idea.'

'I'm afraid –'

'They cut me,' Melody said, with a stricken face. 'In town today, I walked through the tea room at the Gloucester Hotel, and the room fell silent and no one called out to me, not even Lizzie Lam, and I was at primary school with her. We were best friends. She gave me chicken pox! She pretended she didn't see me.'

'I'm sure you're mistaken,' Claire said.

'No, it's true,' Melody whispered. 'People are merciless, you know. In our world, they can be very cruel.'

The hypocrisy of the woman was overwhelming. Melody must have seen her ambivalence because then she said impatiently, 'Oh, you'll never understand.' Then she asked suddenly, 'And you? I suppose your life is quite different now, as well.'

'Yes,' Claire said. 'I've telegraphed my parents to let them know my situation. I will probably have to go home.'

'It's a pretty kettle of fish, isn't it?' Melody said. 'Isn't that what you English say? And you, somehow involved in it. I'd wager you never imagined you would be in this sort of situation.'

'No,' Claire said. 'This is all very foreign to me.'

Melody nodded and got up. 'I'll let Locket know you're here.'

Claire started to explain but Melody interrupted her. 'They say I took her from Trudy, but I didn't, you know. Trudy gave her to me.'

Claire opened her mouth, but nothing came out.

Melody went on in a rush: 'She knew what was coming. She knew she wouldn't live. And she knew I had lost my baby in California. My baby was born dead. I came home after that. I didn't want to stay in America by myself, without family. Trudy wanted me to have hers. It was a gift, from one cousin to another. So many people don't understand, but in China it happened all the time, throughout history, particularly during wartime or famine. We are a country used to suffering; our people are practical. Children were given to other members of the family because they would be better looked after. You Westerners don't understand. It's what Trudy wanted, or would have wanted. She knew that Locket would have a good home. And I think Victor thought Locket would be good insurance as well. She's half Japanese, you know, Locket. Half Japanese, a quarter Chinese, a quarter Portuguese. Although you'd never know it to look at her. You'd never know it. You didn't, did you? And we love her as our own. It was all for the best.' She stopped, looked confused.

'The doctor told me I could never have any more children, that I would die if I did. So I really had no choice . . .' She trailed off. 'Oh,' she said. 'I was going to get Locket.'

She wandered out of the room.

Claire sat in the sudden silence. A clock ticked loudly. Some long minutes later, Locket appeared. 'I was waiting for you at the piano,' she said. 'I waited and waited and then Ling told me you were here. You were with Mummy?'

Claire looked at her with new eyes. Trudy's child. A little girl who had never known her real mother, a child born of violence and deception and desperation. None of this showed on her wide, placid face. The past, her history, had been so easily buried. 'Yes, Locket,' she said. 'But I've come because I have to tell you something. Why don't you come and sit down next to me?'

Locket sat down. 'Would you like a biscuit?' she asked. 'I'm hungry.' She called for a servant and spoke to her in Cantonese. Claire could now tell the difference between the dialects: Shanghainese, Cantonese, Mandarin. Families like Locket's always spoke all three, as well as English and usually some French. 'And will you have a drink, Mrs Pendleton?'

Suddenly Claire saw Locket as a miniature Melody, with her assured handling of servants and household matters. But then she blinked: the maid had brought in a plate of jam biscuits with milk, and Locket was a child again, stuffing two into her mouth at once.

'Locket,' she said. 'I've come to tell you that I can't teach you any longer.'

'Mmm,' said Locket, through a mouthful of biscuit.

'And that I've really enjoyed teaching you, although you never practised as much as you should have.'

'Sorry, Mrs Pendleton.'

'But that doesn't matter. I want to tell you that you're a good girl, and that you can do a great many things. You are sweet and have a real goodness about you. Your innocence is special.'

Locket nodded, her eyes confused.

'I know you don't understand what I'm talking about, Locket, but I want to tell you. You are a good person. I really wish you the best in life as you go forward.' Claire felt the futility of what she was doing, but pressed on. She wanted desperately to leave Locket with something, anything, that would stick. But the very thing that would brand Locket for ever, leave an indelible impression was what she absolutely could not say. She could not take on that responsibility.

'Mrs Pendleton, you make it seem as if I'm going to die or something!'

'I just want you to know . . .' She trailed off. 'Just know. That's all.' She got up and kissed Locket on the top of her glossy black head. 'Goodbye.'

She left Locket in the drawing room with her biscuits and her confusion, and a strange sense of tumult in her own stomach.

1953

In his dreams, she comes back to him. In his dreams, she forgives him.

'I was always searching for a saint,' Trudy says. Her hands are inter-twined behind his head, her eyes looking up into his. 'I thought you were the one.'

'I'm sorry,' he says. 'I never pretended I was.'

'Oh, I think you did,' she says, without anger. 'You always had that saintly aura. People looked to you for guidance. You radiate confidence. Unlike me. I radiate . . . unreliability. But I'm much more fun.'

He touches her hair, the fine, glossy strands of umber and bronze. 'I never locked my door because of you,' he tells her. 'I thought even if there was the slightest chance you were alive . . . Stranger things have happened. I couldn't lock my door because I was tormented by the thought that you'd find your way back to me, that I'd be out, and that you would leave, and then I would have missed my chance. That's why I could never move. People always wondered why I stayed there, stuck in the past.'

'Of course I would find you,' she says, in her clear, bell voice. 'You've forgotten how resourceful I am.'

'You made me want to be the worst kind of man,' he confesses. 'If I'd had a family, I would have left it for you. If you'd wanted a bauble, I'd have stolen it for you. If you'd told me to kill somebody, I might well have done so. There's nothing I wouldn't do for you, and that's the most terrible thing in the world. So I had to get away from it. I had to get away from you to preserve myself.'

'Well,' she says, amused, 'I don't know if that's the nicest thing anyone's ever said to me, or the nastiest.'

She has always told him she's not dependable, that she will leave him in an instant, that she is not to be trusted, but in all her declarations, he has just to look into her eyes, and he doesn't believe her.

'I like to think about when all this is over,' she says. 'I'm going to have ice cream and champagne at every meal and bathe in honey and wine. I am going to be so profligate, you have no idea! I'm going to act every inch the heiress and demand every extravagance – only soaps and scents from France will touch my skin and fresh, exotic flowers on my bedside table every night. This restraint is just killing me. I've become a dour, wartime matron and I intend to scrub every inch of that loathsome person off as soon as . . .' But she cannot say what will end the war.

He shakes her. He wants to bite her cheek, viciously, until flesh tears off and blood runs down his chin. He wants to devour her whole, until she feels the pain he has been feeling. The pain he has caused her too.

He surfaces, she recedes, he remembers the other one, the one who's still alive. But he goes down again, into the past. Its pull is too strong.

The memory of those days. Sitting on his thin bed, helpless, outraged, angered by the endless monotony around him, the small concerns of the others: were they getting their fair ration? Someone had moved surreptitiously into an empty room that had not been allocated after the Americans had been repatriated. Ah, yes, the day the Americans left, their government far more expedient in arranging a prisoner-of-war trade, the indescribable feeling of watching the lorries depart, filled with joyful, bedraggled people, pockets stuffed with messages from those remaining to loved ones around the world. They'd promised to get the letters out. The kinder ones had left all their blankets and extra clothes, equipment and even money, but a few took every last scrap, as if they wouldn't throw it away the moment they got home. Funny, the mentality that springs up in such a place. And a few Americans stayed behind: the Catholic priests. They gave up their chance to return home so they could minister to the faithful remaining in the camp, regardless of nationality. Yes, there had been good people.

Another memory, from even before: the first Christmas in camp, a year or so after they had been interned. He remembered the half-dead grass in the central lawn and the dust kicked up by the children as they ran around, shouting excitedly in their ragged shorts – it had been unseasonably warm. The women had set up tables with watery lemonade and Christmas biscuits donated by those still on the outside. A programme of songs and recitations had been mimeographed and distributed. They had also managed to get hold of some decorations so the straggly trees on the perimeter boasted tinsel and other garish ornaments. An old gramophone piped Christmas carols as the internees gathered round and chatted, sipping from their cups, a flask surreptitiously passed round. Bill Schott had acquired a Santa Claus costume and came out with a pillow stuffed next to his belly, much to the delight of the children, and handed out a motley, but squealed-over, selection of presents: a collection of shiny buttons, a rag doll stuffed with dried grass, a Christmas collage made of leaves. The mothers had been busy.

The Japanese soldiers watched from the side, bemused. They had given packets of boiled sweets to the children earlier.

Regina Arbogast appeared before him, suddenly, a red scarf wrapped dramatically round her neck. She still had flair.

'Will, Merry Christmas,' she said. Her husband was next to her. It was before the torture. That would happen months later.

Will raised his glass to them. 'A year passes too quickly, doesn't it? What a difference from last Christmas.'

'And here we are,' said Reggie.

'Do you enjoy your trips outside?' Regina asked. Will's fluidity between inside and out had been the source of much envy and speculation, although he always tried to bring back supplies for everyone.

'Enjoy is a peculiar way of putting it,' he said.

'Trudy is in cahoots with the current regime.' Regina let the statement hang in the air, a challenge.

'Is that a question or a statement?' Will asked mildly.

'How would you know such a thing, locked up in here?' Reggie said impatiently to his wife. 'You presume too much, Regina.'

'Well, that's what everyone's saying.' Regina winked. 'But I suppose the less you know the better. Isn't that right, Will.'

Reggie rolled his eyes and looked apologetic. 'Oh, look,' he said. 'The choir's ready to sing.' He took Regina firmly by the arm and led her away to where the older children and some of the women were preparing to perform.

Will remembers this exchange with a sick feeling, and how it all ended up, how they had been playing at something that became all too real.

Then 1945, the recurring sounds of aircraft overhead, whispers of a new kind of bomb. Something extraordinary, beyond imagination, an unthinkable death toll. A giant mushroom cloud of devastation over Japan. Snippets of information smuggled in with the daily vegetable delivery, the spinach suddenly wrapped in the English newspaper.

Guards looking sheepish, being slightly friendlier, the camp's inmates allowed more privileges. Their rations grew larger.

Trudy still a daily thought, but now successfully muffled. None of his messages answered, no reported sightings from the people who visited other internees. It was as if she had vanished into thin air. Like her mother, he thought, and pushed that thought out of his head. In war, people die. Later, he would realize that that was how a dying man would think.

And the liberation, entering a brave new world outside, still wary of the Japanese, dangerous in their loss. Some lashed out, killed while they could, but most trod the fine line between conquered and conquerer, that undefined space.

As if an old creaky machine was being cranked into life, Hong Kong sputtered back into motion. The buses and trams started running to their regular schedules, stores received provisions and prices slowly returned to normal. People ran into each other on the street and clutched each other, remarked on how thin everyone was, happy to have survived and to see each other, even if they hadn't liked each other before. Practising normality, trying to reach the mundane.

Otsubo was repatriated to Japan. Later, they heard he was hanged at Sugamo Prison. There was no relief in hearing the news.

The strangeness of the first dinner party, and how everyone slipped into it cautiously at first, but became comfortable so quickly that it was unseemly. They complained about the lack of basic supplies, then the lack of good servants, then how hard it was to get decent wine, then everything. The amnesia of comfort, soothing, anodyne, too seductive. All too soon they were back to themselves.

How can a woman disappear? How can someone so vivid vanish?

Searching for her in the aftermath, the empty taste in his mouth, the taste of regret. Funny thing: he was always thirsty after liberation. He procured a car and drove the empty roads throughout the island – to her old flat, to Angeline's old house, to her father's house in Sai Kung, all vacant and plundered, smelling musty and worse. A tour of abandoned houses. Her father dead in Macau, unknown causes during the war. Dominick also gone. Just another sad story.

Without Trudy's lightness to buoy him up, Will became morose, too serious, too dark. He lurked in odd corners of Hong Kong or stayed at home, a sparse affair with one glass, one plate, a bare light-bulb. He was no longer invited anywhere, 'He's gone odd,' whispered around town. He could not define a new self without Trudy.

He sank into anonymity until he caught a glimpse of Victor and Melody getting out of their car in Causeway Bay, with their daughter. Their daughter who looked nothing like them. He remembered hearing something about Melody in the United States, a tragedy, but something that had been whispered once and never again. He started to think. And then rang Victor with a hard-luck story and asked for a job, knowing that the man would love to hire an Englishman for what he would consider a menial job, both men knowing there was much more to the request.

Victor loved to show him off to unknowing business associates, particularly those just arrived from Europe or America. Will would pull the car round and get out to open the door. Victor's guests would widen their eyes and step in, visibly impressed. An Englishman work-ing as a driver, even for a family such as the Chens, was almost unheard of, especially someone like him, who'd been out and about in society before the war. Still, most were embroiled in their own concerns and many had emerged much changed from the war – the Dutch banker who had left Stanley a schizophrenic and now lived in an alley building in Sheung Wan, coming out to beg with a rattan basket, his blond hair matted and dark, or the Miller girl who had been engaged to one of the Hos, the shipping family, but came out of the camp too used; she now lived in Mongkok and was rumoured to be a bar hostess. Will was just another casualty of war and not the worst off. People talked at first, but then it became just another quirky fact of Hong Kong life.

He worked odd hours and tried to get glimpses of Locket, but the Chens always had the other drivers take her to school. Despite himself, he looked at her face – searching for signs of what? Trudy, yes, but also what he could not voice in his own head.

One day, Victor got into the car and directed Will to drive to the Peak. On the way up, he had seemed agitated, fidgeting with papers on the back seat.

'Mistakes were made,' he said suddenly, opaquely.

Will did not answer, which made Victor even more jumpy.

'Do you know what I'm talking about?' he had asked.

'No.'

'In times of war, many decisions are made, and things are done without the benefit of reflection.'

'Yes, sir,' he had replied, his deference more threatening than anything more he could have said. He saw Victor's face in the rear-view mirror. He was perspiring heavily.

'I've had some news . . .' Victor started.

'Yes, sir,' he repeated.

Victor hesitated, then seemed to get a hold of himself.

'At any rate, Will, the war has changed all of us. We're all in this together now.'

Will remained silent.

'I've changed my mind, Will. You can take me home now.'

Will swung the car round. They didn't speak on the return journey. His wages were suddenly doubled. He never found out what had unnerved Victor, but neither he nor Victor ever mentioned the incident again.

He was waiting for something to happen. And in the meantime, he remembered.

Trudy and Dominick locked in a terrible embrace.

Funny how so many things seem inevitable, given enough distance. Put a girl and a boy of similar persuasions together in summer and see what evolves. Usually love. Two friends, equally matched, then one suddenly has an advantage: rarely will they remain friends. This must have been what happened. Trudy and Dominick, alike as two peas when things were good. When the situation turned fraught, each reverted to form. Trudy essentially good, Dominick an animal. The betrayal sharp.

But his own? Much worse. He knows.

'I forgive you,' she says. 'I understand.'

He clings to this. Hears her say it over and over.

How can he leave her now?

A woman is sitting in a chair, reading by a window. A cup of tea has gone cold beside her. Dusk is gathering outside, and when it becomes too difficult to see, she goes to turn on the light. The room is suddenly illuminated.

She lives by herself now, in a small apartment she has found in Wanchai, amid locals and wet markets. It is furnished simply, with an iron bed and a thin mattress, a wooden fruit crate for a bedside table, a lamp she bought at Dodwell's during the holiday sales. She has a comfortable reading chair as well. She lives very frugally, within her means, as a secretary for a shipping company, and she has found that it is possible to live like a local, on almost nothing, bargaining for everything from lightbulbs to tea towels. She buys one orange at a time, or two carrots, or chooses her own chicken to be killed, a purchase that will last her three days. She eats at the street stalls: noodles and congee and roasted meats and other dishes she would have found unappealing just a year before. She can wield chopsticks now with the best of them. Sometimes, as she sits on the stools, next to a taxi-driver or a shopkeeper, she listens and finds she can understand some of what they are saying: words emerge from the noise, like jewels. In the beginning she was a curiosity to them, but now they have seen her often enough to ignore her. Her Cantonese – still rudimentary – is improving. Now she can order at the *daipaidong*, and they will not repeat the order loudly, in English; they just grunt and dump the noodles in the broth to boil, same treatment as the locals.

At home, she sometimes wears the black trousers and white tunics – the amah uniform – as night clothes and finds them oddly comfortable. They are made of light cotton and are inexpensive. The shop owner had assumed she was buying them for her amah and kept asking how tall, gesturing with her hands. Claire held the cloth against her frame and nodded her head. The first day she spent in her flat, she walked to the local street barber and sat down, much to his surprise, then asked him to cut her hair short.

And she knows the streets of the town: Johnston, Harcourt, Connaught, and how to say them in Cantonese. They are like a web of veins emanating out from Central to Repulse Bay, the Peak, Mid-Levels, places she rarely goes now, places filled with English people and the lives they lead. She runs into people she knows now and then, and they always ask how she is getting on, in that searching, curious way, and she just nods and says, fine, she is fine, enjoying the city very much. But are you going home? they ask, and she says, no, she has no plans to go home at the moment.

She is talked about less and less. She is becoming a part of some old history that will soon be forgotten, and this suits her well.

Sometimes, she is lonely, but she frequents the Librarians' Auxiliary, taking out three or four books at once. There are so many things to know and learn. She reads about Beethoven, Chinese rice farming, British prime ministers, and finds comfort in the fact that she will never run out of books. There is also a piano there, and the manageress has told her she can play after hours if she arranges to beforehand. She has been going there in the early evening, when the heat is less, and playing for an hour or so, while the staff clean around her. She goes late enough that all the women she would know have had their tea and gone home to prepare supper, husbands and children gathering, filling the rooms with chatter and noise, so unlike her own.

Martin is still in Hong Kong, as far as she knows. She had stayed at the flat with him for a few days while she was finding her own quarters, a request she had made when he had come home, ashen-faced, after the party. He had not said yes but he did not say no. She knew it was more than generous of him. She had poured neat whisky into two glasses and sipped it with him in silence. She remembered still his posture. He had sat heavily at the table, drinking slowly, and fingered the edge of the linen coaster. Yu Ling hovered excitedly near the kitchen door, listening for anything, having already been informed by telephone, before either had arrived home, of the scandalous situation through the lightning-quick amah network.

And he hadn't had the stomach for questions. He wanted her to volunteer the information but she could not bring herself to talk to him. For the first few days, his cold silence when he returned home was welcome; it was when he began to try to talk to her, to understand what had happened, that she couldn't bear it. She slept on the sofa in the living room, and tried to wake before Yu Ling got up, so that she could put away the pillow and the blankets, but too often she had seen the amah's curious eyes watching her as she woke. She supposes, in Yu Ling's world, such a situation would be settled with a chopper, and that she and Martin seem bloodless, bizarre.

Then Martin: 'Were you unhappy?' The first sentence he had spoken to her since that night. He had come into the living room from their bedroom; she had been reading.

And what could she have said? She put down her book and tried to come up with an answer. She found the question too prosaic, and hated herself for that.

'I needed to believe there was more to life.' Said simply. The fanciful notion an affront to good values, and she all too aware of it.

'Where did you go?' His second question. He sat down at the dining-table, far from her. He rubbed his eyes.

She explained. She had walked outside the Chens' house. It was hot, as usual, and she had no car. So she went down May Road, the winding, narrow street carved out of the mountain – a snake of a road – until it became Garden Road and she got to Central. By then, she was very hot, so she went into a bakery and drank some cool tea. Her head had been filled with a white noise, similar to when she had fainted outside the Chens' house. Then, not knowing where to go, she had continued east, found herself in Wanchai where the commotion and bustle were soothing. With so much activity around her, the frenzy inside her had quietened. And she had looked around, and thought, I could live here.

'I think I found myself too apparent in the world, after what happened at the party, and I want to be invisible for a while,' she told Martin. 'There was too much going on, and I don't know why I'm a part of it, but I am. And I realize that you must feel the same, and for that I apologize.'

He stared at her – this unworldly young woman he had brought over from England – and realized he had no idea who she was.

So, she left as soon as she could. She packed up her belongings and got a taxi while he was at work. She hugged Yu Ling, feeling the amah's slight frame under her embrace and an unexpected sadness at leaving her, this life. But she was now finally convinced that people got what they expected from life. Martin had never expected to find love, and so, ultimately, he would be all right. She would not be his great disappointment in life, his tragedy. That would come from somewhere else and she grasped, with relief, that she was not responsible for even knowing what that might be. She herself hadn't known what to expect from life, and still didn't. Her life was, is, still a work in progress.

She supposes that she is becoming a cliché, a woman 'gone native', someone who eschews her own kind. Amelia, her old acquaintance, had come to see her in her flat and could not quite hide the shock at the circumstances in which she had found Claire. She had fluttered around the small space, given her a jar of strawberry jam and some soap, and never returned. Claire supposes Amelia dined out on the story for several weeks. This does not trouble her in the least.

Last week, she had taken a small bag of costly jewellery, scarves, trinkets, and given them to the local second-hand shop. The woman who had taken the items looked befuddled and at a loss as to what to do with them, amid the dusty, inexpensive sweaters and used pots. Claire hadn't known what else to do with them. As she walked out of the door, she felt her mood lift, and she became light.

Now she pauses, looks out of the window to the busy streetscape outside. Cars traverse the streets, the red taxis crossing lanes with double-decker trams tethered to their cables, a few men on bicycles. The sky is blue, delineated by the tops of the low buildings with their antennae and roof-top clothes-lines. The pungent air from the road rises and enters through her window. A scene she could never have imagined just two years ago.

And a simple knowledge is what sustains her through all of this: that all she needs to do is step out on to that street and she will dissolve into it, be absorbed in its rhythms and become, easily, a part of the world.

ACKNOWLEDGEMENTS

I want to thank so many people:

My agent, Theresa Park, without whose support and gentle encouragement, this novel might still be a jumble of notes on my computer. She has been with me from the first pages of this book.
Abby Koons, Julian Alexander, Rich Green, Sam Edenborough, Nicki Kennedy and Amanda Cardinale.

Kathryn Court and Clare Smith, my editors at Viking and Harper Press, for their sensitive editing and guidance.
The wonderful team at Viking and Harper Press, especially Clare Ferraro, Alexis Washam, Carolyn Coleburn, Paul Slovak, Nancy Sheppard, Louise Braverman, Ann Day, Isabel Widdowson in the US, and Sophie Goulden, Essie Cousins and Taressa Brennan in the UK.

Pat Towers, who showed me graciousness, always, while teaching me nuance.
Abigail Thomas, who encouraged me with cake, good judgement and kind words.
Chang-rae Lee for advice both writerly and practical, always on-point.
Elaina Richardson for the time at Yaddo.

For friendship and encouragement, and understanding: Mimi Brown, Deborah Cincotta, Rachael Combe, Kate Gellert, Katie Rosman, Sarah Towers, Daphne Uviller.

I read many books about this period in World War II in both the New York Public Library and the Special Collections Library at Hong Kong University. In particular, I learned much about the time from Emily Hahn's excellent memoir, *China to Me*, and the colourful *Prisoner of the Turnip Heads* by George Wright-Nooth with Mark Adkin.

I also spent many hours working in various rooms at the New York Public Library, the New York Society Library and Hong Kong University Library and thank them for being open to the public and providing space for writers to work.

My mother, father and brother and his family.

The extended Bae family.

My children, who give me joy every day and put everything in perspective.

And most importantly, my husband, Joe, who is my best friend, my better half, and who supports me with an unstinting love and generosity that I am grateful for every day.

'I'm just going to write because I cannot help it.'

CHARLOTTE BRONTË

INTERPRETING THE SOUL

A Conversation with Janice Y.K. Lee

THE LAST WORD LIES WITH JUDGEMENT

Things to Think About

BEHIND THE SCENES

INTERPRETING THE SOUL
··
A Conversation with Janice Y.K. Lee

'The soul, fortunately, has an interpreter – often an unconscious, but still a truthful interpreter – in the eye.'

CHARLOTTE BRONTË

The Piano Teacher is a beautiful novel set in Hong Kong just as the World War II is hitting. How did this storyline come about?
The Piano Teacher started as a short story about Claire and Locket, an Englishwoman and a Chinese girl in 1950s Hong Kong. I was born and raised in Hong Kong myself and had always been tantalised by glimpses of the old colonial order and how it existed in uneasy proximity with local society, both high and low. Trudy was the next character to emerge and she sprang, fully formed, off the page, vivid and alive; then Will arrived, more measured but still surprisingly real at his birth. With no idea what these characters had come to do, but knowing that they belonged in the same story, I just kept writing about what they said to each other, what they did, where they did it. I had no map, no outline, just a sense that it might all work out. Over the next five years, I read extensively about the period and noted details of dress, speech, social custom, internalised all that, and slowly, slowly, the characters started to breathe. I would wake up and realise that Claire was going to the beach that day, or I would hear a snippet of conversation and know that Trudy would be making fun of the people talking.

When you were born, Hong Kong was under British rule. After moving to the United States at fifteen, you are back living in Hong Kong and it has now reverted to Chinese rule. Has it changed? What is different for you and what has remained the same?

As a child in the 1970s, I definitely felt the British influence. For a short time, I went to English schools and got a glimpse of that world, but I soon switched to an American school. I am Korean, so I was never a local in a strict sense of the word, but Hong Kong is so international that it never really mattered. People wash up in Hong Kong and stay, and create new lives for themselves. It's that type of place.

I was there for the handover of Hong Kong to China in 1997. It was an odd time. People were afraid but putting the best face on it. They didn't know what would happen.

I moved back to Hong Kong in 2005 and it is a part of China now – the currency looks different, all the 'Royals' have been stripped off the Postal Service, the clubs, etc (many institutions used to have the 'Royal' in front of their names) – although there's no part of China that looks or feels like Hong Kong. I love the English provenance of the street names: Gloucester, Pottinger, Connaught, and I do love that there are remnants of its history in hidden corners, although they are fast disappearing.

Is the Hong Kong you write about different from the Hong Kong you know?
Very! The Hong Kong in the book is entirely imagined by me, although I hope it is a true version of a Hong Kong that once existed. Being neither English nor Chinese, I really had to create a world out of what I could glean through books and films. My Hong Kong now is very much an expatriate American world, and as a child, it was an immigrant's Hong Kong, and the world I wrote about was in the past and about people in a different sphere.

The Piano Teacher **is set during a major piece of world history – World War II. How much research did you do for the book? How historically accurate is it?**
I read a lot of memoirs by English-speakers, obviously, who were here during the war and the occupation, some novels about the

1950s, like *Love is a Many Splendoured Thing*, watched films about the time, like *Lust, Caution* or *The World of Suzie Wong*, just to see what it looked like and how people dressed. And it is as historically accurate as I could make it. For the most part, the dates are real. Parts of Hong Kong did fall on Boxing Day, 1941. They did call people to Murray Parade Ground on 5 January, 1942. So those things are real, and as I read, I found a lot of the detail fascinating. But I believe the obligation of the novelist is to the story, not to the truth. I was trying to tell a story about Will and Trudy and Claire, people who found themselves in a desperate situation, and the background is there to anchor them in this period.

Did your research shape the plot or just add detail to the story?
For me, research really is mostly for that amazing detail that anchors any story set in another time or place. It was just there to provide a wonderful, evocative background to Will, Trudy and Claire's stories.

You have created an eclectic mix of characters who are such individuals, each with a unique identity and role. Are they based on anyone? Did you create the characters and then the story came to you, or did you create the characters to fit into your story?
The characters led the story. I didn't have a plot in mind when I began and I wrote about what they did and what they said and where they did it and the story emerged from that. They aren't based on anyone in history, although Trudy's character has roots in Emily Hahn, an American writer who lived in Hong Kong at the time and was a very outrageous, iconoclastic figure in expatriate society.

Did the story change at all as you wrote or did you map it out ahead of time?
There was no story at all when I started. I just had an idea in my

head about an English woman who becomes the piano teacher to a young Chinese girl. I never had a map, which I find amazing now, having finished a book that relies quite a bit on plot turns.

The novel goes back and forth between Hong Kong around New Year's 1941/1942 and 1952, each was a war time (World War II and the Korean War respectively), which was an interesting time in world history, and many weren't aware of the atrocities that took place in Hong Kong during World War II. What surprised you about the era that you tried to incorporate into the novel?
I'm always surprised when I read about the past, at how similar it is to the present. Although the outfits are different, the substance is the same – that people loved each other, that they betrayed each other, that people were petty, or grand, or irritating. Hong Kong in the 1940s and 1950s was a real mix of modern and old-fashioned, depending on whose memoir you are reading.

Which character do you feel most attached to?
Trudy. Just because she was so immediately apparent to me, and so easy for me to write. She was born fully formed and a real person. I knew exactly what she would say, what she would wear when she was saying it, how she looked, how she smelled. Any scene with her just flowed so easily, so I do like her the most.

Who are your literary influences?
I don't know that I can say who my influences are but I can say who my favourite writers are. Funnily enough, they are quite different from me in writing style. I love Lorrie Moore, Mona Simpson, Shirley Hazzard, Michael Cunningham, Amy Hempel. I think Dana Spiotta is amazingly talented. There are so many good writers!

What is your writing routine?
The Piano Teacher was at least five years' worth of work. When I started the book, I had no children. By the end of it, I had four. So

it was challenging. I'm not a very disciplined writer, but once I had more responsibilities, I definitely took advantage of the times when I knew I could work for a stretch. And when a line comes into my head and I know it's a good one, I will always write it down right away. I've forgotten too many good lines to not do that. Those lines will open up a new chapter for you, or direct you in a significant way, and I've learnt to pay attention when they come.

You were a magazine editor and *The Piano Teacher* is your first novel. How is it for you to be on the other side of the process?
I loved my job as an editor. I was lucky enough to work with people who really valued words and writing and who loved books. It's an invaluable perspective for me as well to know how the editorial side works as I start thinking about getting the book out into the world.

What do you want people to take away from reading *The Piano Teacher*?
I hope they're taken away from their lives into a different world. 'Transported' is an overused word, but I love the feeling of being transported, being drawn into a book so furiously and intensely that when I come up for air, everything seems different. I hope that people can really sink themselves into the world that is portrayed in the book.

In your opinion, what is it that inspires authors to write? Did you have any influences or inspirations that compelled you to write *The Piano Teacher*?
I did not know where *The Piano Teacher* would end up, and many times towards the end, I was scratching my head trying to get my characters out of the sticky situations I had got them in. But I just kept at it. As to the larger question, what is it that inspires authors to put pen to paper, I have no idea. A perverse push against the unknown, the unsaid? An irrepressible, foolhardy compulsion to

say something in a world where too much is said already? For me, busy with life and children and living, writing provided a place for my old self to reside, something that was mine, and that I did not have to share. That was priceless.

What are you working on now?
I'm working on a few ideas, seeing which of them stick and might be worth the long stretch. It's very preliminary at this point.

THE LAST WORD LIES WITH JUDGEMENT

••••••••••••••••••••••••

'There are two ways of spreading light: to be the candle or the mirror that reflects it.'

EDITH WARTON

From Socrates to the salons of pre-Revolutionary France, the great minds of every age have debated the merits of literary offerings alongside questions of politics, social order and morality. Whether you love a book or loathe it, one of the pleasures of reading is the discussion books regularly inspire. Below are a few suggestions for topics of discussion about *The Piano Teacher*...

- Janice Y. K. Lee sets *The Piano Teacher* in the same place – Hong Kong – but at different times: before the Second World War, during the war years and in its aftermath. What do you think the author has achieved by doing this? Is this an effective technique?

- The collision of East and West, and its repercussions, is a strong theme in *The Piano Teacher*. To what extent are these two worlds different? Which characters embody this theme?

- Trudy and Claire are two very different women who both fall in love with the same man. How would you compare their relationships with Will and who, would you argue, is his true love and why?

- *The Piano Teacher* brings to life a specific period in global history. In what ways has life changed? In what ways has it stayed the same? From the portrait Janice Y. K. Lee paints, would you say these changes are for the better or for the worse?

- Do you sympathize with Melody Chen? Do your feelings towards her change as the story progresses? If so then when and why?

- In Part III, Hugh Trotter states that 'wartime makes different animals of us all'. How does the author highlight the impact of the Second World War on her characters' lives? In what ways does the war shape and change them?

- How would you describe this book's genre? Is it a thriller, a mystery or a love story?

What's next?

Tell us the name of an author you love

and we'll find your next great book.